DEFENDING ALICE

DEFENDING ALICE

A Novel of Love and Race in the Roaring Twenties

RICHARD STRATTON

HARPERVIA
An Imprint of HarperCollins*Publishers*

HarperCollins books may be purchased for educational, business, or sales promotional use. For information, please email the Special Markets Department at SPsales@harpercollins.com.

FIRST HARPERVIA EDITION PUBLISHED IN 2022

Designed by SBI Book Arts, LLC

Library of Congress Cataloging-in-Publication Data is available upon request.

ISBN 978-0-06-311546-0

22 23 24 25 26 LSC 10 9 8 7 6 5 4 3 2 1

The first thing that a man—
striving to come of age in any
period of human history—
has to do is to choose what is
true, what is real and what is
not real in the picture of society
established for him by his elders.

—John Dos Passos

Three things will last forever—
faith, hope, and love—
and the greatest of these is love.

—1 Cor. 13:13 (NLT)

PART ONE

COLORBLIND

CHAPTER ONE

For the Defense

I long demurred in writing of the Rhinelander trial. Alice Beatrice Jones Rhinelander is my client; I am her attorney of record; and as such I am bound by the attorney-client privilege.

As sometimes happens over the course of a protracted legal proceeding, Alice and I became quite close. Now she has asked that the privilege be waived. Alice has given me permission to divulge even her most intimate confessions. To that end, when we agreed to embark on this account of the case, Alice provided me with her diaries—the memoirs closest to a woman's heart, revealing her innermost feelings and thoughts—all so that we might, in her words, "set the record straight." Yes, I am Alice's advocate; I am also her confessor, and I admit to bias. Alice has my heart. I write this for her.

* * *

When Alice first gave me her journals, she was ashamed of her writing, calling it, as did Rhinelander's lawyers, "crude and unschooled."

Unlike the Rhinelander attorneys, however, who would seek

to shame Alice by entering her letters in evidence at trial, and then bring attention to errors of spelling and grammar, for the benefit of my readers, I have endeavored to edit her journal entries, although without changing or even shading the meaning and intent of her words.

The Rhinelander lawsuit was heard before a judge and jury in Westchester County Superior Court in White Plains, New York. The month-long trial provoked a frenzy of front-page newspaper stories and feature articles in national magazines. The case dominated the tabloids every day for weeks on end in America, and with dissemination through wire services the Rhinelander lawsuit was news in Europe as well.

It began with the initial discovery of the marriage, which led to a virtual invasion of our town by reporters; cameramen; and avid, even violent, followers of the case. The mania for news about the trial and the litigants continued throughout the year-long legal proceedings; reached a climax during the testimony of the plaintiff, Leonard Rhinelander; and barely subsided with the verdict and lengthy aftermath of appeals and settlements as human-interest stories continued to appear on the fate of the infamous couple.

Yet, in all that has been written about the parties and the issues involved in the Rhinelander lawsuit, no one has told the true and heartfelt essence of what this case is really about. *Rhinelander v. Rhinelander*, when stripped of all the sordid details, is a story of innocent young love tainted and corrupted by money, prejudice, and social standing.

* * *

I know the Jones family; I knew them even before the trial. George Jones, Alice's father, is well regarded in our New

Rochelle, New York, community. He is the owner and operator of our town taxi service. Of West Indian descent, he is a powerfully built man with a dark, coffee-colored complexion, wiry iron gray hair, and a pure white mustache. His wife, Elizabeth Jones, is English, white, and decidedly working-class. As our town's only mixed-race couple, they are an anomaly accepted more readily perhaps because of their British background.

I welcomed Alice and her parents into our offices across from the courthouse in White Plains on that chilly, overcast day in November 1924. The Rhinelander family attorney, a Mr. Leon Jacobs of Manhattan, recommended our firm. Jacobs, who came to be referred to disparagingly around our offices as "that New York kike" or "the big-city yid," was acquainted with my law partner, New Rochelle city judge Samuel Swinburne, who was to be named lead counsel on the Rhinelander defense. Judge Swinburne said in reference to the plaintiff's attorney, Leon Jacobs, "It is one thing to be an able and aggressive advocate; it is quite another to be a spineless lackey."

George and Elizabeth Jones arrived with their daughter Alice, then a woman in her early twenties. I knew George Jones as an industrious man of proud bearing who managed the taxi stand at the local train station; and who, with hard work, frugality, and good business sense, had managed to purchase a few commercial buildings in our town that he then refurbished and sold or leased at a profit. Jones and his wife are both immigrants from England. They have three daughters: Emily, the eldest, who is married and has a daughter of her own; Alice, the middle child; and Grace, the youngest, both still living at home. The entire Jones family attended our venerable Christ's Church in Pelham Manor. Founded in 1843 in the Episcopal/Anglican tradition, our church welcomes all members of the body of Christ.

The well-mannered Jones girls were always smartly dressed

and regularly attended church Sunday school. They enjoyed good reputations well into adulthood. It was through the church that Judge Swinburne came to know George Jones and, under authority of opposing counsel, our firm was retained to represent Alice. I was tasked to argue on Alice's behalf. Judge Swinburne and Richard Keogh, an associate in our firm, were to join me at the defense table. Judge Swinburne recommended my former mentor, Judge Isaac N. Mills, who had only recently retired after twenty-seven years on the bench, as worthy local counsel to assist Mr. Jacobs and appear on behalf of the Rhinelander boy. Judge Joseph Morschauser, a seasoned and well-regarded jurist, was assigned to preside over what was to become a lengthy, bitterly fought, and sensational trial.

At our first meeting, Alice struck me as a young woman of uncommon strength of character. She has a rare, mysterious charm that goes beyond her physical appearance. She has her father's aquiline facial features: a straight nose like the prow of a ship; high, pronounced cheekbones giving her a long visage the English might term "horsey"; and full, shapely lips. She wears her slick black hair in a fashionable long bob. She has a subtle forbidden attraction like belladonna. Alice is not someone to be trifled with; she's no shrinking violet. She carries herself with poise; she looks one in the eye, and she holds one's gaze.

As Alice removed her gloves, I noticed her long, slender, and quite lovely dark-hued hands. Her voice is deep, resonant, and soothing. But it is her eyes that are Alice's most remarkable feature: big, dark brown, and nearly black orbs with whites tinged blue, eyes that are at once luminous and sleepy, what some novelist might describe as "bedroom eyes," with long black lashes that flutter like the delicate wings of a butterfly.

As a woman in her early twenties, she had a remarkable

reserve of self-confidence that I noticed straightaway. Through their attorneys, the Rhinelander family had proffered a considerable monetary settlement should Alice agree not to contest the lawsuit brought by her husband, and thus allow her marriage to young Leonard Kip Rhinelander to be dissolved. When I explained the nature of the cash settlement, and presented her with a draft of the annulment agreement drawn up by the Rhinelander attorneys, Alice rejected the offer without a second thought.

"In the first place, it's not true. *Not one word of what has been written about our marriage in those papers is the truth*," Alice declared, referring to the preliminary complaint brought against her by her husband through his lawyers. She sat forward, pushed the settlement papers aside, and gazed at me steadily with a determined look that I would come to know well over the course of the litigation.

"I didn't deceive Leonard into marrying me; not at all. And I certainly didn't marry him for his family's money," Alice stated emphatically. "I don't intend to be bought off, Mr. Davis. There is no amount of money I can place on my heart.

"Besides, I don't for a moment believe this is Len's doing," she insisted. "Leonard loves me still. This is his father's wish. His father's *fear* is behind this."

I found it interesting that Alice named fear as Rhinelander Senior's motive even at our first interview. *How perceptive*, I thought, and I warned her, "It could get ugly."

To lighten the mood, I remarked how Ambrose Bierce, one of my favorite authors, once likened a lawsuit to "a machine which you go into as a pig and come out a sausage."

Alice laughed and said, "Well, I'm no pig, or I would take the money. And besides, Leonard told me to fight."

Elizabeth Jones confirmed that Leon Jacobs and another

man—whom I was to learn was Joseph Strong, a Rhinelander family handler retained to serve Alice with the lawsuit—had appeared at the Jones home in New Rochelle and read aloud a note from Leonard that urged his bride to fight the annulment. But Jacobs had refused to provide Alice with the note.

Of course Jacobs would not hand over the written note, I thought, knowing full well how it attested to Leonard's state of mind.

So it was decided: come what may, we were going to court.

* * *

As an early indication of the lengths to which Leon Jacobs was prepared to go on behalf of his diffident client, the barrister filed an amended complaint alleging several instances of material fraud on behalf of Alice in supposedly deceiving Leonard Rhinelander into marrying her. Jacobs petitioned the court for a speedy trial based upon the outrageous assertion that the Rhinelander marriage represented, and I quote from the complaint, "a public threat as long as it was allowed to continue."

What public threat? I wondered—besides, that is, the threat to the Rhinelander name. In his filing, Jacobs advised the court that the couple's marriage "is notorious and famous. The great American public, the state, and society are vitally interested in the outcome thereof. That both the plaintiff and the defendant should know as speedily as possible whether they are husband and wife or not."

Judge Morschauser, referring to the already heightened interest in the case and with ever-mounting security concerns as our town filled up with reporters and followers of the proceedings, granted the motion.

With barely a month to prepare, *Rhinelander v. Rhinelander* was placed on the docket with a date set for trial.

* * *

The Rhinelander lawsuit had come to our firm at a time when I was contemplating retirement. My service at the bar had been gratifying but tiring. I graduated from the US Military Academy at West Point with every intention of making a career of the military. The law virtually kidnapped me. During a summer vacation after my graduation, I took what was to be a part-time position as a lowly clerk in the offices of Judge Isaac N. Mills. It was there, and in the courtroom while listening spellbound to Judge Mills argue, that I fell in love with the language of the law. It dawned on me with the force of revelation, and the affair continued with the charms of seduction, the simple intimation that the law exists as naught but words; yes, it is all merely, and yet profoundly, spoken or written language; and hardly an exact science. Indeed, the law is more akin to literature than it is to mathematics; and in school I had always been more attracted to reading and writing than to arithmetic.

It is easy to see how one may become enraptured and then confused by the conflicting narratives in a closely contended case. Facts are facts, to be sure; but they are subject to interpretation. One must weigh all possible counters to every supposition. The law and its practitioners attempt to ferret out the finest morsel and tidbit of truth, each and every nuance and shading of fact in a domain as turbid and conflicted as the human heart; and they search in intellectual territory as dense and varied as a vast swath of subequatorial jungle. Yet when we hear the truth we think we know it, for it rings true. And then along comes opposing counsel to dash our newfound assurances on the bulwark of a better-built argument. Woe to the finder of shifting facts, simple jurymen tasked to grasp snatches of truth swept away like fallen leaves caught in gusts of blustery rhetoric.

In 1924, when Alice and her parents walked into my office and presented me with *Rhinelander v. Rhinelander*, I was content to, as they say, meander off into the sunset with my fishing pole in hand. My handcrafted lures would be at the ready, and then I'd while away my remaining days fly fishing, pass my evenings quietly hooking rugs, and leave the law books and the litigants' arena to the brash boys coming up with their law degrees and licenses in hand, and precious little understanding of the gravitas and responsibilities of the calling—for it is a calling, like the priesthood or the medical profession. The attorney at law has a duty, not simply a job or a profession, but a commitment to a higher order—that of justice; and despite being the brunt of many bad jokes, lawyers are essential to the orderly progress of civilized society.

Of course, I hoped to exit the adversarial stage with a successful performance and a victorious result—a favorable and even memorable decision. In that regard, the case against Alice Rhinelander initially struck me as insuperable. I would have preferred that she agree to accept the settlement offer—a win by default with its monetary rewards.

But that was not to be. After the first amount was summarily rejected, not long before trial was set to commence with preliminary motions and jury selection, a chauffeur-driven limousine pulled up outside our offices. I had only just arrived back from court after entering my counterclaims on behalf of Alice when the family patriarch, Philip Rhinelander himself, stepped from his car accompanied by Mr. Jacobs and Judge Mills, and entered our offices, where they proceeded to ask me to present our client with a second offer of nearly double the original amount.

Philip Rhinelander impressed me as a man who was accustomed to getting his way. Of course I knew who he was. The Rhinelander name and their exalted status was high upon the list of the two hundred most influential New York society families, with their bloodlines traced back to the original Huguenot settlers of New Rochelle, and their vast real estate holdings in the area—the Rhinelander family pedigree and their financial influence were well regarded in our town as well as in our offices. My associate Judge Swinburne knew Philip Rhinelander personally and had done business with the Rhinelander Real Estate Company in the past. The marriage of young Leonard—or Kip, as the Rhinelander boy was known to family and friends—as the sole male heir still under the family patriarch's control, now wed to a local woman so far beneath the social stratum the Rhinelanders occupied—that such a disparate union was clearly unacceptable to Rhinelander Senior came as no surprise. Philip Rhinelander was known as a proud and imperious man with a storied military history.

"As I'm sure you know, Mr. Davis, marriage is a damnably serious state of affairs," Rhinelander felt it necessary to instruct me. "Particularly when it involves a young man who is from a family of a certain place in society."

"I do know that," I said. "And of course I will relay your latest offer to Mrs. Rhinelander."

I took a perverse pleasure in calling Alice by her married name, knowing how it would irk Philip Rhinelander.

"However, I feel I must warn you, sir," I went on, "Alice has instructed me to reject any settlement to accept the annulment. As I hope Mr. Jacobs told you, your son Leonard sent his wife a note with Mr. Jacobs when Alice was served with the suit. She was given the note to read but not to retain. In that note Leonard professed his undying love and urged his bride to contest the lawsuit."

Rhinelander's face hardened, and he nodded. "Yes, I know all about it. I saw the note," he said and cast a quick look at

Jacobs. "But the boy . . . Leonard, well, he's still quite young and . . . he's not thinking clearly, or he would understand that this marriage cannot, *and it must not* be allowed to continue. *We must end it now*," Rhinelander pronounced, and he stood as if to announce that the meeting was concluded.

"I expect you to do what you can to see that your client comes to terms," Rhinelander asserted. "Mr. Jacobs will attend to all the financial details."

"Thank you, sir," I replied and stood to shake Rhinelander's hand and see him out.

"I trust you understand, Mr. Rhinelander," I went on as we neared the front offices, "that my obligation as a member of the bar is to my client, and it requires that I represent her, and only her, and that I counsel her to the best of my ability, which I will surely do. But finally, as you must know, I am bound to do for Mrs. Rhinelander whatever it is that she decides she wants me to do, and not necessarily what you—or I, for that matter—may wish her to do, and which may in fact be in her best interests. Alice . . . well, let me just say that the woman your son courted and married, though perhaps not to your liking, I will tell you this: Alice is a strong-minded woman, and she has clearly won your boy's heart."

"Oh, *courted*, was she?" Rhinelander sniffed, and he stiffened. "*Won his heart* . . . well, why not call it what it is, Mr. Davis: *the boy was seduced*. Lust of this sort, what has afflicted Leonard—*is a species of madness*. He'll recover."

"He's twenty-one."

"So he is." Rhinelander shrugged. "But Leonard is still a babe in the woods when it comes to women. And this . . . *this woman* . . . this"—he shook his head and closed his eyes—"*whatever* she is. She beguiled him. Clearly, *she tricked him* into marriage."

"That is for a jury to decide."

Rhinelander scowled and gazed at me; he was obviously displeased with what he perceived as a lack of acquiescence on my behalf.

"Yes," he said, "I expect it is."

"Do see what you can do, old boy," Isaac Mills suggested in a parting aside. "It really won't benefit anyone should this go to trial."

"It appears it already is," I said. "I filed our reply this morning, and Judge Morschauser's clerk has set a date. There is nothing more I can do now but to see to the interests of my client."

What struck me as I saw the gentlemen out was how—perhaps unknowingly—they had provided me with an intimation of what would be the foundation, and even the core meaning, of their case.

* * *

Finally, weeks later as the case proceeded with the usual delays, and to dispose of this question of Alice's motives, I will relate that, with the trial nearing conclusion, Rhinelander Senior sent a last desperate message through counsel telling me to "name a price, within reason," to abandon the defense. Once again, Alice resolutely refused to consider a monetary settlement of any amount, and she insisted we continue with the trial even as it brought terrible strain upon her nervous condition, and fearsome notoriety as well as threats of violence to her and her family.

Alice was not to be swayed even at the lowest ebb of her faith in her husband's love, and in her loss of trust in the basic goodness of humanity. All of which proved, at least to me, that Alice and indeed the entire Jones family never were in it solely for the

Rhinelander fortune or their esteemed family name, as would be alleged by the Rhinelander lawyers.

Our defense sought to prove that Alice's marriage to young Leonard "Kip" Rhinelander was not simply a matter of unscrupulous ambition and fraud, as the plaintiff would contend; but that it was in fact an affair of the heart—and more, as I was beginning to understand, at least on behalf of the plaintiff: for young Kip Rhinelander, marrying Alice had been an act of defiance.

Now, of course, the challenge was to convince a jury of twelve men, good and true, of the truth of Alice's heart, and of the falsity of the charges brought against her.

CHAPTER TWO

Sunday, September 18, 1921

Dear diary,

Sunday, glorious Sunday! Church, and then a day of rest. Hah! As Father would say, "There's no rest for the weary." I have my home chores to see to . . .

Where have I been? I know you may be wondering as it's been so long—almost a week now since I wrote you last. Working, of course. Two jobs! Ugh! One, for the Hanson family looking after their children, which wouldn't be so bad except for the youngest boy, Derrick, who is a real terror. He has temper tantrums and I don't know what to do with him. He hits me, he screams and yells, he throws his toys around, and he won't do anything I ask until I give him whatever it is he wants. Boys! Girls are so much easier, at least for me. Little boys, that is, can be a handful. Once they get older, it's much easier to settle them down.

And, of course, the other, my usual job as a housemaid. Oh, it's so tedious. . . . Please, someone rescue me!

Which reminds me, here's some big news—I met a boy!

Leonard is his name, of the Rhinelander family, whoever they are, I have no idea, but I was told—everyone says that they're rich and famous—at least around here everyone seems to know them. Not that I care. I've met rich boys before. They come around looking for local girls they think might be easy. Leonard seems different. In the first place, he's shy. He stutters when he gets excited. He came to our home looking for Grace—of course! Grace has all the boys looking after her. And if they're not looking, she makes sure they see her in any case. She's such a flirt! Grace was out when Leonard came supposedly to bring her a message from some other fellow, whose name is Kreitler, Karl Kreitler. I heard that name enough from my mother. She was so upset with Grace for taking a ring from Karl Kreitler. Grace is already engaged! And besides, she only just met him. But that's Grace. Everything is a game to her—or a play, a movie, and she's the star. She doesn't mind teasing boys, or even hurting their feelings. Mother was so upset with her. Her words exactly . . . how many times have I heard them? "You are to behave yourselves as decent and respectable young ladies!"

Those words roll off of Grace like water off a duck.

I was just coming home from my job at the Hanson's when Leonard arrived looking for Grace. He said he was there to tell her that Karl Kreitler couldn't get away to see her that day. Good. So what? Grace had been told not to see him in any case. Now, when he met me, I could tell straightaway that Leonard liked me. It's easy to tell with most boys. They get silly, in a way, or embarrassed. Leonard forgot why he was there; he stared at me and he stuttered when I asked him who he was. I decided to tease him. "And what are you," I asked him, "a messenger boy?" That set him back on his heels a bit, which is just the way I like it. With boys, you've always got to be looking out to protect your feelings or they will hurt you on purpose to try to show you they are in control—at least, that's what they think. That doesn't work with me, not anymore. I learned my lesson and I won't let any boy boss me around and try to control me. So I look to put them on their guard, so to speak, to let them know who I am so they won't think they can lord it over and have their way with me.

"I'm Leonard Rhinelander," he said, all la-di-da, as if I was supposed to be impressed. Of course I knew he was no messenger boy. Grace already told me all about him. And I saw his brand-new auto parked out front, and I could tell by his clothes and by the way he spoke.

"Well, Grace is out," I told him. "But you're welcome to come in and wait if you like."

He wasn't sure what he should do. He stood there scraping his feet and looking around as if to see if there was a way he could escape without looking foolish.

"Come," I said, "there's nothing to be afraid of. We don't bite."

Mother made him a cup of tea. He was very nervous at first. Mother asked him to wait until Grace came home so she could give him back the ring the other fellow gave her. That's something else that made me believe Leonard doesn't know what he's doing when it comes to courting a girl. It turns out that the ring belongs to Leonard's mother. It's a beautiful sapphire ring. Now, how do you explain that? Karl Kreitler gave a ring to Grace, who is already engaged, but she took it anyway, and the ring doesn't even belong to him—it belongs to Leonard's mother! These boys are ridiculous. They must be crazy.

You think that's ridiculous? Wait till you hear this! Grace came home and Mother made her give back the ring. Now what do you suppose Leonard did? He gave the ring to me! He tried to give me a brooch as well. Mother made me give them both back. Grace and I couldn't help it—we were laughing. I know it's not nice to laugh at someone, and I wasn't actually laughing at Leonard. He laughed as well. He made a joke of it.

That's Len. He's a funny boy, and he likes to laugh. He seems lonely to me. I got the impression he doesn't have many friends—apparently, if he's going about with someone like Karl Kreitler, a workman at Leonard's school.

Of course I know what Leonard wants. It's what all boys want.

He invited me to go for a ride in his car. It's a beautiful car his father bought for him. Mother said no, and I told him maybe some other time. Leonard asked if he could phone me. We don't have a telephone, but I gave him Emily's number and said he could try to call me there at eight in the evening. I do hope he calls.

CHAPTER THREE

Defending Alice

Of course Rhinelander called Alice; he called her every night. The boy was clearly smitten, and Alice was intrigued by his attentions. Soon the couple were writing letters to one another daily—letters that would wind up as relevant and even shocking exhibits entered into evidence at trial.

Leonard continued to drive down from the Orchards School in Stamford, Connecticut, to New Rochelle in his brand-new sports roadster to visit Alice at every opportunity he got. He pursued her, and not the other way around, as the Rhinelander lawyers would attempt to prove. Alice confided that she was impressed by Rhinelander's avid attention, and she did nothing to discourage him. It made her feel good, and, as she admitted when I asked, "important. To have a boy like Len court me was . . . *flattering.* I felt better about myself. And I very quickly began to have real feelings for Len. The more I got to know him, the more I liked him, and the more I knew I was right. Leonard really was a very lonely boy when we met. Even his own family seemed to have forgotten him, packed him off to the Orchards School; and he had no real friends. That fellow Karl Kreitler . . . he wasn't Len's friend, not really. He worked at the

Orchards and he just latched onto Len and used him for his auto and his money."

* * *

After our firm had been retained, I set about reading Alice's diary entries related to her relations with Rhinelander, and it occurred to me how some things may appear obvious and apparently simple, such as young love, and yet they remain mysterious, and they can turn out to be as treacherous to navigate and unfathomable as the deep Sargasso Sea. Who is to say how or why or with whom one falls in love? It is an emotion as ancient and as personal and mysterious as life itself—and equally inevitable for most, yet often well beyond our ken. True love, particularly young love, knows no rules or social constraints. It's biological, not logical. It emanates from a profound region not of the mind but of the spirit as well as of the heart. To seek to control love is to attempt to master the life force itself.

In my own rather circumscribed love life I had been happily married for more than thirty years; but I will confess that I had never been seized with the kind of heedless, come-hell-or-high-water intense feeling that seemed to have infected the Rhinelander boy. He clearly lost his mind. Certainly he had never met another girl like Alice. How could he? They come from entirely different worlds. Leonard is the pampered scion of an aristocratic bloodline. Alice was a housemaid with a fifth-grade education when they met. And where is the compatibility in such a mixed match mating? One may wonder what they would even have to talk about. But remarkably, and despite her humble origin and lowly station in life, Alice presents as an enigma in human female form—a creation as alluring as Eve. Alice would soon come to dominate the relationship without even trying, as though Rhinelander surrendered himself to her out of sheer desperation—a need to be loved by a real woman, perhaps, or some overwhelming desire for the other: to know someone who was everything he is not.

* * *

I would attempt to understand Rhinelander's desire for Alice and to put it into perspective even if I couldn't appreciate what he felt. For young Kip, a sheltered and yet adventurous boy from a distinguished family, for him to come upon Alice after motoring along the shore from Connecticut on that early fall afternoon in his shiny new sports roadster given him by his emotionally distant father, and with Leonard perhaps feeling the first intimations of independence from his strict upbringing, yes, a youngster off on his own at first in pursuit of Alice's younger sister, Grace. And then to encounter Alice; to be in her heady presence for the first time, and with her subtle way of casting a mood; to have her invite him in, make him feel welcome, and yet somehow inferior; all this most surely had the impact of an encounter that can and did alter the young man's life. One could liken it to the sudden throwing down of the mythical gauntlet that a boy must either accept or eschew as he embarks on his journey to manhood. "Here I must prove myself," comes the unspoken challenge. "Am I a boy, or am I a man? How am I to be perceived by this exotic creature: woman?"

One feels that with Alice—that uncomfortable sense of being tested in one's own manhood while in her presence. It's curious; how does one explain that even a man of my relatively advanced age, and indeed all the men in our offices, were charmed and slightly intimidated by the young woman? Judge Swinburne in particular seemed to get giddy around Alice—which is why no doubt it was better that I took over management of the lawsuit.

Naturally we have all heard it said that women are the weaker sex; men, however, know otherwise when it comes to the force of their feminine allure. Young and old men alike will often wilt and lose all composure and resolve—as did Judge Swinburne—when in the presence of an attractive and charming woman.

The Rhinelander lad didn't stand a chance in resisting Alice's charms. He was known to be painfully bashful. His father had packed Leonard off while still a teenager to board at the Orchards School in Stamford, Connecticut. Orchards is a renowned in-patient clinic for wealthy young boys said to be suffering from nervous disorders. Leonard was apparently treated for a debilitating stammer; as well, he exhibited a lack of confidence and grace in social settings. He was still boarding and in treatment at the Orchards School when he met Alice.

"I thought Len was silly," Alice told me when I inquired of her impressions after their initial meeting. "But adorable . . . in a way, like a puppy. He wasn't at all like the other fellow, Karl Kreitler, who was so forward and keen on Grace and who turned out to be a cad."

Kreitler, I was to learn, was the older, married man employed as an electrician at the Orchards School. It was this fellow Kreitler who cajoled Leonard into driving down to New Rochelle, where he promised they might pick up local girls along the way who would be happy to go for a ride in Leonard's fancy automobile—and perhaps be willing to go farther. Kreitler was experienced in this pursuit; however, it was a new adventure for the Rhinelander boy. Leonard—or Kip, as he was known, after his mother's maiden name—was a gentle, unassuming lad only recently turned eighteen when he met Alice. His trial counsel, Judge Isaac Mills, would describe Leonard to the jury as "a boy upon whom no girl had ever smiled before."

One could only imagine that the idea of a rendezvous with

local girls who might be of questionable moral scruples was as foreign to young Rhinelander as a bout of fisticuffs. He was what the rough boys might call a pantywaist. Alice described him in her diary as *sweet and polite. He has lovely manners. He treats me so nice. He opens doors for me; he pulls out my chair and won't sit until I am settled. I never, in all my life, I have never known a boy as nice to me as Len is.*

Well, that certainly says a lot for the boy. One must not fault him for being good to Alice—not in the beginning, at least. It must also be said that Leonard had endured a tragic childhood. His was a youth fraught with emotional pain. Despite the Rhinelander family fortune and their lofty standing on the social register as one of New York's founding families, life had not been easy for young Leonard. The trauma of death and loss came early to the lad. As Alice told me, and we were to learn in detail at trial, Leonard was just thirteen years old when his beloved mother, Adelaide Rhinelander, née Kip, perished as a result of burns she sustained when she apparently upset an oil lamp while dressing for an evening out. Leonard was at home at the family's summer estate at Tuxedo Park at the time of the conflagration. Apparently he tried to get to his mother to rescue her but was repelled by the flames. Surely he was traumatized by his mother's immolation and his inability to save her.

I cried when Len told me about his mother's death, Alice confided to her diary. *He loved her so much. I just wanted to hold him, to kiss him, and tell him it would be okay, that I would make it all go away. Len is the youngest boy still living. He had a younger brother who died while a baby. Len was his mother's favorite. He showed me her photograph. She was a beautiful woman, and so refined, a Kip, the family—his mother's family—is even more famous than the Rhinelanders. Leonard told me that Kip's Bay in New York is named after the Kips.*

I had been told that one of Leonard's older brothers failed to return from the Great War. Another brother had married and moved away. All paterfamilias Philip Rhinelander's imperious will and strict discipline fell upon his remaining masculine offspring still living under his roof.

It proved a heavy burden. Leonard became tongue-tied, and some (including his lawyers) would maintain that the boy is brain-tied as well as socially awkward. One suspects he was something of an embarrassment to his aloof and dictatorial father. Indeed, as we would learn during trial, Philip Rhinelander never once visited his boy while Leonard was enrolled at the Orchards School. It took Leonard's bold pursuit of and marriage to Alice to get his father's undivided attention.

* * *

To hear Alice tell it, Leonard and Kreitler on their initial outing that fine September afternoon—what we know in this region as Indian summer—first encountered Alice's younger sister, Grace, another rare beauty. Grace chanced to be walking along in New Rochelle when she came upon Leonard and Kreitler parked by the side of the road. When asked, Grace agreed to go for a drive in Leonard's car.

"That's my sister," Alice complained. "I wouldn't have gone, as I know Mother would have been upset."

Kreitler convinced Leonard to let him take the automobile and go off with Grace while Leonard was made to wait in town; this detail said volumes to me about the Rhinelander boy. Kreitler returned an hour later without Grace. He would intimate to Leonard that he had sex with Grace, though she denies it. Leonard was inspired to return to New Rochelle the following day. He went alone to the Jones's home in search of Grace and with his claim that he had a message for her from Kreitler.

As we were to learn, Rhinelander was actually stepping out on his own in pursuit of a girl for the first time in his young life. Instead of Grace, Leonard met Alice, and from that moment on Alice was to become the singular focus of all Rhinelander's fledgling amorous intentions. According to an early entry in Alice's journal, the affair progressed with alacrity.

What I like about Len, Alice wrote, *and by the way, I never call Leonard Kip, as others sometimes do. That was his mother's maiden name, but it's not a name for a young man—who ever heard of a serious young man with a name like Kip? That's a name for a puppy, or a clown, and though Len can be silly and perhaps immature, he's gentle and respectful. He took me to the picture show in Mount Vernon. We saw* The Sheik *with Rudolph Valentino—I love that movie. Len even combs his hair like Valentino. He did place his hand on my knee during the show, but I removed it, and he was respectful after that. The other fellow, Karl Kreitler, from what Grace said—he was not so nice. Leonard told me that Kreitler is married! Imagine! He kept after Grace until our father threatened to beat him. That was the last we saw of Karl Kreitler. George Jones is not one to ignore if you know what's good for you.*

* * *

The tumultuous year of 1921 was winding down when Alice and Leonard first began seeing each other. The twenties had only just begun to roar its challenge of changing social mores and exciting new styles of dress, music, and popular culture, and it was all tantalizing to a smart, independent young woman such as Alice. Prohibition of the sale of alcohol was in effect, and yet Americans were drinking more. The esteemed *New York Times* declared gin the national drink and sex the national obsession. Rumrunners and bootleggers were seen as folk heroes. There was a generalized sense of newfound freedom brought about in large part by a booming economy, prevalence of the automobile, as well as heightened ethnic and racial migrations. At the same time a new word to describe an age-old movement had entered the popular vocabulary: fascism. The Nineteenth Amendment, allowing women the right to vote, had recently passed to become the law of the land. Young women were experiencing a new sense of freedom and even of incipient personal and collective power. Indeed, the hormone that made them women, called estrogen, had been identified. Alice clearly saw herself in the vanguard of this modern trend. And as a working girl with her own small income, she embodied the freedom from traditional roles that young women were beginning to experience.

"I never felt limited because I am a girl," Alice told me during one of our preliminary interviews. "Whatever I put my mind to—that's what mother always said—whatever you believe you can do, once you put your mind to it, and if you don't allow others to discourage you, you can do it. Mother and Father came to America with nothing. They were both domestic servants in England. They came to America because they believed that it is here in this country where a hardworking and clever person can have the opportunity to be whoever you make up your mind you want to be. Our father proved that. He went from a cab-driver to owning the taxi stand and the building it was in as well as other properties."

All this may have struck members of my generation as daunting and even a bit outlandish; but these children of the new age—known as flappers for the girls and sheiks for the boys—were not intimidated by the changing times, nor were they to be thwarted by rules they considered outmoded. Dating—unchaperoned outings of young men and women, a courting ritual unknown in my youth—had become quite commonplace.

The automobile had found new use as a love nest on wheels by affluent youngsters such as Leonard Rhinelander. Alice, though hardly a flapper, embraced the changing fashions, the evolving social customs, and the emerging status of women.

That a girl of Alice's humble origins would invariably choose a gracious, respectable style of dress, and exhibit refined manners in public as a result of her breeding with strict English parents, impressed Leonard. All this no doubt caused the young would-be sheik to think twice about what sort of girl Alice was. She showed him that she was in no regard some common local girl just out for a good time. Rather than being an easy conquest, Alice would force Leonard to up his game. In practical if not social ways Alice proved to be Leonard's superior, and even a few years his senior, and with more worldly experience despite the obvious chasm in class—whatever that is, I'm still trying to determine; and which I must say, over the course of the litigation and lengthy posttrial proceedings, the definition of class would come to take on new meaning.

For our second meeting, soon after our firm had been retained to represent Alice against the Rhinelander annulment lawsuit, I asked Alice to come to our offices alone, without her parents, so that I might speak with her privately about where I wished to go with this more particular and in-depth interview. I did not want Alice to feel constrained in relating sensitive details of her affair with Rhinelander due to her parents' presence. This was before I was entrusted with Alice's diaries, and at a time when we were preparing for trial. Given that the case appeared headed for the public venue of the courtroom, it was absolutely necessary that I establish and comprehend the specific dynamics and that I know the boundaries of her intimate relations with her estranged husband, to fashion Alice's defense so as not to be blindsided with evidence presented by the plaintiff's lawyers.

"Were you attracted to Rhinelander?" I asked Alice. "It's important that we establish who pursued whom."

"Well . . . attracted." She shrugged her shoulders. "Yes, of course; but not in the way you might expect. Let me see if I can explain how I felt. . . . It's hard to say exactly what was going on in my mind and in my heart at that time. I was very confused and upset having just broken off my engagement with my former beau. I felt . . . *betrayed.* I thought I was over men. But never mind. . . . Speaking of Len, well, all I can say is that at first he amused me. He took my mind off the things that were bothering me. I didn't take him as a serious suitor; it didn't feel like that, not in the beginning. He just . . . *showed up.* He seemed a lonely and timid boy to me. I know that's not at all who he was supposed to be, considering who his people are; but that's the Len I met, and the boy I got to know—but not the man who became my husband, because . . . he did become a man during the time we were together."

Alice broke off; she seemed to withdraw into herself briefly, as though remembering happier times with young Rhinelander while dismissing her present despair.

She shook her head, sighed, and brightened. "Len can be very funny once you got to know him and learned to appreciate his sense of humor. We laughed all the time. Len was particularly . . . how would I say it? He made fun of himself! And he's sweet—he's the sweetest boy I ever met. And not just for the gifts he bought me, or his car, and all of that. . . . No, honestly, *that's not it.* He's a nice boy. At least he was when we first met. And he changed while we were together; Len became a different person. He grew up. He even stopped stuttering."

Now Alice's face eased into a lovely, tender smile, the first I had seen, and she tilted her head and nodded as if assured that her memories of Rhinelander and the effect she had on him were not imagined or mistaken.

"He got better, truthfully, and I was so happy that he seemed pleased and more confident when we were together. Of course, any girl is flattered by a young man's attention, but I was used to that. And Len is not a typical beau. You know, the way some boys can be such show-offs and braggarts. Len wasn't like that, although he did sometimes tend to go on a bit about how rich his family is, and how, on a shopping trip, the shop girls and clerks fell all over each other to serve him. I'm sure he wanted to give me the impression that he would buy me nice things—and he did. . . . But truly, he needn't show off, and I told him. I said, 'Just be who you are, Len. Be a nice boy.' His car, his clothes—you knew when you met Len that he came from money; he didn't hide who his family was. But still, he had to be—I don't know how to explain it—*true*. . . . He had to be true to who he really was: the Rhinelander name, their money. . . . But so what? That doesn't impress me—honestly. I'm more like my father in that respect. George Jones taught his girls not to be taken in by those who try to impress you with their money or who their family is. In fact, he's leery when it comes to the behavior of rich people. He'd seen plenty of that growing up poor in England—an orphan, and going to work in the private homes of the gentry, and he said that one of the reasons he came to America, actually the main reason, was to get away from all that snobbery and supposed class superiority."

Alice shook her head and waved a dismissive hand. "In our home we girls were taught to judge a person by their actions and not by their outward appearance or their last name. I wanted to know what kind of a person Len really was—his character, no matter how much money he may have had, or what he could buy for me. Grace had told me . . . I mean to say, of course we understood who the Rhinelanders were. In New Rochelle the Rhinelander name is well known, even famous, as it is in New York City.

"Now, since the case has been brought against me by Len's family . . . well, I'm sure we will find out who we really are—both the Rhinelanders and the Joneses. People believe they know who the Rhinelanders are because of their wealth. We knew—the Jones family knew who we were long before Len started to come around. Nothing can change that."

Alice shook her head and stuck out her chin. "I hope you understand, Mr. Davis, and I mean this truly: I'm not impressed with all that society nonsense or whatever it is—*I don't care.* And the money, of course it's nice. But it's not going to cause me to love someone or to be attracted to them if they are not good to me. No, we don't sit around in the Jones home and plot how we would attract rich men to take advantage of them."

Alice fixed me with that penetrating dark gaze, as though challenging me to disbelieve her. Indeed, considering the facts, it would be our burden to prove Alice had not pursued Rhinelander and seduced him into marrying her for his family's money; therefore, as her advocate, I wanted to believe her.

"Len chased me—not the other way around," Alice said and boldly reached across the table and gave my hand a brief squeeze.

"I am telling you the truth, Mr. Davis. You can count on this. What I care about, what my parents—particularly my father—what George Jones told us girls always to be aware of is what kind of a person is this you are getting to know. Are they decent, honest, sincere people? That's the most important consideration, no matter how much money they may have. Our father lived by those words, and it has served him well."

"I believe you, Alice," I assured her, "and, of course, as your attorney it is my job to believe you and, should we end up having to try this case, it would be up to me to convince a judge and possibly a jury of the sincerity of your motives in marrying Leonard. If not the money, if not the social status of the Rhinelander family name, then you must tell me, help me understand: What was it that attracted you to the Rhinelander boy?"

Alice sat back in her chair and gave the question some thought before answering.

"Well," she began, "my word to describe Len—and I wrote this in my diary—and what I like so much about him—he is kind, that's all. *Simple.* He's polite. He's gentle. And he is thoughtful. He seemed to really care for me . . . almost from . . . well, it didn't take long. He wrote me such nice, loving letters. And he kept coming back—that's what impressed me about Len: he's persistent . . . and patient. He doesn't give up easily. He took his time when courting me, and that meant a lot to me with regard to his . . . intentions, what he hoped to get from courting me, and the respect he showed me. Len wasn't just looking for a fling with some common girl. I honestly believe he fell in love with me."

Alice gave me an arch look and moved her body slightly, as if to acknowledge that her physical charms would not go unnoticed even by a man of Rhinelander's social remove.

Boy meets girl: nothing new happening here except when one considers that Rhinelander pursued Alice after his odd fashion, which is to say with blind, inept, and yet single-minded determination; and Alice responded, although they were both well aware that the Rhinelander boy was from a social class far above a woman of the Jones family's position and background.

"We knew," Alice admitted, "yes, of course, we talked about how people would react to our keeping company—particularly Len's family. There was no question—we both knew we were going against everything his people stood for and believed in.

But in some ways I believe that I was more aware of it—or more *afraid*, you could say—than Len. Also, because my parents—particularly my father—*George Jones was dead set against my seeing Len.* At one point early on, my father told Len he was not to come around anymore. I was so upset. . . . After that, for a while at least, we would meet secretly at my sister's, at Emily's home. This is what I mean about Len—he's not easily discouraged; he's determined. Now I was the one who was worried about what my father would do if he found out—which of course he did. But by then it was too late. Once we were married, my parents accepted Len. They welcomed him into our home."

As Alice's counsel, if we were to go to trial, I would have to convince a jury that neither Alice nor any member of her family plotted to cause Alice to lure Leonard into marriage solely to gain access to the Rhinelander family's wealth and social standing; this, undoubtedly, would be alleged and purposefully, forcefully argued at trial by Rhinelander's attorneys. On the contrary, I would seek to show that, for George Jones and his wife, Elizabeth, coming as they did from England with its firmly entrenched social class delineations, to the Joneses, the match of their daughter to a Rhinelander was unthinkable.

"Then you weren't . . . you were not encouraged to pursue a relationship with Rhinelander in the hopes of inducing him to marry you?"

"No, not at all; *quite the opposite,*" Alice assured me. "Oh, my sisters might have been impressed in the beginning when Len kept coming around. And they teased me about how I would soon forget them once I became a Rhinelander and moved into my mansion in the city. But . . . *not my parents.* To them, Len's interest was seen more as a threat . . . as a possible hindrance to both our happiness."

"How so? What did they say?"

"We talked about it a lot. They were sure that Len's family would never accept me as his wife . . . and for me to be part of the Rhinelander family. It was impossible."

"How did that make you feel?" I asked her.

"Well, it hurt . . . of course. On the one hand, I was so in love with Len, it made me happy just to be with him. But on the other hand, I was upset by the fact that I wasn't considered *good enough* to be his girl . . . and then . . . *his wife.* It upset me, and it made me *angry* . . . even though—well, we all knew how . . . *difficult* it would be.

"When we were together, nothing else mattered. It was the happiest time of my whole life—and his, I'm sure. He told me how happy it made him feel to be with me, and I could see it in him. He was a different person when we were alone together—or when we went out, particularly in the city; he seemed proud to have me as his girl. But at the same time . . . of course I was terrified. We both were so scared that someday—*this day*—would come . . . and we would be *forced to let each other go.*"

Alice's eyes welled with tears. "We were so happy together, Mr. Davis," she whimpered. "Every day . . . I would wake up and just thank God I was alive and I was loved and that I had Len for me to give my love. . . . And now, since those men came and took Len away . . . I cry myself to sleep every night."

Alice took a handkerchief from her bag and stifled her tears. "My life—our lives—and everything Len and I had together . . . now it has all been turned into something *shameful . . . and horrid.*"

In a moment, as Alice seemed to pull herself together, I remember wondering, *Is this all just an act? Is it in fact all about the money?*

I stood, as did she, and I saw her to my office door.

"I'm sorry, my dear," I said and sought to console her by putting my arm around her shoulder and hugging her gently as I walked her to the door of my office. Already she had become more than a client to me. I wanted to believe her. She was a spurned woman I had come to admire and respect. If she were acting, then it was a convincing performance.

"But—and this is important," I counseled her. "Here . . . and going forward—*you must think long and hard about how you wish to proceed*. . . . It will be . . . *painful*, Alice."

We stopped at the door to the outer office. I held both her hands and looked in her tearful eyes.

"I—for one," I continued, "I am loath to see you hurt and for you to suffer any more than you have already endured. This is a lot of money Rhinelander has offered. And, as your attorney it is my duty to remind you—*to warn you*—of what lies ahead if this goes to trial. A trial—any trial, but particularly a trial like this—can be *a harrowing experience*. I can assure you it will be *dreadful*. Not only for you, but also for your entire family. . . . And so, once more, I must ask you, and assure you as your lawyer, that it is still not too late for you to change your mind and accept a settlement—and to spare yourself the pain and suffering that a trial like this will inevitably bring to you and to your entire family. . . . This is your decision, of course; but you have my advice. I want you to think it over very carefully—"

Alice stifled her sobs and started, "Mr. Davis, I—"

"Not now, my dear," I stopped her. "I want you to go home, spend time with your family, discuss this with them, and pray—I know you are a good Christian woman and can ask God for His guidance—and then search your mind and your soul and be *absolutely sure that this is what you want to do*. Will you do that? . . . For me?"

"Yes, I will, Mr. Davis."

"Promise?"

This elicited a quick smile, then she said, "Yes, I promise."

It would be a few days before I saw Alice again, and in that time I had cause to think long and hard of how I hoped Alice would decide whether she wanted to go forward with a trial, or to accept the cash settlement and be done with it. Finally, I received word at the office that Alice had called to ask if I would attend a family meeting at the Jones home to discuss her decision. Exactly what that decision was, I still did not know.

In the meantime, for reasons that would soon become apparent, I had come to believe that we had a strong case. Rhinelander's attorneys appeared anxious to settle and avoid a trial. Of course, given the notoriety a trial would bring to their son and to the entire Rhinelander domain with the public exposure, it was expected that Rhinelander Senior would want to make it all go away as quickly and quietly as possible. Leon Jacobs, the Rhinelanders' Manhattan attorney, contacted me and offered that they were open to negotiate a higher sum if Alice would consent to the annulment. When I conveyed this to Alice, she maintained that she would refuse to accept any amount.

Her determination was inspiring, however impractical. The very real possibility of losing against a formidable adversary at trial, and all that would mean for Alice going forward, was not to be discounted. Rhinelander had unlimited funds with which to mount his prosecution. As it began to appear that a trial was inevitable, Rhinelander hired the best local law firm to assist his Manhattan attorneys; indeed, Rhinelander's lead counsel was to be my former mentor, Samuel Swinburne. Swinburne would be assisted by Isaac Mills, a renowned trial attorney known for his incisive cross-examination and brilliant oratory.

Nevertheless, as is my practice, and never wishing to be forced to trial ill prepared, even before I was entirely convinced that we were going to litigate the lawsuit in a courtroom before a jury, I began in my mind to formulate Alice's defense.

* * *

There can have been no question what the Rhinelanders' wealth and elevated social status would mean for Alice's future had the marriage endured; and so, to defend her, I would have to overcome that presumption of her motives: that she was an avaricious and conniving girl who was only attracted to Leonard, and had cajoled him into marrying her solely for what gain she and her family, as would be alleged, believed they could achieve for themselves through the marriage. Certainly one could argue that the opposite was also possible; and, as we would show, more likely: that Kip Rhinelander might well have been disowned for marrying Alice; that the couple could just as easily have found themselves ostracized from the proud family fold, cast out barefoot and broke, and living in a hovel.

As I focused on preparing Alice's defense, even before I was convinced of her final decision, and in meetings with the other attorneys in our firm who would be tasked to assist me should we have to try the case, I had to determine, and to find a way to express exactly, what had attracted Alice to Leonard Rhinelander other than his family's money and vaunted social standing. This question was key to Alice's defense. I would need to convince a jury that this was a marriage based on true love.

It would surely be noted that Alice was in fact four years Leonard's senior; and, as she intimated, more experienced in matters of love. Her physical attractiveness was undeniable. The men on the jury could not help but perceive what motivated the Rhinelander boy to pursue Alice on a purely sensual level. She was voluptuous, well endowed, and yet lissome; she moved gracefully; she gave the impression of being aware of, and comfortable with, her physical attributes. To defend against the likely characterization of Alice as the more experienced female vamp, I would need to know all about her past love affairs should it come out in testimony.

* * *

Alice and I went for a walk together in the evening after my meeting with the Jones family, and I found the opportunity to ask her pointedly if she had been chaste when she and Leonard met and courted.

"No," Alice blushed and admitted, "I was not a virgin when Len and I met. I had another beau with whom I was . . . we were intimate. We . . . we planned to marry but I . . . in the end, I knew it was wrong, that it would not work, and so I broke it off. My father certainly didn't approve, nor did Mother. It was a mistake. I regret it." She fell silent.

"I don't need to know details," I assured her after a moment. "But it may come out, so it's important to be prepared. If you were to decide to testify, then it would surely be brought out along with anything else the Rhinelander lawyers could find to hope to impeach your character.

"Of course, in a case like this, these matters are ordinarily relevant, as they go to the foundation of intimate relations between husband and wife. We must be prepared for the Rhinelander lawyers to attempt to dig up, and to enter into evidence, *anything* and *everything* they can find to try to make it appear that you are an immoral woman. They will seek to portray you as a common tramp who seduced a naive young boy from a good family purely for your own financial gain.

"I must warn you, Alice. When this goes to trial, these sorts of things are exactly what Rhinelander's lawyers will wish to get into evidence to persuade the jury . . . in an attempt to bring you and your family into the gutter. So . . . you must be prepared. And you need to help me be prepared as well by telling me everything so that I might defend you effectively and that I not be caught unawares."

* * *

Leonard was hardly a dashing Valentino chap despite his wardrobe and slicked-back hairdo. He wears enormous, round tortoiseshell frame glasses that resemble goggles and give him a curious owlish appearance. His lanky body gives the impression of being soft and hardly athletic. Alice would call him a "teddy bear"; that presumably was his charm: he was cuddly. He was not threatening, and I could understand how he might feel encouraged by her attentions. Alice is undeniably an unusually attractive young woman. A bashful boy with low self-esteem could certainly find it stimulating and be proud to display a newly found swagger with a girl like Alice on his arm.

As Alice recorded in her diary, the affair progressed quickly. *Len asked me out for a ride in his automobile,* she wrote. *I finally agreed to go when Father was not at home. We held hands, although it was awkward because he had to keep shifting gears. It was a beautiful day. We parked and Len put his arm around my shoulder. We kissed. I could tell that Len didn't really know how to kiss a girl. So I showed him. I told him to pucker his lips, and I showed him how to make his mouth feel soft and welcoming.*

Rhinelander would confess in his letters to Alice that he was thrilled with each new posture in this age-old ritual; and he kept coming back for more. Again, these were hardly uncharted territories in the exploration of young love—at least in the beginning.

"Len wasn't an experienced lover," Alice had confided to me when I questioned her about her relations with Rhinelander. We were again in my office and without her parents present.

"To be truthful, he hardly knew what to do with a girl. I found it charming. He had sweaty hands! And so soft. Hands that . . . well, hands that never knew a day's hard work, as my father would say . . . and gentle hands that never knew how to caress a girl."

She laughed and crossed her legs; then she leaned in as if to impart a secret.

"He was awkward," she said with her smoky low voice. "He got so nervous. He bumbled into things. He might walk into a door instead of through it. He made me laugh. Oh, how we both laughed! We had such fun together, Mr. Davis. Leonard could be funny in his own way. Yes, he was spoiled. *Of course.* Do you see? His hands were so delicate, and he adored my hands, and how I made him feel. I wanted to take him by the hand and lead him; I wanted to show him another way: how to become the man he wanted to be. But I also wanted him to learn to find his own way . . . if he could. Does that make sense?" she asked and scowled at me.

"I'm not suggesting he was offish or brash," she went on. "Not in the least. Nor was he a mollycoddle. No, it's not that. Len has refined manners. He was well brought up, of course. And he could be adventurous. I knew he wanted to live an exciting and different life from how he had been raised . . . sheltered, and lonely. I think that was a big part of who he was—his adventurous spirit; his wish to be something more than just a spoiled rich boy. But there is also what I would call a kind of innocence to

Len that I found so delightful and fresh but that could also be frustrating."

I asked her straight out, "What then was it that attracted you to Leonard, Alice? We must overcome the presumption that you were only interested in Rhinelander for his family's wealth."

"Can I say yes and no? Of course I knew Len's family is rich. But I married him knowing that he might be . . . *disowned.* We talked about that, how his family . . . well, how they could well cut him off, as had happened to his uncle. . . . I'm sure you know about that."

"Yes, I do."

"So you see, Mr. Davis, *it didn't matter to us*. I married Leonard knowing full well that he too might have been . . . well, that he might have had to find his own way; and we were ready to accept that and to go about it together. I could go on and on about Len . . . because, well, I married him. I married Leonard because he treated me with respect. And I . . . *I love him.* And that's the simple truth. He's such a silly boy, yet so much fun . . . and he was so good to me, so kind and thoughtful. I'd never known another boy who cared so much for me. And how we laughed when we were together! We could talk for hours and never grow tired of what the other person thought.

"It was all brand-new, in a way, a great adventure for us both to have someone we felt so close to—but particularly for Len. I don't believe that, from the time of his mother's death, anyone ever told Len that they loved him. He was unguarded, if you know what I mean—open . . . and willing to try new experiences. But mostly he was so head over heels in love that—we both were! It was, well, do you know? I hope you do: *to feel that kind of love from another person—how it can make you feel?* So good. So *worthy*. As though God were looking down on you and saying, 'Here, I give you this love, to let you know what life is really all about—now cherish it.'"

I shook my head and stopped her. "Fine, I understand that, and that's all well and good. But you are a bright young lady, and so thoughtful. Surely you must have known—both you and Rhinelander must have been aware that his family would . . . well, *object*; and even strenuously resist Leonard. . . . I don't mean to say that I find you—"

"You needn't explain, Mr. Davis," Alice interrupted. "I understand. People might look down on me and say I'm common. But not Leonard. To him I was special—and look who he is! A Rhinelander! Yes, it's surprising, and it can be overwhelming. But it was—*it is*—true love."

Alice sat up and gazed at me with an amused scowl as though she were letting me in on a secret.

"Do you see? It was . . . *impossible to control* . . . for us both," she insisted. "I don't want you for a minute to imagine that I was in control—no, I was afraid. *Very much afraid. Terrified* of where this was going . . . and so was Len. We were both scared, and yet *attracted even by the fear,* even drawn to the danger of how we knew his people would react . . . and even my people, how they would all—well, you see it. It was exciting, you understand. *My God!* People are so . . . *upset.* But at the time, we didn't care. We were doing what we liked, what felt right to us, and what made us feel good about ourselves."

Alice shook her head and closed her eyes; then she sighed. "And now, Jesus, God . . . look what it has become. *Just the opposite!* A scandal; something made to make us feel like criminals. There are people out there in the street that would like to *kill us* for being in love. *Yes, it's true.* . . . I see it in their faces when they look at me. And yet . . . we couldn't help feeling so deeply for one another. . . . It just happened. Len couldn't stop himself.

Nor could I stop wanting him. Even if we tried to stop those feelings, they were too strong. It really was beyond our control."

Alice leaned in close to me and took hold of my hand. "And do you know, Mr. Davis? This is something . . . that surprised us both. This made us laugh."

She chortled and squeezed my hand.

"Within weeks, maybe it was even days—anyway, God's truth, you can ask Len—very early on as we came to know each other better—I'm not making this up, Mr. Davis, it's the truth. Len's stutter, his stammer that was so embarrassing to him, and so *pronounced* at the beginning when we first met, he could barely get a sentence out without getting all flustered and tongue-tied—why, it nearly disappeared! His stutter was practically gone. He told me that his teachers at the school he attended—the Orchards School in Stamford, where Len stayed when we first met—his teachers were so impressed with his progress after we started seeing one another, they were amazed. What do you think of that? Len's father sent him off to the Orchards, but—"

Alice emitted a girlish titter and flashed me the loveliest smile. "*I cured Len!*" she exclaimed. "With my love . . . I made Leonard better."

* * *

While the couple continued to meet at the home of Alice's older, married sister, Emily, Leonard became friendly with Emily's husband, Robert Brooks—another important fact I wished to get before the jury. Leonard and Alice often spent an evening at Emily's home, where Leonard played poker with Brooks and a few of his friends. Leonard also became quite fond of Emily and Robert Brooks's child, young Roberta. He would bring the little girl gifts, and he became known to her as "Uncle Len."

We are very happy, Alice wrote in her diary of this time, *even if my parents, and certainly Len's family, are not. These are the happiest days of my life. Len is so sweet with Roberta. I can see he's going to be a devoted and doting father. He and Robert hit it off as well. Robert is very good with automobiles. He takes care of Len's car for him when Len takes the train into the city. It's a forest green sports roadster. Robert polishes that car so that it shines like an emerald. He changed the oil and tuned the engine. He and Len have become quite good friends. There's no snobbishness, no superior feelings on Len's part.*

This all transpired during the late fall and early winter of 1921. These are facts, important details, that were to become a significant part of a timeline that would prove to be crucial evidence.

* * *

Before trial I met with Alice for tea one last time at the Jones home in Pelham Manor, where we were to continue our interview and finalize preparations for Alice's defense.

There was still some question whether the case would go to trial. Motions had been filed from both sides challenging everything from the grounds for annulment to the venue, and even the emotional and mental statuses of the parties. Rhinelander's lawyers were doing everything within the law to try to avoid a public trial. Alice was adamant that she would not accept a monetary settlement; but there was pressure being brought to bear from various sources for her to acquiesce to Rhinelander's terms and agree to dissolve the marriage. As well, there were legal hurdles for the plaintiff to overcome.

As Alice continued to resist, Rhinelander's attorneys raised the specter of a jury trial. Indeed, I believe this had been their fallback plan all along, as they believed they lacked credible grounds to have the marriage annulled by the court, and so they would seek to base their case on bias and hope to impanel a jury they could sway with prejudice in lieu of evidence. This tactic of the Rhinelander attorneys became apparent with the filing of their final, amended complaint.

It was incumbent on me as Alice's attorney, and with respect to opposing counsel as well as my assurances to Philip Rhinelander, that I should be cognizant of Alice's state of mind, and for me to establish that she was well informed and prepared so that she was aware of exactly what she was getting herself—and her family—into by forcing Rhinelander's hand if there was to be no agreement.

By this point I had not yet seen the final version of the lawsuit with its bill of particulars; it was still a work in progress with every attempt being made to end the marriage without a public trial. It was a most unsettling time. I wasn't yet aware of exactly what Rhinelander's attorneys would bring as grounds to annul what was—in New York, at least—a perfectly legal marriage between two consenting adults.

* * *

When I entered the Joneses' home to meet with Alice, I could easily surmise Leonard Rhinelander's impressions given what to him must have seemed a cottage. Yet the atmosphere is one of welcoming and even cozy comfort; I immediately felt at home. Elizabeth Jones knows how to make guests in her home feel content and at ease. And who knows better how to serve tea and toast than a woman of English stock?

"I always knew I was pretty," Alice admitted when I asked her what she thought attracted Rhinelander to her. By this time her mother had withdrawn.

"It's a great advantage . . . for a girl, as I'm sure you know," she went on. "I don't mean to sound conceited, because it can also be a fault if you become vain and depend on your looks, or if you are standoffish and think yourself better than other, less pretty girls. We all grow old and lose our looks—there is no way around it. Mother always told us—my sisters, Grace and Emily—well, you've seen them. They are pretty as well. Mother always would say: 'Your looks may get you in the door, but your brains and your manners will keep you there.'

"I think Len liked me—he liked all of us, the whole family—because he could relax around us," she continued. "Once Father accepted Len, after we were married, when he was in our home, we made Len feel welcome and comfortable. As I said, I don't think he ever really felt welcomed and loved even in his own home and with his own people. You see, with us, Len could just . . . *be himself.* He could be funny and laugh, be sweet and feel good, relax and have fun. We listened to records on my Victrola. I remember, my favorite song at the time was 'Love Will Find a Way.' It became a kind of theme song for our marriage. Whenever we would wonder how we were ever going to manage to stay together, Len would say, 'Love will find a way.'"

Tears glistened in Alice's enormous eyes.

"I believed that as well," she went on. "It seems so sad to me now when I think of how good . . . we both felt; and of how happy we were. I would play piano and Len and the others would sing along. We had toast and tea in the evening. Len would dry the dishes after Mother and I washed up. He was like . . . well, he became part of the family.

"Truly, it was that kind of family atmosphere in our home." Alice gestured with her lithe bare arm, indicating the room, and the Joneses' home. "And something perhaps that Len never had, that he never felt in his own home—that kind of warmth and joy. He didn't need to put on airs; there was no need to act according to any set standard of who we thought he should be, if you know what I mean. He could just be himself.

"Now, O God, all I do is worry . . . my family, what this has done to us all, with the *publicity* . . . the reaction around town . . . *it's horrible.*"

"Yes, my dear . . . and it will only get worse—"

"Len would sometimes talk to me about his family," Alice went on, hardly wishing to dwell on what she was getting herself into. "In particular, he worried about his father, Philip. Now, I know, and I knew it then that it was a great deal of pressure and . . . well, as I said, *fear* for Len. He was fearful of not living up to the family name and his father's expectations of who he should be. He told me about his older brothers; how they had been members of something called the Knickerbocker Greys. I have no idea what that meant, but I know how Leonard felt, that it was a big deal and that he could never measure up to his brothers and his father's expectations of what it meant to be a Rhinelander. It worried him . . . and I know he was devastated over the loss of his mother. Len told me how he adored his mother . . . losing her while still a boy . . . well, he never got over it. And yet—and this is the craziest part of it all—as afraid as Len was of what was happening, as terrified as we both were—*it was exciting.* We felt like we were doing something . . . not only daring, *but also good*, something worthy and important with our love, acting out of love. And now—"

Alice broke off. She appeared about to weep; then she pulled herself together. It struck me at the time, and I would be reminded often of this power of hers to control her emotions; it was a quality that would greatly influence my strategy during the trial. It's what her English forebears might refer to as "keeping a stiff upper lip." However, I also believe that Alice's trust in herself, and in her feelings for Leonard, came from knowing that she was being true to their love, and that was what gave her the will to go on in the face of great emotional duress, that she was living her truth.

"Quite frankly," Alice went on, "I had no idea at first of just how hoity-toity the Rhinelanders were until . . . much later. I mean to say, yes, of course I had heard of the Rhinelanders. As you know, the name is well known in our village. But in all honesty, I never imagined the lengths to which they would go to separate us to—*what?* And I let that influence my feelings for Leonard. People may say what they like, I don't care, because I know the truth, and the truth is . . . I fell in love with Len—honestly. I fell in love with the boy I knew, the boy I married—it's that simple. And I wanted to believe that his family—Len would always say that his family would eventually come around. Who the Rhinelanders were in society never interested me in the least. I don't care about any of that. I like poetry. Music. The arts. Movies. Len and I often went to the movies. And I wrote him poems, and I sent them to him in my letters. I wasn't just after him for what I thought I could get out of it. *No, not at all,* Mr. Davis. That is a misconception and a horrid lie."

Alice shook her head and held up her hands as if to push away any suggestion of her as a gold digger. Then she smiled while recalling better times.

"It was an exciting time . . . especially for girls. When you think of how things were changing in the world, certainly here in America with the way women were changing, as far as our status, and how we girls were coming to be accepted in society. That was something. I think what Len liked about me besides my looks is that I was interested in everything new and exciting that was happening in the world, and I wanted to be part of it; I was determined to be part of it. So was Len. We both wanted to be part of the changes taking place in society, and not stuck in the old ways. Do you see? I never wanted to be some old-fashioned girl who was afraid of how the world was changing and who just wanted to be a stay-at-home wife and do and say nothing but 'Yes, sir' and 'No, sir.' No, not Alice Jones Rhinelander. That's not me at all."

Alice laughed. She seemed to delight in recalling how the love she had with Rhinelander had affected them both.

"I wanted adventure in my life . . . excitement. . . . I wanted *to be somebody*, and I wanted the opportunity to go places and do things that were new and fun. We both did. And Len was . . . despite being shy and a bit awkward he was interested in how things in America and in the world were changing. He was adventurous in his own way, and he wanted to be part of the modern world. We had so much fun together, especially when we went into the city. Len could just be himself and laugh and be gay without having to worry about how to keep up pretenses."

Mrs. Jones, who rejoined the conversation to serve more tea, concurred. "The Rhinelander lad was very happy when he visited our home—more than visited," she emphasized. "Why, Leonard lived here for a time. He came to live here with us as one of the family after he and Alice married, and until his father sent those men to take him away . . . and broke my poor dear Alice's heart."

* * *

When I met separately with Alice's father, George Jones—he came by our offices to deliver a payment toward his daughter's defense costs that had been provided by Rhinelander's attorneys—I had occasion to ask his impressions of Leonard and the wealthy scion's pursuit of his daughter—knowing, as I did, of his reservations.

"Well, I wasn't for it," Jones confided. "Not in the beginning, in any case. I'd come home from work and see his fancy automobile parked out front of our home, and it upset me; more so, it worried me. The chap was nice enough, and certainly kind to Alice. But it just seemed . . . *out of kilter*—wrong, these two together. As a father, I never want to see any of my girls hurt . . . as would be expected. I know there are rumors around town that we . . . that Mrs. Jones and me, that we saw this fellow as a fine husband for Alice, and even hoped his relations with our daughter might come as a source of financial gain for our family.

"*I am here to tell you, Mr. Davis, that was never the case,*" George Jones stated emphatically.

"We are not those sort of people. That is not how I as a man conduct myself. I make my own way in life—always have. In fact, I will say to you, and to all who care to listen, that I appealed to Rhinelander to end the affair: I certainly did. Why, I told the boy to stop seeing Alice, though I might have known the youngsters were not going to listen. I knew that if they persisted, if they kept it up, it would end badly, and certainly be hurtful for my daughter."

George Jones looked me in the eye and spoke with assurance. Now I could see where Alice got her strong character as well as her good looks.

"My wife and I, my girls . . . I dare say, we all understand the value and importance of honest hard work when it comes to making one's way in this world," Jones averred. "Alice worked in domestic service from the age of fourteen. When I met Mrs. Jones we were both employed as household staff on a large estate in Lincolnshire. And though we may not be educated—and yes, we are working people; but we are well acquainted with the lackadaisical . . . and, let me say, the often *hurtful* ways of the leisure class when it comes to relations with those they consider their inferiors. And that is particularly true with the American upper classes.

"Young Rhinelander struck me as a bit of a wag. Oh, he was nice enough, and very polite. But I didn't trust his intentions, not at first. Nor as time went on did I get the sense of a man with a stiff backbone. Now, something else may have been stiff, if you follow. . . . But his resolve, the boy's grasp of the rough and tumble ways of the world: all that seemed lacking to me. I've no doubt he was stuck on Alice from the start.

"You know, Mr. Davis, and I'm sure you can see it when you look at Alice or any of my girls beside the pale likes of the lasses I'm sure Rhinelander grew up around and was expected to court; now I ask you, truthfully: What man wouldn't like what he saw in my daughter? She's lovely, she's smart, she's full of life. But a man has got to have some character to make his place in this world, especially if he is to take up with a girl like Alice, and the Rhinelander fellow . . . well, whatever gumption he might have had as a man, his father, Philip Rhinelander, *scared it right out of the boy.* Or we would not be sitting here now and having this discussion."

I made note of his observation: again, *fear.*

Alice had intimated that Leonard was fearful of how he was perceived by his family, and in particular by his father, Philip Rhinelander. This made perfect sense to me after having met Rhinelander in our offices and heard his opinion regarding his son's feelings for the woman he married. In his subsequent visits to our offices, and in the filings we saw, Rhinelander Senior demonstrated that he intended to exercise his control over his son's future regardless of the fact that Leonard had reached the legal age of consent; and it was apparent that the father would do all within his considerable power to protect the celebrated Rhinelander name.

Their heritage and family dynasty went as far back as the late 1700s, when William and Frederick Rhinelander built a flourishing business in sugar and shipbuilding. They built the vessels, they purchased sugar from the Caribbean islands, and they imported sugar and other products to the United States. The Rhinelanders were said to be millionaires at a time when the Rockefellers were still farming on Staten Island.

So from the standpoint of devising a trial strategy, I now had an intimation of where to look for the basis of Alice's defense. The case against her was motivated by fear, that basic human emotion. But fear of what? Where was the substance of that fear? I had to know this to attack the Rhinelanders' case against Alice.

What were they afraid of?

* * *

My guiding principle in preparing a case for trial has always been to first devise, and then to fully flesh out, a credible and coherent theory of defense, a convincing counternarrative to the plaintiff's allegations. And then to make certain that all my facts—or at least those facts I intend to base my argument on—support and elucidate my theory. Next I look for an interpretation of the facts, or for proof of the baseless grounds I am aware my adversary intends to build his argument on that will ultimately come to support my theory; and finally, to craft an accessible and engaging, credible opposing narrative based on those facts—that is, to tell a better story with a structure that a judge and a jury can follow, and a theme that they can relate to as well as to find proved by the evidence.

Now, I have high regard for my adversary at the bar in Rhinelander; indeed, Isaac Mills was my teacher—my mentor, as it were. I was aware that he could be merciless in his pursuit of victory in a case as hard fought and with as much riding on the verdict as the Rhinelander lawsuit would surely be; he would be vituperative and demeaning in his examination of opposing witnesses; and so I hoped to spare Alice and her family that embarrassment and trauma. But it was not to be.

Fear, by God! Yes, now I'd heard it twice. Everyone was afraid—I included—and yet compelled by the fear. Only Alice was not afraid to stand in her truth. I was afraid of the hurt that would be visited upon her—it had already begun; but more, much more was to be expected. I was in fear of losing the case and what that would mean for Alice; and so I wanted nothing more than to deflect the fear back upon Alice's accusers, for they too had to be motivated by fear. Young Rhinelander was deathly afraid of his father; and his father, Philip Rhinelander, for all his wealth and power, this pillar of society was equally afraid of Alice and everything she stood for, and what it would mean to have her claim a perch on that lofty and exclusive family tree. Society itself was afraid of and yet fascinated by what this case might reveal about dark human passions and what it might mean for the future of this great nation and our professed beliefs of racial purity.

So it was here, in that universal emotion and with its intrigue and excitement that I would discover my thesis as well as the narrative spine of Alice's defense—everyone was operating out of fear.

CHAPTER FOUR

Courting Alice

You must believe me, for it is the truth—my truth: I never wanted it to come to this . . . *this lawsuit!*

Of course I didn't! What man in his right mind—and some may find that debatable when it comes to assessing my mental state at the time, as well as now—but who, knowing Alice and caring for her as I did—*as I still do!* I'm not afraid to say—who would want to find oneself in such a God-awful predicament? Dear Lord, forgive me—*what have I done?* What have I allowed to be done to this blameless girl in my name? And why? What good could possibly come of this?

Oh . . . I'm a shit! That's what I am . . . you can say that. Or call me a craven coward. There are days I can hardly bear to see myself in the looking glass without wishing to smash my reflection to bits. And I will never forgive myself; I will forever loathe myself for being the useless excuse for a man that I am, and for allowing this disgrace to come upon dear Alice.

But how was I to do otherwise? My father, and the memory of my mother that he would constantly use to reprove me . . . God knows: Where am I to find that strength of character to stand up to my father and the threat of the dishonor to be brought upon my mother's name? If only I knew . . .

And now, of course, it's too late. The die has been cast. It must all come out in court and be exposed for the world to see.

Alice has power. She has a fine, invisible essence and force emanating from her presence that heightens her attraction, almost like an intoxicating scent. As well, there is something in the way she moves, a kind of lithe feminine strut like she is prancing out onstage, that takes advantage of and shows off every feminine shape and subtle curve and movement of her woman's body. I was mesmerized by the way she moves.

The first time I met Alice, going back to that day when I met her at her parents' home, I was so excited even by the gentle touch of her lovely hand, the mere brush of her sensuous body against mine that, when I returned to my room at the Orchards, I had to relieve myself while picturing her in my mind—I'll admit it all here; I don't give a damn anymore, helpless fool for love that I am. The truth will out, all the sordid details. So it must! It's already too late. *It's all there, in the letters!*

Jesus Christ, the letters! O my God, those letters. I was powerless to keep Alice's letters out of my lawyer's hands. Yes, I admit—*I'm weak*—weak and strong both at once. Strong in my desire; yet weak in my belief in myself.

Yes, everything must come out. Let it all be revealed, and may the truth hold sway; I don't care anymore. I was delirious with lust: an addict, I lost my will . . . and my mind. Call that bewitched if you wish, I can't help it. And yes, certainly the letters—our letters proved both the fire of our passion, and the lack of restraint. In that respect, Father was right: I lost control over my emotions, something that a Rhinelander man must never be guilty of. But the truth is, what happened that perhaps only Alice and I understand is that the physical passion we felt for each other grew to become something greater—true love; it grew into love between a man and a woman; and it became the desire to make a life together as husband and wife. Is that so regrettable, that our affection for each other became something far greater than simply base lust? Was I wrong to fall in love with Alice and to want to take her for my wife?

No, no, I was not. Nor do I blame Karl Kreitler for leading me astray. That is simply another all-too-convenient excuse for what is in fact my lack of purpose. I knew who Kreitler was, and I knew he was married. I knew he was something of a rake, and that he fancied himself a skilled seducer of young girls. And that he espied his prey on the streets of New Rochelle, and he planned to use me and my auto as his chariot to attract local, common girls and take them for a ride and perhaps do some necking . . . and more: petting, fondling their breasts . . .

He told me all about this, how the girls might sometimes let him unclasp their brassieres and expose their bare breasts, "feel them up," he called it; how it worked once you got them aroused with kisses and caresses. And then you might go for the forbidden spots. Kreitler carried a flask of gin to spike the girls' drinks. It was all planned ahead of time, all thought out; premeditated, you could say. The idea was to have some harmless fun with common girls.

But of course it didn't work out that way, at least not with Alice. No, it was never simple, never that easy—nothing is easy or simple with Alice except to be captivated by her. It was always much deeper, more complicated, and more interesting—more exciting. Alice got under my skin; I don't know how else to explain it. She invaded my body as well as my dreams. Nothing could ever quite satisfy my desire for her whether I was with her, or when we were apart. It was like living, like breathing; seeing Alice, looking at her, and being seen with her was something I needed to do to continue to exist. If that is bewitched, well, then so be it. I had never known or been around another girl like Alice, and all I wanted was to continue to be close to her and to have her love me.

Certainly I knew my father would never approve of my courting Alice. I'd heard and knew all too well the stories of my uncle William Copeland Rhinelander, my father's wayward brother, who shocked the family when he determined to marry a domestic servant soon after graduating from Columbia and turning twenty-one. William's bride was named Margueretta McGuiness. She claimed to be descended from Irish royalty, in fact, because she was Irish, but working-class, and so she could never be accepted as a Rhinelander. William, however, was resolute. Despite the threat that he would be cut off from the family inheritance, he went through with the marriage regardless. The scandal worsened when Uncle William shot John Drake, a family attorney whom William accused of trying to alienate his wife and seduce her by offering her money to go back to Ireland and never to return. The lawyer eventually died as a result of his wounds.

William killed his lawyer! Who does such a thing? He was never tried for the deadly assault. All is forgiven if you are a Rhinelander and you toe the line. I should have done the same to my lawyer, Leon Jacobs, that conniving snake. I should have strangled the little weasel. Uncle William happily left New York with his bride and distanced himself from the family, thus forfeiting his claim to what was then a fifty-million-dollar estate. He changed the spelling of his name to Rynlander and survived on a pittance. I'd heard he gambled. When he separated from his first wife, William married again, this time to a waitress who worked in a restaurant he frequented. The man had a taste for déclassé women. Last I heard of Uncle William he was living happily with his second wife, the waitress, somewhere in Canada. He denied any regrets to the interviewer for an article published in a 1914 issue of the *World Magazine.* William was quoted as saying, "Do I regret what I did? Not for one moment, sir. I'd do it all over again for a woman I loved. What is life without love?"

I should ask myself the same question.

* * *

Love may have been the farthest thing from my mind on the day I met Alice. My thoughts and feelings seemed to well up from a region below the diaphragm and not necessarily connected to the heart. It was that time of year, the changing of the seasons, summer coming to an end with the glorious colors of fall in the maple and elm trees along the streets of New Rochelle. And a time when I always find myself in a curious state of mental and even physical restlessness; a time of vague longings and uncertain desires as though I feel the onset of the winter months with their shortened days and long nights. And I hope for some new adventure, some distraction to enliven the dreary months ahead.

I admit that it was sex with common, vulgar girls Kreitler and I went looking for on that afternoon in September, nothing more, and no less—that kind of randy adventure I knew nothing of beyond boyish bragging at the time. Nor could I understand why a married man would want random sex from girls he might meet in the street when he had a wife at home; but it didn't matter. Kreitler told me his wife had gone cold on him since having the kids.

"Marriage," Kreitler pronounced as though confiding a profound realization, "sure isn't all it's cracked up to be."

Kreitler made what we were about to embark upon sound as exciting as anything I had ever imagined.

"These girls," he told me, "are cheap."

"Cheap?" I wasn't sure of his meaning.

He said, "Low-class, Kip. Easy. You'll see. They'll give it up for next to nothing."

He is a former sailor, Kreitler, and a regular tough. I once saw him punch a man who insulted him, knocked the poor fellow unconscious. Kreitler had served in the war, said he'd killed more than one man, and then he went into the merchant marine. He'd spent time in the brig, and he has tattoos to prove it: one of a seminaked girl on the calf of his left leg; he told me he got it in Singapore. He could make her body appear to move sensuously when he flexed his muscle. I liked Kreitler; but he also made me feel a bit uneasy, sometimes downright uncomfortable. I had invested money with Kreitler in a plumbing and electrical supply business venture he proposed. I put up six hundred dollars to be used to start a new company in which I was to be his partner. When it came to nothing, I lost the money, much to my father's annoyance.

It's always been that way with me; there are certain people who intimidate me—men and women. I don't quite know how to say no to them, and yet I am attracted to them. It's as though I hope some of their . . . whatever it is, their confidence, their ease in social situations, even their bravado might rub off on me. But of course it never does, or not for long.

It was like that with Alice as well, even more so, though in a different way. Alice allowed me to feel better about myself. By simply being with her, I was more the man I wished to be. Her attention made me feel worthy. I think we both affected each other that way.

Since I was a young boy I'd heard it said that I am shy by nature. Of course I came to believe it, and yet at the same time I knew that it wasn't really so, or not exactly accurate. Rather, it is how I choose to be, how I choose to present myself to others in some situations because it gives me a certain advantage; and if it's expected, if people think me shy, or easily impressed, then I could obtain a subtle power, whereas I knew the real me, and that it was just how others perceived me. So it's a sort of false impression that in a way gives me the upper hand.

This gets confusing; but I had another idea, you see. For one, I was always less interested in myself than I was in others, which I've come to learn is unusual. I saw other people's lives as infinitely more interesting and exciting than my own. Even with a man such as Karl Kreitler; I found him and his life enticing in a lurid sort of way. That may sound strange or unbelievable, but it's true. The man had traveled on his own, and he claimed to have known women on half a dozen continents. Other people fascinate me, you see. I'm interested in what they think and how they feel, and how they choose to live their lives. Sometimes I might be more interested in these thoughts than I will be in how others perceive me. I want to know all I can about them and compare it with my own limited life experience. I am more of a thinker than people give me credit for. And if someone I meet believes me to be shy, they are more apt to be uncomfortable at first, and then to reveal themselves, and to let me know what they are really about out of some idea that they need to make me feel better about myself. Or they may think they can take advantage when in fact it is I who holds the upper hand. This gets confusing, I know, but it all makes sense when examined in the light of how the Rhinelander name influences social interaction.

Mother—I was very close to my mother: Can I tell you? So close . . . I know she felt the same about me: I was her favorite. She would tell me that I had an artistic temperament; that I was sensitive; and not shy but thoughtful, deep—an intellectual; and possibly even an artist. She would hold me in her arms and assure me that I had deeper and more complex feelings than most men. My mother believed that I should have become a writer or a painter, and not have emulated the other Rhinelander males, not have aspired to be a captain of industry like my forebears. Mother would get angry with my father when he chastised me for not living up to his notion of the ideal Rhinelander Huguenot epitome of masculine fortitude and aggression. *Pah!* What nonsense. She always claimed the Kip men—her family—were superior when it came to the finer aspects of intellect and character. The Kips were as storied and perhaps even more refined than Father's forebears. Kips Bay in New York City is named after Mother's family. Kip then became my middle name, and to many of the family I was referred to as Kip rather than as Leonard.

I was devastated when I lost Mother. Never will I understand . . . still to this day I am not able to make sense of why she was taken from me. It all seems so unnecessary, so senseless. What could she have been thinking? How does one let something like that happen? . . . Death by fire . . . and what a horrific, tortuous way to leave this life—burned to death! Was she drinking? The whole family was staying at our summer home in Tuxedo Park, although Father was in the city on business at the time. Some said the oil lamp simply exploded. Others claimed that Mother upset it, that she had been drinking while dressing for an evening out. I'll never know the truth. It doesn't matter. We children were rushed to safety. I ran back to look for Mother, but there was nothing I could do. Mother never escaped from the flames in her bedroom. Did she simply allow herself to be immolated? Did she wish to die to be free of my overbearing father's control over her life?

These questions haunt me still. Only God knows . . .

So if I am to understand it—and believe me, I continue to try to understand who and what I am, and to know what made me as a man in this world; and why I have done and still choose to do the things I do. It torments me—to understand that event, the death of my mother when I was still so young: it took me out of myself, it removed part of me, say my emotional consciousness was stymied and removed from my physical being. And this caused me to feel helpless, as though my sensational being, that part of me that could feel things, was somehow hovering about or near the people I was with, and always at a distance outside the situation I was physically in, as though merely observing . . . detached, as it were, forever the observer who is observing and not participating emotionally because it's too painful. I would feel that I was *within* and *without* whatever was taking place and at the same time; there but not really there; and more concerned with what might happen if I let my vigilance waver even for a second. If I stopped observing and allowed myself to enjoy the moment, it would all end in pain. It would end in loss . . . in death—as it had with Mother.

Part of me remained fixated on some horrid event in the past, so I knew that at whatever cost I had to avoid experiencing pain like that ever again. And yet . . . and yet . . . What did I do but bring an even greater and more excruciating pain upon myself, and upon others whom I care for because, if I've learned one thing in my time in this life it is that *everything must be paid for.* Do you see? You will always be expected to answer for the good, and also for the bad you cause to yourself and to others. No matter that you may be rich. One can never buy one's way out of troubles or pain of the heart.

Alice dispelled all those feelings, she made them disappear like shadows to her light, like pain to her gentle touch, all those self-doubts dispelled, and all those fears, at least for a time—the time when I was with her—all gone. I thought of nothing at all but how I cared for her, how I enjoyed her sense of herself. In her presence, only during the time I spent alone with Alice did I feel completely 100 percent present and in any given moment for however long it might last. My mind never wandered far from the appreciation of her physical presence, of her body, and of her mind, her voice, her sense of humor, her being. Her smell! One whiff between her legs and I was besotted. Say nothing of her delicate touch, and her seeming *command* of the moment. Yes, Alice invariably set the mood—more so, she *owned* the mood. There was a kind of insolence about her, a self-satisfied sense that she was not someone to be taken advantage of no matter how grand or important you thought you were. And she gave that impression simply by the way she looked at me as well as at others in our presence. She would not be intimidated; as curious as that sounds, but it is true: this slight, adorable person was—no, is—a tough customer, make no mistake about it, a woman of uncommon self-assurance. She is serious despite her fun-loving ways. To Alice, life is real and no nonsense. Her look is penetrating and dreamy all at once. Alice looked at me with those dark, inscrutable eyes, and she looked into my soul; she saw me for who I was: just a boy, a bit awkward at times, but likable—and maybe even lovable. And with that fixed look, those black eyes, the girl put me in my place, ever at her command.

While I was in her presence, Alice owned me.

I know Alice cared for me; I believe she still does. She didn't give a hoot about who my family is, couldn't have cared less except in how it affected my feelings for her and how it might bear upon our future together. There were no shenanigans, no ulterior motives, at least not on her part, not really, despite what others might think. It was all on the up and up. Maybe not on my part, not at first when I had just met her and was out looking for a good time, looking merely for sex; but very soon thereafter it changed and became serious.

I would even say it began by the end of the first day when meeting her at her home. It was as though Alice took control of my feelings from the outset, and she made it clear that she was a serious person as well as a nice girl.

"Who are you?" Alice asked when I appeared at her door. "And what do you want with Grace?"

I stuttered horribly, but then managed to say, "I've come with a message from Karl Kreitler."

"Oh, really," Alice replied with that saucy, knowing smile. "Well . . ." She looked me up and down, looked at my car parked in front of her home, and asked, "Are you some kind of messenger boy?"

"No, I . . . I . . . well . . ." And there it was, my crippling stammer.

"Of course you're not," Alice said and stood aside, opening the door. "Never mind . . . come in," she invited me. "Grace is not at home. But you're welcome to come in and wait, if you like."

I was still there, having tea with Alice and her mother when Grace came in. Alice's mother instructed Grace to return the ring Karl Kreitler had given her, which actually belonged to my mother. Before I left, I tried to give the ring to Alice, which greatly offended Grace.

"Oh, you're a fine one!" she complained. "You take the ring from me, and you give it to my sister!"

The girls both laughed. I felt such a fool.

But Mrs. Jones wasn't having any of it.

"Take the ring back and keep it," she told me.

I could see where her girls got their strong personalities.

And so, all during the fall of 1921, I continued to call on Alice.

* * *

Alice was a girl who knew how to have a good time, perhaps better than anyone I have ever known. She was fearless when it came to trying new experiences. There was never any question of who was in control, which both intrigued me and upset me at once. Alice is very smart. What she may lack in formal education, she makes up for in imagination, in common sense, and in clever thinking and behavior. She has a kind of instinctual understanding of most situations that utterly baffled me. How did she know these things? I'll never understand. Not once did I feel as though I had the upper hand with Alice, not in any instance be it emotional or in a practical sense did I accept that I knew more than she did, much as I might pretend to be more sophisticated to try to impress her. But that didn't matter, not at first, because I knew she cared for me, and I knew she would never hurt me or lead me astray; that isn't in her nature. She is a kind person, and generous with her feelings. If she felt good, she would try to make me feel better.

I will honestly admit that the year we were courting, and the time we spent together right after we married, those were, they still are, and they always will be without question the happiest times of my entire life bar none, even happier than when I was a child before my mother died. Although there were always underlying fears: fear that it could not last; fear I might lose her; fear I might be forced against my will to give her up. And of course, you know, when you live with fears like those, and when they just seem to take over your mind and your spirit, you become those fears—you embody them, they take over your character. What you fear most becomes inevitable. Perhaps you even attract it, as though worrying something is going to happen somehow brings it to bear, wills it into existence. . . . I don't know, but I think so.

What's interesting is that the love I felt for Alice then, even when coupled with the fear I always carried of losing her, my love for Alice had the power for some time at least to enable me to forget about . . . or even to get over all the other strange feelings I had about not being a vital part of or engaged in the real world. For once in my life, I was fully involved and a participant in the here and now: a real man, even if that included worrying about the future. This was something I could believe in—loving Alice and being with her. I felt it deeply, and it was something that took me out of my imagination and gave me an intense appreciation of real life. In a way, it was a dream come true—even a naughty dream. Like looking at pictures of naked girls, and then having the real thing to gaze upon and to touch, to fondle. And it was something I wanted so badly that I felt I didn't deserve it, that I didn't deserve to be so happy.

Being with Alice I was really there, totally there body and soul, mind and feelings, to the exclusion of frightening memories and intimidating doubts, or even distracting thoughts. But when I left her, when we parted and I returned to the Orchards School, none of my time with Alice felt real. How could it be? How could this be happening to me, Leonard Kip Rhinelander? You know that feeling: it's too good to be true. No, it was too . . . *different*, too far beyond my experience, if you will. It was over my head; Alice was too exotic, and it felt as though I were imagining that I had a girl named Alice, a girl who looked like she did and who was all that she was—so different, a little older and more experienced, and so unlike anyone I had ever known; and that she was doing those crazy sexy things she did to me and those things she let me do to her . . . how she seemed to enjoy it, and how I was finally living up to every imagined pleasure with a girl, just to be her man and to have Alice as my girl. . . .

Well, clearly, bottom line: I simply knew I had to have more: more Alice, all of Alice . . . whatever that might entail.

CHAPTER FIVE

Knowing Alice

It is always advisable to avoid a trial if at all possible. My opponent at the bar had the Rhinelander name, the Rhinelander reputation, and the Rhinelander fortune at his back. It would be painful and humiliating for dear Alice, and for her family; that was inevitable. Mr. Mills—though properly referred to as Judge Mills, to avoid confusion as he wasn't the presiding judge but Rhinelander's lead counsel, I'll call him mister—Mills would be thorough and convincing in the examination of his own witnesses, and even more tenacious and intimidating in cross-examination of my witnesses—whomever they might be, I was still not certain. Some questions—indeed, many questions—were unanswered as the case continued to build toward an epic courtroom battle.

A good deal needed to be done. First, I had to research the controlling law. The New York State statutes are quite distinct and strict in matters of matrimony. I spent long hours in our library researching the extant case law in hopes of discovering supportive precedent. And then I wanted more time with Alice to elicit from her the most sensitive and intimate details in her relations with young Rhinelander, as well as the varied practical developments in the course of the affair. So I might continue to craft our best possible defense, I had to be certain that we would not be blindsided by some fact or by the revelation of some event or of a significant detail that we hadn't seen coming and failed to prepare to defend.

"You see," Alice told me with that charming girlish giggle, "Len's idea . . . well, it wasn't entirely his idea. We were going to the city to see a Broadway show . . . and to go to one of the dancing places up around Lenox and Seventh Avenues. Leonard picked me up in his father's car, a limousine with curtains over the windows and driven by a uniformed family chauffeur, Ross Chidester, I believe his name is—not a nice man; in fact, a horrid man, really a wretch. Leonard was so excited to have me alone, we necked heavily all the way into the city. The driver nearly crashed several times because he was so intent on looking at us in the rearview mirror.

"I think Len was a bit . . . well, I know he was excited and terrified by the very idea, but when I told him that I intended to spend the night in a hotel in Manhattan and that I wasn't planning to return to my home for some time, I could see his mind working. You know how boys are, Mr. Davis, men also for that matter—they're so easy to see through sometimes. They will give away their intentions . . . if you let them, like the bulge in their trousers, and it's clear what all men want from a girl; they can't help themselves. Len was no different . . . even more so. He . . . well, he was very randy, I guess you would say, and he asked me if he could . . . accompany me. He was so cute! So bashful! You know, a woman's wiles . . . well, by then, our affections were leading a certain way, a way of men and women that is hardly unusual, even if it feels so very special and personal, we all know what is in store, do we not? It's quite natural. I don't care what the fuddy-duddies say. By then we had . . . kissed, of course, many times, and I knew how good that made Len feel, how excited he got. He put his arms around me, sometimes at my home after my parents were in bed, or at Emily and Robert's, or even in Len's auto. We kissed and kissed. Len wasn't much of a kisser in the beginning. He didn't seem to understand how to make his lips feel soft . . . and welcoming. Kissing him was like kissing a dummy! I had to show him how to kiss a girl better, with more . . . how shall I say? . . . you know, like a pucker, or like a Frenchman. Is this embarrassing for you? It's not for me, not really, because I know that it all came from true feelings of affection and love, not simply from sex, though of course sex is a big part of it when you're young and in love. And that it's normal to feel that way; we know that now—do we not? So I showed Len by my own kisses, and how I used my mouth, my lips, my tongue, until he got it. At first he was a bit startled when I slipped my tongue in between his parted lips. But he liked it right away, and what it symbolizes, like . . . entering each other, going inside the other's body. . . .

"Len was, for all his fumbling, he might be clumsy, but he was a quick study when it came to making love. He was a very dedicated pupil!

"O good Lord, now I am embarrassed.

"As I told you, I was not a virgin when I met and began seeing Leonard. Leonard had never so much as kissed a girl before we . . . before he kissed me. Really! He was the virgin! It was a curious and interesting role reversal, in a way. He had no idea how to fondle and caress a girl's breasts. I had to teach him everything . . . not to be too rough, not to simply squeeze them and maul them like he was feeling an orange or a grapefruit . . . to see if it was ripe. 'Be gentle, Len,' I said. 'Touch me softly. Like this,' and I put my hand on his . . . whatnot. You know, I'm one of those girls . . . my breasts are not particularly large; I'm not what you would call a buxom broad, not at all. But my perky breasts sure are sensitive, particularly the nipples. I quickly get aroused when my nipples are . . . well, you know . . .

"Oh, dear, I feel I am embarrassing you; I can tell. Shall I stop? But I want you to know everything, as you asked, so you are prepared should any of this come up, and you know, it's all in the letters; everything is there, in the letters! So . . . I must not hold anything back. I want you to know everything."

My assurances to Alice had to give her some comfort, for I knew that, were it to come to Alice making an appearance on the witness stand, or while my adversary examined his own client on direct, he would seek to draw out and make a point of every private and salacious detail of the affair. He would endeavor to make it all appear as prurient as possible. He would urge the men on the jury to conclude it was all Alice's doing, her initiative, and her seduction of the innocent Rhinelander boy. He would then rub Alice's fine nose and the jurors' inquisitive noses in every filthy sex act to cast my client as the unscrupulous vamp, the seducer, the licentious, experienced, and oversexed woman; and thus lead the jury to conclude that Rhinelander was an innocent young man, and a bit dim-witted, a naïf whom Alice lured into her web of wanton desire and perverse sexual domination. I knew this because it is exactly what I would have done if I were representing Rhinelander.

I told Alice she must be as open and honest with me as she felt comfortable.

"Is that all," I asked, "as far as you went . . . while still in the automobile?"

"No. As I said, I'm a very sensitive girl," Alice allowed, and the color rose to her cheeks. "I get aroused quite quickly . . . if a man touches my breasts, my nipples in a certain way . . . I had to show Leonard how to caress me. I'm not sure he ever really got it, but he tried, dear boy, he tried. I think he'd read some books or something. . . . In any case, by the time we were on our way into the city that evening, and planning on going to see a show on Broadway, and then uptown to Harlem to hear some jazz and to dance, when I told Len that I planned to spend the night in the city—I will admit . . . it *was* part of my plan, even an important part of my plan, to have Leonard spend the night with me. Why, then, he suddenly put his hand up under my dress and he . . . he fondled my vagina. . . .

"Of course I told him no . . . at first, that he must stop it, and I took his hand away. But Len was persistent, and I was so . . . *wet.* When he asked if he could accompany me . . . to the hotel, and stay with me, again I told him no. And then he practically begged me. And by then . . . well, we were both so excited. He kept it up, all the way into the city, fondling me, kissing me, telling me how much he wanted to be with me. I told him it would not be proper, but truthfully . . . all I really wanted was to see if he had what it took, you know, to see if Len had the . . . the passion . . . and the commitment . . . to be a man, and to love a girl like me. . . .

"At one point, I really had to laugh; we both laughed when Len said that if I didn't let him stay with me . . . *and have me* . . . as he put it *to know me completely*, he said he would simply set up camp in the hallway outside my room, have his meals there, and sleep there all night! Stay there as long as it took until I let him in the room with me, and the way he said it, of course, I knew exactly what he meant. Can you imagine? Len could be funny like that. . . .

"That was when he proposed. Yes, truthfully, in the car on the way into the city, that was the first time Leonard said that he loved me and he wanted to marry me. He begged me to marry him and let him, in his way of saying it—we could have the honeymoon first, and then the marriage. . . .

"I know how this must sound, as though I were leading Leonard along and he was simply following my plan. But it was not that, not entirely, in all honesty. We were in this together, we were a couple, two people in love, *very much in love*, and our love had its own way, its own energy, and . . . what's the word I'm looking for?"

"Momentum?" I suggested. "Its own direction and imagined outcome?"

"Yes! Exactly, that's it—its own course, as though we weren't really in control. We were in this . . . *this love affair* together, and we both knew and wanted the same outcome, which was to be together in our love as a man and a woman, and as a couple, a married couple, for the rest of our lives. That was always the expected outcome once we began to feel . . . *and to know* that we were very much in love, and both committed and feeling every bit of that . . . sometimes painfully overwhelming emotion . . . because we knew, we both knew it would not be easy. . . .

"No, it could never be easy . . . because . . . well, because we were not just a couple of young gadabouts having some fun. This was serious for us both. It was understood between us, and we talked about it, so Leonard knew from that time on that I was not a girl who was just out for a good time, and that I expected him to act honorably, as a man and as a gentleman. And that what I wanted was to marry him and to have his children. We both wanted that."

* * *

It was a few days before Christmas 1921 when Rhinelander checked himself and Alice into the Hotel Marie Antoinette on Broadway between Sixty-Sixth and Sixty-Seventh Streets—an appropriately named location. Leonard registered them as Mr.

and Mrs. Smith from Rye, New York (one won't need to give him credit for an original alias).

Alice waited in the car with the scandalized chauffeur, Ross Chidester.

During their six-day stay at the Marie Antoinette over the Christmas holidays they rarely left their rooms; indeed, they hardly left the bed for the entire time they were in residence there.

It was so romantic, Alice wrote in her diary. *We were living like newlyweds on our honeymoon, and in this grand hotel suite with room service and the staff all rushing about to make us feel comfortable. I had never stayed in a place like the Marie Antoinette—never even imagined it! And here we were in the bridal suite. It was beyond my wildest imagination—well, maybe not entirely. I'd seen such things in the movies. But to be there, and with Len so devoted, so adorable, and so passionate.*

* * *

Leonard did leave Alice for a short time on Christmas Day, to have dinner with his family at their mansion on West Forty-Eighth Street; and then it was back to the Marie Antoinette, and back to Alice's arms, back to her passionate embrace.

Then once again, near the end of January 1922, Alice wrote in her diary that she and Leonard returned to the Marie Antoinette.

We went to see a show on Broadway; it was called Shuffle Along, she wrote. *It was fantastic! I've never been to a Broadway show before, and then out to dinner at a fancy restaurant. This is some kind of girl's fantasy come true.*

They were joined for the evening by a local couple called the Riches, who were proprietors of a furniture store in New Rochelle. The bronze beauties in the chorus line of *Shuffle*

Along enchanted the couples. The foursome then went to dinner; and the next day they went to see the Marx Brothers in *I'll Say She Is.*

This was at a time in New York City that had come to be known as the Harlem Renaissance. Celebrities, actors and musicians, writers, as well as common folk were making the trek uptown to enjoy the vibrant nightlife.

On this visit, Alice and Leonard might not have left the Marie Antoinette until they were married; they may never have separated. They were both committed to a future life together as husband and wife.

"We saw ourselves practically as a married couple by then," Alice told me. "We did virtually everything a man and a woman can think of to do together," she confessed. "There was very little we . . . didn't try. Leonard had gotten ahold of a strange book . . . with pictures. I think it was of some Indian religion, Indian from India, I mean to say, and part of an ancient religion that believed in making the most of all the different love-making positions, and of, well, sort of holding off for as long as possible before the climax to make it seem even more intense.

"I'm sorry, Mr. Davis, I know this sounds strange, and I don't wish to offend you, but you did ask me to give you all the details. . . . Well, Len and I looked at the book, and we tried them all! Oh yes, we did! All the different positions. We did everything in the book and more we thought of on our own. . . . I'm not ashamed to say it: we enjoyed it! We loved it! You never knew two people could have so much fun together without even going anywhere. We loved making love to each other, pleasing each other in every way we could think to try. Leonard was fascinated with my body. He wanted to bathe me, he wanted to know every part of me intimately, and I was only too happy to let him explore and discover each and every sensitive spot, and to love me and please me in every way he desired . . . *we* desired.

"The truth is that we each made the other feel good about who we were, and what we were doing. There was no shame—no, not at all. When we were alone together, the rest of the world—with all its cares and woes about who is what and who is not; about what one's name or their place in society means; about how much money they have or have not—none of that mattered. We were just Alice and Leonard, two young people very much in love with one another."

The couple took provocative photographs of each other in bed. They ordered lavish meals from room service. They might never have parted had Philip Rhinelander not discovered their whereabouts, no doubt from the Rhinelanders' driver, Ross Chidester.

One evening there came a knock on the door of their suite. Leonard thought it was room service coming to take away the tray. It turned out to be a fellow named Spotswood Bowers, a member of a firm of longtime Rhinelander family retainers. Another man, a bodyguard appropriately named John Strong, accompanied the Bowers fellow.

They took Leonard away! Alice wrote in her diary. *They told Leonard that he must leave with them immediately, that they had been sent by his father, and that he had to accompany them to his father's home. Leonard didn't want to go—I know he didn't. At first he resisted. They practically had to drag poor Leonard away.*

"I know he would never have left me; he had no wish to leave," Alice said when I asked her about their parting. "But . . . as I've tried to show you . . . to explain to you how Leonard is, or how he can be sometimes. . . . Well, he's not forceful enough, you see . . . especially when it comes to his father. He could have refused to leave. He could have ordered the hotel staff to throw the men out and call the police. But it's as though he lacks the will to resist his father's demands and to be his own man. Of course, he was still quite young, not yet come of age."

In any case, Rhinelander was gone. Just like that; gone from Alice's life. They took him away from her. He promised he would return as soon as he spoke with his father, but after another day and night it was obvious he wasn't coming back. Alice was devastated.

"I was left alone to make my own way back to New Rochelle and back to my parents' home. O my God, I was so miserable, you can't imagine. . . . I wept bitterly on the train.

"I can't tell you, Mr. Davis. . . . Do you know how that made me feel? Can you imagine? To be abandoned like that? After so much joy, so much love, after finally having Leonard all to myself, being so close to the man I loved, and living with him practically as husband and wife; when they took him away . . . I felt so . . . *alone* . . . so terribly alone. I was miserable, and I felt . . . dirty, and used, like a piece of trash, the way they treated me, those men who came for Leonard, like I was some harlot. It was awful. That was one of the saddest, most horrible times of my whole life . . . up until that time. I didn't know if I would ever see Leonard again.

"And I didn't know what would become of me . . . a spurned woman . . . left alone . . . because—what? Because I wasn't good enough?

"Please don't let them get away with this," Alice pleaded with me and she gazed at me with those captivating eyes. "Don't let them win, Mr. Davis. Don't let Leonard's father separate us forever."

CHAPTER SIX

A Time Apart

In the first place, I was deceived. I would never have agreed to quit our rooms at the Marie Antoinette and abandon Alice had I known Father's true intentions.

They lied to me. I was assured that Father merely wished to speak with me, that it was of the utmost importance that I accompany Bowers and Strong to our home to see my father immediately, that it all had to do with our business affairs, and nothing to do with my being there with Alice. I couldn't understand how they knew we were there in the first place; but then, of course, I realized: Ross Chidester! My driver. He led them there to find us.

I say this . . . and yet, of course, a part of me knows full well that it's a lie. *I can't be truthful even with myself.* Not when it comes to Alice. I'm steeped in lies and half-truths. I am disingenuous, as in some feeble attempt to feel better about what a . . . *pitiful failure* I turned out to be as a man.

Even then, when Bowers and Strong turned up at our door at the Hotel Marie Antoinette, and then they barged in—at first I resisted. But Mr. Strong lives up to his name. He took me by the arm; he gripped my biceps with such strength he left a bruise, and while Bowers grabbed some of my things, Strong quite forcefully pulled me away from Alice, who tried to hold on to my other arm. Strong and Bowers dragged me away from the room. They wrested me from the arms of the woman I love. They hustled me outside to a waiting car driven by Chidester! That conniving bastard! And they shoved me in the rear seat with one on either side of me as though I were some fugitive criminal under arrest. Certainly I knew I was not being summoned to speak with Father about our business affairs. My own father had kidnapped me!

When we got home, I was brought to appear before Father in his study. This was always my worst nightmare: to be summoned to Father's study, what we boys had come to refer to only half jokingly as "Philip's sanctum sanctorum," his holiest of holies, and there to be ordered to "explain yourself!"

Explain myself? What explanation could there possibly be except "I love her"?

"*You what?* You love her? This . . . *Negress?* No, you don't, Leonard," he blustered, barely able to contain his anger. "Are you out of your mind? Of course you are! You don't love her. You *can't* love her. It's impossible. *It's unnatural! . . . The woman is colored!*"

Father was flushed with rage and I imagined for a moment that he might actually strike me. He seemed on the verge of physical violence, though corporeal punishment was rare for Father in disciplining his children. I almost welcomed it; I wished he would strike me and that I had the nerve to hit him back. I had a fleeting fantasy of killing my father. There was a heavy obsidian obelisk paperweight on his desk. I imagined myself picking it up and hitting him with it on the head, striking him again and again until he was dead . . . like some desperate character in a Russian novel.

But no, Philip just smoldered. I could see his mind was at

work conceiving a plan of what to do with me; and I cringed knowing it would mean separation from Alice. My father stared at me with a look I can only recall having seen him give Mother at times when she appeared to drink too much and she challenged him. It was a look that said, "I don't understand you, and I don't wish to because what you are is hateful to me. I do not recognize your right to oppose me."

When I think of this now, in retrospect, I believe that it was actually something much deeper than my love for Alice that upset Father. I believe he felt guilty knowing how he had been unable to love me; and how it was his neglect and his absence in my life that were to blame for why I had turned out to be such a disappointment to him. I think he also saw in my being drawn to Alice yet another example of a deep-seated rebellious impulse in the Rhinelander men to break out of the tried and true, and to take risks that were both the driving force behind their successes in business and their downfall in matters of love and war. No doubt that is why Father fought so hard to control his sons; he knew in his own character that this at times unbridled urge toward revolt and anarchy would lead to heartbreak. He'd seen it in his brother, William; and in my older brother, Father's namesake, Philip, who was killed in the Great War.

"Leave me," he said. "You are wrong, Leonard. *This is wrong.* It's a base infatuation, not love—and it must not be allowed to continue and to bring disgrace upon this family."

Philip gestured to Spotswood Bowers, who was engaged not only to carry me away from Alice, but he and Joseph Strong—an investigator who worked for Bowers and was known to handle the more rigorous duties and who was also a notary public—that these two men had been instructed not just to deliver me to my father, but that they were also engaged to act as my personal wardens.

* * *

Yes, Bowers and Strong were to stay with me, to guard me day and night, to keep me under constant surveillance while in their custody for the next several days or weeks—indeed, for however long it took to rid me of my desire for Alice, which of course no amount of separation could; and, as regards Joseph Strong, he was to accompany me for several weeks to come. The men were ordered never to let me escape their presence and to make certain that I had no further contact with Alice.

At the time, I was assured that Bowers had paid the hotel bill at the Marie Antoinette, and that he had left an envelope with some money, and notified the clerk at the desk that the lady would be checking out as well. I felt such a disgrace, such an utter and complete failure as a man unable to protect and care for the woman I love. I had no idea if it were true, or if they had simply left my girl there alone to cope, and with no way to get home. My father refused to discuss the matter.

At first Bowers, Strong, and I withdrew to rooms at the Hotel Belmont in Midtown; why there, I'm not sure. We stayed two nights. I was not allowed to leave the room. Bowers and Strong teased me relentlessly during my captivity. Particularly Joseph Strong, who was a bit of a ruffian and who enjoyed vulgar talk.

"Say, that was some *gash* you had there, Leonard," Strong chided me with a leer. I had no idea what he meant. "Didn't know you had it in you, old boy . . ." he said and laughed. "So, tell me, is it true, Leonard, what I've heard said: *that it's all pink once you get past the*—?" And he made an impression with his hands to signify a lady's private parts.

"You know what they say, Leonard," Strong went on. "*Once you go Black, you never go back.*"

Both he and Bowers laughed. I hated myself all the more as I laughed with them.

* * *

After our stay at the Belmont, Bowers packed me off to Atlantic City for two weeks with Joseph Strong. Fortunately for my purposes, Strong is a heavy drinker. In the evening, when he'd had too much to drink, he usually passed out and snored raucously. That is when I would slip away to telephone Alice and assure her of my continued and unfailing love and devotion. Once, when I learned Alice was in bed sick with the flu, I absconded from Strong's captivity. As he lay inebriated in our rooms, snoring as loud as a motorboat, I stole away and returned posthaste to New Rochelle to be at my dear Alice's bedside. The poor child was so frail and weak. She told me she suffered as much from pining for me as from the illness. I was afraid she might perish.

It was an exciting time, I must say. I imagined myself as some notorious criminal like Legs Diamond on the lam from the law. I stayed at the Joneses' home and I would never have left Alice's side, I swear. But, of course, Strong found me once more! He knew exactly where I would be—Chidester again, no doubt! And yet again I was hauled away, carried off as a prisoner, and without my consent separated from Alice.

This time my father was to take no more chances of my being reunited with the girl I loved. Thus commenced a terrible two-year period of enforced separation that felt like a kind of living death. Father shipped me off first to Bermuda with another chaperone, Richard Phelps, a friend of my brother's from his class at Harvard, and not nearly as uncouth as Joseph Strong, and far better company; but still I was miserable. All during February and March of 1922, Phelps and I stayed in a plush hotel and golf resort in Bermuda. I tried to enjoy myself, to be good company, but I so dearly missed Alice, and I could not get her out of my mind no matter how I tried to divert myself. I wrote letters to her daily. The hotel was full of young New York society skirts Rick Phelps was happy to chase after. But I found them wanting in comparison to Alice. Their cigarette smoking and booze guzzling, and their constant prattling on with jibber jabber about utter nonsense and stuff—why, instead of charming me, they thoroughly bored and repelled me.

It turned into a brutal *two-year* separation! Two terribly lonely years! Truthfully, as much as it hurt, I consoled myself with the plan that I was biding my time, just living one day to the next and waiting for the day I came of age. From Bermuda, Father sent me off to Washington, DC, where I met and spent time hobnobbing with the so-called movers and shakers in the world of national politics who my father supposed might interest me in a career in public service, since I didn't seem inclined toward business. And then we went to Havana, Cuba, where I attended a live sex show and saw a man perform who had a member the size of a donkey's penis. *Yes!* It was enormous! I had no idea that a woman could accommodate something that large. Then we traveled on to Panama City, Panama, where we were entertained by a roomful of prostitutes. I think the idea was to expose me to every hue and tribe in God's creation with the notion that I would come to realize my own kind is superior. It didn't work. And when, finally, we went to Palm Springs, California, for golf, swimming, and tennis with the whitest of white girls, it all amounted to an unsuccessful effort to wean me from Alice.

Of course it didn't work. How could it? I was in love. In the words of the old adage, absence only made both our hearts grow fonder. One year later—yes, an entire bloody year!—in

1923—Father, who was not to be mollified, as determined as an old Huguenot Calvinist who ever settled and conquered the New World, and seeing me as the last of the Rhinelander males to carry on his good name, to prolong my exile, Father enrolled me in an exclusive ranch school in Scottsdale, Arizona.

For a time during those months, I was terribly afraid that I would lose Alice forever, that she would give me up and choose someone else and marry him before I could return to her and make good on my promise to take her as my bride. We both dreamed about our future together, and we shared our imagined bliss in our letters. Alice sent me a picture she cut from a magazine of a house and car she wanted us to have once we were together. It was a simple home surrounded by an iconic white picket fence and with a modest Ford parked in the driveway. Nothing spectacular, nothing lavish, every simple girl's dream of marital security. I could envision myself as some overgrown version of Tom Sawyer out front of our little abode splashing those pickets with whitewash. I tried to make her see that . . . well, once I reached twenty-one, I would finally be my own man, and I would be rich, very rich indeed. And then I would be able to return to her and take her as my wife. And it wouldn't be a simple house with a white picket fence, but a fine home and a new car in the driveway. I begged her to wait for me. She replied that she would live with me in a one-room flat, if need be; and she admitted that she could have a date every night if she wished; but she chose not to because she would rather "wait for my dear Leonard."

It is a true testament to the love we shared that our affections never wavered, never diminished, never flagged, nor turned away toward others during this time of separation. Of course, we had our mild recriminations, our insinuations, and our harmless ploys to make the other jealous while holding on to their tenuous affections. Alice certainly had her occasional doubts and her intermittent fears. At first she intimated that she might be pregnant. She worried that I would never return and make good on my promise to marry her. We stayed in touch and kept the fires of our passion alight by that oldest means of long-distance intimacy: the impassioned love letter. What could be more romantic and heartfelt than the outpourings of feelings expressed in love letters? Hundreds of sincere epistles teeming with tender emotions, vivid descriptions of unrestrained lust, memories of our time together at the Marie Antoinette; and, at times, taunts and threats made their way through the mails and found each other in our separate solitude, there to fan the flames of imagined and unrelenting passion, or to stab at the open wound of heartbreak. There was no more mention of the child that may have been . . . I was left to wonder.

What we knew, what we each understood, and what sustained us through this time apart from one another was that we both believed that we were destined to be together again. It had to be; it could not be otherwise. Our love would not be denied; it must be realized in the flesh.

Come what may, I was determined to find my way back to Alice and to take her as my wife.

CHAPTER SEVEN

A Time Together

Leonard was faithful to Alice in his promise that he was merely marking his time, waiting for the day he turned twenty-one and could then claim his inheritance, and his independence.

His father enrolled him in a boarding school near Phoenix, Arizona, a sort of combination dude ranch and sweltering open-air prison camp for the recalcitrant sons of wealthy parents who wanted their boys tamed like so many wild horses. Leonard was not to be broken, at least not yet. His letters to Alice were his only escape. For her part, Alice teased him with mention of the attentions of other men—including, remarkably, a coy reference to interest paid her by the world-renowned blackface minstrel Al Jolson, who, Alice intimated, had flirted with her while she was employed over a summer as a chambermaid at a resort in the Catskills.

In her missives, Alice would opine that nothing, that no man could ever usurp Leonard's place in her heart; but that time and chance happen to us all; and for an unwed and attractive girl, time is her enemy. There was no further mention, at least in the letters, of a possible pregnancy. Leonard would write back to declare that his love was true and eternal; that it was only a matter of temporal considerations, never a fact of waning affection or lost determination; and that, as soon as he turned of legal age, he would claim his manhood and return to make good on his promise of matrimony.

And I give the boy credit, for this is exactly what Leonard did. Within days of his twenty-first birthday, Rhinelander arrived back at the Jones home in New Rochelle to collect his betrothed. He lied to George and Elizabeth Jones, told them that he and Alice were to be chaperoned by a married couple, and the youngsters left town together in Leonard's roadster to set off on a leisurely trip through the New England countryside.

They motored along the Post Road into Massachusetts, through Concord and Lexington as Leonard expounded on the early history of these United States, with a stop at Boston to visit Bunker Hill in Charlestown and to see Old Iron Sides, and then on down along the peninsula of Cape Cod, jutting out into the mighty Atlantic like a flexed arm warning unwanted intruders away from our shores.

Oh, I simply love Cape Cod, Alice enthused in her diary. *I could stay here with Len for the rest of our lives. It was past the busy season when we arrived, so most of the summer tourists had already left. We rented a little bungalow on the shore in North Truro. Every day we take long walks in our bare feet along the beach at sunset. We visit Provincetown, a quaint fishing village and artists' colony way out at the very tip of the land, which Len told me is one of the first places where the Pilgrims came ashore when they arrived in America. There are sand dunes that stretch for miles and that look like pictures I'd seen of the Arabian dessert. The air is so fresh and smells of the sea. I fall asleep each night to the peaceful sound of the waves washing up on the beach, and I wake to the sad moan of foghorns off in the distance.*

We are so much in love! We could have died right here and now, both just ceased to exist, left in our bed in each other's arms in our love nest, our spirits together forever, and our lives here on Earth would be complete and completely happy.

I have seen, and come to know, a deeper and even more attractive side to Len during this trip, and all during our days and nights together here on Cape Cod. It is a side of Len that I believe no one other than me—or perhaps his mother—has ever seen. During our time here, Leonard has stopped being a slightly awkward boy and has become a sensitive young man. I've said before that Len can be silly, and that's true, and he can also be funny, and I like that in him. It's attractive; it makes me feel happy when I know he is happy. He is always kind and thoughtful; I have never known him to be any other way. He's sincere; he's never mean or curt. But the man I have spent time with here and on this trip as we travel together and live apart from our families and our lives back in New York, this Leonard Rhinelander is a different man altogether. He is always a sensitive young man, and he knows so much about so many different things. He's the most interesting man I have ever known, once you get to know him, once you get past his shyness and that awkward pose of conceited boredom he sometimes affects—I don't know why, to make himself feel better about himself, I suppose. Because what I do know about Len is that he sometimes suffers from terrible feelings of not being able to live up to what everyone else—including me—expects of him.

I could listen to Len for hours when he talks about the history of America, and when he speaks about his family in ways and with details that he never shared before: about their history, about who they were and why the Rhinelander name is so famous in New Rochelle and in New York City; it's because of their Huguenot background and heritage, and that is all new to me. Len said his mother's family, the Kips, are a famous New York family as well, with a bay named after them. It is all difficult for me to imagine, and I don't really care to think about how different our families are. That only worries me.

By this time, truthfully, Len hardly ever stutters—not with me, in any case. His shyness as well is gone . . . completely. I can honestly say that Leonard has become a different person from the bashful, timid boy who first came to our home to call on Grace. He even looks different! He walks with his head up, shoulders back, chest out, and his back straight. No more slouching, no more shyness in social situations, and certainly no bumbling into things. I'm not imagining this; it's really true. Len has gone from a clumsy, fearful boy to a confident and cheerful young man in a matter of weeks! I am happily amazed!

Just the other day—it was a gorgeous early fall morning—I woke late when Len was already up and out on the beach. He was in his shorts, barefoot, shirtless, and sitting on some huge stones at the water's edge, what he told me was called a breakwater, and he was looking out toward the lighthouse that sits at the very tip of the Cape. He wasn't wearing his glasses. He is deeply tanned. The sun was just coming up. His face, his whole body was lit up by the early morning sun, and he just seemed to shine, to glow with a kind of golden light. The light on Cape Cod is really special, all that ocean and wide-open sky. And Leonard was lit up like a movie star, or like a Greek god—at least, in my eyes; that's how I saw him in the early morning light.

I can still picture him now as I write this, if I close my eyes and imagine these wonderful days spent together on Cape Cod and try to think of it as the only life I have ever known—then nothing else seems real. Clearly, without a doubt, these are the happiest days of my entire life. In my memory, I will always see Len as the man I love, and the man I want to spend the rest of my life with, the man that would be my husband and the father of our children.

We walk into town and have dinner. Len taught me so much about the town, and he told me about some of the famous artists who live here. One I remember is a man named Eugene O'Neill, who wrote a play Leonard and I had been to see in New York, and we couldn't stop talking about it. It's called All God's Chilluns Got Wings, *and it stars a man named Paul Robeson—a beautiful Black man with a wonderful voice whom Leonard says is not only a great actor, but also a great American.*

He knows these things, Leonard does; he isn't the fool his father makes him out to be. Not at all; he's actually very smart, and so well read.

And the seafood! The fish and . . . I had never eaten lobster before. Leonard showed me how to crack open the shells, remove the meat, and then dip it in melted butter. It's delicious. We have steamed clams, cherrystone clams, muscles, oysters, and something called quahogs. Len wants me to try them all. He says that the iodine in the shellfish is good for his . . . for keeping his manhood erect, and for keeping me excited. We don't really need it. I have my ways of getting . . . and keeping Leonard hard for as long as we need. And he has his ways of making me reach my climax. We make love first thing in the morning, last thing at night, and sometimes during an afternoon nap or after a swim in the ocean and with both our bodies still briny . . . we lick the salt from each other's private parts. We are both so . . . randy, so horny the whole time we've been here. I don't know if it's all the seafood or the salt air or the sunshine, or just young love, because it was really no different when we were staying at the Marie Antoinette in Manhattan, because, it seems, all we both want is to . . . well, I won't say. I get excited just thinking about our lovemaking.

Leonard told me that he is in line to inherit the family fortune and the real estate business worth more money than I can even imagine. It's an education for me, and a kind of fantasy. I knew nothing about how important his family was. I mean to say, I knew, but I didn't really know—which is to say, I didn't know the details about the Rhinelander family . . . or the Kips, his mother's people. But of course that scares me as well. Leonard told me what had happened to his uncle William. What a horrible story that is! Certainly, I had to question if a family such as the Rhinelanders or the Kips would ever accept a person like me. How could they? Len swears it doesn't matter, that he loves me, and that he will love me forever no matter what his family has to say. I hope and pray he means it. I think he does, and I believe him when he says it, but I know—that is, I think of what my father said to me, that to people like Leonard's family, the Rhinelanders and the Kips, it's almost impossible for them to be who they may really want to be, or even who they really are, because of who everyone expects them to be. They have this image of who the world believes them to be, and not who they really are, and that they are always trying to live up to an image. I know this sounds strange, but I've seen it in Len sometimes when we are in public. He acts different from when we are just the two of us alone, like he's playing a role of who a Rhinelander is supposed to be.

He told me all about his mother as well, about how good she was to him when he was a little boy. How much she loved him and he loved her and how it crushed him, how it dampened his spirit when she died. . . . How horrible her death was for him and the whole family—I can't even imagine it. Leonard cried when he told me about his mother's death, how he tried to get to her but . . . he couldn't. We both cried. I held his face in my hands and kissed away his tears. Then I knew how to make him feel better, by just loving him. We would talk about the children we will have, about our family, and how I will be the mother he loved and missed for him and for our children. He said he believes his mother would have loved me if for no other reason than that he loves me. It makes me feel sad, very sad for Len to lose his mother like that while still a young boy. And his father, Len told me how he never was able to feel loved by Philip, his father. Of course he knows his father cares for him, but it's different; it's remote, in a way, like his father cares about the idea of having him as his son, but he never really accepts him somehow, and never has been able to show Len any real affection. I'm sure his father was hurt by all the death in the family, losing two children, and losing his wife. That has to be terrible for him. And Len told me something that really made me feel sad. He said that he believes that he is a disappointment to his father, and that his father . . . that Philip even regrets Leonard is his son. I told him no! That couldn't be so. No man, no father in his right mind would ever feel like that about his own son. But when Leonard told me that his father never once came to visit him while he lived at the Orchards School, I was . . . I didn't know what to say; I felt so badly for Len. He seemed so . . . sad, so upset that he had never been able to live up to his father's expectations of who he should be.

Len explains it in a way that I understand because it is so opposite, so different from the love I have with my parents, and especially my father. Goodness gracious, how George Jones loves his girls! He lives and breathes for us.

You know, I used to think, and I believe I even said this to Len: if only our fathers could meet! If only they could get to know each other. I know that seems impossible, but it's interesting to think about. Men admire my father—all sorts of men, grand and common men alike can relate to George Jones. He's his own man. He believes that one should be judged by the way they carry themselves in the world, by their honesty and integrity, and not by who their forebears were or where they come from, where they went to school, or by their religious beliefs, or how much money they have, or even by the color of their skin. All of that, my father said, to get past all that was why people came to America in the first place: to escape all that hatred based on such differences that don't really matter as far as a person's true character is concerned. He goes on and on about that, and how much he loves this country—because here, in America, everyone is to be considered equal no matter their station in life or the color of their skin.

I believe I get much of my strength of character, and my determination, my self-reliance from Father. He's a good and honest man who worked hard all his life to support and love his family.

One day when we were talking about our fathers, I told Leonard, "George Jones is as solid as Plymouth Rock!"

He laughed. He took me to visit Plymouth Rock also. It was so much fun! O Lord, when I think of how this whole long trip together has been a dream come true, I wish it never had to end. My, how we laugh so much, every day. We really have a wonderful time just being together out in the world on our own, and free . . . two young people free to come and go as we please, free to love and be loved, just a man and a woman in the world, and so much in love . . . nobody to bother us.

But, of course, as they say: all good things must come to an end. The time has come for us to return to New York. I can't help being afraid that when we arrive back at home Len is going to leave me again.

"Oh, no, old scout," he told me. "That's not my plan. No, my dear, not at all. Quite the opposite," he said and his face lit up with a smile.

"I'm going to marry you!"

* * *

Rhinelander was as good as his word, at least in the beginning. He made an honest woman of Alice. Our esteemed New Rochelle mayor, Harry Scott, performed the nuptials; he married Alice and Leonard in the town hall on the fourteenth day of October in 1924.

It had been just over three years after they met.

For a time, Alice and Leonard were to live quite happily in a room in the Joneses' humble abode in Pelham Manor while an apartment was painted, fixed up, and furnished for the newlyweds to move into and set up housekeeping together. Leonard would take the train into the city each workday morning. He spent his days at the Rhinelander Real Estate Company offices in Manhattan, where he was employed as a bookkeeper. Then, in the evening, he returned to his bride, who waited for him at the Joneses' home.

And for the first time in her young life, Alice became a lady of leisure. This was a woman who had been in domestic service from her early teens. Now she spent her days buying furniture and fittings, buying clothing and household goods, and preparing for the move into the newlyweds' new home.

"It was what every girl wants," Alice confided when we spoke regarding this important time the couple spent together when considered in light of certain allegations included in the lawsuit. "Well, maybe not every girl; but certainly every decent girl—to marry the man she loves. And yet, also, it was a kind of fantasy. After our time together on Cape Cod, and with Leonard having taken on this . . . how shall I say it? This new . . . way of handling himself. I mean, his forthright manner, his stepping into this new . . . this new idea of who he was as a man. He would get up in the morning, I would make his breakfast, or Mother would already have something prepared. He had his coffee, and then he'd grab his briefcase, put on his hat, Father would take him to the train station, or Robert would pick him up in Len's car, and off Len would go to work in the city at his family's business.

"It all seemed quite normal. We lived like any other American family. It was a bit crowded in our home, but comfortable. Mother and Father were pleased that Leonard had . . . as Father put it, 'been an honorable man, and done the right thing.' And at last they came to accept him, and even to have warm feelings for him. You couldn't help but like Len when he was just being himself, as he always was in our home.

"I know my parents were concerned that it had all been just a dalliance for Leonard, that his intentions were not sincere, and that he might not go through with the marriage. Of course my parents worried that I would be left as a fallen woman, and that no man would ever want to marry me if Leonard betrayed me. Now Leonard was welcomed into our family. When I would ask him—or when Father or Mother might bring it up—if he'd told his family about our marriage, he always appeared quite sure of himself. 'Not yet,' he'd say. 'But I certainly intend to. All in good time.'

"In private he told me it didn't really matter what they thought, or what they did. He was twenty-one, he had his inheritance; he would tell his father of our marriage when he felt the time was right; and then he would take me to meet him. I didn't push it, not at all—none of my family did. Of course, it was on my mind, very much so. How could it not be? But we all understood that it was a delicate matter, it was Leonard's family, and we were happy to let Leonard handle it as he saw fit.

"For the time being at least, there was plenty to do—*we were married!* We had more than enough to keep us busy simply to get our new apartment in order, to sign the lease, and to be ready to move in before the holidays."

* * *

And then it happened.

As soon as word got out that a scion of an esteemed society family, a family whose name was recorded in the *Social Register* of the two hundred most prominent families in New York society, once it was reported that the very eligible young gentleman Leonard Kip Rhinelander had secretly wed, and that the boy had taken an "obscure girl" as his bride, as Alice was first described in the regional press, then Alice became the public's obsession, and finally everyone—every editor and reporter and reader of every newspaper in New York and the entire country—they were all determined to discover who the bride was, where she came from, and who her people were.

I'm not certain exactly how the story first got out. It may have been someone in the office of Mayor Scott who tipped off a local reporter, or the reporter may simply have been making his rounds in the courthouse and heard talk of the marriage and recognized the Rhinelander name as newsworthy. I was told that once Leonard was contacted and asked to comment, he offered money to the reporters to keep the story under wraps. There may actually have been some bribes paid; but it was all to no avail.

The *New Rochelle Standard Star* broke the story on the morning of November 13, 1924, with this provocative headline:

Rhinelander's Son Marries Daughter of Colored Man

By that evening the town swarmed with reporters, magazine writers, photographers: all sent to our quiet village to seek out the Rhinelander bride, her family, or Rhinelander himself. And then, of course, a day after the local paper published the story, the city tabloids and the national papers picked it up.

Not to be outdone, the *New York Daily Mirror*, a Hearst newspaper, followed up with an even more sensational and scandalous banner headline:

Rhinelander Weds Negress/Society Dumbfounded

That was it.

Nothing would ever be the same for Alice and Leonard Rhinelander.

PART TWO

BLUE BLOOD

CHAPTER EIGHT

Flight

It was an onslaught; that's the only way to describe it: *an invasion*. You would think that we were royalty or Hollywood movie stars the way the newspaper people sought us out, how they bivouacked outside the door, how they harassed us and followed us as we came and went from Alice's family's home. It was an embarrassment, and it was terrifying. It was like living inside a whirlwind. I was both angered and bewildered by all the attention. *It was obscene.* And, of course . . . well, one can only imagine. It made my father apoplectic. I was afraid he might have a stroke; secretly I hoped he would.

Soon after the story broke, I no longer commuted into the city to continue working at the family real estate company. I couldn't; it was impossible. Hordes of newspaper reporters and photographers laid in wait outside the Jones home for me to emerge; they followed me everywhere I went. And so quite soon I went nowhere. Alice as well—we were virtual prisoners in her parents' home. The reporters even chased and bothered Alice's father and mother, her sisters, her brother-in-law, and his family. It was horrible. We lived in a state of siege. The reporters and photographers were shameless. George Jones had to black out the windows on the ground level of their home with curtains and shades to keep the reporters and photographers from peering inside and taking photographs.

And that's not all. Not only the reporters, but the curiosity seekers followed us as well. And the hatemongers taunted us. I awoke each day in fear. It was such an abrupt and unwelcome change after our time alone together in New England, and even during those first pleasant days and nights in the Jones home while we were busy preparing our own place; then, all of a sudden to be besieged by all these newspeople; they're uncivilized scoundrels! They are like piranha feeding on the corpse of some unlucky animal fallen into their watery depths. And dishonest to boot! With no moral compunctions! I handed out several hundred good American dollars to bribe the jackals pacing and hotfooting outside our doors, pens and pads at the ready, flashbulbs popping, only to have them skulk away counting their money, file their stories, and then return the next day. *Cheaters! Liars!* It was a hopeless situation. I didn't know what to do. Certainly we couldn't remain holed up there indefinitely. It was difficult enough just having someone venture out for victuals.

And then, of course, the worst came to pass. It didn't take long. Within a week after the news of our marriage first appeared in the press, my father's personal attorney, Leon Jacobs, appeared at the Jones home in the company of Joseph Strong, much as Strong had come to our door at the Marie Antoinette with Spotswood Bowers. The men braved the lurking newsmen, they fought their way to the door, gained admittance, ducked into the house, and promptly and emphatically demanded that I leave with them and report at once to my father, who had called for an immediate emergency family council.

At first I chose not to go. Alice's father was at home at the time, and I thought he would defend me. But Jacobs appealed to

George Jones's understanding of paternal and familial responsibilities and obligations. He averred that it was only right and proper that I meet with my father, that I state my case for the validity of the marriage, and that I present him with a plan for Alice's and my future together. I was, as Jacobs was wont to remind me, my father's only living male offspring, still ostensibly under his guardianship even though I had reached the age of twenty-one. My father, Jacobs insisted, loved me dearly, and he wanted only the best for his son; therefore it was my duty to visit him and to come to terms. If that included Alice as my wife, then so be it. But it was imperative that I face my father as a man and state my intentions.

It was clear that we could not remain as prisoners there forever, hiding in the Joneses' home surrounded by a mob of reporters. Something needed to be done at once. Jacobs would not hear of any other alternative. He assured me, and Alice, and the Jones family that the only way this could ever be resolved, and we might hope for some normal life together, was if we were to receive my father's blessing and to make a plan; and then for everyone to move on with their lives.

I wanted to believe Jacobs and my father; it seemed reasonable. Obviously the present living conditions were untenable; but of course I should have known better. We should have left town immediately after the marriage and hidden out somewhere the newspeople wouldn't discover us. Hindsight: What good can it do me now but to remind me how foolish I was to believe Leon Jacobs?

Mrs. Jones made tea. Ah, the English and their tea! Have a cup of tea, some crumpets or cakes, talk it over, hash it all out, and everything will be fine. Bombs may be falling, the Huns may be at the door, but a good cup of tea will set it all straight. There is something to be said for the British inbred quality of aplomb. Even Leon Jacobs was taken in by Mrs. Jones's hospitality. Joseph Strong was actually successful in chasing away the reporters, threatening them with charges of trespassing and disturbing the peace, and flashing his badge. (Strong had been a former court officer, a federal deputy marshal.) But the reporters hadn't gone far. By the time I was convinced I should depart with Jacobs and Strong, the newsmen were hot on our heels. They flocked around and shouted nasty questions at us as we hurried from the door of the house to Jacobs's car, driven by none other than my betrayer, Ross Chidester.

And that is how I was spirited away to New York to meet my father at his home and present my case for my marriage to Alice.

* * *

I admit that, fearful as I was of facing my father, it felt good to be away from the Jones family's redoubt. I did, however, feel saddened to have left my little girl, my young bride, left her there to brave the press and the mobs of curiosity seekers all on her own. Once again, I wanted to believe that my father would be understanding, or at least be reasonable now that Alice and I were in fact married, and that he would allow me to be my own man and support me in my decision to make a life with Alice as my wife.

Of course—*I was delusional!* How many years does it take to know a man, especially one's own father? And to understand that people don't change, not really, certainly not a man as set in his ways, and as sure of the righteousness of his beliefs as Philip Rhinelander. One can so easily allow oneself to believe anything when the truth is hard to accept; but by this time I should have known better. We didn't even go to my family's home in Manhattan. There was no meeting with Philip, and no family council; not until Jacobs had accomplished his covert objectives.

It had all been subterfuge, a ruse to get me away from Alice and into the hands of Leon Jacobs. They had it all planned out. I was merely a cog in their machinations, a pawn in their devious game to separate me from Alice and render me powerless to resist my father.

It's hard for me to explain because I really don't understand it, not entirely; but once I was out of Alice's presence, and once I was with Jacobs and under my father's command, it's as though I lost all power to think for myself, or to act on my own behalf, even to be anything more than what I had always been, which is to say completely under my father's control: a man who is really a worthless boy with no will or character of his own; a veritable cipher albeit with fantasies of revolt and aspirations to be something more.

In fact, I wasn't to see my father for several days. We spoke on the telephone. He threatened me! Yes, he terrorized his own son. I was ordered not to leave Jacobs's presence under any circumstances; were I to escape again and return to Alice, Philip threatened to have me arrested and committed to an institution. When I objected that probably wouldn't work since I had turned twenty-one, he said he had his ways of accomplishing such things, and he demanded that I do everything Jacobs instructed me to do, or I would find out just how powerful he was, and I would no longer be welcome in our home, no longer be considered his son. I would be banished from the family and forfeit my inheritance.

"On what grounds?" I dared to ask.

"*What grounds?* Why, good Lord, Leonard—you married a Negro! That's unacceptable! Do you understand me?" he railed. "Do you understand what this has done to the family name? Good Lord, son: Are you out of your mind? Yes . . . yes, I believe you are! You have forgotten who you are and who your family is."

* * *

When finally I was brought to face him, Father glared at me with a look I knew so well. It was a look not just of anger, but also of repugnance—and worse, it was a look that said *I wish you were not my child.*

"Now, you will do as I say, Leonard. You will follow my instructions. Or I will have you committed to an institution for the insane."

I kept reminding myself—*He can't do that; I am twenty-one.*

And then, what Father knew would hurt me most, he threatened: "Think of what this will do to your mother's memory! Why, she is turning over in her grave at the very thought *of a Negro* brought into this family. And what, you would bring *little half-breed children* into the world *as Rhinelanders? No, no, Leonard: that must not be!*"

Though I am still not certain what exactly that means—to invoke my mother's memory, to raise her from the dead, so to speak, and to hold her spirit over me like some avenging angel—the thought of it terrified me. To think that my actions would somehow shame my mother, or disturb her soul, that worried me more than what any living being might do or think. I shuddered with dread at the thought of a life lived under the curse of having defiled my mother's memory.

* * *

Strong and Jacobs were intent on getting me out of Manhattan, and out of New York State immediately, as they were determined to keep me out of the public eye. We were on the run from the scandal-mongering press; we were in flight from the fact of my marriage to Alice; and I was ashamed of being their accomplice. I felt like some infamous scalawag—a traitor, an escaped prisoner, a desperate criminal—and a liar and a fraud. On top of it all I was heartbroken; yes, the worst of it was that I felt miserable to have been a fool lured away from my beloved bride, enticed with false promises, and made to say goodbye to my dear, sweet Alice, who had looked so miserable, so sad to see me *abandon her once again!*

All this heartbreak, and at no fault of her own. It was horrible. I was ripped from the bosom of my love and my happiness. And still, deep inside, I knew it was all my doing. I knew that once more I never should have agreed to leave Alice.

* * *

First we went to the Robert Treat Hotel in Newark, New Jersey. I was sequestered in a room under permanent guard. Jacobs was on the phone to my father's office, and back and forth to the offices in Manhattan, leaving me in the custody of Joseph Strong, with strict instructions not to let me out of his sight and to keep me away from the telephone.

Next we went to stay for some time at a boardinghouse on Mowack Avenue in Jamaica, Long Island; I was a virtual prisoner there as well. Then I traveled to Washington, DC, with Jacobs, where we holed up incommunicado for a week's time while something, some paperwork or other, some documents, were prepared; and certain business matters were handled by Jacobs's office back in New York. Then finally we went on to Melrose, Long Island; there I was to be imprisoned in a boardinghouse and guarded by Joseph Strong. It was while huddled in a subway train station in Manhattan on our way to Long Island that Jacobs presented me with papers he had prepared with my father's advice and consent, and he directed me to sign them.

Strong and Jacobs both stood over me while I sat there staring at the documents and with pen in hand. I don't know what I was thinking at the time; I wasn't thinking, actually. My mind was in such turmoil, it was as though I had no will of my own. I had given up. I was wallowing in self-pity, and half of me was enjoying being helpless while the other half hated me for allowing this to happen. The noise of the subway trains was deafening. Jacobs had foisted the papers on me, stuck me with the pen, and told me that if I ever hoped to see my father or any of my family again, if I ever hoped to raise my head up and say my name as a Rhinelander, then I had to go through with it and sign the bloody papers!

"You must not be the husband of a Negro! A commoner!" Jacobs practically shouted. "Don't you understand, Leonard, what this has done, how this affects the family? To bring this woman into the Rhinelander family . . . and with the dower rights that entails? It's not acceptable! It cannot be! *You must sign these papers!* Put your father's mind at rest, at least for the time being. Otherwise *this will kill him!* And put your mother's soul at peace in her grave. Then let me seek to set it all straight before it's too late."

I admit that I didn't even read the papers, though I swore and signed the affidavit to attest that I had—anything to end the rushing about from place to place like fugitives; anything to get away from the deafening noise of the underground trains, the fetid air; anything to appease my father's wrath. Joseph Strong notarized my signature on the spot, and the documents were official. And I admit to feeling at that moment—after I affixed my signature to the documents—that I was yet again the man I really am. I had become once more the real Leonard Kip; I was no longer some proud young buck with a beautiful and exotic girl on my arm; no longer a husband to the girl I loved; I was just poor, simple Kip, a nonentity with his crippling shyness and his stutter, unable to resist the will of his demanding father. I had given up. I felt an odd sort of sickening comfort to admit to myself who I really was: in a word, a coward; and to accept that I no longer had to pretend to be someone else.

Jacobs hurried away to file the suit and to do whatever else he and my father had determined was in my and the family's best interests. I lost all personal control over my life; I gave up the glorious life I had known, however briefly, with Alice—it was gone, almost as if it had never happened. I went into a sort of mental stupor. I became the idiot they wanted me to be. I was practically catatonic. I wished I had the will to throw myself on the tracks like Anna Karenina and to be run over by the train.

The next time I was to see my wife would be in court.

* * *

I tried to convince myself that given Alice's race it could not possibly work, that our marriage was doomed from the start. After Alice and I were separated, I wanted to believe that she had deceived me and that it was never meant to be, that it was an impossible bond, a love that defied convention. But why? I knew that was a lie. Of course I knew Alice had colored blood. Good God, I am not blind. I could see her father, and her brother-in-law. I could see Alice. I could see her in the most intimate of circumstances. And I knew George and Elizabeth Jones had made their union work, and work well. Their girls were all lovely and quite happy. And Robert and Emily, and little Roberta; they were a family. Grace married an Italian. I had allowed myself to believe that it could be so for Alice and me—that we could marry and have a family and live happily ever after like other people.

But, of course, it could never be the same. No, because it's different when you are a Rhinelander—so they tell me. We are different. We are better. . . .

Because, you see, there is so much more at stake.

CHAPTER NINE

November 24, 1924

Dear diary,

How can it be that something so good could be made to seem so bad? I don't understand it. Why should people be so upset by my marriage to Len? How, why is it even any of their business? We are adults. And we live in America.

But, most of all, what hurts the most—how could Len let them do this to our love? To let them try to make something that was so beautiful into something that is so horrible—a crime! And bring me to trial to defend myself?

O Lord, please, help me to understand this. I want to forgive Leonard, and I do, but I still don't understand it—not completely. If Leonard really loves me the way he said he does—and the way I believed in my heart that he did or I never would have gone through with any of this—it just doesn't seem possible that you could love someone and allow this to happen to them—to us. It's not the Len I know. I'm not stupid. I know how boys of Len's class and wealth see girls like me—that we are easy, that we are common, just good for some fun, and then to be cast aside. But I can honestly say that it was never like that with Len—never! He said he loves me. He treated me as his equal. He married me. He lived in our home with me and my family. He was practically one of us. And he seemed so happy.

If I live to be a hundred, I'll never understand how Len could have allowed this to happen to us—to me. To be called a liar and a fraud. To be made to stand trial to prove that I am not a liar. That's not right! To say that I tricked him into marrying me. Goodness, no! It was his decision, his plan, and I believed him when he told me he loved me, and so I agreed to marry him and to have a family. I believed that nothing could ever change that. I still believe it. I don't believe for a minute this is Len's doing. But why doesn't he stop it? He's a man now, isn't he? Why doesn't he come back to me and make all this sadness and hurt go away? How can he let this happen to us and let them destroy all the love we had for one another?

Dear God, when I think of it, of how our home and my family has been—there's only one word for it—our family has been terrorized by . . . well, first of all, by the Rhinelanders' lawyers, and then by the reporters; but now what's much worse, it's these other men, whoever they are, I don't know: nasty, hate-filled men, and women! It's not all men, not at all. There are women out there as well who are just as bad, just as angry and hateful. They yell at me and call me "nigger slut!" People throw things at our home. Stones with nasty notes attached to them have been thrown through our windows. Father won't show me the notes, but I know what they say. The same thing people say when they call to me in the street—"Nigger whore! Go back to Africa!"

That just goes to show how stupid and uneducated they are. My father is dark, yes, but he is not African. He comes from the West Indies. But these people, well, they are so ignorant, so full of hate—and why? What have we ever done to them? Or the African people they stole and brought here as slaves? Nothing. And when you look at it from any reasonable point of view, it should be the Negro people who are angry, the people who were stolen from their families and their homes and brought here to America to be sold as slaves, as property, as though they were never people and created by God. Now they are the ones to be hated and treated so horribly for wanting to be free and to be treated like human beings. Please, God, I don't understand it. I love this country, but I don't love this hate based on skin color and class. It makes no sense, and it has nothing to do with me or with my family; and yet it has everything to do with me and Len and his family, and the family Len and I wanted so much. I still do!

Is it really all over? Was it all just a dream? Please, O God, no! I don't want to believe that.

Life can be so unfair sometimes. Well, not life, really, but people. I know that's an obvious statement, as Len would say. But it never felt so true to me as it does now. I went from being the happiest girl in the world to being called a "dirty nigger bitch," separated from the man I love, now called a liar and a cheat who supposedly tricked Len into marrying me by lying to him and telling him that I was of "pure white blood." That is so ridiculous! Even if I tried to tell Len that, to lie to him like that, doesn't he have eyes? And didn't he live in our home with me and my father—who is obviously not white? And didn't he meet Robert Brooks, didn't he become friendly with Robert, and couldn't he see what is plain to anyone who sees Robert—that he is a Black man? Of course he could! Len didn't care: that's the truth of it. He didn't even think about it until his father took him away and turned him against me.

Some things in life just don't make any sense at all. I keep saying "life," but that's not what I mean. I mean people. What people say they believe, what they say they stand for, and then how they act, how they behave. It's not right, and it's so upsetting. What did I ever do to Philip Rhinelander? And he and his lawyers are going to call me and my father liars? George Jones a liar? Not on your life. And you turn people against us so they throw stones at our home. Then you say you are somehow better than we are. How does that make any sense?

I don't know Len's father. Of course, I never met Philip Rhinelander. But what sort of person could he be first of all to send his boy away to a school such as the Orchards simply because Len is shy and he stutters—that is, he stuttered until he met me! Mr. Rhinelander should be thanking me for curing his son and helping him to become a man. And then, to never even go to visit Len at the school. . . . So you buy him an expensive automobile—but what about going to see him? What about showing him how much you love him and not with a new car but with a visit, a hug, and some time together with your boy? I'll never understand that man.

O dear Lord, I feel so sorry for Len on the one hand, and so angry with him at the same time. Why? How can he let this happen to us? When he knows, I'm sure Len knows what's coming, if this goes forward and goes to court, which supposedly it is now! "The die has been cast," as Mr. Davis says. I love the way Mr. Davis talks. He has all these wonderful expressions. He's a very intelligent man.

It's going to be much worse, and not only for me—everyone keeps telling me, "Oh, Alice, don't you see what you are doing? What you are letting yourself in for? Just accept the money! It's going to be terrible!" Yes, I see it—of course I do. I already see all the hate being stirred up by this lawsuit. But does Len? Does his father? Do they understand how this is going to look to people? If so, then why are they doing it?

I'll tell you why. Because they never believed that a simple little brown-skinned girl from New Rochelle—a servant in a private home, no less, with barely a high school education—that such a girl would have the nerve to stand up to the high and mighty Rhinelanders.

Well, guess what? They were wrong. I do, and I am!

I may look like I'm just some common girl, or not look like it so much as appear to be low-class, considering outward appearances: a working girl with not much formal education. But that's not the real Alice. I read books. I love poetry. That's who I really am inside—a girl with a brain and a love of life and of people. In that respect, I take after my father. George Jones is a good man, and respectful, but he never let other people tell him who he is. He has always been his own man. And I have my pride as well. I like who I am. I'm a fighter when I know I'm right. It's always been that way with me, even as a little girl growing up. I don't let others boss me around and tell me how to live my life. I'm not afraid because my skin is dark. Father used to call me his little drill sergeant because I was the one always telling everyone else what to do. I don't lie, and I never pretend to be something I'm not. With Len, he always knew exactly who he was courting and who he married.

I'll say it here in my diary for anyone to read a hundred years from now if they want to know what was in my mind and who Alice Jones Rhinelander really is: I am not going to allow them to make me out to be a liar and a fraud. No, never! They think they can buy me off, but I will fight them to my last breath if need be. I won't take their money and go away to hide like some horrible, deceitful person. I will stay here and go to court and fight to prove the truth of who I am and show the world the real reason for my marriage to Len—we married because we love each other, and there is nothing wrong or deceitful about that. It's the truth.

Of course, I see what is happening. How our town is overrun with newspeople and now with protesters and angry racists. But it's not my doing. That's the Rhinelanders' fault for bringing the lawsuit against me. I am simply defending my honor and my family's name. I will show them that I am not the low-class piece of trash they think I am, and my parents—my mother and George Jones—we are not people just out to get money from the Rhinelanders by my marrying Len. That is the lie. As my lawyer, Mr. Davis, says, "That is the real fraud."

Who wouldn't do what I am doing in my position? Who wouldn't defend themselves? What, I'm supposed to be scared by the Rhinelander name? "Oh, fiddlesticks!" as Mother would say. Now they are going to say that I lured Len into bed and made him some kind of sex slave—at least that's what Mr. Davis says they will do. Oh, please, that is so crazy. And if that is where they try to take this, to make me out to be the one who seduced Len, they'll be sorry, because it's not true, and it never was true.

We fell in love, that's all that happened.

Dear God, I don't want it to come to this. Please, Lord, stop it! I love Leonard. I never want to hurt him or to do anything to upset him or his family. But I have to defend myself. I have to stand up for my family. We are not—the Jones family—we are not cheaters, and Alice Jones Rhinelander is not a liar, not a cheat, not a slut or a whore. I am a good person. My family are all good people. If the rest of America can't see that, then there is something very wrong in the heart and soul of this country that I love so much.

And you know, my dear old friend, dear diary—as I always say, life goes on. Oh, yes it does. Right now it looks terrible. I'm afraid to go outside sometimes for fear of the angry people—men and women; sometimes the women are the worst! The things they say!

Just the other day I went out to do some shopping, and these girls practically attacked me! I didn't recognize them. They are not from New Rochelle; at least I've never seen them before. "Leave our men alone!" one of them screamed, and she spit at me. "Go after your own kind!" And they called me "Nigger bitch!" I was so hurt. I wanted to ask them, "What are you afraid of? What can I do to hurt you?" One of them, the one who spit at me, was fat and ugly. I wanted to tell her, "You want to know why boys don't like you? Take a look in the mirror."

Here's a better question: *What difference will any of this make a hundred years from now?* That's what Father always says when something happens that seems awful at the time. And that's where I get my strength. When I think of the world and how it just keeps going around no matter what people do or say, and I look up at the sky at night and see all those stars and try to think about God and the universe and how amazing it all is just to be alive and to be part of this glorious amazing creation—now what? I'm supposed to be scared or upset by what some angry, stupid people say and the nasty names they call me? Or I'm supposed to keep my mouth shut and take the money and just go away and hide myself for the rest of my life?

Please, no, not me. That's wrong. You can't hide from yourself and from God. People just don't know me if that's what they think I'm going to do. I've never run away from anything before, and I'm not about to start now. No, that's not Alice Jones Rhinelander. I am better than all that. I am a woman with a mind and a spirit, and I don't care what nasty names they call me. Because I know better. I know the truth. And I am not about to let them frighten me into accepting the money and running away to hide for the rest of my life. Leonard should know better—I'm sure he does. He married me; he knows the sort of girl I am. The rest of them—his lawyers, his father, and all the people who are so interested in this whole trial now that it is definitely going to court—well, they are about to find out who Alice Jones Rhinelander really is and what this girl is all about.

CHAPTER TEN

The Plaintiff

New York matrimonial law is quite stringent. The legislators of our good state hold the institution of holy matrimony, as well as the legal bond of unholy wedlock, in high esteem. You don't dissolve a marriage for too little in the Empire State. There is no law in New York barring miscegenation. Such legislation to outlaw interracial marriage had been introduced, and would be proposed in Albany again shortly after the Rhinelander case was heard; and again it failed to pass into law.

New York City was held up to the rest of the nation, and even to the greater world, as the prime example of a "mongrelized" society dreaded by the eugenicists of the era. It was a hot topic due to what became known as the Great Migration of Blacks from the Southern states to the North, and to no destination more sought after and popular than our lively and modern metropolis. The Harlem Renaissance was in full swing. Books were written and published about the mixing of the races; plays were staged on Broadway; and popular music, jazz, dance: Negroes and their culture were influencing all manner of American styles, ideas, art, sports, fashion; and inevitably social mores were changing as well. Some whites welcomed and embraced the changes; others violently rejected them and fought with vitriol and physical violence to keep Blacks in their supposed place, whatever that place might be according to those who would seek to alter the course of history and humanity in this spicy and teeming melting pot known as the United States of America, where we boasted, "One nation under God with liberty and justice for all." Were these merely empty words, or did "all" in fact mean *all peoples*; and were we bound to live according to the meaning and intent of our Founding Fathers' indelible and unimpeachable words; or were we to be a nation of racist hypocrites?

Nowhere, may I posit for the purposes of this narrative, that in no public setting, in no court of law before or perhaps since would these questions of how the races were—first of all, of how they were to be distinguished from one another; indeed, who might be deemed Black, and who might not really be white; how one could establish racial identity in the first place; and then, most importantly, how the races were to coexist. In what future Americans of all color and creed might hope to live not only in harmony and in peaceful, heterogeneous neighborhoods, but also in intimacy, in cohabitation, in the inevitable mixing of the blood that comes with marriage, in the blending of races that were already much diluted and mixed and perhaps even revitalized—spiked, as it were, in a mixture, a combination to become so complicated, so emotionally fraught, so burdened by our Founding Fathers' original sin and enduring curse, so American, and so debated, so argued over, fought over with riots and murders and lynching of innocent souls; and lamented, and even cursed. Nowhere were these vital questions of race in America to be as thoroughly delineated and debated as in the trial of Rhinelander against Rhinelander.

There you have it all in the very title of the case: *Rhinelander v. Rhinelander.* This is the story of a marriage, a wedding that brought together a man and a woman of disparate ancestry and social strata who nevertheless were human equals and very much in love, and who made a bond that threatened to expose the lie of racial superiority that is the basis of long-held and viciously defended prejudice and that ultimately turned the husband against his bride. It is the original and continuing American curse that would be played out in the most sedate, purposeful, and public setting of them all: a tribunal of both common and statutory law in a courtroom full of witnesses and spectators, and with a jury of twelve white men designated to determine the outcome of the lawsuit as well as the fate of the lovers, and even the validity of the issue of racial disparity.

What could be more personal, more private, more emotionally charged; and yet more public, more current and accessible to public debate than to evoke the beliefs and values, the intimate relations of husband and wife, the very material claims of property and wealth, the intangibles of class and race between a man and a woman in a trial that would open the bedroom doors of this young couple to the world outside; and that was ultimately to test the very bonds of love and marriage against the ties of filial responsibility?

An annulment, I would add, is a far step legally above and beyond a divorce, and therefore harder to attain than a simple, or even a complicated, dissolution of a marriage. An annulment supposes that the marriage never in fact took place; that it was and is invalid under the law and hence void to begin with. The civil and religious bonds are thus nullified. The marriage is not only undone but it is disappeared, eradicated from the record books as though there never was such a union. Neither party has any legal or financial claims upon or obligations to the other party once an annulment has been granted.

As such, there is a high burden of proof on behalf of the

complaining party in an annulment lawsuit, even more so, as in this case, where the plaintiff in his complaint has made the unusual request that the court order a jury trial—which, in my opinion, was the Rhinelander lawyers' first crucial tactical error, although I understand their reasoning. It was simple: they would play the race card.

* * *

A few days after Leonard had been spirited away from the Joneses' home, Leon Jacobs and Joseph Strong reappeared to serve Alice with Rhinelander's original complaint. As I mentioned, Jacobs did have the rectitude to fulfill his promise to Leonard and deliver his admonition to Alice that she not acquiesce to the action against her; that she should fight the case; that she must bring competent lawyers to her defense, which Rhinelander was obliged to pay for; and that she vigorously contend the issues raised in the lawsuit. Alice had every reason to believe, at least at the outset of litigation, that Leonard wanted her to win so that the marriage would survive and endure. Hope springs eternal in the young heart.

It should be noted that we had no proof of this claim on Alice's behalf beyond the testimony of family members who were present at the time of the service and who may have heard Jacobs deliver Leonard's message. My fellow barristers refused to hand over Leonard's written note, claiming that it had been misplaced, which, had it survived, would have constituted unimpeachable evidence of Leonard's intent, or lack thereof, and of his conflicted state of mind. Still, it seemed to me at least in keeping with what I had come to believe was a sorrowfully divided moral and ethical nature assailing young Rhinelander. Alice maintained from the start that the action was not initiated at Leonard's behest or even with his willing compliance; that he had been forced to abandon her and seek the annulment solely upon the initiative and strident demands of his imperious father. I certainly had no reason to doubt her, and definitely not once I met the man and heard from Philip Rhinelander's lips how he intended to end his son's marriage. One could see, as was intimated when he came to our offices, that Philip Rhinelander's stern and formidable hand was at work bending the malleable will of his rather weak-minded boy at every twist and turn in the case. This understanding would provide me with my basis upon which to build Alice's defense.

As Alice's defender, I knew the challenge was to endeavor to show the jury Philip Rhinelander's controlling dominance over his timid son.

* * *

I also must make clear that despite New York City's popular reputation as a tolerant and open society, this was hardly the case a mere thirty miles north of Manhattan at the time of the Rhinelander trial in White Plains; in fact, it was not true in certain neighborhoods in the five boroughs. The great influx of immigrants to New York City had caused alarm and outward resistance among those who believe in preserving what they see as the purity of the white race, and who perceive the arrival of so many peoples of darker hue from southern Europe and Africa as a threat to their station in our society, and a snatched glimpse of their slight vision of the American Dream. This xenophobic sentiment in turn sparked an uptick in anti-immigrant legislation, notably the efforts of Madison Grant that resulted in the Immigration Act of 1924. The literate public was alerted to the appearance of publications such as

The Rising Tide of Color Against White World-Supremacy, a racist screed authored by eugenicist Lothrop Stoddard that warned against the supposed perils of miscegenation, and was mentioned in the pages of F. Scott Fitzgerald's popular novel *The Great Gatsby*.

Racist propaganda and ugly public demonstrations abounded. A proposal to condemn the Ku Klux Klan as a racist organization, brought before the Democratic National Convention of 1924—held at Madison Square Garden in Manhattan from June 24 to July 9, mere months before the Rhinelander case was heard—the initiative lost by only a single vote. The caucus came to a standstill due to threats posed by the ghostly specter of white-robed members of the Klan wending their way in lengthy procession like some diabolical serpent along Eighth Avenue. Klan membership and popularity surged after World War I due primarily to the Klan's support of the Prohibition amendment to the US Constitution—as if those redneck hillbillies didn't partake! More likely they fought the repeal of Prohibition to preserve the need for their illicit moonshine stills.

Hence, the Klan for the first time became a political force in many regions of our nation. This movement reached the apex of its power contemporaneously with the Rhinelander litigation and widespread news coverage of the marriage and of the lawsuit. Anti-immigration movements, racial tensions, and anti-miscegenation legislation exerted malign influence throughout many regions of the United States, as well as impacted both the Republican and Democratic parties when their respective candidates sought re-election. And it provided the obvious, emotionally charged subtext of racial prejudice and fear of miscegenation to the Rhinelander marriage and annulment trial.

New York was labeled an *un-American city* by those white supremacists who would advocate tar-and-feathering Leonard and lynching his "nigger wife." I am ashamed to admit that white law students at my own alma mater, Columbia University School of Law, dressed themselves as Klansmen in white sheets and conical caps, and then set fire to a cross on hallowed university campus grounds in a hideous display of racial hatred designed to force a Negro American student to depart from the Columbia student dormitories.

To make certain the Rhinelander parties were aware of these rising racial tensions, a few days before we were set to begin voir dire, a paving stone wrapped in a paper note crashed through the front window of the Joneses' home.

The note read: "GET OUT! You and your nigger daughters are not welcome here!" and was signed: "Loyal white Americans."

* * *

It was while mired in the midst of all this external tension, and the resulting internal fear and strife felt by the Jones family, that my co-counsel and I were presented with the original Rhinelander lawsuit. We quickly convened to discuss our answer. Leonard's lawyer, Leon Jacobs, and now including Isaac Mills as lead local counsel, chose to bring the annulment complaint on grounds of material fraud. An annulment would eliminate any claims Alice had to the Rhinelander family assets; no rights of either party would survive an annulment; nor would Rhinelander be required to pay Alice alimony.

Such a lawsuit must therefore satisfy certain legal requirements before a judge can allow the case to be heard by a jury. There is no provision of New York's annulment law that references race or ancestry as statutory grounds for dissolving a marriage. Incestuous or bigamous unions are void, of course; but in New

York interracial marriage is not illegal; therefore race in and of itself is not grounds for annulment. As a matter of fact, unlike many other jurisdictions in the United States, New York has no statutory law that defines race, and so the issue of Alice's color and her racial makeup *per se* were of no legal consequence. Race, for all its emotional baggage, has no actual legislative weight when it comes to how it is defined, and thus is nearly impossible to litigate as grounds for annulment without some additional material basis.

Hence we were in somewhat uncharted territories of the law with regard to the issue of race, which is the primary reason it took so long for the lawsuit to make its way into court. Leonard's attorneys had decided to base their suit on grounds of "force of fraud or duress" for the case to proceed to trial. Judge Morschauser would be required to rule that the annulment case could be decided by a jury based on allegations of material fraud on behalf of Alice. To win the annulment, Leonard's lawyers would need to prove that Alice had lied to Leonard as to her race; that she had claimed she was of pure white Caucasian blood; and that she had done this knowingly and intentionally to deceive Leonard into marrying her when in fact she knew that she is not without a trace of colored blood in her veins. Leonard, his complaint alleged, was unaware of Alice's "racial taint," as it were. He claimed to know nothing of her actual color until it was revealed after they had wed and when he was shown a copy of her birth certificate.

This basis for the lawsuit struck me as utterly preposterous. I was baffled that intelligent men—indeed, experienced attorneys—would dare to bring such a cause based as it was on such blatantly false claims. What, young Rhinelander was presumed to be blind as well as tongue-tied? Did his physical challenges also include color blindness?

* * *

Here, for my colleagues at the bar and for those armchair litigators who find such documents of interest, is the first amended complaint, which alleges:

1. That the plaintiff and the defendant, at the time of the commencement of this action, are both residents of the State of New York.
2. That on the fourteenth day of October 1924, in the City of New Rochelle, County of Westchester, State of New York, the plaintiff and the defendant were married.
3. That the consent of said plaintiff to said marriage was obtained by fraud; that prior to said marriage the defendant represented and told the plaintiff that she was white and not colored, and had no colored blood, which representations the plaintiff believed to be true, and was induced thereby to consent to said marriage, and entered into said marriage relying upon such representation.
4. On information and belief, that in truth and fact the said Alice Jones, also known as Alice Jones Rhinelander, was colored and with colored blood.
5. On information and belief, that the said Alice Jones, also known as Alice Jones Rhinelander, had colored blood in her veins, and failed to alert the plaintiff of this fact.
6. On information and belief, that the said representation was wholly untrue and at said times known by the said defendant to be untrue and that she made the same with the intent to deceive and defraud the said plaintiff and thereby induce him into said marriage.
7. That the said plaintiff did not, until after the said marriage, discover that the said representations were untrue.

8. That said plaintiff entered into said marriage with the full belief that the said defendant was white and without colored blood.
9. That the said plaintiff and defendant have not at any time before the commencement of this action, with the full knowledge by the plaintiff of said facts constituting the said fraud and false representations or with full knowledge by him that the defendant was not entirely of white blood and ancestry, voluntarily cohabited as husband and wife.
10. Wherefore the plaintiff prays for judgment that said marriage be annulled and said marriage contract declared void and for such other and further relief that the court may seem just, together with the costs and disbursements of this action.

In our opinion, this late amendment to the plaintiff's complaint did nothing to improve the merits of Rhinelander's suit, and in fact greatly weakened their case. It raised the issue of what in fact constitutes race or even color; and who, save perhaps some Swede born in the highlands of Scandinavia, could claim and prove pure white Nordic or Anglo-Saxon or Caucasian blooded ancestry going back however many generations to the origins of their progenitors. Certainly in America, given the long intermingling of the races and tribes, both Black and white as well as Native American, Asian, Mexican, and diverse foreign interlopers from around the globe, to claim no taint to colored blood was no simple matter. Furthermore, the complaint was riddled with factual and evidentiary inaccuracies that I found preposterous (and based, I believed, on issues other than their veracity) and that I was convinced we could prove to be knowingly false and in fact fraudulent.

Judge Swinburne's public claim that we would prove Alice is white alerted the plaintiff's counsel to what would prove to be a red herring. And it worked like a charm. It impelled Messrs. Mills and Jacobs to proceed along a garden path we directed them to follow. And it would prove to be an effective opening gambit.

* * *

Finally, with all pretrial motions, answers, and countermotions heard and decided, and all relevant papers before the court, it was time to empanel our jury. Alice would continue to reside at the Jones family home throughout the weeks of pretrial motions, of voir dire and jury selection and empanelment, and for the duration of the trial. She was accompanied every day at each and every session of the proceedings by her father, George Jones, looking every bit the enigmatic but solid citizen that he was; her mother, Elizabeth, clearly a white woman of considerable composure and heft; her lovely sisters, Grace and Emily; and her brother-in-law Robert Brooks, who is clearly a Negro.

During the early stages of the proceeding, there had been no sign of young Rhinelander in or around our local environs; his whereabouts remained a mystery. Only his lawyers were to be seen in town and at the courthouse for hearings all during the weeks and days leading up to the trial. Would the wealthy young scion appear? Or had he resolved to absent himself from the proceedings and thereby void his claims against his wife?

No one seemed to know.

CHAPTER ELEVEN

The Reluctant Knickerbocker

Father asked for an audience with Leon Jacobs and me at his club, the Knickerbocker, on East Sixty-Second Street. Known as "the Knick," Father's club was considered to be the most exclusive men's club in the country, if not one of the most selective and aristocratic clubs in the world—of course, or why should Philip wish to be a member? Jews were not allowed to join the Knickerbocker, and I know Mr. Jacobs always felt uncomfortable when Philip asked him to meet there.

He's not the only one. I hated going to see Father at the Knick almost as much as I feared being called to appear before him in his study; the one saving grace was that at his club Father was less apt to scold me. Actually, I despised anything to do with the name Knickerbocker, reminding me as it did of how my older brothers had both been members of the elite Knickerbocker Greys corps, whereas I was considered too weak and effeminate to join. The Greys was founded by Mrs. Augusta Lawler Stacey Curtis, the wife of Dr. Edward Curtis, a noted New York City physician who served on the staff of the surgeon general of the Union Army and who had assisted in the autopsy on the body of President Abraham Lincoln. It was said that Mrs. Curtis started the Greys as a way to keep aggressive, adventurous, and well-born boys out of trouble. Perhaps this was where Philip missed his opportunity with me; he should have insisted that I be conscripted by the Greys. I felt spirited just walking in the door of the Knick, although that is as far as my rebellion went.

Father wanted to discuss how Mr. Jacobs intended to present our case at trial, and to hear his estimation of the local counsel Isaac Mills, whom I had not met as yet. Father also wished to discuss the overall lawsuit strategy, since, thankfully, it had become clear by this time that Alice was determined to fight the suit in court.

Both men felt it wise that Philip not appear in or around the courthouse in White Plains during the trial. They were concerned that the jury might be adversely influenced to find for Alice as a means of striking back at the prominence and influence of the Rhinelander name in Westchester County; or that Philip's presence, which was certain to attract unwanted publicity, would make it appear that it was all my father's initiative and his cause to annul the marriage, and that I was merely doing as my father wished—which, of course, was the truth. "My name must be kept out of it as much as possible," Philip decreed.

I disagreed. I argued that by not appearing to support me and my case, such as it was actually his cause, Philip would appear to see himself as too high and mighty to bother with such a mundane conflict as the fate of his son's marriage, and that he would alienate the jury by his absence and supposed indifference. Of course, as usual, my opinion was given no credence.

Father told us that he had arranged for rooms at the Gramatan Hotel in Bronxville for our party for the duration of the trial. I was to be provided with two bodyguards and a driver. Philip ordered me never to appear in public unescorted, and to limit my exposure to traveling to and from the courthouse, and appearing only in those sessions where my presence was required. He insisted that I was to take all meals in my rooms, and I was to make no statements nor grant interviews to the press. He intimated that he had people reaching out to friendly editors in an attempt to manage the publicity, which, he said, "was already disastrous for the family."

Finally, of course, Philip demanded that I have no contact whatsoever with Alice, or with any of her family members. I was to "ignore her. Do not speak with her; don't even look at her. Best to act as though you don't know her or any of her people."

"Father, that's ridiculous," I protested. "She's my wife."

"She won't be by the time this is over," he ordered, "or you will no longer be considered a member of this family. Now do as you are told!"

* * *

This was the moment, it occurs to me looking back, when I should have made the decisive step that would have altered my life once and for all. Interesting how when we look at our lives in retrospect, we can determine those moments as such that, had we reacted differently and chosen another path, our lives might have been altogether different. This was that moment for me—a lost opportunity I will regret unto my grave. I felt the urge well up inside of me, the impulse to stand and say, "Fine. I choose Alice. I choose my wife, and I choose to live my own life. And if that makes me unacceptable to you and to the rest of the Rhinelanders, and the Kips, and all the best families of New York, then so be it."

I could have turned and walked out of the Knickerbocker Club, walked away from anything and everything to do with my father and his superior attitude toward the rest of the world. I could have gone to Alice and sworn my enduring love, and together we could have gone away somewhere where we were not known and made the life together that we both wanted. In my imagination, I could actually picture all this happening.

So why—*why didn't I do exactly that?* Was it simply fear? Of course I had to consider what I would do to support us. How would we live? Was I not man enough to stand up to Philip and to make a life of my own?

This question must plague me until the day I die. What fatal flaw in my character allowed me to sit there and succumb to my father's will when it went against everything I wanted and believed in? As I think about it now, I know that to have made such a decision and carried it out not only would have infuriated my father, he also never would have accepted us; he never would have allowed Alice as a member of our family; and he would have felt compelled to do everything within his considerable power to make my life with Alice miserable. I also understood that most of Philip's malice would be directed at Alice and not at me.

Of course I knew all along that Philip would never accept my marriage to Alice. I was deceiving myself and Alice and her family when I said that given time Philip would come around and welcome her as part of the family. It was what I wanted, but what I also knew was never going to happen. I also know—at least I realize now—that part of the attraction I felt for Alice had to do with how I expected that my loving and marrying her would affect Philip. I wanted to hurt him—or, not hurt him so much as defy him, to go against everything he stood for; and I wanted to own up to having my own opinions about life and my own decisions as to how life should be lived. I wanted to be part of how it was all changing, and I no longer wanted to be forced to adhere to the demands of wealth and power and race and class that I was supposed to be a prime example of but that I never believed in and never felt that I was. But, well, what I wanted to do and what I did in fact do . . . this is my curse.

"Have it your way," I said and stared at Philip with a look that was as far as I dared go in my defiance. "Fine. But I think that you are both wrong. *This is all wrong.* And it's not going to work. You are wrong about Alice, and you are wrong about me."

Interesting that neither Jacobs nor my father seemed to hear that statement or to take my thoughts and opinions seriously. They looked at me as though I were some imposter, a fool who had wandered in off the street; and that what I believed was of no consequence to them or to the outcome of the case. Why then was I asked to attend the meeting? Of course I knew: I was there only to be embarrassed, to be put in my place, reminded that I was to be told what was expected of me, and what I was to do, how I was to behave . . . *as a Rhinelander.* I was to be the obedient son and to go along with however my father and his lawyers decided to present my case. I was to agree to say and do whatever they ordered me to do regardless of their complete and utter disregard for the facts.

So be it, I thought. How predictable that my father and his lawyers believed they knew so much more about my marriage, and about me and my bride than I did—even though they had thus far grossly misjudged us both. If they only knew the truth, Philip and Jacobs and Mills; if only they understood how I disdained everything they held in such high regard; and how deeply I cared for and admired all that Alice embodied.

* * *

For the next half hour I listened to their instructions as to how I should comport myself in the courtroom and on the witness stand. I was told how I was to be portrayed by my attorneys, and how I should behave in accordance with that portrayal even if it was wrong and, quite frankly, demeaning as well as unbelievable. I left the meeting and walked out of the Knick feeling disgusted with myself and utterly misunderstood and cast adrift by my own father. I was alone in the world and with the realization that any defiance of Philip's will was futile.

Fine, I thought, *we'll do it their way. I don't care what happens to me anymore. The truth is: I hope to lose.*

CHAPTER TWELVE

November 27, 1924

Dear diary,

Thanksgiving! What have I got to be thankful for? I must remember: I have life, I have my family, I have my mind and my spirit. I will thank God and not let this get me down.

Mother prepared a typical feast with all the fixings, and the entire extended brood came by for Thanksgiving dinner. Emily and Robert with little Roberta, whom I adore. Grace and her fiancé, Albert Miller, who both seem to be as excited and frightened by all the unwanted attention as we all are. Mr. Davis came along later for coffee and to discuss the trial, as Monday morning jury selection is to begin.

Yes, it is really happening! As much as I try to tell myself that this is all a bad dream and that I will awake beside Len and he'll tell me not to believe any of it, here I am, here we are, and there doesn't seem to be any way of stopping it now except to give in and take the settlement, which I will never do.

Believe me, most everyone except Father, they all think that is what I should have done. How many times have I heard it? "Why, Alice? Why fight the Rhinelanders? You know how powerful they are. Do you really believe you can win this trial? Don't you think it would be wise to take the money and be secure for the future?"

To that I say, "Be secure as what? A liar? A cheat? I may have the money, but what will I have left of my self-respect?" The only person who agrees with me is my father. Mother as well, though she's more concerned with how this has all weighed on my heart, and how it's affecting my health and mental well-being as well as our safety. It's crazy what is going on in this town. It has certainly been hard, and from what Mr. Davis says, we must expect it to get much worse once the trial actually begins. Worse in every way—more people in town fighting to get a look at me or shouting questions or ugly taunts. More horrible stories in the newspapers, which I never read anyway. And then, more bad things said about me by and through Len's lawyers, and perhaps even Len himself if he takes the stand, which apparently he must do because, as Mr. Davis says, without Len's testimony there is no case against me. It is all based on Len's claims that I lied to him. How can he say that? It's so wrong.

Mr. Davis confirmed that no one has seen any sign of Len since those men took him away from our home. He's not appeared at any of the pretrial hearings. Everyone looks to me as though I might know something. I wish I did, but Leonard's whereabouts are as much a mystery to me as his intentions. He hasn't called, he hasn't written. All I have is the note I read that Len sent with his lawyer telling me that he loves me and that I should fight the case. So that is what I am doing.

The only time I really feel as though I know Len is when

he's with me. As soon as he's out of my sight, it's as though I never knew him, or he becomes another person, and my Len no longer exists as the boy I know and love until he is back at my side. So I am constantly going back and forth in my mind wondering what to think of where this will all end up. I lie awake in bed at night and can't understand why Len left me and why he has allowed this to go as far as it has. Oh, I know, it's all because of his father, and his family, but Len told me he wouldn't let that stop him from loving me. He married me! And he said he would never allow them to come between us. It's so hard to understand another person sometimes, even someone you're close to, so close you think you know them, particularly someone you love and whom you believe loves you. And then . . . what? Who are they really?

The truth is that you can never really know what goes on in another person's mind and in their heart. Because then they might up and do something that takes you completely by surprise. If you had told me just six weeks ago while Len was living here in our home with me and my parents, and while our apartment was being decorated and furnished, with the lease signed and all the arrangements made for us to move in together, even after the story appeared in the papers, if anyone had suggested then that Len would suddenly be taken away, and that I would be accused of lying to him about my color, and tricking him into marrying me by pretending to be white, and that he would bring a lawsuit against me to annul our marriage, I would have said you must be mad. That can't happen; it's impossible. It is so far from the truth, and so wrong given everything I believed about Len and how he cared for me that it is just not something he would ever do. It can't happen, and it won't happen. Yet here it is, and it has happened.

Now I must be ready to face the man I love, and whom I thought loved me, in a courtroom to defend myself against claims that are so hurtful and so wrong that I hardly know how it could have come to this, and what must be done to prove that they are wrong. Mr. Davis says that I must just be myself; that who I am is apparent in how I appear and how I behave. He warns me that Len's lawyers will say all sorts of horrible things about me and try to convince the jury that I am a bad person.

The worst part of it all is how I miss Len and how sad it makes me feel to have lost him. I've gone from the happiest girl in the world to being accused of being a Black slut who lied to the man I love and tricked him into marrying me so I could get his money and his family name. Everyone looks at me differently now—even my own family. Of course they know it's not true, but still they have to wonder what I was thinking to get involved with a man such as Len, a man who would allow this to happen to the woman he supposedly loves. Of course, the truth is I wasn't thinking; I was just feeling, feeling how good it felt at the time to be in love with a man who treated me as well as Len did. Those days we spent together on Cape Cod—I don't know if life can ever get any better than that. At least I can say that I will always have our time together on Cape Cod to remember.

That's the most surprising and upsetting thing about all of this: how sad it is that a man who is as kind and as sweet and loving as Len was to me, how he can suddenly change and allow these lies to be brought against me in his name. I have to ask myself if I was simply all wrong in my idea of what kind of man Leonard is if he could turn on me like this. Then that thought of course causes me to wonder what is true and what is real in life. If you can't believe your heart, and if you can't believe someone you are so close to, so deeply in love with, if you can't trust that, then what can you believe in? And what is life really all about? Is it all just lies and people pretending to feel things and saying things that they don't really feel or believe?

O God, what a horrible thought! How it hurts to think that people aren't really true in what they say they feel and believe. If that is so, then none of this makes any sense. Why bother to live if it's all just a big lie? What's the point in living if there is no true meaning to life? No, I can't believe that. I thank God I have my mother and father to prove to me that love is real, that there are good and honest people in the world, and that life is worth living even if it can be hard to understand and so painful at times.

Of course, right now I feel terrible about how Len turned against me and allowed this to happen to what we had together. I feel awful about everything that is being said about me in the newspapers, and by all those angry people in the street, and the names they call me and my family. But I have to remember that none of that is who I really am, or who the Jones family is. This person, the girl who sits here now, brokenhearted, but still writing these words in her faithful diary and looking for answers about life, and where I pour my heart out—this girl is not a liar, this Alice is not a girl who would trick a man into marrying her so she could get his money and his family name.

No, not on your life! And I am not a tramp who used her sex appeal to cause a man to lose his mind. I loved Len then and I love him now. All I ever wanted was to be his wife and for us to have a family of our own—not to be part of the Rhinelander family. Honestly, that was the farthest thing from my mind; I knew it could never be. Len told me about his family, all the tragedy, all the pain, his mother's horrible death, his brother killed in the war. His uncle William and all he went through with his marriages. You understand that it doesn't matter how much money the family may have, and their mansion in the city, their cars and their servants, their businesses and their name in the social register or whatever—anyone could see there was no real happiness there. Len and I wanted an entirely different life together. We wanted a life based on love and respect for one another just because of who we are as people and how we treat one another.

That is all I ever wanted from Len, and not money or some place in society or anything other than love and a family of our own. Len knows that I am a simple girl who believes in love. We talked about what we wanted together. I wanted what my parents have. And Len saw it when he lived with us, and he said that was what he wanted as well.

Now it's all changed. Len has left me and I don't know what to believe anymore. If you can't believe in love, well then—what else is there worth believing in?

Of course, I thought about taking the money. It would be untrue to say that I never gave it a thought. I did, I thought about it a lot, but it always ended the same way: no, I don't want it, not if it means lying and saying that I lied to Len. How does that make any sense? Tell one lie to prove another lie? No, of course I would not do that. There were those who said I should, those who warned me against going to court to fight a family as rich and powerful as the Rhinelanders. There were a lot of heated discussions around the dinner table and the drawing room in the Jones home about the choices I made. "Oh, Alice, think of it. That's a lot of money. More money than any of us will ever see in a lifetime." Or, "But what if you lose, Alice? Then you will have gone through all of this, and you'll wind up with nothing."

I heard it all again at dinner with the trial set to begin. Mother was suffering from a toothache, what she calls "the curse of the English." She joked that she had married George Jones because he had "such big, strong, white teeth," and she wanted her children to have teeth like their father.

Grace and I served the meal while Mother sat with an ice pack to her swollen face. She perked up when Mr. Davis came along. Mother is very fond of Mr. Davis—we all like him tremendously. He's a strong-minded man. And the most educated man I have ever known. I love to listen to him talk. He quotes the Bible; he speaks of books he's read. He knows more about the history of slavery and how the African people and Negroes are treated in America than any of us will ever know. I'm fortunate to have him as my lawyer. That's another reason why I chose to go to court. First, I had Len's note, then I felt confident that Mr. Davis would do his utmost to win, and finally I knew in my heart that it is the right thing to do.

Of course there is a lot at stake—everything! My reputation. My family's future. But if I accepted the money, then it would mean I admitted to everything they said about us. And, as Mr. Davis says, it would also affect how cases like this might be decided in the future, even how marriages like my marriage to Len might be accepted or condemned.

Am I nervous? Oh, yes, you had better believe that I am nervous. I'm upset, I'm sick at heart, I can't eat, I can't sleep, and I worry about how it will all turn out—for me and for my family. I have never tried to do anything like this before—I never had to! I've never been accused of being a liar or anything of the kind. I am deeply saddened that, as Mr. Davis says, no matter what happens, my marriage to Len will not survive this awful trial. Of course . . . I know. How can it? It is already over.

I don't want to believe this. I keep telling myself that there is still some hope Len will change his mind and that this will all end happily. If he'll just come to me, and sit with me, and look in my eyes the way he used to, and we could talk and hold each other. Then, surely, he'd come back to me. And we'd be together again, as they say in the nursery rhyme, forever and ever. . . .

CHAPTER THIRTEEN

Twelve White Men Good and True

At the voir dire I had only one question for prospective jurors, all of whom were white and male. (Although women had been granted suffrage, it would still be a number of years before the fair sex would be seated upon juries.) I would turn to the defense table, and I would open my arm in a gesture to indicate the demure and charming young woman seated there, and I would ask of the jury candidate: "Can you be absolutely fair to this girl?"

I asked each member of our jury pool that simple question. Sometimes, when it seemed appropriate given the appearance of the prospective juryman, I might add, "This daughter of a respected and hardworking family long known and welcome in the village of New Rochelle," just to plant in their minds that Alice was a local girl of the working class, and therefore someone to whom they could relate.

Much as race may have been the salient issue in the lawsuit, I believed that class was of equal, and might perhaps be of even greater, importance in influencing the jury if it were properly elicited; and if the understanding of how race impacted the Rhinelander couple could be seen as an anomaly of social class behavior—that is, a rich boy's dalliance and cruel rejection of a girl who may or may not be colored but who is clearly more akin to the men on my jury than she was to her aristocratic spouse.

Truthfully, I would not have wanted women on the Rhinelander jury. Then it would have been all about territory. I believe that most women, in particular white women, but even some Black women as well, resented Alice. Perhaps she was adored by the young flappers of the times for her modern and stylish appearance, and for her bold romantic pursuit; but my sense was that most women of both races perceived Alice as a devious social climber, an upstart who misrepresented herself as white when she was actually a mulatto who passed as a white woman and who used her obvious sex appeal and experience in sexual matters in a plan to seduce and steal away a rich and attractive prospective husband from more deserving white girls. Black women might also see Alice as a conniving traitor to the race. White men, on the other hand, would bring an entirely different set of prejudices and emotions and even unconscious impulses and desires to the trying of the facts that I believed could more easily be directed away from blaming Alice for the marriage and focused instead on Rhinelander, by appealing to the sensibilities of men of a certain class.

I had a very clear idea as to the ideal juror to sit as the finder of fact in the Rhinelander suit. I wanted and would endeavor to seat married men of the lower middle class, and the younger the better. I wanted men who believed in and would respect and defend the institution of marriage; men who would know first-hand the demands of matrimony; and men who worked hard to support their wives and families.

I also wanted men who would find Alice attractive, and that sentiment I would have to base on an appraisal of how they looked at her. Finally, I wanted men who would not be intimidated or overly impressed by the Rhinelander wealth and name. Such men, I believed, not only would resent Leonard's family's sense of entitlement, their presumptive lording it over the common working folk with their money, and their social standing; but they also would perceive Leonard as an abysmal representative of, and traitor to, the Rhinelanders' social class and supposed superior white masculine Nordic blue blood that he had shown himself to be—first, by straying from his social circle to court a girl so far beneath his class; then by seducing her, having his way with her, cohabiting with her, marrying her; and, finally, by seeking to annul the marriage, discredit the marriage and the girl as though marrying her, making promises to her, and taking her away from her family were all merely some weak-minded rich boy's misadventures. Then to cast the poor disgraced girl aside like a worn-out overcoat to please his proud and domineering father. I wanted men on the jury who would see Leonard's behavior in particular, and the Rhinelander family's haughty disdain in general, as obscene embarrassments to themselves and to everything they professed to stand for as pillars of upper-class white superiority.

My intention then was to evoke an acute sense of class distinction, which was certainly there in the facts; and to emphasize the mores and obligations of gentlemanly behavior to distract from the potential issue of prejudice toward Alice's race (which we were purportedly denying was Negro) and thus to evoke social bias that would work to undermine Leonard's case and to have him perceived as immoral and cowardly—a sex deviate of weak moral character, a race and class traitor, and a totally reprehensible representative of the so-called blue-blooded aristocracy—a man who, as Alice's father had so astutely perceived him, was without a firm and upright backbone.

Now, it bears notice that there were two very powerful and interrelated undercurrents to this trial that would need to be kept in mind while choosing a jury and that would need to be sought out, mined, and exposed both openly and with telling innuendo while trying the case: those subjects were racial prejudice and the taboo of interracial sex. Of the two, although race may have been the more obvious, sex in and of itself, and sexual relations between the races particularly, would prove in my opinion to be the more personal and hence the more powerful if a hidden theme throughout the litigation.

Sex, ah, yes, fornication, and the lure of the forbidden woman with her swarthy skin and red lips, the myth of the oversexed Black vamp with her wanton ways, her secret powers of seduction and sexual excitation, whether real or not: it was as much a theme of the Rhinelander trial and the plaintiff's case as it is the plot of trashy novels and pornographic films. During this case the subject of sex between the races would play of equal, and perhaps greater import in deciding the outcome than did the Rhinelander fortune.

Therefore I wanted men on that jury, vital men who could look at Alice, see her as a desirable female, exotic, neither Black nor white, a spurned woman, a good and loyal wife from a good, hardworking family who deserved to be respected and treated with dignity regardless of the hue of her skin or the taint of her blood. I also wanted men who would look askance at Rhinelander, see him as a shirker, a pantywaist, a spoiled papa's boy, something of a fop who never worked a day in his pampered life, and, finally, as a coward who did not have the strength of character or goodwill to take responsibility for his own actions and aberrant behavior.

Sex then was another basic human drive along with fear, and even combined with fear, that could provide a theme that, if handled adroitly, would work to Alice's advantage. Leonard was attracted to Alice—what man with a libido wouldn't be? The boy wanted to have sex with her—what red- or even blue-blooded young man wouldn't? And sex was uttermost in Leonard's mind when he pursued Alice, and he knew damn well she had Black blood—in fact it intrigued him, caused him to want her all the more. He seduced her, he bedded her, he cohabited with her; he took her away to hotels and on motor trips to New England; he had debased sexual relations with her all predicated on a promise of marriage, a promise he fulfilled. But in the end he would not prove man enough to stand up to his father. Finally, he let himself be intimidated and manipulated, and, I hoped to prove, even forced to commit perjury by his father to abandon his wife and attempt to utterly reject her, to toss her aside, and to forever disparage the woman he professed to love out of fear of his father, and fear of being disfranchised from the family wealth and social standing. In essence, my defense of Alice must reveal Leonard as a liar, a coward, a man other men could not respect as a representative of not only his so-called class, but also the male gender in general—indeed, not man enough for a woman (girl) like Alice.

Hence, my one question to potential jurors: *Can you be absolutely fair to this girl?* This question includes an additional unstated query: *Can you put aside your biases as regards her skin color or tainted blood and render a fair verdict based solely on the evidence?* That question would also contain every aspersion I hoped to cast upon Rhinelander, who obviously had failed to stand by and be honorable and fair to the girl he seduced and married. I believed that if the fellow I selected to sit on the jury could honestly put aside whatever notions he might have regarding Alice and her sexual allure; that if he could judge the evidence in the case solely on its merits and not hold any preconceived bias toward Alice due to her color and his unspoken fears of or attraction to interracial sex, then he would necessarily see Leonard Kip Rhinelander for who he was: the actual fraudster in this case. He could exonerate Alice by finding Rhinelander guilty.

Such a juror would see only sincere emotion as motivating Alice's behavior—love for Leonard. And this same juror would perceive fear and cowardice as the driving forces behind the Rhinelander lawsuit, not only Leonard's cowardice but Philip Rhinelander's as well. Neither Rhinelander male was man enough to see beyond his presumed blue-blooded superiority to recognize this woman for who she was; indeed, Leonard would abandon her, and Philip would not even meet her, not stoop to face the girl because, in his mind, she was so far beneath him.

Of course it would be my job at trial to give credence to these ideas and beliefs, or at least suggest that they might hold some truth, and to reveal—and hope to use to influence the verdict—the fears and hidden desires that I assumed my jurors held about race and sex and class based on their answers to that simple yet profound question: *Can you be absolutely fair to this girl?* In other words, would you have acted so dishonorably as did Leonard Rhinelander toward a maligned and innocent girl? Would you treat her with the haughty disdain of Philip Rhinelander? Would you fornicate with her, marry her, and then reject her—*for what?* Because you are a poor excuse for a man, and so now you want to drag the woman you supposedly loved through the slime of a nasty public scandal. Shame on you, Leonard Rhinelander! You are the fraud who should be on trial here, not your brave and honest wife.

Certainly, and it goes without saying: Alice is in every way a woman, not a girl; but it behooved me to call her a girl with the intent of eliciting each juror's manly and even fatherly instincts and dispositions to protect and comfort this good person from the wiles of a degenerate playboy, this knave in his shiny new sports roadster. In this game of poker, Alice's person, her physical presence was our hidden card; she was our queen of hearts.

* * *

Our jury was impaneled in fewer than three hours in the first session of voir dire, and the trial was set to commence. There was only one problem: the plaintiff, Leonard Kip Rhinelander, was still nowhere to be seen. On what was to be the opening day of trial, with preliminary statements to be made by counsel, and witness testimony set to begin, when Rhinelander failed to appear for the morning session, the trial was suddenly halted.

Scuttlebutt among spectators in the courtroom as well as with the crowds gathered outside in the hallways and on the courthouse grounds immediately raised the speculation that Leonard's absence indicated he had determined not to go through with the action to spurn his bride. So much attention in the press was given to the romantic notion of true love as a theme to the Rhinelander marriage, faint hearts of both genders wanted to believe in this fairy-tale affair and defiant wedlock. They wished to see Leonard come sweeping in to rescue his bride, upstage his father's lawyers, and redefine the Rhinelander family name. They hoped Leonard would declare his undying love to his wife, to judge and jury; to pick up Alice in his arms and carry her away to some distant idyll where they might live together in peace, anonymity, and wedded happiness.

I admit that even at the defense table there was some conjecture that there would be no trial, that Rhinelander had undergone a change of heart, that the suit would be dismissed, and that all our preparations were for naught. I for one hoped this was so, though I doubted it. Alice at first made no comment. She simply sighed, rolled her eyes, and shook her lovely head.

* * *

"All rise!" commanded the court clerk as Judge Morschauser strode in and assumed his position on the bench. He gazed out at the packed courtroom. His judicial demeanor seemed to me to soften when he looked upon Alice; she looked back at him with an expression of placid determination. The judge nodded slightly and then his look grew stern as he settled upon the plaintiff's table and inquired, "Where is the plaintiff, Mr. Rhinelander?"

Isaac Mills (though, as noted, Mr. Mills is properly referred to as a judge, I'll try not to designate him as such when it might cause confusion as to who was actually presiding over the trial) asked for the court's forbearance. "Your Honor," he declared, "the plaintiff, Leonard Kip Rhinelander, is expected at any moment."

One could see that the judge was not pleased. No judge is patient with tardiness on behalf of the parties, though he himself might keep the litigants waiting for hours. Mr. Mills declared that he was prepared to deliver his opening statement without Leonard's actual presence; I of course objected. I wanted Rhinelander there in the room to hear what his attorney expected to prove, and so the jury could observe him all the while; as well I wanted the delay in commencement of the trial to be recognized as the result of Rhinelander's failure to appear, and have whatever impact it caused directed upon the plaintiff; that the jurors might say, "Oh, so you call us all here because you want us to annul your marriage and dispose of your wife, and then you don't even have the decency to show up on time! What sort of man are you?"

The judge agreed and said court would reconvene when counsel for the plaintiff could produce the complainant. Judge Morschauser departed the bench with instructions to his clerk to alert him as soon as Rhinelander appeared; he then withdrew to chambers.

* * *

What? No Rhinelander? Only his lawyers . . . Incredibly, the morning dragged on and still the man whose powerful family had summoned us to this tribunal to determine the vital question of the legitimacy of his union, the complaining party, had not appeared. Isaac Mills attempted to take some of the onus for Rhinelander's absence and appease the court and the jury with the explanation that co-counsel Leon Jacobs had assured Rhinelander that voir dire would certainly consume the entire morning session and most likely go well into the afternoon; thus he had instructed Rhinelander that he need not appear until midafternoon. Mr. Mills explained that Jacobs is accustomed to the tedious process of impaneling juries in New York City and so he was not aware that "we do things much more expeditiously here in Westchester." He assured the court that Rhinelander was registered in rooms at the Gramatan Hotel in nearby Bronxville; he said he had dispatched one of his assistants to Leonard's hotel to track him down.

However, as Mills professed with certitude that there could be no question Rhinelander had every intention to go through with the trial, and that his tardiness was not to be misinterpreted as an abandonment of the lawsuit, sentiment both in the courtroom and on the bench (as well, one hoped among the jurors being held in the jury room like so many hostages to Rhinelander's bad manners) began to turn to one of mild hostility and irritation toward the party causing everyone to wait for his tardy arrival.

Being forced to wait is tedious enough under the best of circumstances. But especially with so many people poised to begin what had long infatuated their minds, a restless gathering being made to amuse themselves in a crowded, stuffy, overheated room, or in a confined jury room with no refreshments, and replete with eager expectation, such delay could only work to predispose the jurors against the arrogant and impolite scion and in favor of the demure and well-dressed, punctual young lady left in the lurch. She was now sitting patiently with the slightest of bemused smiles, and with reserved good manners while required to abide her husband's boorish, flippant failure to appear—and made to wonder if perhaps there was still some glimmer of hope he would call it off and return to her side at the last moment.

Reporters rushed into and out of the courtroom to call their editors. They reported that Alice looked stylish in a close-fitting cloche hat and fur-trimmed coat and that she sat quietly at the defense table and seemed unperturbed by the failure of her husband to make his entrance. Photographers jockeyed for the best shot of the bride and her family in court, waiting for Rhinelander to either appear or send word that he had decided against denouncing the marriage.

* * *

A recess was called for lunch. The trial was scheduled to resume with opening statements at 2:00 p.m.; and yet when court reconvened, Rhinelander was still missing. Now rumors that he had changed his mind and decided to quit his cause were again whispered and murmured in the courtroom, and debated aloud in the halls of the courthouse. Reporters speculated that there would be no trial after all. When queried by reporters, Alice would say only that she had not heard from Leonard. Isaac Mills continued to insist that Rhinelander would appear. Judge Morschauser's patience was sorely tested.

There was some discussion that if Rhinelander did not appear before the end of the day, I should move the court to dismiss the suit. As the hours of the afternoon dragged on, the mood in and around the courthouse became one of confusion and agitated expectation. With so many people gathered to take part in what was being hailed as "the trial of the century," anticlimax hung over the proceedings like a wet blanket set to stifle the mood. Soon anger simmered beneath the surface tension. Even Leon Jacobs appeared to be losing composure as he rushed into and out of the courtroom, still apparently unable to locate his bewildering client.

"It's just like Leonard," Alice confided with a knowing smile over a lunch she hardly touched. "He never knows what to do; or, I should say, he's unable to make up his mind when he's pushed into choosing one thing to do over another. We used to laugh about it. Go to see a movie? A show or a play? Stay in and enjoy each other's company? It's as though he wants to do everything and nothing. I had to simply take him by the hand and say, 'Come, let's go for a walk.' He has a difficult time settling his mind on a plan. Not always, but when he gets confused—it's like his stutter, his . . . indecisiveness: it comes and goes with his moods and when he feels pressed.

"I'll tell you, and I don't mean to toot my own horn, but with me Len was much better. I think he enjoyed taking the role of the man in control of the situation. We worked on it together.

You see, Leonard is actually much deeper and more intelligent than most people—even those who know him—give him credit; a lot goes on in that brain of his—too much, and though it might be a jumble of thoughts and ideas, and he keeps it to himself, sometimes it becomes too much and he needs someone to tell him what to do.

"With me, he very often opened up completely, and he let me see who he really is—to see beneath the image he hopes to portray. At heart, he's a good man; he wants to be a better man. He wants to make people proud, especially his father, but he feels he hasn't . . . that he lacks his father's power and will and, even more important, his love. After his mother, I was the only person who was ever really able to make Leonard feel loved and respected for who he is."

Alice stopped speaking for a moment; and then, ever prescient, she said, "Leonard will appear. As soon as his father hears that he's missing, you can be sure that Leonard will appear."

CHAPTER FOURTEEN

The Plaintiff's Evidence

It was nearly half past three in the afternoon when Leonard Rhinelander finally made his appearance. The complaining husband was delivered to the courthouse seated in his family limousine behind drawn curtains. He departed the vehicle and was rushed into the building flanked by Mr. Strong and another bodyguard retained to protect him should any of the militant Klansmen or angry local racists decide to make good on their threats to harm him as a traitor to all loyal white Americans.

Rhinelander barged into the courtroom not as Prince Charming come to rescue his fair maiden, as some had hoped; no, he sauntered in with his retinue and with a notably haughty swagger, more like a movie star at his premiere. He was dressed in a double-breasted suit, waistcoat, and spats; and he presented a contradictory beleaguered demeanor, peering out from behind his large round spectacles like an owl in the woods. His drawn and haggard countenance seemed to suggest sleepless nights and a feigned disposition that not only was he harried and put out to have been forced to appear at a trial of his own making; also young Kip gave the impression that he saw himself as someone who was above the fray, as if it were all beneath him, and of no real consequence to a person of his exalted social stature and world-weary sensibilities.

I was staggered. *What? How dare he amble in here over half a day late as though he were the one being called to defend himself?* I hasten to say that this grand entrance not only did not go over well with the judge and spectators, but was nearly transparent. Upon closer regard, one could perceive that the lad was both terrified and chagrined to have to appear in this courtroom to contest his case against the humble and faithful woman seated patiently at the defense table and whom he had taken as his bride. One could sense the frayed nerves beneath young Rhinelander's wan, indifferent surface composure.

Alice closely watched Leonard enter. Her expectant and loving gaze never left him as his bodyguards pushed through the crowds at the courtroom entrance, and then the plaintiff made his way along the aisle between the packed spectators' benches. It was the first time Alice had seen her husband since he was spirited away from her home by his father's henchmen; Rhinelander, however, did not so much as cast a glance Alice's way. He took his chair beside his lawyers, and he behaved as though the woman he had professed to love were not there, as though she did not exist.

The clerk hurried out to get the judge. The newspaper people scurried in and out to file their stories. Judge Joseph Morschauser returned, settled firmly on the bench, and one could surmise by his demeanor that he was not pleased with the tardy entrance of the plaintiff. The jury was brought in and seated in the jury box; I noted several of the jurors also appeared put out to have been kept waiting.

* * *

At long last, with all parties present, with the courtroom filled to capacity, with a hundred or more hopeful spectators milling around in the chill November air outside the courthouse, with the lovely defendant and all her family poised and ready to hear the evidence such as it may be, and with a now nervous and distracted Leonard Kip Rhinelander finally seated with his lawyers at the plaintiff's table, the clerk stood to announce the case.

"Hear ye, hear ye!" he bellowed. "In the matter of Rhinelander against Rhinelander, the Honorable Joseph Morschauser presiding, court is now in session."

At last the trial was ready to begin in earnest with counsels' opening statements.

* * *

As lead counsel for the plaintiff, Mr. Mills was to go first. He stood and addressed the judge and jury. Mills was getting on in years at the time of the Rhinelander trial, and he would soon retire; in fact, I believe *Rhinelander* was to be his swan song; but make no mistake, Mills was still a formidable opponent. A graduate of Amherst College and the Columbia School of Law, for all his experience trying cases in and around Westchester County, Mr. Mills, with his use of language and metaphor, often citing classical literary and biblical references that sailed above the heads of the jurors; and even down to the large, old-fashioned ear horn like a giant seashell that he occasionally stuck in his head to enhance his failing hearing: my opponent was decidedly of another era in his personal and his courtroom style. He wore a skullcap; and he spoke slowly, with a deep, resonant voice.

Mills began his remarks with an apology to the jury for the plaintiff's late arrival, again blaming it on Jacobs and the difficulties of finding twelve men good and true in Manhattan as opposed to here in Westchester; and he got a rise from the jurors when he complimented them on their suitability as "real Americans" to sit on this important case. "The world," he announced, "is watching." (This statement would appear as the headline in several newspapers the next morning.)

Mills then presented an outline of Rhinelander's suit from the plaintiff's perspective, and he did this in a grave manner, with a physical bearing and oratory style, with words and ideas intended to assure the jurors that there were indeed set standards of behavior, of social responsibility, particularly in matters of matrimony in a civilized society; that there were laws, beliefs, values; and that there were perceivable social class differences, differences in culture and education, differences indeed in race and blood that must need be respected, protected, and adhered to if our great country and our American way of life were to continue to flourish; if our American culture and economy were to endure and thrive amid the hurried onslaught of new, untested ideas brought with the influx of new races and creeds; and if we as a nation were to withstand the modern, less stringent forbearance to the ways of civilized society espoused by those he termed "iconoclasts and nihilists determined to reduce the American people to an unrecognizable polymorphism." Times were changing, Mr. Mills intimated, yes; but to mix the races, and to ignore long-recognized class differences, Mills harkened with foreboding, this loosening of sacred values would mean the end of life as we knew it. The nation, Mills sought to suggest—that is, white, blue-blooded America—was on the verge of chaos, and it would not survive if the Rhinelander marriage were allowed to continue.

Hyperbole? Of course, and not said in exactly those words, but implied, spoken and unspoken, and there in the body and presence of young Leonard Kip Rhinelander and his mulatto wife, the very embodiments of white upper-class America and its mongrel underclasses.

After this intimidating foreshadowing of where he intended his opening to go, Mills grounded his remarks in an explanation of the controlling law and a definition of the pertinent legal terms the jurors would be asked to understand. First, he wanted the jurymen to know what the legal term "material" meant, as it pertains to an annulment proceeding such as the Rhinelander lawsuit.

"A fact is material to the matrimonial relation," Mills explained, "such that if known to the other party it would naturally have prevented the marriage. . . .

"A fraud," Mills went on to note, "could happen both as an actual false representation—in this particular instance the statement by the young woman or others that she is entirely of white blood; and also a fraud can happen by concealment of a material fact, such as that she is not of pure white blood."

Mills then delineated the six specific questions that, based on the pleadings, he expected the jury would be called upon to answer once they had heard all the evidence and retired to the jury room to deliberate and reach a verdict.

They were:

The first one. At the time of the said marriage of the parties, was the defendant, Alice Jones Rhinelander, colored and of colored blood?

Second. Did the defendant, prior to said marriage, represent to the plaintiff, Leonard Kip Rhinelander, that she was white and not colored, and had no colored blood?

Third. Did she make the said representation with the intent

to deceive and defraud the plaintiff and thereby induce him to enter into the said marriage?

Fourth. Was the plaintiff, by said representation made by the defendant to him, induced to enter into the said marriage?

Fifth. Did the plaintiff enter into said marriage with the full belief that the said defendant was white and without colored blood?

And finally, sixth. Has the plaintiff cohabited with the defendant after he obtained full knowledge of the facts constituting the said fraud and the falsity of the said representation or with full knowledge by him that the defendant was not entirely of white blood?

There could be no question, Mills declared, and he promised he would prove to these good men of the jury, that the plaintiff, Leonard Kip Rhinelander, was "of pure white stock, and a descendant of one of the original French Huguenot settlers of New Rochelle."

Indeed, that fact was obvious and something Mills would be in no need to prove; and I for one believed this statement gave his client no advantage. Whereas Alice, Mills declared he was prepared to show the jury, "has a substantial strain of Black blood that comes to her from her father."

With that statement, Mills turned and made a dramatic gesture to indicate George Jones seated in the row of spectators' seats reserved for the defendant's family. One could see that Alice's father was obviously a dark-complected gentleman with a snowy white mustache. His facial features, however, were remarkable in that they were not what one would ordinarily describe as Negroid. He had a fine, aquiline nose, rather thin lips, a prominent jaw, and chiseled features. The skin tone as well was of a dark chocolate color more readily identified with people of West Indian heritage.

Mills went on to say that he and his firm had invested significant funds in an exhausting effort to trace and determine the actual ancestry and racial background of George Jones, the defendant's father. They not only had, however, been unable to establish his bloodlines, but were not even successful in verifying George Jones's claimed birthplace or the location of his childhood home. Thus Mills presented the jury with the notion that not only was Alice a fraud, but her father as well was not who he claimed to be.

Here Mills made an extraordinary statement that I found impossible to accept. "My eyes never rested upon the father until today," Mills announced to the jury. "I deemed it incumbent upon us to trace him back as far as possible."

Mills claimed that, had he seen George Jones before the trial, he would not have bothered to expend the funds and time he wasted in an effort to determine Jones's race, as it was obvious in his appearance.

The statement provoked a subdued utterance of amusement from the audience. Of course the man was obviously not white; one need only to look at him to know that he was colored. I was stunned. Was I hearing Mills correctly? Did he actually expect the jury to believe that George Jones was some kind of phantom who had hidden himself from view until this trial? Were the jurors expected to believe that Mills had never taken a cab from George Jones's taxi stand at the train station and so not cast his eyes upon the proprietor? Never seen George Jones and his wife and daughters at church? Never seen the man at any of the pretrial hearings? It was ludicrous. Was he attempting to make a subtle and yet poignant point? Was he suggesting to the jury that a Black man was of no significance, no consequence—indeed, invisible—until he intruded upon white society? And thus, was he saying that he simply never before noticed George Jones? Was he suggesting that race was something that could be determined simply by physical appearance when need be, such as when a woman of color sought to entrap a wealthy white man in marriage?

All this and more were suggested in Mills's claim of never having seen George Jones or his daughters. To my mind, it was just the first of several obvious lies that were the foundations of the plaintiff's case. If we were to believe Mr. Mills that all that was needed was to see George Jones in person, and to take notice of him, to know that he was a colored man—well, then what of Leonard Rhinelander's ability to see? Hadn't the plaintiff met George Jones on any number of occasions? Hadn't Rhinelander actually lived in the Joneses' home with George Jones and been in such close proximity, sat at the breakfast table with him and discussed the day's events? Hadn't Rhinelander actually been living in the Joneses' home when his father's lawyer Leon Jacobs appeared to take him away? Was it only then, after Jacobs appeared on the doorstep at the Joneses' home, that the scales before Leonard's eyes fell away, and his ability to see clearly and discern George Jones's color gave him some indication that his wife may have Black blood?

Absurd! Extraordinary! This statement confounded me; it was the sort of averment only an attorney who was no friend to the lower classes could expect a jury to believe: to insinuate that George Jones was beneath notice until circumstances demanded. So much of what the Rhinelander lawyers alleged and sought to prove was clearly false; I had to gather my thoughts, rethink my opening. Listening to Mr. Mills at first gave me solace to believe that there were such huge discrepancies in what the suit claimed and what I knew to be the facts; discrepancies that could not be explained away or ignored. Actual material facts that were clearly at odds with the plaintiff's allegations. To suppose that Leonard is somehow unable to perceive something as obvious as the color of George Jones's skin when it was apparent to Mr. Mills, and for Leonard not to know therefore that Jones's daughter Alice has some Black blood in her veins while living in the Jones home, was clearly preposterous. *Fantastic!* Unbelievable on its face. And we knew for a fact that even after Alice's racial taint was revealed to the public on the front pages of local and national newspapers, when she was labeled a "Negress," even then, in direct contradiction to allegations made in the complaint, Leonard continued to cohabit with Alice. Of course he did! They lived together in her family's home. They slept in the same bed. They planned a future together; they had rented an apartment, bought furniture and household lares and penates and bedroom accoutrements with every intention of remaining joined as husband and wife, and then to raise a family—until, that is, Rhinelander Senior's hirelings appeared to take Leonard away.

This was readily demonstrable to the jury. We would show them how baseless the Rhinelander complaint was given the facts. Incredible, yes; but this opening also gave me a clear indication of how Mills and Jacobs were prepared to try their case. First off, they never expected the case to go to trial—of that I am certain. I'm convinced that Rhinelander Senior and his lawyers firmly believed that Alice was in it for the money and that she would readily take a settlement and be gone. Then, once they understood that they had misjudged her, and that Alice could not be bought off, and that they would be called to prove their allegations, they determined it would not be on the facts; no, it would be on innuendo and on raising the vile, underlying prejudices and fears that they intended to provoke in the minds and hearts of the twelve white men seated in the jury box.

For my part, I would need to overcome those prejudices and fears. Why do whites fear Blacks? What is it about Blacks that seems threatening? There is not *a race*—there are ethnicities. There is only one race: the human race. Race is a construct that fascinates and attracts us as well as it scares us.

In his opening statement, Mills said that he would be entering into evidence George Jones's naturalization papers, signed by none other than the presiding judge, Joseph Morschauser, in which document George Jones is identified as a colored man. He would, Mills declared, also be submitting George Jones's driver's license application from September 30, 1924, only a few months prior to the commencement of the trial, and that document also identified Jones as colored. As well, Mills said he would be entering the birth certificate of the defendant's sister Emily Jones on which she was recorded as mulatto; and the birth certificate of Alice's younger sister, Grace, on which she was recorded as "Black, Negro, mixed." Finally, Alice's own birth certificate, which designated her as "color, Black," would be entered into evidence.

Additionally, Mills said he would prove Alice's race by actions she and her family engaged in, primarily by her sisters consorting with colored people; one of the sisters was actually married to a Black man. Here Mills turned and pointed to Alice's brother-in-law Robert Brooks, who was obviously Negro, seated in the spectators' gallery with his wife, Alice's sister Emily, and whereupon Mills declared, "We have subpoenaed him in court. We shall exhibit him to you."

Alice, Mills said he would show, had also "kept company" with a Black man prior to her meeting Leonard. Mills said that he would prove Alice was an older, experienced, and sexually aggressive Black woman who had taken advantage of a naive and sheltered white boy from a prominent family in hopes of seducing him into marriage purely for financial gain. Furthermore, Mills proclaimed that the fact that Alice had not invested the funds provided by Leonard to prove that she was white actually proved the opposite: that there was no evidence of her color except that she was Black. All these factors, Mills assured the jury, he would submit and enter into evidence to prove beyond any doubt that

Alice—light-skinned though she might appear and able to pass herself as white—was in fact a colored person, with Black blood in her veins, and therefore she could not be considered white.

But why? Why would the jury need to be shown all this documentary evidence of Alice's color if in fact George Jones's color was so obvious that Mills knew upon seeing him that he was colored?

Mills might appear to be arguing our case instead of his own!

How are we to define race? Is it only discernible in the eyes of the beholder? If all the Jones girls were obviously colored, if Alice's father was colored, if her brother-in-law was a Negro, how could Leonard possibly have been deceived as to Alice's color? It made no sense. It seemed clear to me that Mills was presenting his case in a contradictory and thoroughly baseless and confusing manner, one that would not depend on evidence but only on prejudice—and, once again, on fear.

Yes, the fear that if this family with an obviously Black father and three Black daughters, if the Jones brood could so readily insinuate themselves into white society as to have one of the girls marry a Rhinelander, the pinnacle of white, blue-blooded aristocracy, God forbid! Nothing and no one was sacred. The very lines of class and race in America would cease to exist. Mills challenged the jurors to look upon Alice and to see for themselves how insidious the mixing of the races is in that "the trace of Negro blood in Mrs. Rhinelander is almost imperceptible," thus raising the very real specter of Blacks passing themselves off as whites until there was no such thing as a pure white American. The white race was doomed and could never survive such an assault. It had to be stopped here, in this case!

Mills further claimed that he would prove that the Jones family were desperate money grubbers who had plotted to pass themselves off as white; that Elizabeth Jones conspired with her daughters and sent them to seduce and marry white men to infiltrate white society and enrich herself in the process. Alice, Mills proclaimed, had struck gold, found the mother lode, a real "catch" to be exploited by her "gold-digging family" when she snared her millionaire's son, Leonard Kip Rhinelander.

Perhaps Mills forgot that only a moment before he had exhibited one Jones daughter's husband, Robert Brooks, and used his obvious Blackness to demonstrate that Alice must also be Black. But then he quickly backtracked and claimed that Emily's marriage to a Black man had caused turmoil in the Jones household, which would prove to be yet another falsehood among several out-and-out lies the plaintiff's counsel attempted to use to sway the jury.

Mills's opening remarks were all over the courtroom, and all over the issue of race in America. His so-called facts were riddled with misrepresentations and baseless accusations.

But even that was not enough. Next, Mills stunned the audience and perplexed the jury as well as the judge when he claimed that he would prove that his client, Leonard Kip Rhinelander—this descendant of the Huguenot bloodline, born to a founding family of New York high society, and with his name listed in the elite social register—was "a brain-tied miserable wretch, a boy, tongue-tied and diffident, upon whom no woman, or at least no woman of his kind, had ever smiled before."

What? I shook my head in dismay and wondered if I also needed an ear horn. Was I hearing my opponent correctly? He would prove young Kip Rhinelander an idiot? The assertion that Leonard was little more than a moron not only astounded everyone in the courtroom, it also caused the spectators to emit an audible gasp, and it provoked commotion as the reporters rushed out to file their reports.

Judge Morschauser commanded order in the court. Mills took a breath. He looked around and gave time to let this incredible statement, this insult to the intelligence of his client and to the Rhinelander family name and reputation, settle in. I had to wonder if his nibs Rhinelander Senior was aware of how his lawyer intended to characterize his boy. Leonard, Mills claimed he would prove, was a simpleminded dupe to the degree that he was barely one step above an imbecile; mentally handicapped to the point where he could not perceive Black from white because he was enslaved by illicit sex with a Black female vampire, a conniving mistress of trickery sicced upon him by a devious, ambitious, social-climbing, money-grubbing family.

This was too much.

I stood and objected.

"Your Honor, this is outrageous!" I told the judge. "I must object to my esteemed colleague's professed claim: *Leonard Kip Rhinelander an idiot? A brain-tied imbecile?* Why, we have seen no proffer of this evidence."

Mr. Mills angrily asserted that if I would only let him proceed, he would show that he intended to bring the director from the Orchards School to court to testify as to Leonard's impaired mental condition. Mills was given leave to proceed. Leonard, he claimed, was not merely mentally backward, he not only had a debilitating stutter, but he also was younger than Alice by a few years; he was socially inept; he was sexually inexperienced; he suffered from childhood trauma brought about by the death by fire of his beloved mother, and by his older brother's death in the Great War—of course he stammered; and he couldn't perceive right from wrong; and on and on, poor lad, such as the only thing he was good for was to be seduced and inveigled by a lascivious, calculating, and devious Black woman.

Oh, but still Mr. Mills went on to attack Alice's family! He disparaged and maligned her mother, Elizabeth Jones. He announced that there had been another Jones daughter, or perhaps not a Jones daughter, but a child of Elizabeth Jones born out of wedlock, sent away, and pressed into domestic service as a child in the household of another family; and whom, Mills said, he would call as a witness and bring into court to prove the moral degeneracy of the scheming woman who would marry Alice to a Rhinelander.

Once again I rose to object. Where was the relevance? Mr. Mills was seeking to inflame the jurors with preposterous and unfounded claims with no bearing on the issues at trial. Judge Morschauser agreed, but he reminded me as well as the jury that this opening statement by Mr. Mills was not to be taken as evidence in and of itself, but rather was to be considered as what the plaintiff intended to prove through the introduction of actual evidence; and as such, the jurors need be reminded to withhold any judgment upon the issues until all the evidence had been presented. I of course said I understood that but still asked the judge to instruct plaintiff's counsel to confine his statements to the relevant issues he expected to prove and not seek to defame the defendant's family in some obvious and unethical smear campaign.

Mills then focused his disapprobation upon Alice and her sisters. They were, Mills insinuated, out walking the streets of New Rochelle, hardly more than prostitutes in search of men to seduce and entrap in marriage when poor idiot child Leonard strayed into their clutches. Alice pursued Leonard, not the other way around, Mills claimed he would prove. And she schemed with her mother to keep the naïf under her spell with filthy letters describing the unnatural and illegal sex acts she would perform on him to keep him enslaved until such time as he could claim his manhood and inheritance, break loose from his father's control, and give way to Alice's demands that he marry her. In Mills's recounting of the relationship, Alice made innocent, mentally impaired Leonard her sex slave, and then she demanded that he marry her so she could fulfill the Jones family plot of ensnaring a rich white man to enhance the Joneses' social and financial status.

At last, in one final breath of his spiel, and with all that smut before the court, Mills sat down.

* * *

I was disgusted; truthfully, I was appalled, not just at Mills's obvious attempts to provoke the jurors' supposed racial prejudice and fear of miscegenation, but also for the nasty way in which my opponent had sought to disgrace Alice's mother; there was no need for that.

I stood and objected vehemently to Mills's entire opening. I called his remarks heartless, asked that they be stricken from the record, that the jury be instructed to disregard everything Mills had said, and I asserted that the plaintiff's intended case against Alice as outlined in Mills's opening, and the Rhinelander suit itself, was "un-American, a travesty, not fit to be heard by a jury in a court of law." I said I found Mills's allegations not only baseless and false but also "repulsive and below the standards and dignity of this honorable court."

Judge Morschauser reminded the jury once again that counsel's remarks were not meant to be evidence. He instructed them to keep an open mind until they had heard and had a chance to consider opposing counsel's remarks, and then been afforded all the relevant evidence presented by both sides, and upon which to base their findings.

With that, court was adjourned for the day.

CHAPTER FIFTEEN

December 1, 1924

A trial? I am on trial? My marriage to Len is on trial? No—never. Not possible. . . . How can this be? Whenever I would think about my life, what it might be, where I might go and what I might do, even whom I might marry, and the family I might have—never would I ever have imagined it would come to this—a trial! And with me as the one being tried by a jury. Why? How can this be? This sort of thing doesn't happen to young girls who only want to marry a good man and be a loving and faithful wife and raise and love her family. This just doesn't make any sense at all. It's like a nightmare, a horrible dream I wake up from every day and that still continues even after I am awake. You fall in love with a man, you marry him, and then what—you are put on trial and called a liar? A tramp? A Black whore? How can such a thing happen?

And there was Len in the courtroom unable even to look my way! As though I were a stranger. He ignored me. He paid me no mind—the woman he swore he loved and whom he married. And now he allows his lawyer to say these things about me. It's incredible. Never in my life would I have imagined that my love for Len would come to this.

Oh, certainly, I was warned—everyone warned me. "Don't do it, Alice," they said. "Take the money and get on with your life. You can't win against people such as the Rhinelanders. People like that always win. Just take the money. Don't be foolish. Don't let your pride influence your decision. They will say and do horrible things to you if you fight them."

Well, now, how many times have I heard that? "Take the money, Alice! Don't force them to take you to trial. You can't win!"

Maybe they are right, the naysayers, as Father calls them. Maybe I should have listened. Maybe I should have done as everyone advised and taken the money and run off to hide. Everyone, that is, except my father. No, not George Jones. He wasn't having it. Mother as well—though she was less sure of it than my father. He's a fighter. He's one of those never-say-die Englishmen who will fight you with their last breath. And I am my father's daughter. And particularly if you know you are right, then it is your duty to fight.

I am supposed to say that I lied to Len and told him I was of pure white Anglo-Saxon blood! Why, that is simply crazy. This entire trial is insane. It's a nightmare, and it's madness. It's a pack of lies dreamed up by lawyers to try to intimidate me into taking the money and admitting that I tricked Len into marrying me.

Well, no. I'm not stupid. And I'm not a liar. And I'm not afraid of the Rhinelanders and their money or their high social standing. I may not have Len's education, and I may not be worthy of the Rhinelander name, as they seem to think, but I'm not an idiot—as Len's own lawyer said, he is an idiot! I almost fell out of my chair when I heard that. What did he say? Len is "brain-tied." Whatever that means, when said about Len, it's ridiculous. Len is one of the smartest people I have ever met. He's almost too smart, if there is such a thing. By that I mean to say that his mind works overtime. Every time he has an idea, almost at the same time he has the opposite idea. I saw that with him so often. He had such trouble making up his mind because his mind is too active, too full of ideas and questions. He's not an idiot at all. I couldn't believe it when I heard his lawyer say that. And I could only wonder how it made Len feel to have him described as such a failure of a man, as his lawyer seems to want everyone to believe.

What I can't understand about Leonard is how he will allow other people to rule over him the way he does. His father, his father's lawyers, and the men who work for his father—it's as though Len loses all faith in himself when those men come around. It's the strangest thing I've ever seen, how a man, and a man I know and love, how he can suddenly change right before my eyes and seem to become someone else altogether—so fearful. There is the Leonard I know, the man I love and the man I married, and then there is this other Leonard—or Kip, as they call him. I don't know that man. I never knew him. He's not the man I married. He's not the man I spent that glorious time with on Cape Cod—my Greek god. He's not even the shy and embarrassed boy who came to our home looking for Grace and who fell in love with me. The man who walked into the courtroom and took a seat at the table with his lawyers, that Leonard Kip Rhinelander—I don't know him; and he obviously doesn't know me if he thinks I am just going to sit there and allow his lawyers to say these things about me and my family without raising my head and shouting loud and clear, "No! This is all a pack of lies!"

I ask myself how it could have come to this. I ask God, Dear Lord, how could you let this happen? That I, Alice Jones, and now Alice Jones Rhinelander, married to the man I love, how could it come to my being dragged into court . . . first of all that my husband is taken away from me by these other men, and then I am taken into court to prove what? That I didn't lie to Len about the color of my skin? How crazy is that? Len can see with his own eyes! No, there is something else going on here, and it is just not right. When I asked Father how God could allow this to happen, he said that it's not God at all; he told me it's just people, and that people have free will. People do things that are wrong and they are the ones who pay for their actions. Nobody gets away with anything in the long run, not according to Father. But it doesn't look that way, not at all, not now. It looks like I am the one who is being made to suffer simply for loving Leonard.

People say take the money and be done with it. O God, how many times have I heard that! Maybe that's what I should have done. Perhaps it's not too late. But how would that put an end to anything? Yes, the trial would end. But my life would still go on. And it would never be the same were I to say that I am a liar who deceived Len about my color and tricked him into marrying me, so I could be what? A rich liar? How could I ever look at myself in the mirror if I did that? Please, no, never. I am not a liar. I never told Len I was "of pure white Anglo-Saxon blood," whatever that is supposed to be! I am what I am and I am not ashamed of it.

I don't care about the money. I don't care about the Rhinelander name. I married Len because I love him. We planned to have a family. Len was a better man when he was with me. He had more confidence in himself and he was happy. I helped him to get over his stutter. We could have a good life together if they would all just leave us alone and let us be who we really are—Alice and Len.

Instead, look what it's become! This is a marriage of two people who love each other, and look what it has been turned into! A trial! A scandal. They say, "America is watching!" Watching what? That I am called a liar who tricked Len into marrying me by telling him I was pure white? Now, how does that make any sense when all you need to do is look at my Father? And Len . . . no, I don't understand it. And I am not—well, it's gone past all that now; but I, the person I am, George Jones's daughter Alice, the woman I am is not the sort of person who will let people tell her what to do when she—I—when I know in my heart that it is wrong. To say that I lied to Len would be the real lie.

A trial! To prove that a lie that never was is a lie? No, I'm sorry, Mr. Rhinelander, Philip Rhinelander, whom I never met, I'm sorry if you don't like me and don't approve of your son marrying me. But that is what Leonard did, he married me because he loved me, not because I tricked him into it or whatever, that I made him lose his mind. No, he knew exactly what he was doing, and so did I, and so I still do.

I don't care what happens to me. It doesn't matter. I am who I am and no one can prove otherwise. Even my lawyer, Mr. Davis, whom I like very much, and I believe he likes me and he believes me—he believes in our case. But he as well warns me over and over of the risk I am taking by going to trial against the Rhinelanders. I understand he's just doing his job as my lawyer. He wants me to know all of the facts and of the issues we face by insisting on this trial. Of course we could lose. And then I would be found guilty of fraud. That would be terrible. I understand that. But for me to lie and admit to something that is simply untrue, and something so important as who I am and what was in my mind and my heart when I married Leonard—no, I can't do it. I couldn't do it and look at myself in the mirror every day and say, "Alice, you are a good person, a strong woman, and a person who stands up for what you believe in." I couldn't do that if I lied and took the money because I was afraid to go into court and stand trial to prove the truth. That would be a real case of fraud.

In the end, "when it all comes down to the final analysis," as George Jones would say, I am my father's daughter, and my father always taught me to fight for what I believe in and not to let other people bully me into doing something I know is wrong.

And besides, I saw the note from Len. He's the one who told me to fight.

I believe that Len still loves me.

CHAPTER SIXTEEN

Defending Alice

When it came time for me to make my opening statement, I was not to protest merely for the sake of attempting to sway the jury, not purely for show. Rather, I wanted to make a record; and it was crucial to let everyone in the courtroom know that as Alice's defender, I would not be intimidated and acquiesce to such a slanderous defamation of my client's good character.

I couldn't believe the vile, unfounded allegations that had issued from this learned man's mouth in his opening statement to the jury. I was prepared to counterattack, and I needed only to contain and focus my outrage.

However, by this point in the proceedings, already delayed by Rhinelander's belated arrival, and upon listening to Mills's offensive opening, I was temporarily dismayed—"enraged" may be a better way to express how I felt. I would need to settle down; to recover my equanimity; to reconsider my remarks in light of Mills's opening; and then to use my opening statement to denigrate opposing counsel's outrageous claims and thereby point out the weakness in the premise of the plaintiff's case.

As an experienced trial attorney, it goes without saying that I am well acquainted with the aggressive and often vicious tactics used by lawyers to win their case. This attack by Mr. Mills, however, struck me as something more, something out of character—a desperate attempt to sway the jury by appealing to their racial biases, their fear of Black sexuality, and the threat of Negroes passing into white society. Mr. Mills, I perceived, had apparently stooped to such low devices because he perceived that the facts of the lawsuit were not to his client's benefit.

Thankfully, as it was already late in the day, Judge Morschauser decided to adjourn until the following morning, at which time I would present my opening remarks. He reminded the jurors once again that they should not consider the plaintiff's counsel's statement until they had heard from the respondent and that they should refrain from talking about the case among themselves or to friends and family. Also, they should avoid reading any news reports about the trial, or listening to the radio; and generally they were reminded to keep an open mind until all the evidence had been presented and they were charged with the case.

I wanted to focus on the two thoughts that had occurred to me simultaneously as I considered my rebuttal. To that end, I forced myself to ponder how to attack the ignominy of the smut that Mills spewed upon not only Alice but also her mother, Elizabeth Jones, as well as George Jones, Alice's sisters, and her brothers-in-law. Indeed, it included anyone remotely connected to the young woman as though they were all part of some criminal plot motivated by greed to entrap Rhinelander in a deceitful marriage as a means of taking him and his family for all they were worth.

The first thought that was made readily apparent listening to Mills's opening was that this case would be fought at the very lowest levels of adversarial contest—down and dirty, as it were—that it would be nasty and verge upon the unethical. That thought was accompanied by its subtext: Mills and his co-counsel were hardly invested in the evidentiary and factual merits of their case; they were aware that the suit stood on flimsy if not to say imagined evidentiary grounds of fraud; and so they felt forced to fight dirty because they did not believe they could prevail in any other way.

Mr. Mills clearly knew that the facts were not in his client's favor. I was sure he knew damn well his client was no idiot, and that he was fully cognizant of Alice's mixed race when he courted and married her. Mills knew that Leonard was well acquainted with Alice's family; that he had lived with them; that Leonard knew Alice's father, George Jones, was not white, and he didn't care that Alice was colored—in fact, plaintiff's counsel knew that Alice's mixed race was fine with Leonard until his father objected and demanded that the boy cease his cohabitation with Alice and remove himself from the marriage, or be cut off from the Rhinelander fortune and expelled from the family. I also believe that Mills was well aware that in fact his client, Leonard Rhinelander, was no idiot, no brain-tied dupe or sex slave; and that it was he, Rhinelander, through his lawyers, who perpetrated the real fraud.

Mills knew that the lawsuit he was litigating was based on lies. Such a lawsuit would only proceed to trial because of two facts: the fact of the Rhinelander name and their fortune; and the fact of racial bias in American society. As Alice's defender, I was not only fighting a phantom case; I was also opposed to the benefits of class and money and to the powerful emotional sway of racism in America.

What I had, however, was what every lawyer wants in a case: I had the facts in my favor; and I had a client who in my mind, at least, was beyond reproach. This realization—the idea that the Rhinelander lawsuit was based on lies and would be fought with an attempt to sway the jury with emotion—did not surprise me even as it presented me with a dilemma: Was I to take the high road and thereby risk being subverted, undercut by Mills's obvious appeal to the jurors' biases and base fears; or would I fight scandal, sensationalism, and abject filth with its equal? And it also set about to intrigue me with an idea I had been entertaining regarding the possibility of an entire change to our proposed defense tactics. This idea would continue to take form in my mind.

* * *

Thankfully, as by this time the day's session was at an end, there would be no time for my opening remarks until the following day, which was fine with me. I would have the evening to prepare my rejoinder, to assuage my anger, and to light the fuse to the bombshell I intended to detonate right there in open court and to blow the case wide open.

* * *

"The Leonard I saw in the courtroom today," Alice bemoaned at the close of trial on the first day. "I feel I don't know him. He was nothing like the man I married . . . *so cold* . . . so distant. He was a stranger to me."

We met for tea with Alice's parents, George and Elizabeth, at a shop near the courthouse. The crowds that had pursued us upon leaving court soon trailed off in pursuit of Leonard. Alice was devastated, poor girl; I could see it in her eyes, now dimmed with sadness and the harsh realization of lost love; I could hear it in the tremulous timbre of her deep, sonorous voice now strained with emotional pain; and I knew the travail would only get worse, only heighten and intensify with more disgusting revelations and heartless allegations as the trial progressed.

Amazingly, Alice would get stronger morally even if more deeply hurt and physically overwrought. Interesting, however, that she would never harbor any feelings for Leonard but the deepest emotions of love tinged with sadness and compassion. Although there were those—most notably a few lady members of the press—who sought to keep hope alive that the marriage might survive if in fact Alice were to prevail in the suit, I had my doubts; no, better still, I knew the marriage was doomed. Yes, I believed, as did Alice, that Leonard's heart—whatever heart the boy had—was not in the action against his wife. But I also understood what George Jones, wise father of three girls, said when he pegged Rhinelander from the beginning: Leonard was a weak sister; the fellow had no backbone, no testicular fortitude.

I was sure of one other fact, as I had been foretold in Philip Rhinelander's visit to my office, and as Alice had proclaimed from the start: the annulment suit was not Leonard's doing; the lad was a mere pawn in his father's cruel machinations. This, I believed, could be proved, and it would prove Alice blameless and hardly some scheming Black vamp. Leonard's compliance in the annulment suit, whether willing or forced, certainly bespoke a flawed character. I filed that thought away for future reference in preparation for what I assumed was coming: Leonard's appearance on the witness stand, and my opportunity to cross-examine him. Mills would have to call the fraudster to hope to prove the fraud, for he had no other evidence.

"I can't believe this is happening," Alice went on. "How did it come to this?" I could see she was close to tears. "All I did was love Leonard. Was that wrong?"

Her father put his strong arm around her shoulders and hugged his daughter close. "Of course not, my dear. You've done nothing to be ashamed of," George Jones assured her. "Don't mind what they say, Alice. You know who you are. We know who you are. And we know who we are as people. Don't imagine any of this is your doing."

Elizabeth agreed, nodding, and took her daughter's delicate hand in hers.

"It's all right, child," she said. "We'll get through this."

Alice looked at me with those alarming dark eyes now glistening like polished onyx and asked, "What will become of me?"

I was startled by the question. How to answer so deep and perceptive an inquiry? What will become of Alice Rhinelander? Did I have an answer? Did she have future happiness? One might see the years yawning ahead if she were to be utterly defeated: a poor girl, cast off, broken, and defamed. Yet even victory would come at tremendous cost. I had no faith in either outcome.

"You, my dear, are an extraordinary person, a woman of uncanny character and charm," I told her, and I meant it. "And you will remain so. You will go on being the remarkable woman you are, regardless of what happens. Nothing, no words that issue from anyone's mouth in that courtroom, no judgment either way can change who you are, Alice. You are Alice Rhinelander. Your love for Leonard is innocent; it is and was always decent and pure. *You* are innocent and pure. Whatever they may say, and whatever they do, just continue to be who you are, dear Alice. Understand that this is being done in an effort to win a fraudulent case against you when in fact it is Rhinelander who is guilty of fraud. And we will prevail—*you* will prevail."

I said this, I believed it, and of course I hoped it was true. But Alice was wise in perceiving that there could be no real victory for her in this contest.

She had already lost the love of her life.

CHAPTER SEVENTEEN

A Bombshell

At least Rhinelander had the decency and good sense to appear on time on day two. Once again, he looked to me as though he'd hardly slept. I hoped he'd tossed and turned all night in his bed as he wrestled with the unnerving and demoralizing realization of what a cad, what a pathetic excuse for a man he'd turned out to be, and of the disgrace and heartbreak he'd brought to the girl who gave her love to him and asked nothing but his love in return. Not even the Rhinelander millions, not the lawyers nor the bodyguards could protect him from who he was—a man with no fundamental masculine honor and pride.

But judge not lest we be judged ourselves. Of course, I understood it; I could see how, given his tragic childhood, the loss of his beloved mother at a tender age; and then the brilliant example of his older brothers; and the pressure brought by the strident will of his domineering father; all that coupled with the boy's physical and mental hindrances; even considering the family scandal caused by his uncle William's bizarre marital choices. And given Leonard's own reliance on the family name and wealth as his only means of support, and indeed of identity, I could accept that Rhinelander might become a timid, easily manipulated young man. I was also aware that he enjoyed some small streak of the Rhinelander derring-do. And I was aware of the evidence of the electrician Karl Kreitler, and of his having taken advantage of Leonard and fleecing him for money on a bogus business venture. (There was still at this point in the proceedings some speculation that Kreitler might be called as a witness on behalf of the plaintiff.) But, for God's sake, man, get over it! Grow up and be a man, goddamnit! You did one interesting and bold thing in your pampered life; you fell in love with and you married a mixed-race girl. Now, that is something daring and even a choice to be proud of—but now you want to disavow it? No. Honor your choice to be unique. Live up to your actions. Be a man and own your behavior, and for God's sake stop making these childish excuses for yourself, and stop allowing others to make false excuses for your unmanly behavior.

I could sustain no feelings of sympathy for Rhinelander because there was this other aspect to his nature: his supercilious personality; call it what you may, his feigned arrogance, his haughty aloofness, his seeming self-satisfaction with his station in life that came as a result of no efforts of his own but instead by chance, the luck of birth into a rich family: all that I found utterly distasteful and infuriating, and I believed the men of the jury would see him as a pompous ne'er-do-well also—if I were able to demonstrate it for them.

It was a risky tack to take, but that was to be my task. I would ask, though unspoken, at least until my summation: Where was the humility, for God's sake? Where was the awe and gratitude for all you have been blessed with, Leonard Kip Rhinelander? Have you ever truly suffered a day in your spoiled life? Oh, yes, you lost your mother while still a boy. That indeed was a tragedy. But don't give me your self-satisfied pomp, you fraud. Show me your vulnerability, and your decency, your compassion, your higher spirit, your selfless love—all that you showed to Alice to cause her to love you. And ask yourself: What did you think you were doing when you took this young woman to bed and then married her? Playing some rich boy's sex games with a poor girl of mixed race; indulging your fantasy of forbidden love in an effort to make yourself appear more daring and interesting; seeking to upset and dismay your overbearing father? All of the above? But you must be made to understand that this is a serious affair of the heart as well as of the body—particularly once you married the girl. And now you want to destroy the child? Ruin her for the rest of her life? What sort of man does that to a girl he professes to love? To any girl, for that matter. How could you? Why would you? Because your father says so? *Why?* I wished to show the boy. *Alice is ten times the person of integrity that you are, Kip. That is why you fell in love with her in the first place. She made you feel better about yourself.*

I could hear these questions, these demands, and these assertions to be asked and posited in my summation, and with Kip's failure to answer the unspoken inquiry of his wife as a man, instead of his hollow claims of having been deluded into loving Alice, resounding in my busy brain, the opening statements were upon us, and the trial was set to begin.

Of course, one might also suppose that Leonard's arrogance was all an act to try to cover a deep-seated knowledge of his own lack of character and embarrassment at his social timidity and ineptitude. Yes, I have no doubt the boy was attempting to compensate for a lack of self-esteem and for his inability to stand up to his father's domineering will and demanding aspirations for his irresolute youngest son. I understand that. But rather than evoking sympathy, this sentiment only made me more intent on bursting the boy's bubble and revealing him to the jury, to the press, to the spectators, and to the world for the pretentious bag of hot air that was this Leonard Kip Rhinelander, this son of wealth and social prominence, this pretender who would defame the good name of his wife and her family with the vilest of smut hurled upon these decent people by his conniving advocates.

* * *

When I walked into the crowded courtroom I was full of righteous indignation and barely stifled anger. I was genuinely upset with Rhinelander and his lawyers for the despicable manner in which they had determined to conduct their case.

Court came to order when the clerk announced His Honor, and Judge Morschauser resumed the bench. Counsel for the plaintiff and for the defense welcomed His Honor and bade him a good morning. Once everyone was settled, and the judge had determined that there were no outstanding issues to be decided before the defense was to proceed with our opening remarks, the jury was brought in and took their seats. The judge welcomed them and thanked them for their patience. And then, with all in the courtroom intent on the proceedings, His Honor turned to me and asked, "Is the defense ready to proceed?"

I stood and said, "We are, Your Honor."

I chose this moment to look around the room with care, as if to make certain all present had afforded me their undivided attention. I looked first at the members of the jury, giving each man a moment's notice; then I turned to face the crowded gallery; and finally I let my gaze settle upon Alice—ever lovely, ever poised, good Alice Rhinelander, dressed, as always, fashionably demure. I let the silence endure almost to the point where everyone was on the verge of discomfort and wondering what was to come next, or if I had forgotten my speech.

"Yes!" I practically shouted. "We—Alice Rhinelander—is ready to defend against these outrageous and baseless charges. *But first*," I continued, raising my voice even more to make certain everyone could hear and to be sure I had their notice, "before opening, the *defendant* Alice Beatrice Jones Rhinelander, this young lady seated beside me at the defense table, desires to make a statement, through her attorneys, and for the benefit of the record."

Here I paused and once again I looked around the room to allow everyone a tense moment to wonder what on earth Alice might wish to say to the court at this crucial moment in the proceedings. Then I continued.

"That statement being: that, at the outset of this litigation, there was interposed *a technical legal denial* . . . on advice of counsel, as to *the blood of this defendant*."

Here I hesitated again to let the statement play out, certain that I had everyone's attention, and I turned once more to face the jury. An expectant murmur rippled through the gallery, and then the room went still.

Finally, once more to address His Honor, I spoke in a forceful though less stentorian manner.

"Your Honor, let the record reflect that, in the interest of *shortening this trial*," I continued, my voice again gathering in volume. (Oh, how I cherish these moments in a trial!) Then I announced, "I would advise the court that the defendant's counsel hereby *withdraws the previous denial as to the blood of this defendant*; *and*,"—I turned to face the jury and the gallery—"for the purpose of this trial, let it be known that Alice Rhinelander *admits that she has some colored blood in her veins*."

What revelation is this? And yet never in my experience has a statement of the obvious had such a remarkable effect. Alice has some Black blood. Well, imagine that! Perhaps, if we had not met her father we might have been deceived; and yet, she's clearly not pure white. But now that I admitted a fact that all could see if only they would look, and yet it stunned nearly everyone in the room to have me state what was apparent, it was as if I had said, "There is racism in this country, and in this courtroom, and if we allow it, we are all guilty." Indeed, that is exactly the subtext of what I was saying.

Audible exclamations, gasps of surprise and dismay, erupted from the spectators in the gallery. The jurors for the most part maintained their composure. Still, one could perceive a wave of surprise and excitement ripple across their hitherto expressionless faces: this was big news! Alice admitted she had some Black blood. Well, now, wait just a moment—but wasn't it obvious? Hadn't we seen her father? Hadn't we heard Mr. Mills describe George Jones as a colored man? How then could this admission be such a revelation? And yet it was as if I had dropped a bombshell in the courtroom.

Ah-ha! Here was my sneak attack in the very crux of our defense. The plaintiff had no case! We admitted Alice was colored. *Now what?*

Journalists rushed from the courtroom to go to the phones and wire services, some noticing as they left that Alice had taken out her white handkerchief, bowed her head, and wept.

I felt terrible for Alice, but it had to be done—as would other even more embarrassing displays need to be presented to prove what need not have been proved in the first place. Does the sun rise in the morning and set at night? Of course. Do we all live and then die? Apparently. And if the girl's father is a colored man, well, then—*what?* It makes sense, doesn't it? Why were we even here in this courtroom when our eyes could provide all the evidence needed for anyone to perceive that Alice was a person of mixed blood? *So what?* I'll get to that.

The case was not about whether Alice was Black or not; it was about whether America was ready to admit its race-based curse.

* * *

As I had earlier perceived, the case would be fought tooth and nail and with no holds barred; therefore I must rise to the occasion, not to be outdone by Rhinelander and company. For Alice's sake, I could not allow Rhinelander's legal team to control the trial, to manipulate the drama, as it were, and so to win their case due to my lack of an equally aggressive and forceful defense. Though perhaps there could be no foreseeable victory in saving the marriage given our admission of Alice's racial background, to lose her case due to a verdict of fraud would mean certain ruin for the young woman who was my client, as well as for her family.

The judge ordered the spectators to quiet themselves. Gradually the hubbub died down and the court came to order. At first, Mr. Mills, perhaps still in shock, chose to congratulate me and called the admission of Alice's race brave. But quickly, once he realized what we had done to his case, Mills objected strenuously and demanded a mistrial.

How could he do otherwise? I was laughing inside. We had just pulled the rug out from under his entire lawsuit.

Judge Morschauser called counsel to the sidebar.

Mills was irate. "Your Honor," he complained, "Mr. Davis has deceived us!" he blustered. "Deceived everyone! Deceived the court! This is an outrage! We have prepared our entire case upon—"

"Just a moment," I cut him off. "The outrage is of your doing, sir, not ours. How dare you attempt to drag this girl and her family through the filth and slime that you have spewed forth, and then have the temerity to complain of my defense strategy? In the first place, it was Judge Swinburne and not I who claimed we would attempt to prove Alice Rhinelander to be of pure white stock, and that was some time ago and before we had a chance to view all the evidence. Upon looking at the evidence—the evidence you, sir, provided—I could readily appreciate that there was no value for us to attempt to prove Alice Rhinelander's race. *That is your job, not mine*; and you have done a fine job of it. Now, our job is to show that your client knew bloody well that his wife has some Black blood; and to show that this is all a sham, a put-up case to destroy this girl in an effort to appease Rhinelander Senior!"

"That's enough," Judge Morschauser interceded. "Save it for the jury. I am going to allow defense counsel to proceed with this opening . . . and with this defense."

"Your Honor—" Mr. Mills objected.

"I have ruled," said the judge. "*Proceed.*"

The unexpected announcement, and the judge's decision to allow me to continue, settled, and at the same time it completely eliminated, the issue of Alice's racial identity. This admission also thereby nullified the plaintiff's primary claim of fraud. In effect, we destroyed the plaintiff's argument.

I admit that this admission had been our plan all along, or at least from the moment we considered the full impact of the evidence. It was Judge Swinburne's tactic to assert that we would prove Alice to be white when in fact we had no intention to attempt such proof, knowing it was impossible given the facts. What was left to litigate? If Alice admitted to having some Black blood, then there was only the issue of whether she had tried to deceive Rhinelander; if she had lied to him as to her race. Also if she were successful in deceiving him as to this fact; if she had denied she had any Black blood; and if she had claimed the opposite, that she was wholly of white blood; and, finally, that Rhinelander had married her believing she was of pure white blood. With Alice's admission that she had some Black blood, it was now an altogether different case.

We resumed our position in open court and I began my initial statement to the jury by addressing my disgust with Mr. Mills's opening.

"There is a bit of a feeling, gentlemen, a feeling of nervousness as I address you good men this morning; a feeling that I may not be able to *restrain* or even to *contain* my anger, and so open this case calmly on behalf of this defendant," I told the jurors as I made a showing of doing all I could to control my wrath.

I turned and gazed solemnly at the defendant, still quietly weeping into her dainty white handkerchief; then I turned and gestured toward Rhinelander, who sat slouched at the plaintiff's table and who looked deeply troubled.

"It was not my purpose to hurt this man," I asserted. "I did not come here to court to defend Alice Rhinelander by attacking and denigrating young Kip Rhinelander, or his father, Philip Rhinelander, and the family's good name unnecessarily . . . *unless it became absolutely necessary to protect this girl*, this young woman, I should call her, whom you see seated at the defense table and who is my client. I did not come here to sling mud to save Alice from injustice perpetrated on behalf of the Rhinelander family, by their lawyers, and with the family's vast fortune. No, that was never my intent."

Here I paused and gave the jury a disgusted look as though I were struggling to overcome the reluctance I felt at having to continue along a path I had no desire to take.

"But, given what we have been forced to hear from the lawyers representing the plaintiff, *I am shocked*," I said, once again raising my voice. "*And disgusted!* Yes, horrified! Why? I'll tell you why I am shocked and repulsed: because, in my twenty years at the trial bar, *I have never in my life listened to a more vicious opening than that delivered to you by plaintiff's counsel!* I have never listened to an opening that was more uselessly cruel not only to the defendant, Mrs. Rhinelander, *but also to her family!* Why, you attack the girl's family, sir!"

Here I looked directly at Mr. Mills and bellowed, "*How low must you go? How far would you stoop to prove these baseless claims?*"

To the jury I said, "May I tell you gentlemen that in all my years of trying cases before juries and in courts all over this great state, I have never listened to a statement from counsel that was more *un-American!* I tell you that I have never had the misfortune to listen to a statement by counsel that was more *opposed to everything* that we as a country and as a people stand for than the vicious diatribe that issued from the lips of eminent counsel.

"*How dare he?*" I cried, and then changed my tone to appeal first to the jurors' manly emotions.

As opposed to the doom and gloom of Mills's opening, the imagined peril of the purity of the white race under siege by unscrupulous Negroes, assaulted by this girl and her devious family, "Alice Rhinelander," I declared, and I directed the jurors' attention toward Alice as she sat, still silently weeping, "the young lady you see sitting here . . . why, she is no evil vamp. Please, gentlemen, take just a moment to look at her, to look at Alice. Observe her. . . . She is no oversexed harlot, no tramp; any more than this man, Leonard Kip Rhinelander"—and here I turned and pointed to the slouched figure of the plaintiff—"the scion of the socially prominent and wealthy Rhinelander family, *is a simpleminded dupe, an idiot* who was utterly under the spell and sexual domination of this girl. Please, gentlemen, *no! Why, all that is preposterous! That is fiction.* You are men. You know how these things work. This entire lawsuit, this disgraceful and insincere attack on Alice Rhinelander and her family—it is all *a blatant lie designed to deceive you.*"

I glared at Rhinelander and his lawyers for a moment and then continued.

"I would submit that the learned counsel's opening is patently ridiculous . . . that is, if it were not for the fact that I had identified the plaintiff's case, and his attorney's opening remarks for what it is: *a calumny!* A festering pile of vile smut meant to deceive you twelve men good and true. You, gentlemen. Yes, you are the ones being tricked, and not Leonard Rhinelander.

"And now, as we proceed, I want to warn you to beware that, as to convince you of his ridiculous and insincere assertions, Mr. Mills may wish to portray Leonard Kip Rhinelander as an idiot, an imbecile, or a craven sex maniac in thrall to this young girl. How could he say such things about the boy? Oh, goodness, the poor fellow! I'm not sure which fiction his lawyers will choose to attempt to deceive you. Mr. Mills seems to have tried on a couple of excuses for his client's *ungentlemanly*—and even *unmanly—behavior.* Is he color-blind? Is he mentally retarded? Is he a sex addict? Or is he all of the above, and a poor little rich boy to boot?

"Let us look at this for what it is, gentlemen. Because all that is stuff and nonsense, balderdash, gentlemen; tripe: lies. The boy is a simpleminded idiot who stumbled into the arms of a sexual predator. *Oh, no.* That, gentlemen, is the plot for an obscene pulp novel concocted by plaintiff's counsel in what we shall prove is an underhanded effort to save an ancient name dating back to the Huguenots; and in the process to crush, and to utterly destroy a humble and decent New Rochelle family; and to attempt this with *no regard for the truth.*

"Truth, gentlemen. *Facts.* Please pay close attention to the facts. The truth of the facts as they will be shown to you—that is what you must remain fixed upon; and that is our duty as the attorneys here before the court to show you and what you good men are charged with determining: truth. Yes, factual evidence. And not the outrageous assertions of a desperate and groundless lawsuit concocted by clever Manhattan lawyers for their rich clients."

Here I again paused to let that idea sink in, given that our jury was made of men who might be expected to sympathize with the Jones family as not unlike themselves, and to see the Rhinelanders as representative of the rich landowners and robber barons who had long profited from the labor and at the expense of local working people while they stayed ensconced in their Manhattan mansions.

"But in all fairness, it is not this plaintiff," I declared. "Oh, no, not this brain-stormed Rhinelander papa's boy, this *stuttering nut* who is behind the suit . . . not at all, gentlemen. Rather, the evidence will show that it is the Rhinelander family, and the Rhinelander fortune brought to bear upon this innocent girl by the plaintiff's father, Philip Rhinelander, who, though nowhere to be seen, the defense will show that it is Rhinelander Senior, Philip Rhinelander, who is the real driving force behind the vile efforts to disgrace and cast off his daughter-in-law, whom he has never met, and to try to make her into someone desperate and conniving and to disparage and ruin her family. And that this characterization of Alice concocted by Rhinelander and his willing attorneys has *absolutely no basis in fact nor one iota of truth.* It is all lies, plain and simple.

"They, Rhinelander's minions, these men"—and here I gestured to the attorneys at the plaintiff's table—"these learned counsel must be the ones who are deceived to think of us all as a bit out of touch with reality here in the boondocks of Westchester County to believe they could come in here and sell you gentlemen this bill of goods, this bogus lawsuit based on the plot of a dime novel: innocent rich boy seduced by Black vamp. *What? I beg your pardon.* Think again, gentlemen. The men of Westchester County are not idiots."

I could see Leon Jacobs squirm in his seat. Mr. Mills appeared flustered, as though he wished to object but knew it would do no good. Everyone knew I was speaking the truth. Leonard was simply a cog in the Rhinelander machine set in motion by his father to destroy Alice and the Jones family name.

I pointed to Rhinelander and then to Alice and said, "When it comes down to it, to the real truth, these two, Alice and Leonard—look at them, *and see them as they are*—what do you see? I'll tell you: they are simply two young people from vastly different social worlds who chanced to meet one day, and they fell madly in love. *That's it.* No scandal. No criminal plot to take advantage of a rich boy. No sex fiend loosed on a poor brain-tied aristocrat with a taste for the exotic. No. *Just young love, gentlemen.* Why, this is a story as old as Adam and Eve; it is a story as universal and as poignant as that classic tale of star-crossed lovers told by the great Bard in *Romeo and Juliet.* There is no fraud, gentlemen: no lies, no trickery; just two young lovers who wanted nothing more than to marry and then to spend their lives together, and who would probably be doing just that had it not been for the imperious interference of Rhinelander Senior, Philip Rhinelander, who is the true author of this lawsuit, and the impetus behind his lawyer's vicious assault upon this young girl and her family . . . because—*what?* Why take her to court and seek to do away with the marriage? *Why?* Because, are we to suppose that dear Alice, this young girl seated here for all the world to see, is not good enough? Look at her, gentlemen. She is not up to Philip Rhinelander's standard of a suitable bride for his son? That's the real reason for this despicable and dishonest lawsuit. And I believe and declare that it is hogwash. It is snobbery and vile rubbish. And I shall prove that she is, that this young girl, that it is Alice Rhinelander who is *the better person here,* gentlemen, the more honorable, the more admirable, the more truthful, and the one who has been defrauded." I swung my arm around to point an accusing finger at Rhinelander. "Defrauded by this man! *The real fraudster in this case. And the spineless surrogate for his father's ruthless will.*

"Why," I asked, "why have they—Rhinelander Senior and his lawyers—why have they brought this callous and baseless lawsuit? I'll tell you why, and the evidence will prove: they brought this lawsuit to destroy the young couple's love and happiness, to declare the union illegal, and therefore nonexistent for one reason. Because they were helpless to thwart the love these two young people felt for each other in any other way. That's why. They are deathly afraid of how this union might reflect upon the great and socially prominent Rhinelander name. *That's it!* Pride! Nothing more is behind this case. Pride and arrogance. *And money.*

"And they tried, oh, how they tried. The evidence will show the lengths to which Rhinelander Senior and his henchmen—his bodyguards, his chauffeurs, and his obedient factotums—how far they were willing to go in their efforts to separate his son from his bride, the woman he loved, and to stifle and to stamp out the love between these two young people as if it were a contagion, a disease that threatened to infect the entire Rhinelander clan and hence the very upper echelons of New York society.

"But alas for Rhinelander Senior: mere separation could not end the deep and overpowering love started in the hearts of two young lovers who come from such different walks of life. *Why?*"

Here I paused and leaned on the railing before the jury box. Then I pressed my hands together as if to demonstrate the close bond between the lovers.

"Now here is something for us to contemplate, gentlemen—all of us; you men of the jury and the rest of us as Americans, and it is something I have mulled over in my mind since I first met

Alice Rhinelander. *What happened here?* What took place between these two young people, Alice and Leonard? I'll tell you what. It is a phenomenon as old as mankind. It is a subject that the poets and the artists and the composers of great music have long meditated upon and drawn their inspiration from. What happened to Leonard and Alice is a feeling, an emotion that, for some of us at least, is so powerful that we have no control over it. Because what happened between these two young people is *true love*, gentlemen. And the love these two young people felt for one another *knows nothing of social class distinction.* That's right. True love regards no line of ancestry; nor even, may I add, and may it shock the prejudices of the segregationists wherever they are—not, I venture to say, in this courtroom nor seated upon this jury—*true love knows nothing of any taint of blood, any hue of skin color!*

"Shocked, are we? It is a fact! *True love is blind, gentlemen!*

"And true love is true no matter what Daddy says nor what he does to try to make it go away. And true love will prevail. It's what makes the world go 'round. Believe it or not, I'll tell you: not money; not social class; not skin color, as some may believe. No, it is love, gentlemen. For, dare we admit, without love life is not worth living.

"And, indeed, no matter what happens here in this courtroom, mark my words, gentlemen: true love is true. And love will prevail. Love will conquer all prejudice. These two young lovers may not be allowed to prevail in their marriage, but true love will never be defeated by racial hatred, nor by class snobbery, nor by lies and treachery."

Here I heard more than one slight gasp and audible shudder of deep emotion, particularly from the ladies in the gallery. Though the men on the jury might not have shown they were moved, I suspected they were, and I knew they all had wives, and that a few of them may actually have once been in love.

"Instead of arguing that their client, Leonard Kip Rhinelander, is a dimwitted nut case," I went on. "Oh, please, that is such an insulting insinuation. Why, Mr. Rhinelander's lawyers would have you believe the boy is an imbecile? No, I dare say they would have done better to argue that Leonard Rhinelander is *color-blind*. Yes, they should have asserted that when it came to how he perceived his bride, he simply couldn't see straight, as his mind was too muddled by love, too inflamed by infatuation. But that, we shall prove, had no bearing on Rhinelander's actions, or on his ability to perceive Alice's race once he had come into contact with her family, and once he had taken her to bed. Of course it didn't.

"The evidence will prove beyond any doubt that Leonard Kip Rhinelander, the plaintiff in this lawsuit, pursued Alice Beatrice Jones, and he seduced her, he made love to her, and then he married her *knowing full well of her ancestry, knowing full well that she has some Black blood*. The man is not blind, for God's sake. The man has eyes and he can bloody well see . . . if you'll pardon me for cursing, *I get so worked up!*

"Indeed, we shall prove that young Rhinelander liked what he saw when he met Alice. He was attracted by Alice's exotic and forbidden charm; her considerable beauty was not lost upon the young man despite the hue of her skin. And why should it be? This is nineteen twenty-four. And this is the United States of America, where we profess to love and welcome all our human brothers and sisters no matter the color of their skin. *And this is a damn good-looking woman!*"

I paused and looked around the room and was pleased to see that not only did I have everyone's rapt attention, several of the ladies were in sympathy with Alice and crying into their handkerchiefs as well. The men I hoped were at least made somewhat uncomfortable by their hidden prejudices and sublimated desires.

"Ah, but let us put all that aside for now, as we will address each and every point in the false claim against this young woman who is on trial, and against her family. We shall prove that Mr. Mills's allegations of fraud and deceit, as well as his entire disgraceful opening salvo against Alice and the Jones family, are vicious. They are un-American. And why? We shall prove, *because they are fraudulent.* Yes. The *real fraud* is Rhinelander's, not Alice's. It is a fraud plainly intended to condemn and to provoke disgust toward this . . . girl, this sweet and loving young creature whose only mistake was to believe the promises of marriage and a happy life made to her by this plaintiff, Leonard Kip Rhinelander, who sits here smugly acting under the total control of his wealthy and domineering father . . ." I trailed off and turned to gaze upon Leonard, then shook my head sadly.

"Well, I must leave that for you to decide, gentlemen, as to the young man's character. It's simple: What we have is a case of wealth and social class attempting—that of the Rhinelander millions—attempting to crush a young girl and her family with dirt, with slime, and with vile lies . . . because—*what?* Because she is not good enough for—" I swung around and again pointed at Leonard, who was already turning scarlet and glistening with perspiration. "Not good enough for what? For . . ." I let it hang in the minds of the jurors as a question. "*For him? For this fellow? This innocent, brain-tied dupe?* Well, as the con man said, if you believe that, I have a bridge I would like to sell you."

I let the murmur of amusement die down, and then I turned and addressed my next comments to my adversary, Isaac Mills.

"If that is the kind of case Mr. Mills wants," I challenged, "if Mr. Mills wants to sling mud and dirt and see what sticks to whom—*well, may I assure you, then he's going to get it!* If they want to throw slime"—and here I turned and pointed directly at Rhinelander as I declared—"*I'm going to wreck the boy!*"

This comment and implicit threat provoked an undercurrent of shock and dismay as well as audible gasps from the gallery.

I asked the jurors to consider, "Did Alice represent to this man Kip Rhinelander that she had no colored blood in her veins and was pure white? *Oh, please.* That is an absurdity. How could she? After introducing him to her father? And when he had already met her sister, who is married to a Negro? I hardly think so. . . . The gentleman, Alice's father, Mr. Jones, whose appearance was enough to convince Mr. Mills that he is colored—what, you are expected to believe that young Rhinelander couldn't see what Mr. Mills finds so obvious? This is utter nonsense, gentlemen. What is worse: it is all lies meant to deceive you. There is no shred of truth in this lawsuit.

"And that, gentlemen, that question is really your first issue, because the question of colored blood is not in issue anymore on our admission. We admit that Alice has some colored blood. *We admit the obvious.* So really, your first inquiry is: Did Alice Rhinelander—not 'this woman,' as Mr. Mills chooses to refer to her, after referring to Rhinelander as a *young gentleman*; young gentleman indeed, I ask you, good men of the jury, is this how a gentleman treats a girl? He seduces her; he drives her around in his fancy new auto to impress her. He gives her rings and other baubles. He beds her, makes love to her, marries her, *and then he abandons her because Daddy doesn't feel she measures up to the exalted Rhinelander social standards?* Pish-posh! What rot! *No!* Where's the man in all this? Why, this is not how a gentleman behaves toward a girl. You good men all know that for yourselves. You are not to be impressed by the Rhinelander name and their millions. This is not Park Avenue in Manhattan. We are impressed only by truth and courage here in Westchester—the truth to stand up for what you believe in and who you are. AS DID THIS GIRL, ALICE RHINELANDER!" I fairly bellowed.

"Alice Rhinelander is here in this room to defend herself against the lies and false accusations brought by this man's father through his lawyers. And we judge a man or a woman not by their name or their money but by their actions.

"Let us look at the facts. Did Alice Rhinelander represent to Leonard Rhinelander before her marriage on October 14, 1924, that she was pure white? *No!* Of course she did not. How could she? This entire case is ridiculous on its face. Did Alice say to young Kip, 'Well, you see my father, who is quite dark; and you see my brother-in-law, who is unmistakably a Negro; you see what color they are; but pay it no mind, Len. *I am a pure white girl.* Absurd. Shameful. Mr. Mills may claim his client is a moron, but you gentlemen are not morons. And you will see that there is no evidence, not one iota of fact to prove that Kip Rhinelander is so brain-tied that he can't tell Black from white. Oh, so he stutters. So what? That means nothing when looking at a girl and taking her to bed. He's not stuttering then, is he?"

Here I paused to let the mutters and guffaws from the gallery die down.

"The evidence will prove the notion of Rhinelander's feeblemindedness—his inability to see color, and to know Black from white—that it is absolutely false and absurd. *It is utter nonsense. . . .* Now, that is clear: *Is it not, gentlemen?* The lie that is the basis of this lawsuit against Alice Rhinelander is seen for the false travesty that it is."

The jurors' mute responses were nevertheless in the affirmative. I actually noticed a few of them appearing to nod in assent. The remaining allegation, given what we already knew from the plaintiff's proffered evidence concerning the entire Jones family—Alice's Negro brother-in-law seated in the gallery, and every one of the documents Mr. Mills had declared he would use to prove Alice was not white—to then suppose that Alice had passed herself off as white to Leonard was not only a far cry from evident; indeed, it appeared impossible, given the plaintiff's own submissions.

"How," I asked the jurors to consider, "how could Alice possibly have expected Rhinelander to believe she was pure white when he knew her father? Knew her sister, knew her Negro brother-in-law, and played cards with him and his Black friends? There could be no question, gentlemen, this man, Leonard Kip Rhinelander, this son of wealth and social standing, this sheltered little rich boy *knowingly* and *intentionally* crossed clear and apparent racial lines when he met and socialized with Robert Brooks, who is married to Alice's sister Emily and who is concededly and in appearance a colored man."

I drew some laughter from the audience in the gallery and smiles from the jurors when I said, "I think the issue Mr. Mills should have presented to you with regard to young Rhinelander is not mental unsoundness . . . but color blindness! I see Leonard Rhinelander wears glasses, but are we to believe that he is also color-blind?

"Gentlemen, you are called here to this august setting, this court of law, to determine whether Alice Rhinelander before her marriage told this man, Leonard Rhinelander, that she was a pure white person, and that she had no colored blood. You are here to determine next whether that fooled Rhinelander, whether it convinced him. Whether or not he could not see with his own eyes that he was marrying into a colored family.

"You heard Mr. Mills declare that all it took was one look at Alice's father, George Jones, to see the man is colored. Are we to believe Leonard Rhinelander couldn't see what"—and here I gestured to George Jones seated in the gallery with his wife, his other daughters, and his very Black son-in-law—"is and always was readily apparent to anyone else who gazed upon the Jones family?

"No, that will not wash, gentlemen. Brain-tied, a stuttering nut, poor little rich boy—*but blind? Unable to determine the fact of colored blood in this girl?* No. Impossible. *Ridiculous.* And *an insult* to your intelligence. Young Kip Rhinelander may be an imbecile, easily fooled—but you gentlemen are not.

"But that is all nonsense. Rather, we shall prove, Leonard Kip Rhinelander is the real fraud in this despicable case."

That statement as well provoked muttered responses, a few gasps, and more rushing into and out of the courtroom by the reporters. Mr. Mills stood to object, but thought better of it when I turned and smirked at him.

"Having dispensed with the issue of Alice's race," I continued, again addressing the jurors, "let us move on to the allegation by Mr. Mills that Alice duped this poor innocent idiot into a sexual relationship, a scandalous liaison with the brain-tied youngster solely as a means of forcing him to marry her so she and her family could get their hands on the Rhinelander fortune.

"That this little girl here seduced Father's boy? *Oh, please.* Are we serious, intelligent people here, gentlemen; or are we also to be perceived as brain-tied idiots and mental patients to be bamboozled by the insincere claims of lawyers? Consider this, and let me give you a moment to think it over. . . .

"Well, now I am speaking coldly and frankly, gentlemen," I continued, my voice mounting with indignation and gathering volume. "Man to man, gentlemen, as it were. Papa's son was seduced, aye? Oh, dear, poor lad. Lured into an intimate sexual relationship with this lovely young woman . . . duped—*shocking!* We are enjoined by Mr. Mills to believe this preposterous fiction, this scandalous, trashy pornography. *Duped? What?* Seduced against his will—whatever will the brain-tied youngster may have, I don't know; but I must say that although I have prosecuted much in the way of crime over the years, this is the first and only time that I have ever heard of a girl criminally assaulting and raping a man."

This elicited not only the expected titters but also a few unrestrained guffaws from the audience; headshaking and sneers of disbelief by the jurors; and embarrassment on behalf of both Alice and Leonard Rhinelander.

"The evidence will also prove that, contrary to claims made by plaintiff's learned counsel that Leonard Rhinelander no longer cohabited with his wife after learning that she has some colored blood: that is clearly false, gentlemen. In fact, the evidence will show, Rhinelander continued to live in the Joneses' home in New Rochelle; and Rhinelander continued to share a bed with his wife for a full WEEK after his wife had been declared a Negress in the press. Yes, it is true. The evidence will prove that Leonard continued to live with his wife in her family's home. *Of course he did!* He was happy—why not? He was in love—deeply in love with his bride. He would declare to the press that he knew his wife was colored and that it didn't matter to him; that he loved her no matter that she had some Black blood in her veins. He wasn't being held there against his will, a sex slave, as Mr. Mills would have you believe. *Not at all.* He would lounge around the house in his pajamas and a fine pair of moccasins he had brought from the West, and a bathrobe. He did not care and continued in the face of this, this evidence that he was not fooled, in the face of all these newspapers branding the family he lived with as Negroes, and he had his own eyesight before. Of course, he could see for himself, and still *he did not leave his wife's side* and turn against her family. . . . *No,* he stayed. . . .

"And they stayed in that house, husband and wife, besieged, mind you. Yes, and with the press coming out daily with these glaring stories and with bold headlines, '*Rhinelander's Son Marries into a Negro Family,*' and so on. And Leonard and his wife still slept in the same room, gentlemen, slept in the same bed and lived together as husband and wife while outside and all around the world she was being declared a colored woman. It mattered not to young Kip Rhinelander and to his wife, Alice Jones Rhinelander—*yes!* That's her name! *Alice Jones Rhinelander!* I will call her by no other name, as she calls herself. Whom you see seated here—look at her, gentlemen, see her as she is. Leonard continued to live with Alice; the couple continued their married life together as husband and wife—joined in the eyes of God and under the laws of our state. He—Rhinelander having newspapers brought up to him mornings as he lay in bed with his coffee and read these glaring headlines—even then there was no remonstrance, no getting up and running away from the Negro family he had married into. He stayed, he and his bride stayed together. The newlywed husband and wife ignored the storm of controversy gathering outside their conjugal bliss.

"Oh, but *beware the father.* Yes, gentlemen, the world quakes and people cower in abject fear—at least his son does when Philip Rhinelander speaks. When Rhinelander Senior learned of his son's marriage, *ah-ha!* You had better believe: now things were about to change.

"Rhinelander did not leave his wife then, no, not right away, as counsel averred; not at first, when the news of the marriage first broke. We shall prove to you, gentlemen, it is a fact that it was not until Rhinelander's father's lawyers"—and here I turned and pointed directly at Leon Jacobs—"it was not until *this man*, Mr. Leon Jacobs, at the behest of Rhinelander Senior, who is his employer, it was not until Jacobs appeared on the Joneses' doorstep with another man, a bodyguard and, the evidence will show, a notary—when those two men showed up *one week*, yes a full week, *after* the news of the Jones family's race had been declared in all the newspapers; and these men, a lawyer and a notary, both licensed in the State of New York, these men both *lied* to Leonard Kip Rhinelander and to his wife, Alice Rhinelander, and to her family, saying only that Rhinelander Senior wished to see his son and inquire about the marriage. But then, under these false pretenses, they proceeded to take the boy away. Make no mistake, the evidence will show that *they spirited young Rhinelander away* from his bride under false pretenses; they lied to him, claimed they were merely taking him to meet with his father so that he might explain his decision to marry Alice. But that was not true. No, instead they hid the boy like a wanted criminal. They held him hostage first in New Jersey, in a hotel and under guard and with a false name to keep him incommunicado and away from his wife; to force him to comply with the action devised and declared by his father and his lawyers to rid young Kip Rhinelander of his bride by bringing this bogus, baseless lawsuit that we are now hearing. They—the evidence will show—Philip Rhinelander, the boy's own father, and his retinue of lawyers *forced* the young man to turn against his new wife and to assault her and her good family with this utterly false and despicable lawsuit brought to defame and defraud honest and decent people. They are the perpetrators of this fraud. Not this young girl, not Alice. . . ."

I paused, took a breath, and gazed once again at the men seated in the jury box. And as I did, I knew, as if by some telepathic messaging, what they all wished to know—*If her face were not enough, was the girl's body not its own evidence?*

"I have been to the Joneses' home, gentlemen," I continued, on a new track and with a less strident tone, and after jotting a quick note to remind myself of the intuition, "I have seen the humble abode, and there been invited to enjoy a cup of tea with

Mrs. Jones, who is a fine woman of English stock despite how Mr. Mills has attempted to denigrate her character with his slanderous accusations. It is a small, cramped home; it is simple and hardly luxurious, such as what I'm sure the Rhinelander lad is accustomed to; but it is as clean as the finest mansion on Fifth Avenue. Alice was a member of a happy family in this humble abode, and she worked to help support herself and the family by doing what? Now, this will be important, and we will prove it as dealing with the question of whether or not this son of the long and distinguished Huguenot line was deceived. Alice, gentlemen, at the time Rhinelander met and courted her, the girl was working as a *housemaid*—a perfectly honest, decent employment, true; but working as a *servant in a private family* when the rich son of Manhattan's aristocracy came bursting into her life . . . pursuing her, seducing her in his fancy car given him by his father, and he proceeded to whisk her away, take her from her home; he took her away, the evidence will show, first to hotels and the theater and to dinners at fine restaurants in Manhattan—*why?* To seduce her, of course! What else? To get her into bed and have his carnal ways with her. That's all. There is nothing new here, no trickery, certainly not on Alice's part. She wasn't the one chasing after Rhinelander in her fancy automobile and carrying him off to hotels in a chauffeured limousine. Not at all. Alice was the one who was employed as a housemaid.

"Now . . . you will also hear how Rhinelander took Alice on a road trip, a drive through New England. He lied to her family. He told them they were to be chaperoned by a married couple when he knew it was not true. They lived together, Rhinelander and Alice lived together in every way as man and wife; they slept in the same bed, though without the benefit of a lawful marriage, and they lived together every day and night as man and wife for more than a week. And what did they do upon returning home? *This is important.* How did they proceed after their illicit time together on Cape Cod? Why, they made it legal! They did the right thing. They married. Leonard Rhinelander kept his word to make Alice his legal wife.

"May I also say that we shall show the young couple then rented an apartment and began to furnish it, and that they were preparing to live there and to have a family, to live together happily . . . *until THIS MAN*"—and here I suddenly shouted as I indicated Leon Jacobs. I noticed a couple of the jurors came awake, some actually flinched, and Jacobs himself startled—"*until this man*, who is employed by Philip Rhinelander . . . no matter how he might wish to deny it; this man, acting solely on behalf of Leonard's father, Mr. Leon Jacobs *insinuated* himself upon the scene, and he disrupted the happy couple, and then he dragged the boy away. *Shame on you, sir!*" I reproached Jacobs, who grimaced at me.

"But . . . that's not all, not all the nonsense the plaintiff's lawyers would have you believe. Just let Mr. Mills bring in the director of the Orchards School to prove Leonard Rhinelander stuttered and was awkward in social situations. So, gentlemen, I ask you: Does that make him *an idiot?* A man who cannot see a woman's color even under the most intimate of circumstances, when he gazes upon her naked body: he still can't see the color of her skin—*what?* Because he has a speech impediment? How are we to believe that? A speech impediment does not result in a man being color-blind or suffering from idiocy. I think we have shown beyond any doubt that Leonard Kip Rhinelander is not mentally retarded despite what his lawyers might wish to have you believe. Well, may I ask: The Orchards School is not an insane asylum, is it? It's not the loony bin? Or a school for the blind? No, it is a private facility for the sons of rich men, pampered boys who have difficulty in social situations. *Oh, dear me, so sorry. Poor fellows . . . sad idiots . . .* and Leonard, the most idiotic of them all, was at this school to afford him help with his stuttering: his speech—*not his eyesight!*"

Here Mr. Mills and Leon Jacobs both leaped to their feet to object.

"Oh, please," I said, addressing Mr. Mills, "sit down, sir. You and your lackey are not the only ones who can hurl insults!"

The judge seemed taken aback, stymied by the level of the vitriol on behalf of both parties.

"Gentlemen," he said, "this is a civil court. Let us keep it so."

"Of course, Your Honor," I said. "I will endeavor to do so. And I hope the other side will as well."

And I shot an angry glance at Jacobs, who promptly sat back down. Mr. Mills as well shook his head and returned to his chair.

"May I continue?" I asked.

The judge nodded. "You may."

"Thank you, Your Honor."

I turned to address the jury.

"When it comes to it, I will ask the directing physician at the Orchards School if it is not a fact that Leonard's condition improved markedly upon meeting and becoming close with Alice. Indeed, she helped him to overcome his trepidation of everyone—everyone, that is, except his father."

It could not be helped. I knew I had them on the defensive now, and I knew it was bound to be hard on Alice; but I also knew that it was the only way we could expect to fight this case and hope to win given how Rhinelander's lawyers were attempting to influence the jury by evoking prejudice and racial fear as well as social scandal. For Leonard, I could feel scant pity, certainly given what we had heard from Mr. Mills and mutely affirmed by his client. I had to show the jury that Rhinelander was no dupe, no brain-tied imbecile, and far less innocent than his lawyers would attempt to depict him when it came to his pursuit of a sexual relationship with Alice.

"The evidence will show that Leonard Kip Rhinelander knew exactly what he was doing when he courted and seduced Alice Jones," I continued, "and when he pursued her sexually, even within the Jones family home, and when he took her to Manhattan in his chauffeur-driven limousine, and he registered them under a false name and as husband and wife for their lengthy tryst at the Hotel Marie Antoinette, so that he could have his wanton ways with her sexually; yes, gentlemen, to know her in *every conceivable fashion.* He even brought along a pornographic manual to educate Alice in his base lustful pursuits. Now, I ask you: *Do these sound like the actions of a dim-witted boy? Or of a naive dupe?*

"Certainly they do not. And we will also prove that Leonard continued to pursue Alice after he had been forced by his father to leave her. Yes, he defied his father; and he broke away to travel to see Alice when she was ill; and he wrote her *dozens* of smut-filled *lust letters*—I won't call them love letters—to keep her attention fixed on him in his absence. Yes, the boy loved her, *oh, yes, he certainly did!* By this time he was infatuated with her, and deeply in love—as was she with him. That is all, gentlemen. It was love, true love, and decent and good until . . . *until . . .*"

I shook my head. I sighed. I looked down at the floor and lamented, "Until . . ." And then I stopped, as though suddenly remembering an important detail.

"Oh, yes . . . *wait,*" I said as though it had slipped my mind. "I nearly forgot. . . . My colleague Mr. Mills says he wants to read letters, does he? Yes, I believe he does. He wishes to read

Alice's letters to the plaintiff. He plans to put Alice's love letters in evidence. Fine. *We shall read our letters as well.*"

I intimated in a threatening tone, "Not to be upstaged, we shall read letters written by Kip Rhinelander, letters that we will present in evidence—*scandalous letters! Sex letters!* And letters begging Alice to remain true to him and only to him, and reminding her of the base sexual pleasures he had afforded her.

"Mr. Mills wishes to read you letters from Alice, aye? Fine. I will read you far more explicit and salacious letters from the hand of the plaintiff, this brain-tied dupe, Leonard Kip Rhinelander; letters that will convince you gentlemen that Rhinelander is no gentleman, no brain-tied idiot, and that he knew exactly what he was doing every filthy, disgraceful step of the way in his lustful pursuit of this young woman.

"It was Leonard Kip Rhinelander, I assure you gentlemen that the evidence will prove, Rhinelander, Leonard or Kip, however he's called, *that man!*" And I swung my arm around once more and pointed at Rhinelander, who was sitting between his lawyers, with his bodyguards seated behind him, and looking every bit as though he wished he could simply sink and disappear under the floorboards. "Yes, *that man*, who is no fool, he's no babbling, brain-tied idiot or lunatic escaped from an asylum as his lawyers would have us believe; no, *he* was the knowing instigator; *he* was the seducer; and he knew full well what he was doing, just as he knew Alice's mixed race; and he wanted Alice for his lust, for his purely sexual desires. He took her away time and again to hotels and on trips here and there *to have his way with her.*"

Here I turned and gestured toward Alice.

"But she, good girl that she is, Alice wanted to be Leonard's wife. *Of course she did.* And where's the crime in that? Where's the fraud? Alice wanted the benefit of a legal marriage to protect her good name. She believed Kip Rhinelander's promises to make her Mrs. Leonard Kip Rhinelander because she loved Leonard. Alice loves him still, sadly, let there be no doubt."

All eyes turned to Alice, who was still silently weeping (or was she laughing?) into her now tear-soaked white handkerchief. She was the very picture of feminine vulnerability, and also of emotional candor and truth.

"Poor girl, poor deceived Alice," I went on with all the pathos I could muster. "And so what did Alice do? After Leonard's demands and his promises? Well, she gave herself to him . . . *completely*. She trusted him; and under his promise, the sacred promise of marriage, she loved him; she believed he loved her; and she waited for him to return to make good on his promise. And he did; he kept his promise to Alice. Yes, he did . . . I will say that for young Kip Rhinelander. The evidence will prove that he did at least make good on his promise and he married Alice; he made her his lawful wife. Why? Because he was her sex slave? Because he was and still presumably is an idiot? A brain-tied dupe who can't tell a girl of mixed race when he sees her? No. I think not. *Of course not!* Because he was forced to? *No, again, by God*—the evidence will prove that Leonard Kip Rhinelander married Alice Jones and took her as his lawful wife for no reason *except that he was in love with her and he wanted to spend the rest of his life with her.* Yes, he married her because he loved her. . . . I believe he *still loves* her."

This statement brought an audible gasp from Alice and reverberations from the ladies in the gallery. Alice wept. Even some of the men in the jury box let on that they were moved. I was silent for a moment to let the mood take hold.

And then I continued in a sad and miserable tone.

"But he . . . oh, yes, Leonard Kip Rhinelander, he is also a weak man, sadly, a spineless man who lives in abject fear; yes, gentlemen, the Rhinelander son lives in a crippling fear of his powerful and determined father, Philip Rhinelander—the man who, despite his absence here in this courtroom, make no mistake about it: Philip Rhinelander, the father, and not his weak-willed and terrified son; Rhinelander Senior with his family wealth and name in the social register; *Philip Rhinelander is the real engineer and the true author of this lawsuit.* Yes, I said it before and I'll say it again so that there can be no mistake: *Philip Rhinelander and his millions, his status among the top society families in New York: that is what is at stake here.* And holding Leonard's fear of being cut off from the Rhinelander fortune is the father's controlling power over his *cowardly son.*" I fairly spit the words. "And it is that fear—the fear of the taint upon the Rhinelander name—*that is Rhinelander's driving force behind this lawsuit.*

"There is nothing more here, gentlemen: simply power, wealth, social prominence being brought to bear upon this young girl and her family *out of fear.* Make no mistake, and the evidence will prove that there is *no issue of race deception, and neither lies nor fraud on behalf of Alice*; no, no, no, that's all poppycock. There is only bias, prejudice, false social pride, and fear of the loss of status and wealth on behalf of Philip Rhinelander, who is forcing his son, Leonard Kip, this man who is not weak-minded but of *weak character,* indeed, so weak of will as to allow his father to turn him against this innocent girl he seduced and promised to marry; and who he *perhaps still loves!* And to do what? To throw his slime upon her and her family in a scandalous and dishonest attempt to have you gentlemen strip her of all honor and pride."

Here I paused, I shook my head as I took a moment to look each member of the jury in the eye before I ended with this challenge: "But I will say again that . . . *if they want to start throwing slime*, yes, if Rhinelander and his lawyers wish *to sling smut*—and they will be the first ones to do it—at this young girl—oh, but you better be sure that I will not let them get away with it. *No, I will not!* I will lick this young boy, this Kip Rhinelander, *on his own letters!* If he starts calling his wife black—I mean in morals—and he makes it necessary, he will find that the kettle is just as black—*no, it is blacker!*

"Mr. Mills has taken the lid off the kettle with his vile insinuations. He's let it all out: the name-calling and attacks upon this young girl's modesty, her morality; and so now it is to be *a real fight.*"

I paused and then declared, "*Let the fight go on!* You will see it. And I appeal to you gentlemen as Americans, and as men of good conscience: gentlemen, I ask that you give this girl a square deal in the face of the assault backed as it is by the Rhinelander millions."

I nodded gravely. I gave them each a look of faith in their integrity and said, "Now, I thank you, gentlemen, on behalf of this young girl, Alice Beatrice Jones Rhinelander: I thank you for being honest and for being good and decent Americans."

I sat down to more murmuring and rushing in and out by members of the press. Alice took my hand and gripped it. She put away her handkerchief and composed herself.

"Thank you," she said.

With that, with both sides having presented their opening remarks, it was up to the plaintiff to call the first witness.

CHAPTER EIGHTEEN

Yes, She's Colored

However, my opening remarks to the jury had taken up a good portion of the morning session; and so, given the hour, Judge Morschauser declared court in adjournment for lunch.

Though I was roundly congratulated for my opening, with some of my colleagues and a few reporters opining that it was most eloquent and convincing, and that if the jury were to be polled now they would surely find in favor of the defendant, I, however, was feeling a bit drained and somewhat ill at ease both for the mustering of so much anger and repugnance over the plaintiff's case, and for the tension and bias evoked upon our admittance that Alice had some colored blood.

This clearly was a dicey maneuver. A jury is a curious, multi-headed creature. One can never be sure how they will find until the verdict is in. All it would take is for one or more persuasive racists to arouse the resentment, the bias, and the latent or obvious fears of the other eleven to convince them that a woman of mixed blood must never by their verdict be accorded legal sanction to marry a white man. Remember the words of Leonard's lawyers: "America is watching."

That Alice's race was an even more powerful issue we would

have to contend with now that Alice had admitted her color, I was further convinced and disgraced to realize upon learning that restaurants in White Plains—in fact, even the shop in which we had enjoyed tea the day before—now chose to ban Alice admittance due to her admitted Black blood! I was horrified; I complained bitterly to the management, but the fellow claimed he was acting upon orders from the owner. Why, just the day before they had welcomed Alice and her father. The Jones family had been perceived as good enough to enter and enjoy a cup of tea or a meal in their establishment. There had never been segregation of this sort in our village. Yet now—because of fear of reprisals, I suppose, threats apparently made by Klansmen and disseminated by Rhinelander's minions; warnings of attacks made upon the parties and premises—Alice was barred from entering their restaurant.

Such a disgrace! The girl was stunned. It was a poignant moment and a reminder that no matter how I might be able to frame it, and no matter how attractive and sympathetic Alice might appear, race—or rather the mixing of the races, now that we had admitted Alice had some Black blood—the fear of miscegenation was a powerful determining factor to be dealt with going forward in this battle to save the girl from total disgrace.

I would need to find some compelling evidence to overcome the fears of white men; I needn't make it up. And, secretly, we all know it; and as a nation we suffer because of our past sin of subjecting other humans to the degradation of bondage, of rape and murder, of lynchings; and of our continuing legacy of racial bias and hatred.

* * *

I brought Alice a tuna salad sandwich. She nibbled at it in the lawyers' conference room but said she had no appetite. I was amazed by the girl's emotional fortitude. She said she understood that, given the way Leonard's lawyers were forcing the lawsuit, it was incumbent on us that we fight them with equally harsh and forceful tactics and that sometimes those efforts might be painful for her as well as for her family.

"But do please . . . *don't be too hard on Len*, Mr. Davis," Alice pleaded. "I know how you must feel about his . . . his behavior; how he's allowed his father to do this to us. It hurts me as well—*deeply*. But I can't find it in my heart to blame Len. I hope you won't attack him so—"

"But Alice—*I must*," I complained. "If we are to win, if you are to be exonerated, the jury must come to find Leonard, his father, and their lawyers as the guilty parties. A jury needs a villain. I shall cast Philip Rhinelander in that role to the best of my ability; but as Philip's proxy, and as Philip hasn't even seen fit to show his face in the courtroom, he must bear the brunt of the guilt when it comes to convincing a jury that you are the innocent party in this case."

"The whole thing is painful," Alice admitted. "I'm . . . I'm just so sorry, and so miserable, so sad to think that it has come to this . . . that something that was so good, what Len and I had together, and the plans we had, for it all to become so . . . shameful. *Why?* What on earth did we do that is so wrong?"

"Well, my dear, you did nothing . . . nothing but to follow your heart," I reminded her. "Please stop finding fault or guilt with your behavior in all of this—no matter how Leonard's lawyers will attempt to make you out to be the guilty party. It's what Leonard did—or what he allowed his father to do in his name—that is the cause of all the pain and sorrow. And as much as it is hurtful to you both, it is Rhinelander Senior who is pushing this through in his son's name. Therefore I'm afraid it is inevitable that we will have to fight . . . and to fight equally viciously against Leonard as his father's proxy for the jury to come to understand, and to find that you are not the one who is made to be the originator of this fraud, and therefore to suffer unduly because of the case mounted by Rhinelander and his lawyers.

"Do you see that, Alice? *We can't have that.* You do see what Rhinelander's lawyers are trying to do? And that for you to prevail it is absolutely necessary for us to fight these accusations, their false claims as to you and your family and what you are about—this shameful claim that you and your family all plotted to take Leonard for his money! *Good Lord!* You do see how we must counter and defeat these horrendous accusations with the truth, as hurtful as that may be to Leonard in particular, and to you both, given how you still feel about him—do you see it?"

After a moment, Alice admitted, "Yes, of course I do. I see it; I understand it. I just wish it wasn't so. I wish you could spare Len. As upset as I am with him, I don't want to hurt him. . . . I can see he's already suffering."

Well, I thought, *yes, it's true.* Despite the Rhinelander lad's false show of aplomb and distracted boredom, one could see he was hurting inside. He reeked of shame at what was being done in his name to his bride, whom he couldn't even look at for fear of losing all composure. But regardless of how we might wish to spare young Rhinelander, I couldn't explain to Alice what she had already done; no, I couldn't admit to her the truth of what she was actually guilty of, and what had created all this turmoil and anger and nasty accusations in the first place.

I had to cause the jurors to understand without expressly saying it, so that it occurred to each and every member of the jury as if by their own idea: that Alice, a colored girl, a domestic servant girl, had entered into the hallowed domain of noble, blue-blooded American society. She had trespassed where no one of her tribe was to be allowed except as a servant; and more: she had cohabited, and she had planned to have a family with an example of white masculine social and racial pride in the person of her husband, Leonard Kip Rhinelander, the bluest of blue bloods, and son of the distinguished Philip Rhinelander. And by so doing, Alice had inadvertently revealed the Rhinelander boy to the world for the miserable excuse for manhood, and for personal integrity, and for false moral superiority, that he is; and thus Alice had in turn revealed the family, the Rhinelander clan, for the arrogant, prejudiced snobs and blowhards that they are. Finally, Alice had unintentionally subverted not just the Rhinelanders' image of themselves, but also the whole notion of superiority based on skin color and wealth, family background, and racial or social heritage—even gender. These cherished beliefs were all in jeopardy of being revealed as rubbish by a common colored housemaid.

Yes, this humble and yet determined and powerful young woman had unknowingly shaken the very foundations of the so-called American aristocracy. The jurors must be made to appreciate how Alice had innocently uncovered class superiority based as it is on wealth, skin color, and family name rather than character and true moral fortitude; and by doing so she had revealed the prejudice of social superiority for the utter farce that it is; and that, and only that, was Alice's true transgression: her embodiment of the American spirit, by God—a colored girl! A domestic servant! A girl of uncommon beauty and strength of character! With her sixth-grade education and deep-seated sense of right and wrong, Alice Jones Rhinelander, even with her very name, this remarkable young woman challenged the assumptions of white male superiority. And by so doing, her selfless contribution was to the original concept of what it means to be an American: the belief in racial and social equality, so cherished and proclaimed by our Founding Fathers and yet so rarely demonstrated; Alice would put it all to the test.

Was what we profess as Americans really true, or was it all a fraud?

* * *

A reminder: Alice could simply have taken the money; let us not forget that she could have snatched up the proffered settlement—a handsome sum—and even demanded more if she chose, which no doubt Rhinelander would gladly have paid. She could have avoided all this stress and upset, the travail of a trial, the threats of violence to her and her loved ones; and she could have gone off to live in relative prosperity and obscurity. She might have found a new husband and had the family she so desired. She could have lived a normal life in obscurity. But no, she chose instead to fight. She chose to defend her good name under assault by the wealthy family of the man she loved; and in so doing, Alice determined and continued to fight it out with the whole world watching; and with many in the press condemning her; and the radical racist yellow journals professing to wanting to see her disgraced and condemned as "a conniving Black whore" and run out of town simply for whom she was—a colored girl of humble origins in love with an aristocratic white man.

* * *

I admit, alone, I might question my motives: *Is this right, what I am doing? And am I doing it—do I wish to pursue this case in a trial for the right reasons? Or am I doing it for my own benefit, to bask in the limelight and to satisfy my pride? Should I be more forceful in urging Alice to take the settlement?* As well, Alice might cry into her pillow—I have no doubt that she did—and wonder if she should not have just taken the money and saved herself all the emotional turmoil and shame of being put on trial to defend her name and her character. The trial was already exacting a harsh toll on the young girl no matter her emotional fortitude.

She could simply wish it all away, as could I. But, come what may, Alice continued to show up in court each day and to maintain her dignity in the face of the Rhinelander onslaught. Alice Jones Rhinelander would prove herself to be no fainthearted young woman; no timid female of humble measure easily scared into submission; and no greedy harlot to be bought off; but rather she would show herself to be a woman of intelligence, of strong will, and of integrity—a person of stellar character, unlike her husband and his father.

Alice's strong will and character thus fortified her advocate's zeal.

* * *

Mr. Mills was still flushed with anger and unnerved by indignation when court resumed for the afternoon session after my shocking admission as to Alice's mixed race and my equally vicious opening counterattack. Mills looked shaken, even a bit demoralized when he stood to call the first of not one—no, not even a few—but *twenty-one* unneeded and totally redundant witnesses to prove—*what?* Yes, plaintiff's counsel insisted on calling *twenty-one witnesses* to the stand to introduce his carefully accumulated documentary evidence and testimony to prove *what the defense had already conceded*: that Alice had some colored blood.

All right, we admitted it! It was no longer an issue before the jury. Get on with it, man! And yet Mr. Mills chose to bore the jurors and the spectators; he proceeded to exasperate the judge and to prolong the trial unnecessarily with his evidence for no reason that I could discern beyond that he had gone to all the trouble and the expense to gather such proof that Alice was colored; and so now the lawyer felt he needed to go through with it to justify his time and fees even if it would put the jury and the court into a state of somnolence and prove to be utterly without any evidentiary value. Indeed, in fact, it would appear to prove our case. If Alice was so demonstrably colored, why hadn't Kip Rhinelander been able to see it?

Indeed, the newspapers had proclaimed it with a front-page banner headline in the *Daily News*: **YES, SHE'S COLORED**.

Fine, so let's move along. Show us what else you've got to prove your case.

Yet, even then, Mills's evidence as to Alice's race was contradictory, confusing, and thus further proof of the ambiguity of race in America. For instance, there was the marriage license stating that the bride was white. And Mr. Mills called a representative from the Metropolitan Life Insurance Company who testified that Alice was described as white on an application for insurance filed in 1900; and then, on a second application filed eight years later, Alice's color was recorded as Black.

During my cross-examination of the agent, I was able to elicit that it was the company's policy to have the agents fill out the forms based on their observations and not to question the applicant as to his or her race. Alice's race, therefore, and which point I would emphasize, was all in the eyes of the beholder. So two different agents on two different occasions some years apart came to opposite conclusions as to Alice's color. Mills apparently wanted to show the jury that Alice was something of a chameleon, able to change the appearance of her color at will and dependent on circumstances.

I objected more than once to this evidence, calling all Mr.

Mills's insistence on proving Alice's race as superfluous and even as tedious as a weather report given that we were stuck inside this courtroom and not going out to play golf, and that we had admitted Alice had some colored blood; and I made no attempt to disguise my frustration as Mills insisted on calling this gaggle of superfluous witnesses. Of course, what Mills hoped to prove was that Alice could easily pass for white and that she had deceived Rhinelander by allowing herself to be registered on various documents as white when she knew otherwise. After all, we were made to believe, Rhinelander was not too bright.

I protested that we had intended to speed up the trial and spare the jury all this tedious testimony with our admission of Alice having some Black blood. The jury had her physical presence in the courtroom as all the evidence needed to judge her color as well as her ability to pass as white. And here was counsel for the plaintiff doing his utmost to slow down the proceedings and put everyone to sleep by proving what we had already conceded.

Truthfully, I was happy to have Mr. Mills bore and irritate the jurors with this tiresome, unneeded testimony and documentary submissions that did nothing more than prove the weakness of his case; and even, I believe, persuade some of the jurors away from any bias against Alice based on the very ambiguity of her race.

* * *

At long last, and we were now actually a good three days into the trial testimony, Mills finally switched his attention to the issue of Kip Rhinelander's alleged "mental backwardness," his mental retardation as the underlying reason the poor fellow was susceptible to Alice's seductions, and was unable to perceive her color, and so was duped into marrying her. This evidence, in my opinion, was equally ludicrous. Once more I objected to this whole line of questioning, but again I was overruled as Mills was allowed to call Dr. L. Pierce Clark, the physician who had founded the Orchards School and who was a specialist in treating nervous and mental disorders.

Dr. Clark testified that Leonard's father, Philip Rhinelander, had enrolled the boy at the Orchards School in hopes of finding a cure for what the doctor described as Leonard's "primary, main difficulty, a speech one—a stammering—chronic stammering speech disorder; stuttering. In addition to that, we found that his condition was based on a great sense of inferiority and incomplete mental development of judgment, memory, and his power of attention."

To this, Mr. Mills asked, "Isn't stammering often accompanied with some mental weakness as well as nervousness?"

"Yes, always," the doctor replied.

Mills submitted and proceeded to enter into evidence Leonard's treatment files from the Orchards. The files revealed Leonard to be "rather retiring and [he] makes no effort to talk unless directly addressed. His main difficulty appears to be in getting started, for once he begins a sentence he is able to go on with it. There is, however, a tendency to hurry with his speech and there is present . . . a sense of fear."

Ah, yes: fear; here it was again. It was everywhere. And I would point out that Leonard's primary fear was of his sire, his male parent, the man who never once came to visit the only living son still under his paternal authority while the boy underwent treatment at the Orchards; the father who instead bought him a new car and sent him money to be squandered on bogus investments with devious hospital staff. It was also interesting to note, and I made sure to bring this to the attention of the jury during my cross-examination of Dr. Clark that, as noted in Kip Rhinelander's treatment records, by September 1921 Leonard had purchased a car and that "he is greatly pleased with it, has taken some of the club members out, and shows a general feeling of being decidedly more superior."

Superior, aye? Club? I thought the Orchards was a school, not a club. Well, Daddy bought him a new car to make the boy feel superior. I made sure the jury heard that word, *superior*, more than once; and I hoped the men of the jury who were fathers would think of how they in turn sought to make their male offspring feel worthy and loved. Oh, yes, by all means, buy the boy an expensive new car to make him feel better about himself, even if you couldn't find the time to pay your son a visit. Again, I could not help but to feel that this evidence Mills insisted on presenting was doing nothing to evoke sympathy from our jurors for Leonard or the Rhinelander family.

On cross-examination, I asked the doctor to read from the file, and I pointed to a section where the records noted that a few weeks after meeting Alice and Grace Jones in September 1921, Leonard had become, in the words of the recording physician, "a changed man. He has recently made the acquaintance of some young girls. He calls on these friends, is looking for phone calls, talks well over the phone."

"Would it be fair to say then, Dr. Clark," I began my query, "in your expert opinion, and as related in Leonard Rhinelander's treatment files, that, throughout the period—the months of September and October 1921—after Leonard Rhinelander met the young friends you mention in your report, would you say that the boy appeared greatly improved and that he showed no signs of mental or even verbal deficiencies?"

"Yes . . . quite," the good doctor agreed. "He seemed especially fond of talking with one girl I recall, and would frequently absent himself from the Orchards to seek her company."

"I see. . . ."

No question who that girl was, and I made sure to point it out to the jury.

"Do you recall the girl's name, Doctor?"

"Yes, of course. I made note of her name in my progress reports. Leonard spoke of her often. Her name was Alice . . . Alice Jones."

"Ah, yes. Alice Jones. Now known as *Alice Jones Rhinelander*," I pronounced with emphasis for the benefit of the jury, who needed no reminding. "The young lady who is the defendant in this case." And I gestured toward Alice, seated at the defense table. "This is the young lady who had such an ameliorative effect upon the Rhinelander boy?"

Dr. Clark said, "Yes, I believe so."

Score another one for the defense. The Jones girls, and Alice in particular, actually helped Rhinelander to overcome his shyness and his sense of inadequacy. Such are the ameliorations of a pretty girl's attentions on a young man's sense of himself—Alice cured the lad!

* * *

Mills next called Joseph J. Strong to the witness stand. After he was sworn in, Mr. Strong identified himself as a licensed notary public and said that he was also the acting secretary to State Supreme Court judge James M. Fawcett. When Mills asked Mr. Strong if he worked for Philip Rhinelander, Strong stated that he did not. He testified that he had been with Leon Jacobs when they had picked up Leonard from the Joneses' home and that he subsequently "returned him to his father's custody."

Strong went on to recount how it had been he and Jacobs who went back to the Joneses' home a few weeks later to serve Alice with the annulment papers.

When it was my turn, I also asked Mr. Strong if he worked for Philip Rhinelander, and if it was at Rhinelander's direction that he had traveled with Mr. Jacobs to New Rochelle to "rescue Leonard from the Joneses' home."

Again, Strong denied he worked for Rhinelander.

"Is that so?" I said. "As you sit here today, under oath, and you are a man licensed in this state as a notary, is it your testimony, sir, that you are not and never were employed by Philip Rhinelander, the plaintiff's father? And that it was not at *Mr. Rhinelander's* direction that you went to New Rochelle to convince Leonard Rhinelander to end his marriage to this girl? Is that your testimony?"

"Yes, that is correct," Strong averred.

"Well, sir, then may I ask, and so the jury may understand, *why* and at *whose direction* you went to the Jones home and spirited away young Rhinelander. Was this your own plan?"

"No. I was employed, at that time, by Mr. Jacobs," Strong answered.

"Oh, I see. Well, now, of course—*that explains it.* That makes all the difference. You weren't working for Mr. Rhinelander. *You were working for Mr. Rhinelander's lawyer.* Is that correct?"

"Yes."

"That man." I pointed to Jacobs.

"Yes."

"Let the record reflect that the witness identified Mr. Leon Jacobs, plaintiff's counsel," I stated.

"And it was with that man, Mr. Jacobs, who works for Philip Rhinelander—I believe, exclusively for the Rhinelander family company, if I am not mistaken—it was while in that man's employ, and under that man's direction, while you were with that man, Mr. Jacobs, who is the attorney representing the plaintiff in this lawsuit, that you went to the Joneses' home and took the plaintiff, Leonard Kip Rhinelander into your custody, and you spirited him away from his bride—is that correct?"

"Yes, that is correct."

"I see. Then you were in fact with Mr. Jacobs and under *his* employment at that time?"

"I was, yes," Strong admitted.

"Well, of course. Why, how could I not have seen that? You didn't work for Mr. Rhinelander. No, how foolish of me to presume that. You worked for Mr. Jacobs . . . *who takes his orders directly from Mr. Rhinelander and who works exclusively for Mr. Philip Rhinelander.* Thank you, sir, for making that distinction."

* * *

By this time I would have expected Mills and Jacobs to give up on the line of questioning introduced and designed to portray Leonard as feeble-minded. But after Strong left the stand, it appeared the plaintiff's counsel was determined to blunder on with this characterization of his client as a nitwit by introducing his next witness, a not so young woman whom the jury learned was Miss Julie Despres, a governess who had been employed by the Rhinelander family from 1908 until 1913.

Miss Despres took her place on the stand with her face covered by a black veil, as though she were attending a funeral and not appearing as a witness at an annulment trial. Her evidence proved no more vital. When I challenged the relevancy of this witness's testimony, and that of the next to take the stand—a Mr. Sidney Ussher, the family clergyman who had officiated at Leonard's mother's funeral—Mills told the court that his point in examining these witnesses was to prove his contention that Leonard "was backward in his mental development at this time, when he first came in connection, contact, meeting with this defendant. And that, as bearing on the probability of the practice of fraud."

Which evidence, it seemed clear to me, had no merit, and I could tell by looking at the jury, noticing how they seemed a bit restless, that they too had seen enough to discount the idea of Rhinelander as a pathetic mental case.

It soon became obvious, however, that Mills also hoped to use his next witnesses to testify as to the Rhinelander family's distinguished bloodline. I objected, even though I knew such evidence did nothing to benefit Rhinelander's case and might actually further direct any prejudice away from Alice and onto Rhinelander.

"Your Honor," I said, "let the record reflect that the defense, and that Alice Rhinelander, have never questioned the Rhinelander family's pure white aristocratic pedigree. And also let me remind the plaintiff's counsel as well as the jury that the Rhinelander heritage and bloodline is *not an issue* in this case; and that rather, once again, it is an irrelevancy that is having no effect except to slow the proceedings."

Judge Morschauser agreed and sustained the objection.

Mills next called to the stand one J. Provost Stout, who had been employed as Leonard's tutor when the boy was eighteen years of age and when Leonard had first come into contact with Alice. (I had to wonder at these gentlemen's names: Stout, Strong; would we hear from Mr. Muscles next?)

Stout as well was of no help to the plaintiff's case. While he described Leonard's development as "slow" and his attention as a student as having been "diffident," he drew the line at classifying the boy as mentally deficient.

"What else can you tell us, Mr. Stout," Mills inquired, "with regard to the boy's—young Rhinelander's—hobbies, as it were, his chosen pursuits at this time, while you were his teacher?"

Stout thought for a bit and then responded to what seemed to me an obviously prepared question and rehearsed answer.

"Leonard was quite fond of jazz music," he offered, and looked pointedly at the jury. "He enjoyed listening to recordings of jazz."

Oh, well, of course, that explains it, I thought. *The boy has been corrupted by Negro music.*

I smirked and shook my head.

Now to have some fun with this witness during my cross-examination.

"Sir," I inquired of Mr. Stout once Mills was finished, "have you ever had occasion to observe a boy who was slow at mathematics but awfully fast at baseball?"

"Yes, decidedly," Mr. Stout replied.

"Thank you. And did you ever observe a boy that was a little slow in spelling but who was able and willing to work fast when he made love to a girl? Did you ever observe such a boy?"

"I have, yes," said Mr. Stout, "more than a few."

With his answer Mr. Stout provoked a ripple of laughter from the spectators as well as chuckles and smiles from the jurors.

"And, just one last question, sir, with regard to Leonard Rhinelander's choice in music. Do you suppose the fact that he enjoyed listening to what is modern music, that is, popular music, does that attest to his being mentally retarded? Might it not, on the contrary, just as well show young Rhinelander to be well versed in current trends, a modern boy; and so, one might also say, to use a modern phrase, that he is a young man who is *on the ball?*"

"It could, I suppose."

This exchange brought actual peals of laughter. The nitwit was on the ball and a lover of jazz music!

* * *

These witnesses once again, in my opinion, had done little or nothing to establish the plaintiff's claim that Leonard was mentally unsound or intellectually deficient when he met Alice, when he courted her, and when he then took her as his bride. As a point of fact, in my cross-examination of Mr. Stout, I believe I succeeded in bolstering the defense argument that Rhinelander knew precisely what he was about when he pursued Alice; and he was not too slow or too stupid or even color-blind to fail to recognize and appreciate that Alice was colored; and that he knowingly decided to make love to her; and he resolved to marry her; and he did in fact marry her regardless of her mixed race.

All these needless testimonies were mere warm-up exercises, preliminary bouts to what would be the main event. Once this witness was dismissed, and with his client's lawsuit faltering on the brink of collapse, there was little else Mills could do at this juncture to hope to resurrect the Rhinelander cause but to call to the witness stand the enigmatic plaintiff himself.

Leonard Rhinelander, however, was not in the courtroom.

And so, yet again, there was the question of the boy's whereabouts. Rhinelander, though announced as the next witness, had not been seen all day. Judge Morschauser was clearly exasperated by yet another delay in the proceedings due to the plaintiff's absence.

"He's on his way here, Your Honor," Jacobs averred. "He should be here momentarily."

I suggested that, given the hour, we break for lunch. His Honor agreed.

CHAPTER NINETEEN

Meeting Alice

It was early afternoon when court reconvened after the lunch recess on the fifth of December, Armistice Day, the moment everyone had been waiting for, when Mr. Mills addressed the court and announced: "If it may please the court, we call Leonard Kip Rhinelander."

As was his wont, Leonard sauntered into the courtroom accompanied by his bodyguards. The Rhinelander boy, however, appeared far less sure of himself as he approached, then mounted the witness stand alone and took the oath. One could not help but notice that when he passed by his bride seated at the defense table, and as he was within arm's-length distance of the girl he once loved, Alice reached out her hand to him in a pitiful gesture that Rhinelander cruelly chose to ignore. I saw it, of course, and I had to believe that most of the jurors had seen it as well, given that all eyes were upon the Rhinelander lad as he entered; and that they would be urged to question, *What sort of man is this? How can he be so callous? Has he no tender human feelings?*

Some members of the press corps as well had seen Alice reach for Leonard, and they reported it in the next day's papers, thereby dashing any remaining chance of reconciliation.

If there had been even a glimmer of hope that I might feel sorry for the boy and so go gently on him in my cross-examination, as requested by Alice, upon observing the plaintiff's self-satisfied entrance and his blatant refusal to acknowledge his wife, such notions flew from my mind. Kip Rhinelander's cold refusal to even notice his wife, his choice to ignore the woman whose heart he had broken, and upon whom he had inflicted or allowed such emotional pain to be put upon this girl who he had professed to love, made love to, promised to marry, married, and now—*what?* He no longer had any human or decent feelings for her? No pity, no compassion if not love? What sort of man is capable of such hard-heartedness? Of such utter, pitiless rejection of a good and true woman such as Alice?

I was astonished; I couldn't understand Rhinelander; and I was still smoldering with anger over the whole nasty, underhanded business of this trial as the smug perpetrator assumed the witness stand, and I held firm to my resolve to do all within my power to destroy the boy despite Alice's request that I go easy on him.

* * *

It was two thirty in the afternoon when Rhinelander was sworn in. He would remain on the witness stand for several grueling days with one remarkable respite, when a mystery witness was called to testify in what would come to be seen as comic relief. From the moment he assumed the witness stand, young Kip gazed out at the crowded courtroom with an expression on his face that I can only describe as bland; perhaps self-satisfied may be a better description; but yet not comfortable in his role, like a man tasked with a nuisance duty who would like to give the impression that he is capable although not enthusiastic as to his calling. He showed little emotion beyond a mild pique and vague discomfort at being asked to appear and defend his own annulment lawsuit.

Rhinelander was dressed in a blue, well-tailored, smartly pressed English-made suit. He wore gray spats over his shoes. Instead of his usual round-rimmed goggle eyeglasses, he had donned a pair of scholarly-looking pince-nez that, with his hair parted down the middle and slicked back, gave the impression of a young intellectual or professional rather than the idle, spoiled rich boy; the jazz lover and man about town we knew him to be. Rhinelander's manner, however—his way of crossing and uncrossing his long, rather thick legs; his fidgeting with his large, soft-looking hands; slouching somewhat in the witness chair; asking for and guzzling glasses of water to moisten his parched mouth (the true sign of a liar!); gazing around the room as though he were unsure of how he'd gotten here—all this could only give the impression that he was either nervous or simply distracted, unable to appreciate or even to feel the gravity of the cause his father and his lawyers had forced him to bring against Alice, a woman he had once professed to love and whom he now refused even to look at or to acknowledge in any way.

I was distressed for dear Alice. This behavior by the man she loved and had married had to hurt her deeply.

* * *

By this time in the trial, on the day when Leonard Kip was expected to testify, by early morning a huge, increasingly boisterous and unruly horde of would-be spectators were gathered outside our county courthouse in White Plains. Once court was in session, would-be spectators who had been refused entrance were upset that there was no room for them in the courtroom. The parties to the proceeding were forced to have to jostle their way through the crowds when entering or leaving; and one could hear the noisy throng milling about outside, giving the sense of an angry lynch mob waiting for a victim. The deputy sheriffs had their hands full trying to control the overflow of flappers, of young working girls, older married women and matrons; men of all ages and class gathered and straining at the doors in hopes of gaining entrance and witnessing some of the scandalous testimony the crowd expected to emerge with Rhinelander's appearance on the witness stand.

News reporters bustled into and out of the courtroom, officiously brandishing their press passes. Photographers pushed and shoved their way into position to take photos of the litigants, their family members, the witnesses, and the lawyers. Inside the courtroom, while awaiting the judge and jury, there was the general atmosphere of a convivial if somewhat awkward social gathering, like a reunion of relatives from two different clans rather than a sedate legal proceeding. However, once court was in session, with Judge Morschauser on the bench, with the jurymen in their box, and a witness on the stand, the deputy sheriffs, the clerk, and the judge would endeavor continually to maintain order.

Once a witness had been sworn in and testimony begun, it soon became clear that this was a battle of wits like no other of its kind. Over the years I had appeared in many courtrooms up and down this great state, and even in our nation's capital; but in the Rhinelander trial one had the impression of having entered a theater of such intense emotional and intellectual conflict set as it were along intimate lines of dispute—race, class, wealth, love, sex, courtship, and marriage—all to be testified to, examined, as well as revealed to the public in a rarefied domain of strictly controlled language and emotion, where serious issues of love and respect were debated in legal terms and considered, then judged in opposition to the powers of affluence and social prominence while held under the codified restraint of civil law—that this trial was not only unique but also of profound and lasting consequence. Need I remind my readers, as I had to remind myself? America—and now possibly even the world—was watching.

* * *

At last, with the Rhinelander boy finally settled in the witness chair, Mr. Mills approached and asked his witness to identify himself for the court and for the record.

"Leonard Kip Rhinelander," he declared, his voice betraying a slight quaver.

"Are you the plaintiff in this action?" Mills inquired.

"I am," Leonard said somewhat more forcefully.

"Your age at the present time?"

"Twenty-one."

Mills then went back to elicit testimony already covered by his previous witness Dr. Clark of the Orchards School. He afforded Leonard an opportunity to show the jury that he was, as Mills had maintained in his opening, and as he had attempted to show with his previous witnesses, and to prove the accusation of fraud by proving this characterization of his client: that of showing Rhinelander to be an innocent, rather sheltered, and backward young aristocrat who had strayed from the confines of his clinic, and on his travels had stumbled into unknown territory—the wild and wooly streets of New Rochelle—and there he fell into the clutches of a temptress, a jezebel, a lascivious Black vamp who used her aggressive sexuality and experience in lovemaking to seduce and then utterly enslave young Kip to the degree at which the boy had no control over his ability to judge right from wrong, nor even to discern Black from white.

Early in his examination, Mills asked Leonard, "Had you ever had any experience with a woman? I mean any *sexual* experience, or anything of that sort before you met this woman?" Mills then turned to indicate Alice.

The audience followed Leonard's gaze to see if he would finally look upon his wife, but he never did.

As expected, Leonard replied that he had not.

Nodding thoughtfully, Mills said, "I see . . . so you were, it is safe to say, you were . . . new to all this business of lovemaking?"

To which I objected, "Asked and answered, Your Honor."

Mills withdrew the question and asked, "If you had known—that is, if you had been aware of what is now conceded to be true before you married Alice Jones, that she is of colored blood—would you have married her?"

Rhinelander replied, "Absolutely not; no."

"When you married her," Mills asked, "did you believe her statement that she was white?"

"I did," Rhinelander claimed. "I always believed her."

I watched the jurors carefully as Rhinelander testified as to this supposed fact: that Alice claimed she was of pure white blood. More than a couple of them told me by their reactions—a barely noticeable shaking of the head, or even a sneer, a rolling of the eyes—that they did not believe this statement.

Mills moved on to Leonard's description of the events that had brought him into initial contact with the Jones girls, and later into frequent association with the Jones family in the fall and winter of 1921–22.

In attempting to answer the question of how he met Alice, Leonard's stutter quite abruptly manifested itself. To the amazement of the judge, jury, and spectators, Rhinelander was suddenly tongue-tied to the point where he seemed unable to utter a complete sentence without stumbling over nearly every other word. Mr. Mills cautioned Rhinelander to take his time, to relax, and to merely tell the court and the jury in his own words how he came to meet Alice, her sisters, and the Jones family. After more stammering, Leonard managed to articulate a confusing story of the time when he and his friend, whom he identified as Karl Kreitler, the fellow who worked at the Orchards as an electrician, drove down to New Rochelle from Stamford together merely as a joy ride in Leonard's new car, and to have some time away from the school. He made no mention that the two young men had set out in search of local girls. But once there, along a main road in New Rochelle, they came upon Grace Jones. Rhinelander claimed that they had not set out to meet girls but that some trouble with the automobile had brought them to a standstill at the side of the road where Kreitler was at work on the engine when they were "picked up" by Alice's younger sister Grace.

"Picked up? How so?" Mills asked.

"Well, we were working . . . Karl was working on the car when she came along and asked if she could g . . . g . . . g . . . if we would take her for a ride."

"And did you take her for a ride?" Mills asked.

Leonard struggled to say that no, he didn't take her for a ride. Karl Kreitler did.

"In your automobile?"

"Yes."

"I see," the lawyer observed and then inquired, "And what happened between Kreitler and the Jones girl?"

I stood up. "Objection, Your Honor. Calls for speculation. The witness just said he was not present."

"Sustained."

"What did Karl Kreitler *tell you* happened when he returned with your car?"

"He . . . he . . . he . . . well, that, he said that he—"

"Did he tell you that he had sex with the Jones girl?"

"Judge, he's leading the witness," I objected. "As well, this is hearsay."

"Well, Your Honor, as you can see, the witness has some difficulty articulating . . ." Mills explained what needed no explanation. "And we are not offering this as for the truth of what happened, only what the witness was told."

Judge Morschauser said, "Continue."

Mills did indeed continue to lead the witness, over my repeated objections. He managed to get Leonard to recount a somewhat conflicting narrative that changed even within the telling, and at one point included another friend from the Orchards but whose name Leonard said he couldn't recall, and then at other times it appeared to be just Leonard and Kreitler out and about when they met the girls. In one version of his story, Leonard said that Alice had come along while the boys were talking with Grace, but when questioned he said that perhaps he was mistaken and he hadn't actually met Alice until another time, at her home. He did say that while Kreitler was off supposedly having a sexual encounter with Grace Jones in Leonard's car, Leonard and the other fellow, who may or may not have been along with him, waited in town. The three men then drove Grace home. This, Leonard told the jury, was his first experience "picking up girls."

Three days after the first meeting with Grace Jones, which Karl Kreitler had told him had resulted in a sexual encounter with the girl, Leonard claimed he was sufficiently intrigued to drive back to New Rochelle on his own after he received a postcard from Alice inviting him to come visit.

A postcard? From Alice? This was the first we had heard anything about a postcard. And had Leonard even met Alice at this point? This was not clear, either. Did Alice have his postal address? It was all so muddled; I doubted any such postcard existed. When Mills asked Leonard to recount exactly what Alice had written to invite him to visit, I objected and asked that the postcard be submitted and therefore serve as evidence of its contents.

"Unfortunately, the postcard has been lost," Mr. Mills admitted. "However . . . we are in possession of a number of other postcards from the defendant—"

"Your Honor, is counsel suggesting to prove the existence of one postcard—a highly suspect postcard of which we have never been apprised before today, and supposedly written by the defendant at a time when she did not even know the plaintiff—simply by the existence of other postcards written and posted after they had become lovers? I suggest that this first postcard is a figment of the witness's or the witness's attorneys' imagination, and I ask that the jury be directed to ignore this testimony as totally unfounded unless the postcard can be produced and entered as evidence of its contents."

"Sustained," Judge Morschauser declared. "The jury will ignore the testimony as to the postcard."

Mr. Mills then asked Leonard to go on and describe his first meeting with Alice. Leonard told of having arrived at the Joneses' home, which he claimed to have known the whereabouts of after dropping Grace off there on the previous trip. He said he went to the door to deliver a message from Karl Kreitler apologizing for having been unable to return to keep his date with Grace due to the demands of his work at the Orchards.

"And tell the jury what happened when you went to the Joneses' home to deliver your message."

"I . . . well, I . . . she wasn't home."

"Who wasn't home?"

"Ah, Grace . . . Grace was out."

"What happened then?"

It took Leonard some time, and no little effort, but he finally managed to articulate how instead of meeting Grace, he chanced to meet Alice Jones, who arrived while Leonard was still there talking with Mrs. Jones. Leonard said he was enticed by Alice and by her mother; they welcomed him into their home, they invited him to stay to tea; he was made to feel quite at ease; and that he was immediately attracted to Alice who, Leonard claimed, was flirtatious and even a bit brazen in her sex appeal.

"How so?" Mills wanted to know. "What did she do?"

"She . . . well, she touched me. She put her hand on mine, and on my arm at times, and she looked at me with . . . her . . . ah, her . . . she has lovely eyes, quite extraordinary eyes, and she knows how to use them . . . to make a fellow feel weak . . . and excited. I . . . I was quite . . . She was so friendly I was charmed by her."

"I see. What happened then?"

Leonard appeared perplexed by the question.

"Did you stay for tea? Did you leave? What happened next?"

"Oh, well, yes, I stayed a bit longer. I didn't want to leave. It was pleasant . . . I liked being there. And then Grace came home. And I . . . I believe, yes, Mrs. Jones, Alice's mother, you see . . . sh . . . sh . . . she told Grace to . . . to . . . to return the ring I had given her—actually, no, not I, Karl Kreitler had given Grace the ring, but it be . . . be . . . belonged . . . or it had belonged . . . to my mother—"

Rhinelander suddenly broke off, as if the memory of his dead mother proved too much for him.

"Go on, Leonard," Mills gently prodded him. "What happened then? Did Grace give you the ring?"

"Yes. Mrs. Jones told Grace to give it back . . . because, apparently, Grace already . . . I believe she was already engaged . . . to another fellow. So it wasn't proper—"

"Then she gave it back?"

"Yes, well . . . she didn't like to, but she did."

Mills asked, "And what did you do then?"

Leonard shrugged. He looked around the room nervously and then admitted, "I gave it to Alice."

Mills paused. He adjusted his ear horn to make sure he was hearing Leonard's testimony. He raised his rather bushy eyebrows in an expression of surprise, and then he turned to look at the gentlemen in the jury box as he said, "Let me get this straight. You say you took the ring from Grace Jones upon her mother's demand that she return it. And then you gave the ring *to Alice . . . to the defendant?* But . . . you had only just met her, hadn't you?"

This provoked laughter from the spectators and even a few of the jurors. More than anything else young Rhinelander or his lawyers might have said to intimate how inept and unschooled Leonard was in courting young ladies, his recounting how he took the ring from one sister and promptly handed it over to the other sister whom he had only just met proved not only his inexperience but also his lack of common sense.

Leonard blushed as the laughter continued, as though he hadn't understood how foolish his behavior might appear.

"Well, no, I was mistaken. I did see Alice, I saw her before . . . at the Joneses' home on that first day, when we dropped Gr . . . Gr . . . her sister at home, we spoke then, very briefly, and that was how she happened to send me the postcard. Or . . . I might have met her by the side of the road. I can't remember."

"I see," Mills said. "So . . . in fact, you had met Alice originally on the first trip to New Rochelle. And did you talk to her then?"

"Only to say hello . . . I believe we met only in passing . . . she might have been on her way in . . . or sh . . . sh . . . sh . . . she might have been leaving, I don't recall. But I did see her."

Now, as the story became even more confusing, Leonard was, however, succeeding in giving the jury the impression Mr. Mills had hoped for: that of an innocent, tongue-tied, and socially backward young man who was easily manipulated by his social inferiors, people such as Karl Kreitler and the Jones sisters. I believed this impression had also elicited a certain amount of compassion for the witness, which I was determined to dispel.

"And did Alice take the ring?" Mills asked.

"No, well, yes . . . I mean, her mother wouldn't allow her to take it. It caused quite a . . . what, I . . ." Rhinelander broke off and appeared flustered.

"The girls, you say? It caused—what? Were they . . . upset by this business with the ring? It bothered them? Tell us how."

"Well, yes, I think it did. But they also laughed. It seemed funny to them."

Here Mills turned to the jury and remarked, "It seems funny to me as well."

This comment brought forth even more laughter from nearly everyone in the room with the exception of Judge Morschauser; the Jones girls, Alice at our table, and Grace and her mother in the spectators' seats—and of course the witness himself.

Judge Morschauser admonished the spectators and told them to refrain from laughing. It was evident that Mr. Mills, in making fun of his own client, was succeeding in his efforts to portray Rhinelander as a somewhat pitiful rich nitwit who had stumbled into a den of clever and calculating colored females.

* * *

With this foundation thoroughly established (and which I looked forward to attacking on cross-examination), Mills moved along to begin entering a number of letters written by Alice and sent to Rhinelander: letters the lawyer sought to offer as proof that it had been Alice who lured Leonard into a slavish sexual relationship; and that she then used her explicit letters with enticements of more to come to keep Rhinelander hooked while he was away; and ultimately to inveigle the boy into marrying her upon his coming of age, at which time he should expect to receive a substantial, multimillion-dollar inheritance.

During Leonard's testimony with regard to the content of Alice's letters and her postcards—including the now disappeared postcard alleged to have been an invitation to Leonard to visit—I objected to the letters being allowed into evidence. I demanded that the court order Mr. Mills to explain how his client's attorney had managed to gain possession of Alice's personal correspondence. Here there ensued a lengthy sidebar, and at last the jury was sent out while the lawyers argued the admissibility of the letters in open court.

We maintained that the letters were Alice's property, since she had written them. Judge Morschauser ruled that although the letters were composed by Alice, they were addressed and delivered to Leonard through the US Postal Service; Rhinelander had received them legally; and they were in his possession in his home at the time they were seized as evidence by his attorney who, presumably, was acting under the implicit authority of Rhinelander; therefore the letters would be allowed on a letter-by-letter basis only after each letter submitted as evidence had first been reviewed and considered as to its relevance by the court. Alice's letters would become evidence over my objections and made part of the record.

Finally, after the better part of the afternoon session had been consumed with argument, the jury was able to hear Leonard's testimony revealing the extraordinary degree to which his father's attorney, Mr. Leon Jacobs, who was seated at the plaintiff's table, how Jacobs and his factotum Mr. Strong not only had managed to usurp complete control over the boy and his cause, but also, and perhaps extralegally, one might even suppose—and I would suggest—Jacobs had *illegally* obtained evidence in the case. I would declare that in the opinion of the defense, Leonard's lawyer had gathered exhibits and submitted actual sworn and notarized documents received by the court knowing they contained false statements. Once again the judge ruled that the evidence would be allowed over my objections, to be noted for the record, and subject to His Honor's review and ruling as to the individual letters' relevance.

Leonard testified that Mr. Jacobs had gone to the Rhinelander family mansion in Manhattan, entered Leonard's room when the boy was not at home, and seized Alice's letters without Rhinelander's permission or knowledge until after the fact. Furthermore, I was able to have Leonard tell how Jacobs, in searching for more letters, had gone to the apartment the couple rented but never occupied, an apartment in New Rochelle, and cleared it out, taken not only more of Alice's letters, but also all of the furniture the newlyweds had purchased, even including the couple's wedding gifts, again without Leonard's permission or knowledge. Mr. Jacobs, we were able to establish through Leonard's testimony, was a man on a shameless mission, directed by his employer, Philip Rhinelander, to remove and wipe out any vestige and memory of the scion's unacceptable bride.

Once more, this testimony succeeded in showing Rhinelander to be a young man totally under the power and control of his rich and almighty father, aided by his father's servile attorney. I made a note to be careful not to let this impression of Leonard as one who is easily manipulated and controlled by others linger and carry over to include his relations with Alice. I had to distinguish that he was quite sure of himself and in control when it came to his courting and eventual seduction of and marriage to the girl, and not the other way around, which was how Mr. Mills was endeavoring to characterize the relationship, and managing it with some success as I discerned through introduction of Alice's love letters and, in general, with Rhinelander's apparent inexperience in dealing with women and in the ways of the world.

* * *

Over the next few days, with Kip perched uncomfortably on the witness stand, and Alice at times flushed with embarrassment or overcome with shame and sadness, Mr. Mills proceeded to read sections of, and enter into evidence more than one hundred of Alice's letters to Leonard—*one hundred plus letters!* To what degree of evidentiary value one might only suppose. Further, by reading Alice's letters in open court, counsel for the plaintiff had afforded to the defense an equal gambit, and one that would prove to have far more impact upon the plaintiff's case.

At the outset of the reading of Alice's letters, Judge Morschauser invited the spectators present in the courtroom to absent themselves if they so wished, and His Honor also ordered children under age twenty-one to be removed, which caused a wave of audible discontent from some of the younger flappers and sheiks. The judge cautioned that due to the fact that the content of the letters would at times be sexually explicit, graphic, and even vulgar and obscene, and thus could prove discomfiting, anyone who might be offended by descriptions of such behavior would be prudent to depart from the courtroom during the reading of the letters.

No men and few of the ladies availed themselves of the opportunity to quit the proceedings, and those few who did exit along with the unhappy minors were quickly replaced by willing substitutes.

I objected repeatedly and asked that certain passages and even sentences from the missives that had been taken out of context be reread in their entirety. The letters proved embarrassing to Alice not only due to the content, but also given the girl's lack of a proper formal education, resulting, as mentioned, in her crude skills in spelling and grammar.

Mr. Mills seemed to delight in exposing Alice's inadequate literacy and revealing her lack of social sophistication; but I believe this may have worked to our advantage in evoking sympathy from at least some of the jurors; to allow them to perceive Alice as a working-class girl of limited education who was easily taken in by the better-educated, wealthy, and worldly—even if socially awkward—young blue blood seated slouched on the witness stand, wearing his spats and waistcoat, and with his Valentino hairdo, trying to look for all the world as though he were hardly disturbed by the humiliation his wife was being made to suffer at his cause.

Furthermore, by denigrating Alice, who by this time had clearly gained the affection of most everyone in the courtroom—save perhaps her husband and his lawyers—due to her unassuming beauty and grace, always showing up on time and coiffed and well attired—yet, like so much of the evidence, Alice's letters could be shown to cut both ways; for, in fact, as I would demonstrate, Alice's writings were tepid, hardly scandalous, and innocent when compared with what would be revealed of the allegedly inexperienced Rhinelander boy's rank epistolary pornography; which now, given the court's ruling with regard to Alice's letters, would open the door for me to enter Kip's shocking missives.

* * *

In a letter from Alice in early December 1921, she wrote to let Leonard know that she was at home alone and thinking of him.

"Just think of me, this evening being hear alone, Mother and Father and sister Emily, and hear husband, as gone to Westchester to see Buddies—and I am hear alone, thinking of you, dear heart. . . . I only wished Lenard was coming down this evening. How I could caress, you dear, Because you no, you love for me, to caress you dear. But my heart, feels very lonesome, this Eve. But what, can I do dear, because you are so, far from me sweet heart."

Hearing this, my heart went out to Alice. I believe several of the jurors felt for her as well; that they could imagine her as a girl who was not so much calculating as she was enamored with a boy she believed also cared for her. Remarkably, Alice appeared outwardly unmoved by the evidence of her love for Rhinelander as well as by her rudimentary skills as a writer. Again I noticed how Alice responded to stress and insult—it appeared to make her stronger, at least for the time being.

Mills asked Leonard if this letter was written and received by him prior to the time the couple spent together over the Christmas holidays at the Hotel Marie Antoinette in Manhattan.

"Yes, that would be some time, perhaps a week or two before the Marie Antoinette."

"Now, up to that time," Mills continued, "before you went and stayed at the hotel, had you had any sexual intercourse with Alice?"

"No," Rhinelander replied.

"I see. Well, had you made any attempt to have any sexual intercourse with Alice . . . up to that time?"

Again Rhinelander replied that he had not.

I felt obliged to object to this entire line of questioning, arguing that it was outside the scope of the case, as this was not meant to be an investigation into the couple's sex life—which, of course, it was.

As expected, Judge Morschauser overruled, stating that

intimate relations between a man and his wife were proper grounds for consideration in an annulment lawsuit based on allegations of racial fraud.

In all honesty, my objection was in form alone. I was pleased to have Mr. Mills pursue this line of questioning and to let the jury come to an understanding that it was as a result of the plaintiff's initiative that the sexual relations between Alice and Rhinelander had been introduced in evidence so that when I brought up Rhinelander's letters to Alice, it would be accepted as having been done in reaction to the plaintiff's attack upon his wife and not purely for the shock value of the letters' obscene sexual content. I would thus be allowed in my cross-examination to ask Leonard to describe how the couple had first consummated their illicit sexual relationship over the several days and nights they spent together at the Hotel Marie Antoinette, and I would be justified in introducing Leonard's letters to Alice to further defame the plaintiff.

I must admit that I was stunned and baffled to see that Mills had blundered into this line of attack. What could he have been thinking? I could only surmise that Rhinelander failed to alert his counsel as to the embarrassing content of his letters to Alice; or that Rhinelander had no idea we possessed his letters even though we had alluded to them during discovery. Yet if we, as Alice's lawyers, were not in possession of the letters, then who would be? Were Jacobs and Mills even aware of Rhinelander's obscene correspondence? If not—then why not? Had they asked Rhinelander about his letters and what he may have written to Alice? Was the boy too embarrassed by what he knew was in his letters to admit of their existence? Were they paying attention to our submissions made to the court?

I had no idea. Again, my only explanation for the chaos of the plaintiff's case is that they had not prepared for a trial and so were overwhelmed trying to play catch-up—never a good place for a client's counsel to be with the case before a jury. Then, with our unexpected admission as to Alice's color, opposing counsel was without a case; they were now on the defense. And finally, it occurred to me that there was some dissension in the Rhinelander camp as to who was in control of their lawsuit. I could see it in Mr. Mills's face when he conferred with Jacobs, that there was no meeting of the minds as to how their evidence was to be presented, or even what their evidence should be now that they had no fraud to prove. And one could only wonder as to the influence of the hidden hand of Rhinelander Senior as he sought to orchestrate his reluctant son's lawsuit.

Now, with the admission of Alice's race, and the subject of intimate sexual relations between husband and wife coming in through the letters, the specter of interracial sex was at the forefront of the evidence to be presented to the jury.

As court adjourned for the day, within hours, with publication of the evening papers, the scandalous underbelly of the Rhinelander case was exposed to the world.

* * *

I had a brief meeting with Alice and her parents in our offices at the close of the afternoon session, and we confirmed plans for me to attend a family dinner over the weekend to further discuss the case. The gist of their discomfort, and what would be the main topic of discussion at the Joneses' home at dinner, could be summed up as: *Is this really necessary? Must we allow our daughter, our sister, our loved one to be put through this? Isn't it obvious that the case against her is false?* To which I had no answer but to assure them that the only way for Alice to avoid what was to happen in the courtroom would be for her to accept the settlement offer, as I had originally suggested, and for her to agree not to challenge the annulment, which would then put an end to the trial and, eventually, the overwhelming attention by the newspapers.

Alice wouldn't hear of it, of "throwing in the towel," as her brother-in-law, Robert Brooks, described in prizefighting terms what it would mean for Alice to quit her defense. Alice's parents, as well as any other family member who questioned the wisdom of fighting the case with no holds barred, were made to respect Alice's decision—for, after all, as Alice made clear, it was her decision alone despite the impact it might have on the rest of the family.

It became clear that Mrs. Jones was the one who most feared what pursuing this course might do to her daughter, and, by association, to the entire Jones family and their already highly publicized place in the community.

* * *

It had reached the point as the trial came to court where Alice and her mother, and even Alice's sisters, required some protection as they made their way to and from the courthouse in White Plains, and even occasionally when they appeared on the streets of New Rochelle. Apparently Rhinelander as well had been accosted even though his bodyguards always accompanied him. Mr. Strong and possibly one of Rhinelander's other bodyguards were said to be carrying loaded pistols. The tension in and around the courthouse as well as in the streets of White Plains and particularly in New Rochelle mounted daily with the numbers of policemen, deputy sheriffs, and even some local troops brought in to quell demonstrations that threatened to turn violent.

I could only advise the extended Jones family as well as Alice and her parents that I expected things to get worse before they got better; and I asked them to bear with me and to trust that, even if I at times seemed to be asking questions of witnesses or attempting to enter into evidence facts that were extremely embarrassing and hurtful to Alice and to the Jones family, it was all calculated and done with an eye toward accomplishing our objective of winning the trial. That result—victory at trial—above and beyond all else, I emphasized, was our single, paramount goal; for, I reminded them, losing the case was not an alternative I for one was willing to entertain. That would mean certain ruin for Alice and far more dire consequences for all the rest of the family than what they might be going through now.

"In contrast," I reflected, "there is not another Rhinelander, no member of the plaintiff's family, or even any friend in the courtroom. The boy and his lawyers are all alone.

"There is scandal here, certainly, I have no doubt," I said. "But, in truth, I believe that, knowing the facts, and once the jury is privy to all those facts, once I can bring the men on the jury to see Rhinelander for who he really is—and the beauty of this is that the boy is our best evidence of . . . well, it's quite clear, and I don't mean to insult the man you love, Alice, but it is clear to me that Leonard is not up to defending the false narrative his lawyers are seeking to use to persuade the jury. His heart is not in this, as you said from the very beginning. What, that he is an imbecile? No, no, I don't believe so. He's clearly upset with this characterization. If anything, I am struck by how young Rhinelander is in fact the best proof of how he is merely a reluctant pawn in his father's ugly game of defaming you, Alice, as well as your entire family. It's shocking. I've only met Leonard's father, Philip, once, when he came to our offices early on; however, I've done a bit of reading on him, and I've asked of those who do know him what sort of fellow he is. Judge Swinburne knows Rhinelander quite well. The overall opinion seems to be that he is a man of overweening pride, what we might refer to in common terms as a stuffed shirt. He's been photographed with a puffed-up chest adorned with medals. So he sees himself as some sort of American hero and idol of bravery, of respectability, and a fine, unimpeachable example of . . . dare I say it, of white supremacy.

"Fine. Good for him. Frankly, I find all that extremely distasteful, especially when such nonsense is trotted out in a court of law to stand as some sort of proof of grounds upon which any action for or against this supposed moral and genealogical superiority must fail. It's absurd, really; but I know they—the Rhinelanders of the world—believe that they are far and away superior to the rest of us mere mortals, and I know that for far too long they have been allowed to believe in this supposed superiority. Our jury, however, I am willing to bet is not so predisposed—no, in fact, I believe, they tend toward the opposite belief: that one is not defined by what their last name is as much as by their behavior and their character."

"That's true," said George Jones. "And that truth will out."

"Indeed. And, you see," I wished to explain, "keep in mind that it is not merely Rhinelander versus Rhinelander in this lawsuit; no, not at all. It is Rhinelander versus Jones. It is wealth and entitlement against this family, what could be seen as the American ideal of equality regardless of skin color, race, family name, or religion. And finally it is young Rhinelander, and by extension his entire family and their cohorts in high society, whose behavior is the least defensible. This is how I will present them to our jurors—as the guilty party."

George Jones nodded in agreement. "This was always my concern with the Rhinelander boy," he said, "much as we came to like him. He's a likable chap. But I for one never believed that, when push came to shove, which I had no doubt it would, I feared young Len would not have the courage to stand up to his father. I don't have any boys of my own, but I've been a son, and been a boy faced with trials and tribulations brought upon me by my father. I had to make decisions, to stand on my own, and to make my own way in the world. I've said it before, but given the boy's coddled upbringing, and losing his mother, it was clear to me that he lacked the will to oppose his father's wishes."

Alice said, "Len doesn't want this any more than we do."

"If that's the case, and I believe you when you say it is, then Rhinelander needs to put a stop to it," I said. "He's the only one who can do that . . . other than you."

I went on to say, "You know, when the opposition trumpets that America is watching, we do well to know that they are not mistaken. America—everything that is good and decent and fair in the American way of life—is in fact being balanced on the scales of justice in this case.

"None of that, I believe, must be lost upon the men in the jury box. They are all decent family men of the lower middle class and even the working class. They will relate to you, Alice, and they will be scandalized by Rhinelander and his father if, I advise, if we give them every reason to find against the Rhinelanders—and that, I warn you, will entail taking whatever scandal Rhinelander's attorneys attempt to inflict upon you and your family, and turning it around to settle squarely upon the boy, his father, and their lawyers for bringing this bogus lawsuit."

Once I let this thought take hold, I went on to say, "Hear me: I must and I will be absolutely merciless in my cross-examination of Leonard Rhinelander, as I have been of his witnesses. Whatever disgrace his cause has brought upon you, Alice, and upon your family, will be *doubly, triply* brought back to defame the plaintiff, his family, and even his attorneys, or I have not done my job as your advocate and your defender.

"And that is why I commend your bravery, as well as your belief in yourself. You alone chose this course. I for one, and I'm sure there were others who counseled you to take the settlement and avoid what we knew would be a long and hurtful battle. So it is you who is the one who should be wearing the medals for valor in defending the very ideals of what it means to be an American. Not some pompous peacock who . . . well, when I learned that Philip Rhinelander had never once been to visit his son at the Orchards, I was appalled! More than anything, that told me much about the man. What sort of father does this? His own boy . . . and now he wishes to destroy the lad's bold hope for happiness in marriage to a girl he obviously was madly in love with. *Why?* Because Rhinelander is so vain, so enamored with his own sense of superiority that he is unable to accept and perhaps even come to love the woman his son has chosen as his wife. No, I'm sorry, I don't understand that attitude; it is inexcusable, I tell you, it does not come from love, and I also believe it has to do with the shame the family still feels over Leonard's uncle's marital indiscretions. But I'm sorry, no, not as good and decent Americans, we must not be allowed to judge one another based on such considerations and still call ourselves loyal to the very ideals this great nation was founded upon."

"Here, here," George Jones pronounced and gave me a pat on the back.

"This is not just me wearing my lawyer's hat when I say this. I am quite passionate about the American ideal of human equality, which is why I chose to pursue the law as a profession. I come from a long line of abolitionists, and I am certain that the twelve men chosen to sit on that jury also want to believe in the values our country is founded upon. Prejudice, be it over class, race, religion, as our forefathers determined, *must not be allowed* to hold sway in America and particularly not in our courts. And so we must *have no mercy*—you understand? We must give no quarter to the Rhinelanders, and admit no credence to class or race superiority; we must do all we can to destroy it even as it sits before us represented in the person of young Kip Rhinelander—though he apparently is without these prejudices. That is what I find remarkable about the boy; he does not feel these emotions, and yet he allows them to be perpetrated in his name.

"We can't allow it. We must adhere to the ideal of equality so crucial to protect and safeguard even now as remnants of the abomination of slavery still exist in the segregation and persecution of our countrymen based on race or creed.

"Keep watching, America!" I declared, rising to my theme and standing to leave. "By God, watch while I have at Rhinelander's weak-minded boy, and show him to the jury and to the world for the disgrace he is not only to the Rhinelander name but also for his abject failure to live up to what it means to be an American . . . and a gentleman!"

I looked into Alice's eyes, now brimming with tears.

"I'm sorry," I continued. "Sorry that all this must be made to come out through what I must do to your Leonard. I wish this were not the case; but that is the way his father has chosen to defend—or, conversely, to destroy—his son and their family name."

I might have wished I had a stenographer on hand to record my outburst and to save it as material for my closing argument. However, as I'm sure the reader has detected by now, though I may have been a white man of a certain social standing given my name and my profession, I am sincere in my passion as to defending the fundamental issues at stake in the Rhinelander case. And I am equally appalled by the kind of arrogance and self-satisfied aplomb Rhinelander Senior and his ilk demonstrate to try to rule over the rest of us mere mortals.

George Jones saw me to the door. "We've been through this before," Jones admitted as I was about to take my leave. "Mrs. Jones and me, not the same, but similar. I know it's hurtful to have such things dragged out into the public." He shook his head sadly. "But sometimes it can't be helped. You have our support, Mr. Davis. *Please, save our Alice.*"

As I walked home, and when I entered my study and sat at my desk to make my notes, I knew that in the Rhinelander case, and in America, the time was due for some truth to be told about race and class, may it shock the jurors, the spectators, and the world at large; may it embarrass and hurt the defendant and her family; may it be seen as vicious and vituperative. Rhinelander must be exposed for the fake gentleman, the poor excuse for a man, and the false claimant of fraud that he was even as he sat there in his three-piece English tweed suit, his hair parted down the middle and slicked back, peering out at the world from behind his oversize glasses with his feigned look of superiority and self-satisfaction that I was determined to wipe away, and to expose him before the jury, the spectators, and indeed before the world for the fraud that he allowed his father to prosecute, and the shame he allowed to be brought upon Alice, his loving wife.

Alice must not be made to suffer for Rhinelander's false pride and moral weakness.

CHAPTER TWENTY

December 10, 1924

Dear diary,

Mr. Davis, my lawyer, was here this evening, and he only just left. It seems so strange to me even to see those words in my diary—my lawyer. Who would ever have thought that I would need a lawyer? Not me! This whole thing still seems like something that was meant to be happening to someone else—a real criminal, a real liar and a cheater, not just a girl who fell in love with a boy and married him only to have his family say I am not good enough to be Len's wife.

Oh, dear diary, how my head is filled with troubling thoughts, and how my heart aches with pain. Len, when he came into court and passed me by on his way to the witness stand—he wouldn't even look at me! If I can tell you how that made me feel—like I was nothing to him! Like all that we shared together—our love, our plans for the future—as though they were all lies! I couldn't believe it. In all honesty, I believed that Len, when he was brought to the court—and knowing how he had tried to avoid coming to court—when he was finally brought face-to-face with me, that he would not be able to go through with it; he would stop the trial and come back to me and be my husband forever, and that this nightmare would finally end.

But no, not at all. The man I saw in court was a stranger to me. Well, that's not exactly true. I've seen that Len before, the Len who sometimes put on airs when we were in public, or when he felt he had to prove how important his family is for whatever reason. I didn't like it then, because Len was not the sweet and kind boy I fell in love with, and I certainly felt terrible when I saw him walk into the courtroom with his bodyguards, more than half a day late, and looking around like he had no idea what everyone was doing there.

And do you know what really surprised me? When you are called to testify, they make you swear on the Bible that you will tell the truth, the whole truth, and nothing but the truth, so help you God. And then nearly every word out of Len's lawyers when they spoke to the jury, those were all lies. Yes, lies! I couldn't believe it! Maybe the lawyers don't have to tell the truth. So what's the point? If the lawyers can lie, then it only seems natural that the witnesses are going to lie as well. That Len is mentally retarded or an imbecile, as Mr. Davis called him. That's just plain crazy. Or that I seduced Len instead of the other way around. Okay, I admit, and I have told this to Mr. Davis, that Len was not what I would call an experienced lover when we met. But he made up for it in a willingness to learn all he could about how to please a girl. He was very adventurous when it came to lovemaking. The point is, and what the jury must be made to believe, is that I never forced myself or my lovemaking on Len. He pursued me from the first day we met, and he kept at it because he said he loved me, and he wanted to make love to me, and he wanted to marry me and have a family.

And I believed him. That was all either of us ever wanted from each other.

The rest are all lies. Lies! I thought court is where people are supposed to tell the truth. I haven't heard one word of truth out of anyone's mouth in that courtroom except for Mr. Davis. Len's lawyers are unbelievable! Oh, they are smart, at least they seem to think they are, and they can talk, yes, but I have to wonder how smart they really are to get up there and try to win a case against a girl based on a pack of lies.

Len wouldn't even look at me all the time he was on the witness stand. I was so upset that I wept. I couldn't help it. It seemed like a nightmare to me. At one point I had to leave the court and go to the ladies' room. There is a young woman reporter I like very much, and she seems to like me. Her name is Grace Robinson, and she writes for the *Daily News*, though I think some of her stories have been carried by the wire services and are read all over the country. That's another thing about this trial that is unbelievable—how it has attracted so much attention not only here in New York, which is understandable given who Len's family is, but all over the country as well. All over the world! Why? Because of the color of my skin? Why is that such a big deal? "Oh, but it is," Mr. Davis said when I asked him. "That, young lady, is a very big deal indeed. And that is why we are here in this court faced with this lawsuit."

In any case, I met Grace Robinson in the ladies' room during a break, what they call a recess in the trial—as if we were all schoolchildren and allowed out to play. She could see that I was crying. It was after Len had been on the stand and when he refused to even look at me. She was very kind. She told me that the question of race and class had become so prominent now because of all of the changes taking place in the country, and that it wasn't just about this case, but about race relations all over the world. She is very intelligent and obviously well educated. It made me feel sad to think of how I was never able to improve my education, and how much I always wanted to be more than just a servant in someone else's home. I suppose to that degree what they say about my marrying Len is true—that I did see it in part as an opportunity to improve myself, and certainly as a way to give my children a better chance to be successful in life. But does that make it wrong? I don't think so. Am I wrong to want to better myself, and also my hopes for the future? No, not at all. And besides, that was only part of it. I wouldn't have agreed to marry Len if I hadn't loved him first and above all else.

Then, while we were in the ladies' room, Grace Robinson asked me something that really made me think. She said, "Do you believe that Leonard is still in love with you?"

Then, even before I answered, she looked me in the eyes and said, "Well, I do."

I thought about it for a second instead of answering right away. Of course, I have always wanted to believe that Len still loves me. I realized that of course, in my heart I believe he still loves me, and so I asked her why she thought that. She said that it was obvious to her Len was almost totally under the control of his father and that, even though he was over twenty-one, he still felt obligated to do whatever his father demanded that he do. But, she said, there was something about Len that impressed her. She said she had interviewed Len when he was coming back to our home one evening when the story first broke—I remember the story—and that his reaction then, when he told her he married the woman he loves, she believed him. And then she said something that really made me wonder. Maybe, she said,

Len is just doing all this to appease his father. Maybe what he really wants is for me to win and to save the marriage. And, she said, that I was doing the right thing, the brave thing, and the only hopeful thing to prove my love and possibly save the marriage by not taking the money and by going to court, which would also prove that it was never about the money.

I was so glad that someone else—an obviously intelligent woman such as Grace Robinson, a reporter—could look at this case and see it the way I did. Certainly to get at his family money was never my reason for marrying Len. *No!* That's not true at all. And Grace Robinson could see that. Otherwise why not just take the money? It had been reported—in fact, Grace had written—that I refused large cash offers from the Rhinelanders to accept the annulment. Because money and the Rhinelander name were never why I agreed to marry Len. There have been other boys from good families and with money who tried to court me; but no, I did what I did with Len. I agreed to go off with him to Cape Cod and to live with him as husband and wife for one reason and one reason only: because I love him, and I believed that he loved me. In talking with Grace Robinson, I knew that in my heart of hearts, I still believe Len loves me. A feeling like that, like what we have for each other, doesn't just go away because your father says so.

And for that reason, even though it hurts so much what I am going through by insisting on this trial, I do it because I am honoring what Len told me to do in his note, when he told me to fight, and because I believe it is the right thing to do.

Now that Grace Robinson mentioned it, she got me thinking. Also, and this may be crazy, and which is something I have never told anyone, not even Mr. Davis and what I share only here with my dear diary, is that I believe Len told me to fight because he wants me to win—of course he does! And when it is all over, Len will come back to me, and we will have the life and the family we always wanted.

That's why I go through with it! And that is where I get my strength. Yes, it hurts terribly when I see Len and he ignores me in court—but what if it's all a big act? I do want to believe that it is all part of the way he has decided to act so as to look as though he is going along with everything his lawyers are doing to please his father, because he knows he must even though in his heart it is not true, and he wants to lose the case! Which is why he told me to fight in the first place! Oh, I do hope it's true.

I haven't mentioned this to anyone, certainly not to Mr. Davis, although I have tried to convince him not to be so hard on Len. But at the same time I understand, as Mr. Davis has made clear, he must do his job to the best of his ability, even if that means hurting Len, as long as it means getting the jury on our side and our winning the case, which is also, I believe, what Len wants.

Could it be true? Then, when the truth of our love is proved in court, Len will come back to me, and there will be nothing his family can do to stop him. And we will live together as husband and wife and have the family we dreamed of!

O God—*yes!* How I hope it's true!

CHAPTER TWENTY-ONE

Knowing Alice

When court resumed the next day with Rhinelander back on the witness stand, in response to Mills's probing—and although he often faltered, got confused, stammered, and blushed with embarrassment—Rhinelander recounted for the jury and the spellbound spectators and journalists how, for their first assignation he and Alice had traveled to New York City in his family's car, driven by the chauffeur, Mr. Ross Chidester. Rhinelander admitted the couple first begun their intimacies while in the car, necking heavily and petting. They checked into the hotel as husband and wife, and they stayed there for more than a week at Christmastime, hardly leaving their rooms. Rhinelander said that they engaged in sexual intercourse repeatedly, daily, sometimes two or even three times a day until Mr. Jacobs and Mr. Strong arrived to take Leonard away and pack him off on an extended trip arranged by Rhinelander Senior in a failed effort to separate the young lovers and keep Leonard away from Alice until he might be cured of his infatuation.

"And did that work? Sending you away?" Mills inquired. "What happened?"

"Well, no . . . we . . . It didn't work because . . . be . . . be, we stayed in touch . . . we . . . through the letters."

"I see . . . meaning the letters Alice wrote to you while you were . . . traveling. For instance—and here, Your Honor, may it please the court—I would submit this letter, written by the defendant, and dated January 2, 1922."

"Proceed," Judge Morschauser intoned.

"Thank you, Your Honor."

Mr. Mills asked the witness, "This date, January 2, 1922, would be immediately following the stay at the Hotel Marie Antoinette. Is that correct?"

"It is," Leonard confirmed.

Mills nodded and said, "And I read from the letter: 'Now, Lenard, on the level, I will say, dear, you have been lovely to me. But when it comes to give Edward back his ring, know that you hold the same of me. You want me, as you say, and you do not want me to go about with others. But Leonard, if you want me to keep steady company with you, I love you enough to be true to you, dear, but you will after give me a ring, a right one like what Ed gave me, and if you do, you will never hear any more about that man.'"

I made a note to remind the jury that Rhinelander was traveling at this time, having been sent away by his father, and that he would later be attending a ranch school in Arizona; therefore, for the lovers to stay in touch, Rhinelander would have had to be the one who initiated, and who kept up the correspondence with Alice, as she would have had no way of knowing where to send her letters. This was important to show that Leonard, as much as if not even more so than Alice, had worked to keep the love affair alive even during this time of enforced separation.

Mr. Mills chose to read selections from Alice's letters that were described as "unprintable" in the press in an effort to show

how she used references to sex and her ability to please Leonard sexually to retain control over the weak-minded sex slave by writing vivid descriptions of their intimate times together. Again, Judge Morschauser chose this time to advise those ladies still present in the courtroom that they would be subjected to explicit sexual references and even descriptions of depraved sex acts in the letters such that they might not wish to hear or even to know about; and he gave them another opportunity to absent themselves. Once again, only two or three ladies chose to leave; other ladies, waiting in the halls, rushed in to fill the abandoned seats in the gallery.

In a letter from Alice dated May 19, 1922, she wrote that she had made a new friend, a young woman who introduced her to other young men and women: "But none appeals to me like my dear Leonard," Mills read from the letter, noting that this time she had spelled Leonard's name correctly, "and I was just thinking of you the other evening, how you have caressed and held me, and wanted me badly at times. Now dear all of those things come in my mind. I only wished you was here to do it to me now."

Mills paused; he looked at the jury, and he shook his head with an expression of mild repugnance, as though to remind them exactly what Alice was wishing Leonard had been there to do to her.

In her letter Alice went on to describe how she often reread Leonard's letters while she lay naked in her bed.

"You made me feel very passionate for the want of you," Mills read from another of her titillating epistles, "telling me how happy my little hand has often made you feel, and several other things, but can't help to tell you. Gee, please come to me, Len, because I want to feel you again like that. . . . You can always have it, and be at your service."

Here Mills stopped reading, shook his head, and looked up at the jury.

I stood to declare that I was still desirous of keeping the filth out of this case—though of course this was hardly true.

Mills replied, however, "Well, that is impossible."

Mills suggested Alice's letters, though clearly sexually explicit, were vital as evidence to prove that it had been her intent all along to use her "sexual powers" to induce Leonard to marry her, first with actual physical enticements, and then with repeated reminders of their intimate relations and promises of more to come. Finally, Mills said, when that wasn't enough, Alice tried to provoke his jealousy. One such letter in particular was brought to the attention of the court; in it Alice recounted how she had met the popular blackface entertainer, Al Jolson, while she was employed at a summer camp in the Catskills. Jolson, she implied, had flirted with her.

"*He was in swimming, but he is some flirt with the girls,*" Alice wrote. "*There is four fellows with him. His cottage is next to ours, and they had instruments and we had some orchestra here today.*"

In a letter written in May 1922, Mills claimed Alice revealed her ultimate plan to get Leonard to marry her. "*And I do hope you are going to reward me for it in making you happy. . . . I pray and hope every night I wished Len, you was my husband, what things I would tell you, and make you happy, but I do not want to tell you yet because, I do not own you yet. . . . I often wish you and I was down at the Antoinette again, but I am afraid, we will never see it any more. I do not want to go to a hotel any more what we should have Len, our own little house and we could go up whenever we wanted.*"

By September, Mills claimed that when her letters still hadn't produced the result Alice hoped for, she tried a new tactic: the prospect of losing her forever. Alice wrote,

> Len, I want you, to forget me try and think you never knew me, it was only a dream, as I am not, going to write no more, as you after do the right thing, for your father. . . . But you will after forget me completely, until you get at age. That's if I am not taken, before that, you can have me. . . . All of this, is going to be a waste of time, which I can see now. You could have married just as easily as not before you went away, but your money came first before me, or we could have kepted it a died secrt, which nobody would ever, had known. And I could be living home, And not working, like I am, And you away having a gret time, what you spend in going around, it would keep me, nicely. . . . If I cant have you now Len you will never get me, in the future, as I will fall back on the one I love second best, from you . . . I never want you to bother me again, dear until you are at age, Probly then you will be to late, entirely, I am afraid you will. . . . I hope you read over severl times, And Understand it right. And get the right idea.

This ploy apparently worked. Mr. Mills told the jury that by now Leonard was completely under Alice's "spell" to the point where, as soon as he was of age, he left the Arizona ranch school he was attending and headed straight back to New Rochelle to find Alice. Leonard then took Alice on the road trip to New England, including Cape Cod; and then, upon returning to New Rochelle, now thoroughly "induced" by Alice's will and under her control, he relented to her demands and married her.

Next, in an obvious effort to bolster Rhinelander's claim of racial fraud, Mills questioned Leonard about his understanding of the effect it had on the Jones family when Alice's sister Emily had married a Black man. Leonard testified, "Between the months of May and September 1924, in the presence of Alice and Mr. and Mrs. Jones, Mrs. Jones told me that they had done everything in their power to prevent Emily from marrying Brooks; but, seeing that it was of no avail, they denied Emily and Brooks the house for two years. Mrs. Jones told me they were not colored—she assured me that they were English—they were born in England. She said, 'The first time we ever saw a colored person was on our arrival in America, while walking on Sixth Avenue.' And she told me how they were surprised and didn't know what Negroes were. Then Alice entered the conversation and said, 'Of course we are not colored. We never associate with colored people and never will.'"

This was extraordinary testimony and clearly perjurious. I was astonished. I couldn't believe that Mills would allow such demonstrably false statements to issue from his client's mouth while he was under oath; and I couldn't wait to cross-examine the witness to expose this blatantly false testimony. What, we were expected to believe Grace and George Jones had never seen an African? Last time I inquired, I was assured there were people of African descent living in England; yes, and Negroes to be seen on the streets of London. But Mills was just getting started. He then asked Leonard to describe his reaction when Alice was declared colored in the newspapers shortly after they were married and while they were living together at the Joneses' home.

"Was anything said at that time by Alice Jones as to whether she was of colored blood or white?" Mills asked.

"Yes," Leonard said.

"What did she say on that subject?"

"I told Alice what the newspapers said. She said, 'This is terrible; it is not true.'"

Leonard went on to say that Alice had denied she was colored not only to him, but also to the reporters who questioned her.

According to Leonard, Alice told them, "I am white, and I shall sue the newspapers through my attorney, Judge Swinburne."

Another blatant lie. Alice did not engage Judge Swinburne as her attorney. She barely knew him until after she was served with the annulment papers. Leonard went on to falsify the circumstances under which he left the Jones home with Leon Jacobs, and with his promise to return. He claimed that Alice assured Jacobs she was white, and that her family planned to sue the newspapers for reporting that she was colored. But then a few days later, when Jacobs returned and still nothing had been done to file suit, Leonard maintained this failure to act was what finally convinced him that Alice had lied.

Rhinelander testified that he left the Jones home with Jacobs because, in Rhinelander's words, "There was no doubt in my mind," that Alice had deceived him as to her race.

With that statement in evidence, Mills turned to me and pronounced, "Your witness."

CHAPTER TWENTY-TWO

My Nitwit

Rhinelander had been on the witness stand four days giving his direct testimony; I commenced cross-examination on the fifth day of his appearance. There was no doubt in my mind, as I rose to question the plaintiff, that Mills had been partially successful in deceiving the jury (and, for that matter, the reporters, and the general public following the trial) into believing that young Kip was indeed a weak-minded dupe, a sheltered society youth, a neophyte rich boy seduced by an older, sexually experienced colored woman; and that he had then been entrapped in a marriage based on sexual enslavement and lies.

There was an element of truth to this belief, which is always the best way to foster a lie: conceal it within the subterfuge of verisimilitude. I would show Kip was not only weak-minded, but more important, he was weak of character. He was deeply ambivalent—a man who seemed at times to be at odds with himself. And, as to the truth, Alice certainly was an older, attractive colored girl with some experience in sexual matters, which was, I would seek to show, why Rhinelander pursued her with such purpose. And, yes, certainly it is also true that

Alice saw marriage to Leonard as her ultimate goal in the relationship; but this could be said of any proper young woman who enters into a love affair with a man expecting it to result in marriage and the beginning of a family. That this outcome may have been unrealistic given the vast gulf in the lovers' respective stations in life was a consideration that should have been Leonard's to determine, and not necessarily a hindrance to Alice's dream. Any young woman from whatever walk of life is subject to the storybook tale of the simple but beautiful young maiden who is carried off to a life of bliss and comfort by a handsome prince. With this flimsy and yet persuasive basis of truth in Rhinelander's testimony in mind, I stood; I approached the witness warily, as though sizing him up for the kill; and I began my cross-examination gently, one might even say respectfully, as appearing to give Rhinelander the benefit of the doubt concerning his alleged intellectual handicap. I was careful to treat him as the poor excuse for a man that he had allowed his lawyer to portray him as, even while I sought to prove it was a charade and not to be believed. I also wanted to give Rhinelander an opportunity to feel somewhat at ease with my questioning before I began a more forceful grilling in an effort to expose Leonard as the actual perpetrator of the fraud.

"Mr. Rhinelander," I started in my most solicitous tone, "because of your . . . *affliction of speech*, and your *weak intellect*, I want to be just as gentle as I possibly can with you. Do you understand that, sir? Am I making myself clear?" I asked with just the slightest trace of sarcasm creeping into my intonation.

Leonard replied, "I do."

"You do? Very good. And . . . will you keep carefully in mind that, if I ask you any question that you don't completely understand, you are at liberty to tell me so?" I went on, treating him like an imbecile, befitting his attorney's characterization.

Again Leonard replied that he understood. It should have been obvious, even to a supposed idiot, that I was mocking him.

"I will try to make my questions clear to you, sir." I hesitated, looked him over carefully; and then with a slight tilt of my head, as though not entirely convinced, I inquired, "Your mind is all right now, isn't it?"

Leonard said, "I believe it is."

"You *believe* it is. Very good. I will proceed upon your belief."

I turned to cast a quick glance at the jury, not quite a smirk; I rolled my eyes, and saw I had them a bit amused with where this was heading.

"Your trouble is that you stammer?" I asked and turned quickly back to face the witness. "*Is that right?*"

"Ah, yes, it is," Rhinelander admitted.

"Fine, and as you sit there now, Mr. Rhinelander, you are telling the men of this jury, and His Honor, Judge Morschauser, you are telling them that your mind's all right, *isn't it?*" I said and raised my voice noticeably, adding just a trace more sarcasm.

Rhinelander said, "Yes."

Here I changed tone to affect what I expected to sound like a note of sincere sympathy, and I turned again to look at the jury.

"Now, sir, you don't want your attorney, Mr. Mills, to have you appear as—*and you don't want this jury to gather the impression that you are an imbecile? A stuttering nut!*" I declared, apparently somewhat in shock at the very suggestion.

I heard a few muted expressions of mirth from the gallery as Leonard struggled to say, "N . . . n . . . no . . . I d d do not want anyone to th. th . . . th . . . to believe that!"

"*Of course you don't!*" I exclaimed. "Why, no one wants to be thought of as mentally incompetent, especially in such an important matter as how *or why* one has chosen to marry, and then decided *to dispose of one's wife.* Isn't that true, Mr. Rhinelander?"

"What . . ." Rhinelander managed to utter, and he attempted to go on but could only manage more stuttering.

With that, I turned back to face the witness and, without waiting for his response, I allowed a more forceful tenor to take hold of my voice.

"I said, sir, *you don't want this jury to have any impression that you are an idiot, do you?*"

"No."

"Good, sir, very good, though I have to wonder *why you allowed yourself* to be described as mentally retarded in the first place. But never mind that; it is done. We shall seek to undo it—*what?*

"Your only difficulty, sir, is that you have this unfortunate impediment in your speech; is that correct?"

"Yes."

"Now, let us go back to 1921, to the fall of 1921, when you met . . . this girl." I indicated Alice. "Was your mind all right then?"

"Yes."

Here I became more emphatic. "Sir, you don't want this jury to get the impression from anything that Mr. Mills said, or anything that Mr. Mills had you say, you don't want this jury to believe that *you didn't know what you were doing in 1921*, do you?"

"No," Leonard snapped, and I could see he was beginning to grow more uncomfortable with this line of questioning.

Good, I thought; *it's your fault for letting your lawyer portray you as an idiot.*

"Your only trouble back in 1921, when you met Alice and began to court her, your mental challenge was that you stuttered? Is that right?"

"It is, yes."

"But your vision: *you could see all right*, could you?"

"Yes," Leonard said.

"You did begin to court Alice, in 1921, didn't you, sir?"

"I met her . . . yes."

"*You met her?* Let's get this straight. This is important. You drove your fancy new automobile—which your father had just purchased and given you as a gift—you drove from Stamford, Connecticut, here, to New Rochelle, in your expensive new roadster, not once but any number of times, to see Alice; you called her on the telephone daily; you wrote letters to her; *and you did this to court her.* Alice wasn't coming to you at the Orchards in her fancy new roadster and taking you out for rides, was she?"

"N . . . n . . . no . . ." Rhinelander finally uttered his answer.

"Of course she wasn't! . . . *You* courted *her, sir. Correct?*" I nodded, and again turned back to look at the jury, and I shook my head in apparent frustration. "Of course you did. It wasn't Alice pursuing you, was it?"

Rhinelander made no response.

"Sorry. What did you say, sir?"

"I, I suppose you could say . . ." he managed at last and then broke off.

Then I asked, "How do you feel now? Can you talk fairly clearly?"

"Maybe . . . yes."

"Well, let me get to the heart of it. Do you recall courting Alice?"

"I . . . think so," Leonard said and he trailed off.

"I see. . . . *You think so. . . . Well, let's hope so. . . .* You do have a mind, after all, and a memory. It is when you get excited, is it, that you stutter a little more than usual? That you get confused. . . . Is that how your affliction works?"

Leonard shifted uncomfortably in the witness chair and blushed as if it had just dawned on him that I was playing with his mind and attempting to expose him to the jury as a faker. He cast a quick look at his counsel, as though hoping for some relief, as he said, "It is . . . yes, that's correct."

I turned and gestured to Alice.

"This is your wife, *isn't it, Mr. Rhinelander?*" I declared emphatically. "This girl sitting here, Alice Beatrice Jones Rhinelander; *she is your wife*, correct, sir? You married her, did you not? *Sir, would you please look at Alice and confirm for this jury that this young woman is your wife, the woman you married, and who are now seeking to do away with?*"

Leonard fairly mumbled, "Yes."

"Your Honor—" Mills stood to object.

"Sir? I'm sorry," I cut Mills off, as if concerned that the lawyer was having difficulty hearing. "Mr. Rhinelander, if you would, please speak up so Mr. Mills can hear. Mr. Mills, we know, is somewhat hard of hearing."

Then I turned back to the witness. "What did you say, sir? LOOK AT HER!" I nearly yelled. "*This is your wife, sitting here—is it not, sir?*"

"Yes—"

"*Yes!* Of course it is your wife, Alice Rhinelander, indeed! You seduced and married the girl. And now wish to be done with her, correct?"

"I . . . I . . . I do, yes."

"You do what?"

"I don't . . ."

"*Look at her, sir!*"

Mills was on his feet. "Your Honor! Counsel is badgering the witness!"

"I am not badgering the witness," I protested. "I have simply asked that he look at his wife and tell me—tell this court and the members of the jury—that he has decided *of his own free will* to dispense with this girl as his lawful wife. *That is the matter before the jury, is it not?*"

"Indeed," Mills concurred. "Therefore there is no reason for—"

"Wait just a moment. I for one, and I'm sure there are others in this courtroom who would like to hear *this man*, the husband, indeed *the plaintiff* who has initiated this action against his wife: I would like to hear him tell the jury *why. Why does he choose to dispose of his wife?*"

"Asked and answered, Your Honor," Mr. Mills declared. "The action was commenced due to the false claims as to the purity of her blood."

"Fine," I said. "I see." I turned back to the witness.

"Now let me hear *you* say it, sir. Let me hear you tell this jury that you *rejected* your wife because she supposedly *lied* about the purity of her blood. *Is that it?*" I demanded of Rhinelander. "I would like to hear it from you, sir."

"Yes," Rhinelander admitted weakly.

"Yes, what?"

"Yes . . . due to her colored blood . . . that is why, why I, I, I . . ." he trailed off, unable to finish the sentence.

"Oh, is it really? Well"—and I shook my head in disbelief—"*we shall see about that!*" I threatened. And to Judge Morschauser I asked, "Now, Your Honor, may I please proceed without opposing counsel's repeated objections?"

Judge Morschauser said, "You may do so."

"But Your Honor," Mr. Mills protested, "surely there must be some *decorum* to opposing counsel's line of questioning—"

"This is cross-examination," the judge declared. "Within bounds, of course . . . which the court will determine."

"Decorum, the man says . . . *decorum*. And yet"—I turned to face Judge Morschauser—"thank you, Your Honor," I said and shot Mr. Mills a self-satisfied smirk. "Yes, decorum. We would like to see it *from both sides*; would we not?"

To Rhinelander I said, "Sir, tell me, and tell the jury, did your wife look the same as she does now when you met her in 1921?"

Rhinelander said, "Yes."

"I see. And you are now looking at her with her hat off, correct?"

"Yes."

"And she looked just the same then as now? Her hair was the same as it is now?"

"Yes."

"And yet you are telling the men of this jury that *no inquiry arose in your mind as to her color . . . her race?* When you looked upon your wife when first meeting her in 1921, you . . . you saw her hair, you looked at her hands, and there was no question in your mind as to . . . as to her color; that it was . . . not necessarily apparent. . . . You had no question *that she was pure white?*"

"None whatsoever, no."

"I see. . . . And, you said, you see quite well—*what?* Tell us, how is your eyesight? Are you color-blind, Mr. Rhinelander?" I asked.

"I am not, no."

"Very good. So you can distinguish *Black from white* . . . and *brown from white?* You are able to perceive the difference in these hues of skin tone, correct? And even perhaps in the texture of hair—*yes?*"

"Yes."

"And yet . . . when you met this girl, and when you met her family—when you met her father and her brother-in-law—still *you had no inkling that she had some Black blood?* How is that possible, sir . . . given, as you say, that your eyesight is all right?"

"*No!*" Rhinelander asserted. "I didn't question her because . . . *she* told me she was white."

"Oh, of course. Now I understand: *she told you* she was white, did she? Just offered it out of the blue?" Here I mimicked a girl's voice. "'Oh, hello, Mr. Rhinelander. My name is Alice, and I am a nice girl of *pure white blood.*' Or did you *ask* her if she were white? Because perhaps there was some question in your mind? And, if so, why? Because truthfully you had some doubt in your mind—*what?* Or, perhaps not. Because you just told us that you are able to distinguish Black from white. Did you not see, when you looked at your wife, could you not see that she has some Black blood? Was that not *apparent to you*, sir, at first, and then upon close association with Alice and her family? You say, because *she told you* she was pure white? Yet you met her father. . . . Now tell me, if I told you I was green, would you believe me?"

This provoked laughter from the gallery and from some of the jurors.

Rhinelander was getting flustered. "No . . . I . . . well, I didn't . . . I was . . . N-n-n-n-no, I didn't."

"You didn't what?"

"I couldn't tell—"

"Just a moment. Let's get this straight, for the members of the jury. And when you met her father, George Jones . . ." I turned and indicated Alice's father in the gallery.

"You can see George Jones, correct?"

"Yes."

All eyes turned to gaze upon the very noticeably colored visage of Alice's father.

"You know George Jones, do you not?" I asked the witness.

"I do, yes."

"In fact, *you lived in his home* with him and with your wife, Alice, who is Mr. Jones's daughter . . . for some time, did you not?"

"Yes, I did."

"And it *never occurred to you*, given what is plain to see of

Mr. Jones that he is a man of color—why, it never dawned on your . . . as we have established, your perfectly rational and discerning mind, that his daughter Alice must indeed have some colored blood? Let's be clear, because . . . well, we know that Mr. Mills has sought to portray you as an imbecile but he has never suggested that you are color-blind."

"Your Honor, I must object." Mills was on his feet, ear horn stuck to his head. "*Imbecile*—"

"All right then, brain-tied, backward, mentally slow, weak-minded papa's boy, sex slave, however you wish to portray Mr. Rhinelander's impaired mental capacity, he sits here upon the witness stand, and under oath, and he testifies that he is of sound mind and that he can see clearly. He is his own evidence as to his mental soundness, correct?"

I turned back to the witness and said, "But sir . . . Mr. Rhinelander, when you first saw your wife's father, George Jones—whom you can see now seated in the gallery with Mrs. Jones and Alice's sisters—are you telling the men of this jury that it *never dawned on your* . . . shall we say *innocent mind?* Untutored mind? Call it what you like. . . . It never occurred to you, sir, that Alice, as the daughter of Mr. Jones, whom we all can see is clearly a man of color, must therefore have some colored blood?"

"I . . . *no*, I didn't think she has some Black blood because *she told me she was pure white!*"

"Oh, that's right, why—*I forgot*. Of course: *Alice told you*. . . . Do you honestly expect—as you sit there and look at the men seated in the jury box—do you honestly believe that these intelligent, mentally competent men who all presumably have good eyesight, do you expect the men of the jury to believe that, sir?"

Mr. Mills objected. "He's badgering the witness, Your Honor. Mr. Rhinelander can't be expected to know what the men on the jury believe."

"Oh, badgering, am I?" I said with all the contempt I could muster. "Well, wait just a minute. We are here in this court to prove or to dispute a lawsuit, correct? And we do so by proving or failing to prove our case before the jury. I believe that is the way it works. But please excuse me if the witness—who is the plaintiff in this matter—if Mr. Rhinelander is not expected to understand *why* we are here, even if it is *at his insistence.* Badgering the poor brain-tied . . . color-blind . . . lad. So sorry. . . . But surely this is his lawsuit to be decided—"

And I turned back to the witness before giving the judge a chance to respond.

"Well, now, Mr. Rhinelander," I said sharply, "I will move along. If you will, please take us through the events surrounding your *abandoning* your wife. You left your wife, sir, you left Alice in the lurch, didn't you? *You walked out on her*, and you *coldheartedly abandoned* your wife on November twentieth, 1924—*did you not?*"

Mills again, "Your Honor—"

"Well, what would you call it? If, as a man, if you walk out on the woman who loves you, your new wife—"

"The witness may answer the question," Judge Morschauser ruled.

"I did—"

"Louder, sir, *please!* For the benefit of Mr. Mills and the jury."

"I did!"

"*You did what?*"

"I . . . I . . . I . . . I . . ."

"You can't say it, can you, Mr. Rhinelander? Because you know it's a *cowardly act! You left her! You abandoned your wife!* Of course you did! You deserted your wife as she and her family were *besieged by the press*, and under attack by racist hooligans. You walked out on your wife and left her and her family *in danger that you created. Why?* And why then, when Mr. Jacobs appeared at the Joneses' home, why did you leave this girl at that time, sir? Was she *not good enough* for you? Or was she *not good enough for your father?*" I demanded.

Again Mills stood to object. "Your Honor, Mr. Davis is again harassing the witness. He's making statements—"

"I beg your pardon, sir. *Statements?* No. I am asking appropriate questions in my cross-examination. The witness has been portrayed as somewhat weak-minded, brain-tied, as it were, if not an imbecile, by you, sir! I want to know what induced this poor fellow to abandon his wife after one month of marriage. *Was it his idea?* This is an important question."

Judge Morschauser said, "You may continue."

"Thank you, Your Honor," I said. Before turning back to the witness, I chanced to glance out at the audience and to give the jury a quick look. By my appraisal, I could see that everyone in the room was fully engaged in where I was going with the witness, the plaintiff, the wealthy son of the aristocracy who had brought the lawsuit against the young girl seated at the defense table—and who was from time to time weeping into her dainty white handkerchief. I had everyone's undivided attention, and I had the witness right where I wanted him.

"By the way, is your father, *Philip Rhinelander*, is he here, sir?" I asked. "I haven't seen him."

"No, I don't believe he is."

"I see," I said. "And, if you could, tell us who was with you when you *abandoned* your wife?"

Leonard again looked at the lawyers seated at the plaintiff's table, as if hoping for some signal before answering, "My attorney Mr. Jacobs."

"This gentleman, seated here, Mr. Leon Jacobs, he is *your* attorney?" I asked incredulously. "Or is he more accurately *your father's* attorney?"

"He's mine . . . and my father's—"

"Who pays him, sir? Do you pay him?"

"I . . . I . . . I—"

"You don't pay for anything, do you? Your father pays for everything! Why, he's paying for this entire trial, *isn't he?*"

"Your Honor," Mills objected.

Judge Morschauser said, "Mr. Davis, please confine your examination to actual questions . . . and refrain from editorializing."

"Yes, Judge, of course. Please accept my apology."

I turned back to Rhinelander and asked, "You left with this man." I pointed to Leon Jacobs. "With Mr. Jacobs, *your father's lawyer.* You both got into an automobile that was closely curtained, correct?"

"Yes."

I commenced asking my questions rapidly now, to show the jury that Rhinelander, brain-tied wretch that he had been made out to be, was actually having no difficulty following my inquiries.

"Mr. Jacobs hurried you into that automobile," I said, deliberately putting words into Rhinelander's mouth.

"I left there of my own initiative—"

"Just a minute, sir. Did I ask you that question, Mr. Rhinelander? He, Mr. Jacobs, is *your father's attorney*—"

"He's *my* attorney!" Rhinelander blurted out.

"Oh, Mr. Jacobs is *your attorney*; not your father's attorney? So you are able to make that distinction, *aren't you?*"

Rhinelander said, "You asked me who hurried me."

I turned back to the witness and said, "He, this man, Mr. Jacobs, *your attorney*, he hurried you into that automobile, *did he not?*"

"No. *I* hurried into the automobile."

"*You* hurried. So you are also able to make that distinction. Your mind is working very clearly, isn't it?"

"Yes."

"Very good, because we will have some *important questions* for you that will require a good mind, and not the brain-tied mind of an imbecile. Now, sir, tell us where you went after you got into that automobile with Mr. Jacobs? Oh . . . who is sitting here . . . *oh, I see—just a moment.* Mr. Jacobs has his back turned! *How extraordinary!* He's turned and faced away from the well of the court. . . . *How odd!* Is it that he does not care to hear how his client is responding to my questions? I would like it if I could have the plaintiff's counsel's attention."

Jacobs was indeed sitting facing away from the witness stand, as though he could not bear to see how I might be mangling and impugning his client's honesty and credibility.

I turned back to the witness. "Tell us, sir, if you will: Where did you go after you hurried away from your wife with this man who appears distracted . . . looking off into space?"

"I went to Jamaica, Long Island. Mowack Avenue."

"And what kind of place is it?"

"That is a high-class boardinghouse."

"Of course it is high-class," I snapped. "Why, you wouldn't go to a low-class boardinghouse, would you? A man of your social standing? *A Rhinelander!* Perish the thought. You are intelligent enough to make that distinction. . . . Had you ever been there before?"

"No."

"Who took you there?"

"My attorney."

"I see . . . *your attorney.* By that you mean this gentleman, Mr. Jacobs, who still prefers to look anywhere *but at you!* His client. You won't look at your wife; he won't look at his client—"

"Your Honor, please!" Mr. Mills protested.

"So sorry," I said. "Please excuse me. I am happy to see, Mr. Mills, *that you at least* are paying attention."

This brought about a murmur of laughter from the gallery and smiles from a few members of the jury.

To the witness I said, "How long did you stay at this *high-class* boardinghouse?"

"One night."

I paused my questioning here and referred to some unrelated documents on the defense table; then I looked up at the jury as though I had made an important discovery.

"You say . . . *one night*. And then you went out of state, *did you?*"

"Yes, I—"

I interrupted. "You quickly left the State of New York and absconded to New Jersey, is that correct?"

"Well, I don't know . . . that evening, I did, yes . . . though I wouldn't say I absconded . . ."

"What would you call it, then? You are able to make that distinction? Very well. Your mind is fine, I see. Did you make any stops between the time that you abandoned your wife in New Rochelle . . . and for you to then get out of the State of New York?"

I wanted to make it appear that Rhinelander was on the run, though from what I had no idea: His wife? His father? The press? Perhaps all of them. The idea was to make him appear cowardly, a man running away from the marriage, shirking his responsibilities as a man and a husband; and, more importantly, fleeing from his wife in her time of need to appease his father.

"That evening I did, yes."

"What time did you abandon this young girl, your wife, Alice Rhinelander, who was in peril, besieged by angry racist mobs?"

"Around four in the afternoon."

Once again I chose to deliberately misquote him when I said, "What stop did you make in going from where you left your wife until you got to this high-class boardinghouse in New Jersey?"

Rhinelander quickly corrected me. "It isn't in New Jersey. It is in Jamaica, Queens."

"*Oh!*" I turned to the jury and gave them a slight smile. "Oh, yes, I am wrong. You are right. You corrected me, didn't you?"

"Yes, I did."

"Sir, you were happy with your wife, you were fine and quite pleased with Alice before you were forced to abandon her, were you not?"

"I . . . I wasn't forced. I left of my own initiative."

"*Of your own initiative, you say?* Did you call Mr. Jacobs or your father and ask *to be rescued* from the Joneses' home on your own initiative? To be saved from this girl's clutches? Let's call it what it was, you were *spirited away!* Of your own initiative? Is that your testimony? You were induced to leave this girl under *false pretenses*, were you not? Was that your idea to leave?"

"No, I didn't need to call them—"

"I see. They—your father's lawyer, and the other fellow, Mr. Strong, I believe his name is, the notary—these men would just *assume* that you needed to be rescued, is that what you are telling this jury? They *divined it*, and simply appeared at the Joneses' home to take you away. . . . And where did you go after you were spirited away?"

"I went to Washington."

"With this man, Mr. Jacobs, who, I see, *has finally decided* to look at you. Did you have some important business in Washington that required your immediate attention? That prompted you to abandon your wife *just one month* after your marriage? Whatever did you go there for?"

Rhinelander had no answer for this question.

"Oh, I see. . . . That's all right, Mr. Rhinelander, never mind. Whatever it was, it couldn't have been too important—*but it was important enough to take you away from your wife, wasn't it, sir?* You came back from Washington, after this business trip, for which purpose you don't remember, and then you went to the Robert Treat in Newark, correct?"

I could see that Rhinelander was nearly completely flustered; he was flushed and perspiring, shifting nervously in his chair. I decided to back off just a bit as the hour for lunch break approached, and to let him think that he was past the worst of it, off the hook, so to speak, before I would begin my final assault.

"That's right," Rhinelander asserted.

"Fine . . . is your brain working all right now, Mr. Rhinelander?"

"I believe so, yes."

"Thank goodness, because I don't want to confuse you. I am not trying to upset you. But we must know the answers to some *very important questions*, mustn't we? You understand the *gravity of the charges* you have brought against your wife in this lawsuit, *don't you, sir?* Given how your wife, *how this young girl has been portrayed here in this court by your lawyer.* Most despicably, I would say! Wouldn't you say so, sir?"

Mr. Mills leaped to his feet. "Your Honor, is there a question here? Or is counsel intent on upsetting the witness and disparaging counsel?"

"Mr. Davis—" the judge began.

"Your Honor, of course I am asking a reasonable question." Now I was interrupting the judge!

"I want to know if the witness—the plaintiff in *this shameless assault on a young girl and her family*—I want to know how Leonard Rhinelander *feels* about the way his wife and her family have been portrayed in this case before this jury. Is it *his idea* to *defame* his wife and her parents, her sisters? After all, this man." I pointed at Rhinelander. "He is the complaining party. His name is on the lawsuit aimed at *destroying the reputation of Alice*

Jones Rhinelander. This is his action against *his wife.* As I perceive it, this is important: to know his motive in attempting to discard a woman he professed to love."

Here I stopped speaking and looked around the room, as though to confirm that there was such an interest in the members of the jury as well as those spectators in the gallery; indeed, all those wherever they were who were fascinated by this trial would want to know Rhinelander's true intention, the real reason he decided to dispose of his wife.

"But, fine," I continued. "I withdraw the question. Let the jury decide if there is any actual fraud here other than how this girl has been portrayed as well as her good family: her father, George Jones, and her mother, Elizabeth. How they have been *misrepresented . . . insulted in this courtroom by plaintiff's counsel—*"

"Your Honor!" Mr. Mills interjected.

But I kept right at it. Lunchtime was drawing near, and I wanted to leave the jury with some food for thought.

"*Never mind!* I give that consideration to the good men of this jury to determine for themselves. I am charged to get to the truth of this man's intentions as he rushed about and left his wife alone to face the onslaught of the press, the hostile crowds, and the disgrace and heartache of having been abandoned by the man she loves . . . *after one month of marriage!* My God, it was some honeymoon—*what?*"

I turned back to the witness. "Now, sir, from the Robert Treat, you went right on through to Melrose, Long Island. Is that correct?"

"Yes."

"How did you go there?"

"By train."

"By yourself?"

"I was with . . . my attorney."

"*Of course you were!*" I agreed most emphatically. "Mr. Jacobs, your attorney—as you say—why, he wasn't about to let you out of his sight now, was he? Did you stop over anywhere on the way to Melrose?"

"Yes."

"Tell us: Where did you stop?"

"In the subway tube."

"The subway tube? What subway tube?"

"Ninth Avenue, I believe."

"*What for?*" I snapped.

"I . . . Mr. Jacobs . . ."

"Mr. Jacobs again? . . . Oh, goodness. *Who else?* Come now, Mr. Rhinelander, who else was with you?"

"Mr. Strong."

"Oh, yes, Mr. Strong," I said. "You forgot about him, didn't you? You forgot that Mr. Strong was with Mr. Jacobs, wasn't he?"

"He met us there."

"Where?"

"In the subway tube."

"Just a moment. You say Mr. Strong met you in the subway tube while you were on your way to Melrose, Long Island—*whatever for?* How did Mr. Strong know to meet you there? And I might just as well ask you: What did you do with these gentlemen in that subway station?"

Leonard began to stutter. "I . . . I . . . I—"

"Were you hiding from the public . . . from the press?"

"I, I, I . . . don't think I was, no—"

"Come now, sir. You have a meeting with Mr. Jacobs, your father's lawyer, and the other gentleman, Mr. Strong, who also is employed by your father. You meet them of all places *in a subway station in Manhattan.* Tell the men of the jury: What did you do in that subway station with Mr. Jacobs, your father's attorney, and Mr. Strong, a notary also employed by your father, Philip Rhinelander, *correct?*"

"I, I, I . . . I *signed the complaint*," Leonard managed to get out.

"*Ah-ha! You signed the complaint?*" I repeated, apparently dumbfounded. "Do you mean that you signed the complaint with a bill of particulars that is the basis of the lawsuit that resulted in this trial?" I held up the document and displayed it for the jury. "Do you mean *this* document? You signed this complaint in the subway station with this gentleman, Mr. Jacobs, and with—*where is he?*"

I stopped and looked around the courtroom as though to see if Mr. Strong had made an appearance. "The other gentleman, the notary, Mr. Strong. He's not here today, is he? I thought I saw him earlier. Perhaps he left."

I turned back to face the witness. "You were keeping out of the way of the public, weren't you?"

"Yes, I was."

"You didn't like this notoriety—*what?*"

"No, I didn't."

"You were happy to cause it, and to bring it to your wife and her family, *but you didn't like it*."

"I didn't care for it."

"Of course not. You were a little timid about the public after the news of your marriage to your wife, Alice Rhinelander, once the news had come out in the press, *is that it?*"

"Yes."

"Now, Mr. Rhinelander, who picked out the subway station of all places in New York City—whose brilliant plan was it to choose the subway station for you to read through and sign a document of this importance? Was that your idea?"

Rhinelander appeared perplexed by the question. "I, I, I followed orders," he said with some difficulty and after a pause.

I registered my surprise. "*You followed orders?*" And I nodded while looking at the jurors. "*That, sir, is your testimony? You followed orders?*"

"Yes—"

"You *were ordered* to sign these papers in the subway station?"

"Yes."

"*I see! At last! That is exactly what we have been trying to get at!* Whose orders did you follow, sir?" I asked as though greatly relieved to have finally discovered the true cause behind the lawsuit.

"Mr. Jacobs."

"Mr. Jacobs! *Why, of course!*" I declared in a loud voice and turned to indicate the man seated at the plaintiff's table and who was now giving the proceedings his undivided attention. "*This man! Your father's lawyer!*"

"*My* lawyer!" Leonard protested.

"Your lawyer . . . *Did you hire him?*"

"I . . . I—"

"Of course you didn't! He came on orders from your father, isn't that so? Where did Mr. Jacobs give you those orders?"

"At the Robert Treat."

"Mr. Jacobs told you to go with Mr. Strong to New York?"

"Yes."

"You were *ordered* by *your father's attorney*, Mr. Jacobs; he *ordered* you to go to a subway station in Manhattan; and, once there, he *ordered* to sign this annulment action? Is that your testimony?"

"Yes."

"And you followed his orders?"

"I did."

"Well, Mr. Rhinelander, at last that is clear. But—*why?* Let us come back to that important question. Why did you follow Mr. Jacobs's orders? Only a few days before—two days, to be exact—you were living quite happily with your wife in her parents' home, *even after the story of your marriage to Alice Rhinelander was on the front page of newspapers all across this nation, and with the stories indicating in no uncertain terms that your wife has Black blood in her veins,* WHICH YOU KNEW IN ANY CASE! You knew it all along, even before you married her; and you declared it to at least one newspaper reporter, Grace Robinson. You told her you were aware your wife had some Black blood and that *it didn't matter to you, because you loved her regardless. Isn't that so, sir?*"

Rhinelander did not respond.

"And you continued to live with Alice as husband and wife knowing this: *knowing Alice has some Black blood!* It made no difference to you! Isn't that true, sir? And then you were whisked away! You were taken here and there for some unknown reason by this gentleman, Mr. Jacobs, your father's lawyer; and finally *you were ordered* to sign these annulment papers, legal documents initiating this lawsuit, documents that you read and swore to *in a subway station! But why? We still don't know why, Mr. Rhinelander.* Did you know, at the time you signed these papers, did you know *what* you were signing?"

"I did—"

"You read it, you read the complaint, and you read the bill of particulars, where it states, *in your words*, that you were *deceived as to the purity of your wife's blood*, you understood it when you signed it?"

"Yes," Rhinelander said.

"But—this is important, sir—when you swore to the allegations and the statements in these papers you meant every word of it; correct?"

"Yes," Rhinelander mumbled rather feebly, as if he understood where I was going with this and that he was now the one who was utterly trapped in all of the lies and in the fraud exposed as the bases of the suit.

"Let's be clear for the jury, Mr. Rhinelander. *This is important!* You didn't want to sign this paper, did you? *You were ordered to sign it.*"

"I did."

"But you just told this jury that *you were ordered to sign it!* Which is it: Did you sign it because you wanted to, because you believed every word of the complaint and the bill of particulars to be true? Or did you sign *because you were ordered by your father's lawyer to sign the document?*"

"I . . . wanted to sign it be, be, be . . . because . . . because of what I knew to be true."

"*What* did you know to be true?" I asked.

"That . . . I knew . . . that Alice was . . . that she was colored."

"Oh, so you did! I see. You just found this out, did you? And it was your wish to sign the papers because you *suddenly realized* while standing in the subway station, you *had a revelation* that your wife, Alice, this girl, who is seated here and being subjected to all this . . . *on your account, I might add,* and whom *you had abandoned* some days before, and whom you had continued to live with in her parents' home well *after* it was revealed in newspapers all across the nation, newspapers that you read, that your wife, Alice, was the daughter of a colored man and had some Black blood in her veins, you now knew—LOOK AT HER, SIR! LOOK AT YOUR WIFE!" I bellowed and actually caused Rhinelander to startle. He looked at me with an expression of shock and fear; but he would not look at Alice, and he made no answer.

"You are telling this jury, sir, that as you stood in the subway station reading the complaint, *then and only then* you knew *what had never crossed your mind before,* even after meeting and knowing your wife's father, George Jones—LOOK AT HIM,

Mr. Rhinelander! See Mr. Jones, your wife's father seated in the gallery: a fine-looking gentleman with dark skin—*what?* And after meeting and knowing and playing cards with Emily Jones's husband, Robert Brooks, a NEGRO! *Look at him!* Can you see him, sir? Can you see Mr. Brooks, and can you see that he is a Negro? But you want us to believe that it had only just then dawned on your poor brain-twisted comprehension, your imbecilic understanding that Alice had some Black blood? Is that what you are asking the men of this jury to believe? Or *is it not in fact the truth*, as you told us just moments ago, that you signed the complaint because you were *following orders, orders given to you by this man, Mr. Jacobs, your father's lawyer?*"

Rhinelander looked up at Judge Morschauser and said, "I can't answer that, Your Honor."

"*What?*" I demanded. "You can't answer? *Why?* Which is it, Mr. Rhinelander? It's a simple question even for someone who may be a bit weak-minded—which you assured us that you are not. Were you *ordered* to sign the complaint, or did you sign it because *you suddenly realized your wife has some Black blood in her veins?*"

"Both," Rhinelander managed to say after some stuttering, hence admitting that to him nothing was ever black or white; that he was ever of a divided and conflicted nature.

The admission allowed me to fathom the man's ambivalent character.

* * *

Judge Morschauser chose this time to adjourn for lunch. I sequestered myself with co-counsel, Judge Swinburne and Richard Keogh, that we might consider the progress in the cross-examination of the plaintiff and determine how to proceed once court was back in session.

I had hoped not to meet with Alice and her parents, because of how upset I knew Alice had become with my harsh treatment of her husband. It was clear to all that Rhinelander's appearance on the witness stand thus far had not gone well—that is, not for his side. We had the witness—in Judge Swinburne's words, in yet another prizefighting analogy—Rhinelander was "on the ropes." I had very nearly destroyed his credibility and his case. Were the jury to vote now, all believed, we would triumph.

However, that, my co-counsel and I were well aware, did not necessarily assure victory for Alice going forward. There was still much to overcome by way of proving Leonard Kip Rhinelander as the guilty party to the fraud alleged in the lawsuit. Because Rhinelander had been portrayed by his lawyer as a weak-minded boy entrapped by a clever and experienced Black woman; and as we had shown the jury how completely he was influenced and manipulated by his domineering father and his father's lawyer: those could just as easily work against us. I still felt it necessary to prove not only that the Rhinelander boy was the guilty party in the lawsuit, but that the suit was based on Rhinelander's fraud and therefore not on any deceit on Alice's behalf. I wanted also to show the jury the level of deceit in how the love affair had been portrayed; this was most important, for I believed I had to convince the men of the jury that Rhinelander knew exactly what he was doing when he seduced Alice; that he was in love with her in full knowledge that she was colored; that he and not Alice was the instigator in the seduction; that he was attracted to Alice; that he initiated sexual relations with her, not the other way around; and finally, that he was not the innocent victim of an experienced and lascivious Black woman's wiles.

For all that, thankfully, I had Rhinelander's own letters with which to unmask him. But the stage still needed to be set for the final act.

* * *

Alice was upset with me for the way I was, as she put it, "cruelly attacking Len." She felt badly for him, and asked that I not be so hard on him, so cruel to the man she still loved. I believe she may have retained some hope for the two of them to live together again as husband and wife if we were to succeed in the lawsuit without destroying and thus forever alienating Leonard; indeed, there was that scant hope the marriage might endure, being kept alive mostly among the ladies observing the trial, those who wished to believe that love would triumph over money, class, race, and the determined will of Philip Rhinelander. For evidence of this romantic wish, there was Leonard's note instructing Alice to fight the case; that was still seen by some as proof of his desire to salvage the marriage. I felt it necessary to disabuse Alice of this hope, for I knew that it was impossible for Philip Rhinelander to allow the marriage to succeed.

I tried, as gently as possible, to have Alice understand that it could never be so; the marriage was doomed because, as I firmly believed, Leonard was not and never could be his own man. If that were the case, if he were willing to take responsibility for his feelings and for his actions in seducing Alice and making her his wife, he never would have allowed his father and his father's lawyers to force him to sign the complaint and initiate the lawsuit in the first place.

Also, I wanted Alice to understand that the case at trial was not simply about the fate of their marriage. No. I hoped she would see that this case was never just about Leonard Rhinelander and Alice Jones; it was always about the Rhinelander family name; it was about race and class relations in America; about the mixing of the races in conjugal wedlock; and the encouragement of mixed-race offspring supposedly mongrelizing the white American race. A Rhinelander child of mixed race was unthinkable to Philip Rhinelander. The trial was also about class divisions, as the verdict would have a direct bearing on the Rhinelanders' guarded place in New York high society. It was a romantic fantasy to believe that there was any way for the marriage to endure. Regardless of the verdict, the marriage was finished.

As her lawyer, I had to admit that Alice was of mixed race because it was true to win the case; we could never have mounted a convincing defense if we claimed she was of pure white blood because, obviously, the evidence proved otherwise. But with that admission we necessarily eliminated any hope of saving the marriage, because saving the marriage would strike fear throughout a white society as embodied by Philip Rhinelander. To hope to win would mean attacking the prejudice that motivated Rhinelander Senior; and that initiative, unfortunately, could only be accomplished through humiliating the boy, Rhinelander's son, as a sort of surrogate for the father, and yet someone who had shown no sincere trace of the racial bias that motivated Philip Rhinelander.

How curious it was for me to understand, and to hope to convey to the jury, that it was not the parties themselves, not Alice and Kip and how they were being portrayed in this trial, nor the validity of their marriage vows, nor even the love they may have felt for one another that was on trial in this case. The trial was actually to decide whether the two young lovers *had the right* to marry given who they were, the color of their skin, and their respective stations in society; if they had the right to defy the strictures of race and class defined for them by their elders. There was the clash of generational as well as racial and social mores on trial in this case.

On the one hand, we had to show that Leonard was the seducer; that he made love to Alice and married her knowing full well that she was of mixed race; also that it was Leonard who kept the affair alive and the marriage a possibility; and finally that he was the one who made it a reality even after he had been captured and packed off by his father to parts far from Alice's influence. At the same time, we had the double-edged sword of proving that Leonard was a man who was free of the biases that motivated his father, and he was also a young man who was easily manipulated by others—his father, his father's lawyers and factotums—that, indeed, Kip Rhinelander was a man of such ambivalent nature that he made no distinction based on skin color, which idea carried with it the unspoken notion that he was ready prey for a conniving Black temptress; and, in sum, that Rhinelander was a generally weak-minded and easily manipulated man.

Actually, I would seek to prove that Rhinelander was attracted to Alice knowing her mixed color, in part because he was in revolt against his father's stern race and class distinctions. It was the boy's show of defiance against his overbearing father; and that was to be commended, not condemned. Leonard was comfortable in the Joneses' home, and at ease in company with Alice's Black in-laws—far more comfortable than he was with his own family. The Rhinelander boy was open-minded, one might say—indeed, progressive! And yet a Rhinelander! Perish the thought. Kip Rhinelander was a bundle of contradictions.

The Rhinelander fortune had been founded in part upon the sugar trade. That carried with it images of dark-skinned workers slaving in blazing hot canefields. Shipbuilding was another source of the vast Rhinelander wealth, and that made one think of the human cargo transported in the slave galleys. The sins of the father visited upon the son; the boy motivated by some unseen urges coursing through his pure white blood as a substitute for his father and his father's generation to ameliorate for the criminal behavior of the father and of the Founding Fathers.

On the other hand, what sort of man allows himself to be bullied into swearing to and signing a bill of particulars, in essence committing perjury while trapped by his father's lawyer in a subway tube knowing that the false statements it contains denigrate and convict the woman he professes to love? Why, one could argue—and the men of the jury might decide—of course, it is the same sort of man who is easily taken advantage of by a practiced swarthy seductress. (I could almost hear my colleagues mutter among themselves that it was precisely the sort of person who cannot distinguish Black from white who would lead this great nation into chaos; and from whom the likes of a young Leonard Rhinelander as a symbol of innocent, and therefore easily influenced, white males must be protected.)

We had to show that Leonard, as much as if not more than Alice, initiated the affair; that he was no innocent dupe; that he was in fact a randy young sexual and social adventurer attracted to a woman of obvious mixed race and lower class; and that he was the one who kept the torch burning with his inflamed love letters and his promises to make Alice his wife not because he was easily manipulated but because he loved her. He loved the idea of being in love with a girl such as Alice. She made him feel better about himself, better about who he was as a young American who was open to change even in defiance of his father and all the Rhinelander family stood for. The more difficult evidence I would need to show—not only to the jurors but also to Alice—was the influence of the imperious will of Philip Rhinelander; that, one might argue, was the will of reactionary white America. Yes, it was Rhinelander Senior—and indeed the white aristocracy he represented—that could not allow the marriage to succeed even if we were to win the lawsuit because it would mean the beginning of their downfall.

Hence it had to be recognized by Alice that her counsel, even as I might be attacking Leonard on the witness stand—which I was wont to do—I was actually endeavoring to show the jury that it was Rhinelander Senior's pride, and thus America's false pride, that was on trial here: it was the pride of the white race as personified by Philip Rhinelander that had to be thoroughly defamed and revealed as the curse of America's original sin still playing havoc on all those of Alice's hue.

Of course, all of this was subtext, and it could not be demonstrated based on the principles at issue; that might never prevail. It could only be accomplished based on the facts, and the facts had to show that innocent Kip Rhinelander was the guilty party as a stand-in for his father.

My mind at times balked at the challenge, at the complexity of the issues on trial for I knew most if not all the men on our jury would, in their hearts, sympathize not with the modern boy who fell in love with a dark girl, but with the strict and dictatorial father who rejected her and who represented the will of aristocratic and even lower-class white America.

Alice was so clever because she had grown up in a household where all this national schizophrenia over race was known if not necessarily understood, and where the reality of class differences was made apparent in the jobs she held as a domestic servant. I believe that she was quick to understand and appreciate all the complexities of the issues at stake in this case even beyond her marriage to young Rhinelander. That, of course, didn't make it any easier for her to accept what needed to be done in the courtroom. I could say to her, "Dear girl, as has been bandied about in the newspapers, it is the future of race—and, indeed, of social class distinctions in America—that is on trial here; that is not necessarily an exaggeration. And that is far too important for us to sacrifice by going easy on Leonard; beside the fact that he has shown he is undeserving of our mercy." Alice was more concerned with hurting the man she still loved than with winning her case.

Here is where—and I'd seen it many times before in my service before the bar—the goals of the litigants and the strategies or the tactics employed by their advocates might be in conflict. It is why one hires legal representation; not simply because the lawyer supposedly knows the law, but also because a good lawyer knows that litigation is war of a sort; and they understand that any war is often vicious and always hurtful to both sides; and that a lawsuit is more often won with what at times may appear to be a lack of scruples than with rectitude, and indeed may prevail through the use of vicious tactics that are hurtful to both parties.

I could have told Alice to keep in mind what I had been retained to do, which was to protect her, and for her to allow me to fight her case as I saw fit. Instead, I reminded her, "Alice, dear girl, remember what Leonard allowed his lawyers to say, not just about you and your motives in marrying him, but also about your mother, your father, and how you all supposedly conspired to force this marriage, with you as the devious female sent to seduce Leonard and own him solely as a means of getting at his family's money and in hopes of being elevated to their social status. Leonard may not have said these horrible lies about you; but he allowed them to be said by his lawyers and before this jury and before the public in his name; and by so doing Leonard in essence gave these lies credence.

"No, Alice, you must not be persuaded to wish me to *go easy* on Leonard because you still love him. Though I understand that, and though I may in my heart sympathize, it is because I am your advocate, because I have your best interests at heart, and because of the value and purity of your love—and the years of life you still have ahead of you—that we must show

Leonard's complicity in this case against you, dear girl, for the travesty, the unmitigated calumny it is. We must fight their lies with your truth or not only will you lose what has already been sacrificed by Leonard's allowing this suit to be brought in the first place—which is to say, Your Honor; even though he might not have wanted it, Leonard allowed it; and by so doing, by taking the witness stand *against you*, if he is allowed to win, you, dear girl *will be ruined*: spurned, degraded, abused, cast aside, and denigrated by white society and Black as well. Your family will be scandalized, made to suffer, and possibly ostracized—*for what?* To go easy on young Kip, who felt no remorse in taking the witness stand against you. To protect the Rhinelander name and social status. *No, I must implore you: it's not worth it, and it's not right!* The Rhinelanders do not deserve your pity. They must be treated in the same manner as they have treated you and your family."

I don't know that Alice was convinced. The trial was taking its toll not only on Rhinelander, with his rapidly deteriorating evidence, but also on Alice's physical and emotional well-being. She looked to have lost a good six or seven pounds, and she was never a stout girl. She appeared gaunt and overwrought, though even this only served to enhance her allure, her tragic beauty. Though her resolve may have weakened when she felt the pain being inflicted on the man she loved, her body and mind were taking nearly as much of a beating as was her husband. In a marriage when there is love, any pain felt by one is known by both; it cannot be otherwise.

I would remind myself, and ever so pointedly tell Alice, that whatever she might be going through now with this case at trial, were she to lose, then every day of every year for the remainder of her life would be as bad as the worst day she was living through now. Leonard would manage to bumble through the rest of his years with his family name and the Rhinelander fortune to sustain him. Even Alice's family would have renewed lives apart from the verdict here. But Alice would not; no, Alice would wake every morning and live through every day of the rest of her life with the fact of her having been disgraced, abused, misrepresented, rejected, and vilified as a wanton seducer and unscrupulous fraud all through no fault of her own and due only to the taint of her blood and the humble status of her family in society. She would be made to suffer for Rhinelander's and America's sins. This result—to me, and I would seek to convince Alice—was unacceptable. We must not allow Rhinelander to get away with this fraud, not as long as we could thwart it. This was not a future Alice should be forced to endure out of deference to the man who rejected her and brought such an ignominious fate upon his faithful wife. Rhinelander must be punished for allowing the suit to be brought in his name, and for the shocking attempt to spurn Alice simply for loving him.

Alice, however, continued to have her doubts. Some part of her still clung to her belief in the love she and Leonard had shared.

CHAPTER TWENTY-THREE

Blackface

When court reconvened after the lunch recess, before the jury was brought in, Mr. Mills stood to address Judge Morschauser and to ask if the defense's cross-examination of the plaintiff might be halted temporarily to allow him to call "a special witness, Your Honor, a well-known entertainer who needs to leave for an afternoon public engagement and whose busy schedule will allow only this opportunity to appear."

"Your Honor," I protested, "this is most irregular. A special witness? This is the first I am hearing of a special witness. Counsel for the defense is quite far along in cross-examination of the plaintiff. Surely Mr. Mills can delay calling his mystery witness until after the defense has finished with Mr. Rhinelander."

Mills replied, "Al Johnson . . . or Jolson, I believe he is." Which response provoked a ripple of laughter from the spectators; Mills wasn't even sure of his famous witness's name. "And, due to his professional commitments, this afternoon is the only opportunity he has to appear."

It was clear what Mills was attempting to accomplish by asking leave to introduce a new witness in the middle of my heated cross-examination. He wanted some more time with Kip to settle the boy's frayed nerves and to counsel him on how to resist my vicious onslaughts. Furthermore, he wished to distract the jury and give them an opportunity to forget how poorly Rhinelander had been withstanding my questioning. Finally, he no doubt hoped this interruption might throw me off my rhythm and upset my attack while giving the jury some unexpected amusement.

"But what relevant evidence of any *value* could this witness possibly provide?" I wanted to know.

Mills replied, "Well, Your Honor and Mr. Davis and the jury will no doubt recall that the defendant, Alice Jones, had mentioned in one of her letters to Leonard Rhinelander that the singer, actor, and minstrel entertainer Al Jolson had been appearing at Paul Smith's White Pine Camp, a well-known resort in the Adirondack Mountains, where the defendant was apparently employed as a chambermaid. The defendant intimated that Mr. Jolson flirted with her while he was staying there during an appearance at the resort. Mr. Jolson categorically denies this event ever took place; he told us that these allegations have caused him considerable embarrassment and some unwanted tension in his marriage due to the fact that his wife was made aware of Miss Jones's comments while reading news reports on this trial.

"Mr. Rhinelander believes, and we wish to show the jury, how dishonest and duplicitous Miss Jones was in her desperation to hold on to the promise of a life of riches and luxury should she be successful in keeping Leonard Rhinelander enthralled and dupe him into marrying her, and that she brought up the false accusations against Mr. Jolson in her letter as part of a deceitful attempt to provoke the Rhinelander boy's jealousy. Therefore we believe Mr. Jolson's testimony is relevant to impugn the defendant's credibility to prove the plaintiff's claim of fraud."

Judge Morschauser asked, "What is the defense's position?"

"Well, Your Honor," I began, "this well-known man's evidence, such as it might be, I submit is decidedly tangential to the issues before this jury. It is obvious Mr. Mills is attempting to resurrect his plaintiff's case, and to sway the jury with the introduction of testimony from a well-known entertainer—indeed, to entertain the jurors rather than present them with actual relevant evidence. Much as we might also be amused by Mr. Jolson's appearance on the witness stand; and as much as his performance as a blackface entertainer might reflect on issues at stake in this case, I feel compelled to object to introduction of this witness at this time."

I was not wholly truthful in my professed wish to keep Al Jolson from testifying. Jolson had something of a reputation as a womanizer, one might assume; or why should his wife be upset with Alice having mentioned that he flirted with her? Besides, I could hardly deny the jury the opportunity to meet this man whose entire professional career as an entertainer was founded upon painting his face Black and mimicking Negroes. One could just as soon present Jolson's evidence as a primer on what his popularity told us about the ambiguity of race in America. That Jolson—born a Russian Jew who had immigrated to this country and who had become famous for his blackface portrayal of American Negroes—why, Jolson's professional persona embodied the country's conflicted attitude toward Black Americans even as he prospered by imitating them: we make fun of them; we mimic them; we allow them to entertain us; but we don't accept them as our equals.

Furthermore, I believed it would also be perceived by the jury as a pointless and desperate effort by plaintiff's counsel to shore up their faltering case with weak, even if entertaining, evidence because they had nothing better with which to discredit the defendant; the Rhinelander lawyers were grasping at evidentiary straws as it were. I considered asking Mills if Jolson would be appearing in blackface.

In the end, I suspect Jolson's star performance on the witness stand amounted to little more than comic relief from the palpable tension resulting from Kip Rhinelander's floundering testimony; and it resulted in something of a brief introduction for the jury to the history of blackface entertainment, while it created another dizzying whirlwind of newspaper stories on the trial.

Jolson's appearance was also a reminder of the current racial confusion and the degree to which cross-cultural references had become so prevalent in American entertainment. I doubt if anyone in the courtroom had ever seen the man without his face painted Black. After being sworn in, Jolson stated that his birth name was Asa Yoelson and that he was born in Seredžius, Kovno Governorate of Russian Lithuania. When asked if he knew the defendant, Jolson claimed he'd never before laid eyes on her; and he admitted that, if he had, he would surely remember having met such a lovely young woman, thus admitting he had an eye for the ladies, which admission amused the men on the jury when I called it to their attention during my brief cross-examination. To prove Alice wrong, Jolson said he was not present at the White Pine resort in the Adirondacks on the date in 1922 when Alice claimed he had flirted with her.

"Well, sir, have you ever appeared at the Paul Smith resort?" I asked.

"No," Jolson replied. "I know it's a regular stop on the Borscht Belt, better known as the Jewish Alps. But I've never been there. I never saw the defendant, never spoke with her, don't know her—"

I consoled him. "We don't claim you know her."

"Thank goodness for that," Jolson said with a toothy smile. "While it may be true that everybody in the theatrical business is a flirt, I have never been to Paul Smith. I got hotel bills proving where I was."

"That's all right, sir. We believe you."

"Good," Jolson said. "Now I can go home and make up with my wife."

Even Judge Morschauser appeared amused by this remark.

Not to let Jolson steal the show, I remarked, "Your appearance here might be good publicity. This is a good headline for you."

"But the other wasn't," Jolson quipped. "Make this different."

With the jury and the spectators diverted, it was up to me to bring them back to the issues at trial. "You understand, Mr. Jolson, sometimes people are given nicknames of prominent theatrical persons?" I asked him.

To which Jolson replied, "Yes, that's true."

"Let me relieve your mind. Do you know that at Paul Smith's there was a chap that was nicknamed after you because he is witty and funny?"

Jolson appeared surprised. "I should demand a portion of his pay. Meanwhile, every time I go to my dressing room the orchestra plays 'Alice, Where Art Thou Going?'"

Everyone laughed—except Alice and, though I didn't see him, I presume Rhinelander as well. When the laughter quieted, I said, "I have no further questions."

Judge Morschauser said, "You are excused."

"Thank you, Your Honor," Jolson said with his characteristic wit. "I hope I'll eat breakfast at home tomorrow."

Once the laughter subsided, Judge Morschauser ordered a brief recess, then Rhinelander was recalled with a reminder that he was still under oath. Kip hardly looked refreshed, and I wasted no time in renewing my attack. I faced the jury, wished them a good afternoon, then turned to the witness and said, "Now that we have that amusing *yet pointless* diversion out of the way, let us return to that subway station. Odd location to read, discuss with one's attorneys, and then sign—indeed, swear to before a notary—what is, once it has been signed and attested to, this, sir"—and I brandished the complaint—"a *legal document* with all that implies, that it is *factual* and *accurate*. You understand that, do you?"

"Yes, I do," Rhinelander admitted.

"It was there, in the tube station, with the subway cars rattling noisily past, with the crowds rushing about, it was there that you and Mr. Jacobs and Mr. Strong, the notary, it was there that the three of you men gathered so that you might read and then sign and thereby swear and attest to *the truth of this document*. Is that accurate, Mr. Rhinelander?"

"Excuse me, Your Honor," Mr. Mills objected, "is there a question here, in all this verbiage, or is Mr. Davis back to his editorializing?"

"Oh, hush now," I said. "Of course there is a question, sir! Adjust your ear horn if you can't discern the question. *I'm getting to it!*" I had to raise my voice to be heard above the laughter.

"I simply wished to set the scene and point out the rather unusual circumstance of meeting with a client; having said client attest to a legal document as serious as an annulment claim—*brought on grounds of fraud*—and to go about this important business in a crowded New York City subway station. It is an odd location in which to be conducting important legal business—*what?* I'm sure Mr. Jacobs must have law offices somewhere, yet he chooses to conduct serious legal business in a subway station. Very strange; even *highly irregular*. My question is there: *Why?* We know that you are hard of hearing, Mr. Mills. Would you like me to have the question read back to you from the stenographer's record?"

Now there was audible laughter not only from the gallery but also from the jury. Even Judge Morschauser couldn't suppress a smile. "Go on, Mr. Davis," the judge said.

I turned to face Rhinelander. "In the complaint that you signed and swore to in the subway station—this document that

I hold in my hand and will now present to you to refresh your memory—you state that prior to the date of signing, you believed your wife had no Black blood. *Is that claim true?*"

"Yes."

"Really, sir?" I shook my head and looked utterly baffled. "But you knew your wife's father, George Jones. You could see his color. You knew Alice's sister, Emily's husband—knew him quite well. You played poker with him and his Black friends; isn't that correct?"

Rhinelander shrugged and nodded.

"The court reporter needs *actual words* for the record. *Is that a yes?*"

"Yes, but that didn't mean I should accept Alice had Black blood."

"Do you mean to say that you didn't *want* to accept it?"

"I couldn't be sure . . . to look at Alice, I mean . . ."

Of course, I thought, *Rhinelander has been instructed to plant doubt in the minds of the jurors, given Alice's ambiguous appearance; a most adroit tactic, for the girl was such a physical enigma.*

"You expect us to believe that? Do we appear brain-tied to you?"

Mills again. "Your Honor—"

"Let me withdraw the question and ask another. All that about Mr. and Mrs. Jones not accepting Emily and Robert Brooks after their marriage; *that was all lies, wasn't it, sir?*"

"Your Honor!" Mills stood to object. "He's putting words into the witness's mouth—"

I ignored the objection. "I will bring Robert Brooks and Emily in to testify at this trial. And I will ask them to tell us under oath if this is true: that the couple was not welcome in the Joneses' home because Mr. Brooks is a Negro. And I will call Mrs. Jones and Mr. Jones.

"Now, do you still wish to give this evidence when you know as you sit here now *that it is all lies?* You know that Mr. and Mrs. Jones never made any such protest whatsoever when Emily married Robert Brooks. They welcomed Mr. Brooks into their home *just as they welcomed you.* And little Roberta, their daughter; you know she is a pretty young Black girl whom you were very fond of. She sat on your lap and called you 'Uncle Len' when you visited at the Brooks's home. All these *colored folks* welcomed you into their homes, and you were happy to be accepted by them. All this about not realizing Alice had some Black blood, that is simply NOT TRUE. *It's a lie,* and you signed this complaint." Again I brandished the papers. "You swore to the bill of particulars KNOWING THERE WERE SEVERAL STATEMENTS that WERE NOT TRUE, that were OUT AND OUT LIES! You swore to these lies as being true statements, *isn't that correct, sir?*"

Rhinelander was again sweating, struggling to maintain composure while being unmasked as a liar. "I . . . I was following instructions! . . . I was doing . . . what I was instructed to do *by my attorney.*"

"*What?* Sir, *for the jury, and for the record.* You are testifying under oath that you signed the complaint, you swore to and signed this legal document after you read it, you swore to the veracity of its contents, and affixed your signature, Leonard Kip Rhinelander." I showed him the document once again. "That is your signature? *Is it?*"

"Yes," Rhinelander admitted.

"You signed this document, with a bill of particulars prepared by this man, Mr. Jacobs, who is a licensed attorney, a member of the bar, as having acted in the employ of your father, Philip Rhinelander; and you swore to the accuracy of its contents *under penalty of perjury,* with this man, an attorney licensed under the laws of the State of New York, and with a notary public, Mr.

Strong, who also works for your father, and who is a licensed notary in this state, and you *signed the document, you swore to the truthfulness of the statements in the bill of particulars KNOWING THAT THESE STATEMENTS WERE NOT TRUE!*" I shouted, marshaling my most stentorian vocal skills. "And you did it because you were *ordered to* by your father's attorney. Is that your testimony here in this court, sir?"

"I did it because . . . *I was advised by my lawyer* to . . . to sign."

I shook my head in disbelief and sighed in frustration. "You are a man, are you not, sir?" I asked.

"Yes, I am."

"And a gentleman?"

"I . . . I try to be."

I looked at the men in the jury box and shook my head. "Is this how a gentleman behaves? Swearing to statements he knows to be untrue to rid himself of his bride, whom he claims to have loved? Were you a gentleman when you courted Alice and made her your wife? Let us consider how your lawyer Mr. Mills, how he has chosen to portray your love affair and marriage to this girl, and let us see how accurate that portrayal is given what, well, what we have seen and what we now know as to the accuracy of your complaint: *that very nearly every statement, practically the entire bill of particulars is false! All lies!*

"Perhaps it will serve this jury and do some good to know *the real truth* of your courtship and marriage to this girl. Let me ask you, sir, did you pursue Alice, or was she pursuing you?"

"I . . . I fell in love with her. . . ."

This remark produced an audible gasp from the audience, in particular exclamations from the ladies, who seemed relieved to hear Rhinelander finally admit what they all hoped was true: *he fell in love with Alice!* Of course he did! And why not? He's a man; she's a lovely young woman with a wonderful character even if she's of mixed blood and from humble origins. Social conventions and bigotry be damned! Leonard and Alice fell in love. Surely there's no crime, no fraud in that.

"Well, thank you, sir," I said and offered the witness my first smile. "I am pleased to hear you admit that, Mr. Rhinelander; to know that you fell in love with Alice. It does my heart good; it helps me to *understand you*. Love is such a powerful emotion, *what?* Now perhaps the gentlemen on the jury may also understand what you were doing when you courted Alice. It's not that you were her sex slave. That's another lie. Thank you for explaining what motivated you. You loved this girl. You fell in love with Alice, whom you then married."

I couldn't say it enough. Alice wept. Several other ladies had withdrawn their handkerchiefs.

"Now, tell us: Did you fall in love with Alice willingly, sir? You weren't *tricked* or *coerced* into falling in love with Alice? You weren't *forced* into falling in love with her by your attorney, were you, sir?"

"No. I fell in love with her of my own initiative."

"Wonderful! *Of your own initiative.* Thank you for clearing that up."

Rhinelander seemed to like that phrase—*of my own initiative*—and I could understand why, since so much of what he did in his life, and what he had done, were not on his own initiative but instead under orders and direction from his father or his father's lawyers. The boy was struggling to be his own man; I had to present him with the opportunity to do that even as it would weaken his case.

"That is good to know. And it is of utmost importance for the men of the jury to know and to consider in their verdict: that you fell in love with Alice voluntarily, willingly, as a man attracted to a beautiful young girl, and *of your own initiative*, as you put it.

And that no one forced you or tricked you or cajoled you into loving this young girl. *You were not her slave, were you?* Of course not! How long after you met Alice in September 1921, when you drove down from Stamford in your new roadster automobile, how long after that did you fall in love with Alice?"

"I drove down actually to see Grace . . . at first. Not Alice."

"Of course you did! *See?* There we have it again: you correcting me. Your mind is working quite well today, is it not, sir?"

"Yes."

"Good for you. Now, tell us, how long was it after your first encounter with Alice that you fell in love with her?"

"Several weeks," Rhinelander said, and looked down again at his shoes, a sure indication that he was lying.

"*Several weeks?* Really? Or was it a couple of weeks?"

"A couple of weeks . . ."

"That wasn't a very long time for a girl to pursue you, was it?"

"No."

"You testified that you had some trouble with your automobile, and that you were stopped by the side of the road trying to get your auto running again, and that is when you were . . . I believe your words were 'picked up' by Grace Jones. Is that true, sir? Were you picked up by Grace Jones as you were stopped by the side of the road with engine trouble?"

"Yes," Rhinelander declared.

"Really? A brand-new car; must have been a lemon, aye?"

I went to the defense table and rustled through some papers as if in search of a document to refute this claim; of course, there was no such document. "Isn't it true that there was nothing whatsoever wrong with your automobile? It was a brand-new automobile, correct? Isn't it true that this was all a ploy? You and your friend, Mr. Kreitler . . . Mr. Kreitler is a married man, is he not?"

"I believe he is—"

"You *know* he is, don't you? And you know there was nothing wrong with your new car."

I had no way of knowing if this were true, but it had just occurred to me that it was all a little too convenient; so I ventured forth and found my hunch to be accurate.

"Isn't it a fact that you saw the Jones girl, Alice's sister Grace, you and Mr. Kreitler saw her walking along the road, so you pulled over to pretend there was some problem with the car—perhaps at Mr. Kreitler's direction, since he is the one with more experience in this game of *picking up girls.* So you boys were there—well, Kreitler is more accurately a man, I believe, in his thirties—you were stopped by the side of the road *pretending* to have engine trouble only so you would have an excuse to stop Miss Jones as she passed by and inquire if she were willing to go for a ride—once, of course, that you were suddenly able to get the car running again. But really, truth be told, there was nothing wrong with your car. That was another lie."

Once established that young Rhinelander was not averse to having trickery employed in picking up girls, I quickly changed the subject.

"You pursued Alice as a matter of fact, didn't you, frankly?"

"At that time I did, yes."

"You were trying to get her love in return for yours?"

"I . . . Yes . . ."

"You had never known a girl like Alice, *had you?* A pretty girl who made you feel good about yourself when you were with her. Why, you even managed to control your difficulty speaking. Alice was *good for you*, wasn't she, sir? You were proud to have a girl like Alice. It allowed you to feel better about yourself as a man who could appeal to a good-looking girl like Alice. *Isn't that correct, sir?*"

"I . . . I did like it, yes."

"What did you like? The way Alice made you feel? Is that it?"

"Yes . . . *she was good to me*," Rhinelander admitted, and he nearly choked up with feeling.

There were sobs from some of the ladies in the gallery upon hearing Rhinelander admit this; some emitted audible shrieks and gasps. Alice wept quietly into her handkerchief. Even a few of the men on the jury appeared moved.

I knew Rhinelander was all in now; his defenses utterly destroyed. He was alone on the witness stand, bereft, and naked emotionally; revealed as a liar who was easily manipulated by others. I perceived that it was merely a matter of appealing to the boy's faltering sense of himself as a man, and seeking to give him an opportunity to renew that confidence in himself that had been evoked by Alice's attentions; but which had subsequently been thoroughly debased first by his father in bringing the lawsuit, and then by his own lawyer; and for me to now rehabilitate his masculinity and his sense of himself as a gentleman and as a man who was welcomed into the arms of a woman like Alice; even to evoke the feelings he had for her; then Rhinelander would be exposed and have to admit to being the aggressor rather than having been seduced by Alice; and thus he would accept responsibility out of a need to preserve some portion of his wounded manly pride by telling the truth of how he felt about Alice—or so I hoped.

"You were proud to have a woman like Alice fall in love with you? Most any young man would have been proud to have a girl like Alice. You weren't concerned that Alice has mixed blood, were you? *She's beautiful. Why, look at her! Your wife is a beautiful young woman.* Men—you included—men are attracted to Alice. Look again, sir. LOOK AT YOUR WIFE, MR. RHINELANDER! *She* is the real catch, *what?*"

I paused. Rhinelander did actually find the temerity to look at his wife, perhaps for the first time since he'd entered the courtroom. And, indeed, Alice looked lovely: demure, poised, even a bit wan, which didn't suit my purposes—again, the ambiguity of her color. She even managed to appear refined despite the fact that we all knew she was a girl of humble origins. Alice was always elegantly dressed; her posture was erect and proud; and she was soft-spoken and well mannered. It didn't matter her social class; the girl had class all her own. One couldn't look at Alice Rhinelander and not see that she was a woman of substance as well as beauty. It's the ineffable quality, call it charm; and character. Alice was charming, and a woman at peace with her charm. Rhinelander's face changed as he finally gave in and looked at Alice. The smug, disinterested pose melted. One could see that he still loved Alice; that he still felt deeply for his wife. Yes, as Alice knew, Kip was still in love with his bride. I felt sorry for him—indeed, I was sorry for them both.

In the imaginary, staged presentation of the Rhinelander love story, at this point in the plot here is where the young husband would break down and profess his undying love; the lights would dim; the hero would quit the witness stand and rush to his wife's side; he would kneel before her; he would beg forgiveness; then he would take her up in his arms. They would embrace and both weep tears of joy at being reunited; and off they would go, back to the bliss of the marital bed with or without the Rhinelander fortune; they would subsist instead on the riches of tender love.

Ah, but, here in the harsh light of the courtroom in the midst of a heated and infamous annulment trial, nothing of the sort happened. Kip cast a quick look at Jacobs for guidance; then he pulled himself together.

I resumed my cross-examination. "When you started to make love to Alice Rhinelander, as you said, two weeks after you met her, you were a man about it, weren't you?" I asked, with the subtext of that question being: *Unlike in your dealings with your father's lawyer, where you are completely a cipher who is under his control: a craven coward; here, while making love to this lovely young woman, you were the man in charge as perhaps the only time in your life when you were truly a man.*

"Yes," Rhinelander said, again rising to the inquiry manfully.

"You weren't making love to a girl, and seeking her love in return without honest marriage in view, were you? I mean, as a gentleman, that was your objective, correct? You weren't trying to deceive Alice?"

"No, I was not."

"*Very good*, sir! Now we are getting some truth at last, *aren't we?* So you are a gentleman after all. I am glad to know that, Mr. Rhinelander; it makes my job so much easier, dealing with a true gentleman *rather than with a liar.* I'm sure the men on the jury are glad to know it as well as they will determine their verdict. It is important to know that you are not some pathetic brain-tied wretch in the hands of a conniving jezebel."

I let that statement hang in the moment, gave it time to register with the jurors, in particular that word "jezebel," loaded as it is; and as certainly that would prove to be the crucial point of testimony going forward.

"Fine," I continued. Again I referred to papers on my table that had nothing to do with the questions I was asking; I did it merely to let Rhinelander believe that I had some documents to refute any lies or misstatements he might hope to tell. I asked, "When did Alice return this love that you extended to her?"

"It was, I would say, about the same time."

"Are saying that within *two weeks* of meeting Alice, you confessed your love for her, and she reciprocated? And then the courtship began in earnest and with marriage in view?"

Here Rhinelander hesitated. "Ah . . . not exactly; no."

"Was that before you went to stay at the Hotel Marie Antoinette?"

Rhinelander didn't answer.

"Let us be clear for the jury. What *were you making love* to each other for? Was it for sexual gratification only? Because you told us that you are a gentleman. Therefore we must know: *What did you have in view?* Were you trying to take advantage of this girl by professing to love her? As a gentleman, you wouldn't do that, *would you, sir?*"

Rhinelander was again at a loss for an answer; he simply shrugged his shoulders, and he gave me a thoroughly pathetic and perplexed look.

"Are you not sure, sir? As to your motives? Is your plan in making love to Alice not something about which you feel confident? This is important for the jury to understand. It's important to understand, since you did marry Alice. And of your own free will. We've heard the testimony: how you returned from the dude ranch and took Alice away, spent time with her, for all intents as man and wife. Then you returned here to Westchester to make good on your promise to marry her. We need to know *why. Why did you do this?*"

"Because . . . because I cared for her," Rhinelander managed to admit after more stuttering. "As I said . . . *I loved her.*"

There were audible moans and groans of relief from the spectators.

"Thank you, sir. I should certainly hope so, on your account as a gentleman. Thank you for clearing that up."

I turned away from the witness and looked directly at Mr. Jacobs and Mr. Mills and gave them a slight smirk as if to say: *There, gentlemen, you heard it from the plaintiff. He loved his bride. We may all go home. Your case is lost!*

Then I turned back to the witness and continued. "*So you*

did. You loved Alice. Mr. Mills in his opening said you are a very innocent boy, *lacking brains.* That you are somewhat, shall we say, that you are not very bright. We have *disposed of* that idea of you as a simpleminded idiot, have we not?"

"Maybe we have."

"Maybe? Well, let's look at it closely. This theory of Mr. Jacobs, as expounded by Mr. Mills, portraying you as some sort of innocent nincompoop, to use a common term, between us, Mr. Rhinelander, we have eliminated that false characterization of you—haven't we?"

"Yes."

"Of course we have! You are not a brain-tied idiot, are you?"

"*No!*" Rhinelander replied emphatically.

"Good, sir. As the plaintiff in this action, you want that false characterization of you—*you want it eliminated, don't you?*"

Rhinelander admitted that he did.

"Very well, sir. Let us proceed with the understanding before the good men of this jury that you are *not some miserable brain-tied wretch* but that rather you are a young man with a good mind, a decent mind, who believes him to be a gentleman and who knows exactly what he is doing when he makes love to a girl. Because the next classification we come to in the plaintiff's case is *innocence.* You were not so awfully innocent when you met Alice, were you, frankly?"

"I was."

"You were, eh? You see, sir, we have been running right through on cross-examination the different characterizations of you that your lawyer has presented to the jury. That you were simpleminded; that you were an innocent boy who was seduced by Alice. We have disposed of those two characterizations. Now we are down to the third one: that you were a babe in the woods when it came to making love to a girl."

"I was, yes."

"Oh, I see, you are saying you didn't know how to go about it?"

"No . . . I didn't."

"Really?" I said with a bemused look. "*How extraordinary!*"

At that point, I went to the defense table and looked through a stack of letters, chose one, and held it up for all to see.

"Since Mr. Mills chose to read *Alice's* letters to the jury, I shall read some of *your letters* as well. You recall those letters, sir?"

Rhinelander did not answer. He blushed and looked down at his shoes.

To the clerk I said, "I would here ask to mark this letter for identification and to enter it—never mind: we'll get to that in time."

I put the letter back with the others on the defendant's table and continued questioning Rhinelander—baiting the hook, as it were, fashioning the lure; and certain everyone in the room was dying to hear what was in Leonard's letters.

"Well, sir, did you know how to hold a girl's hand?" I asked him.

"Yes."

"Of course. And did you know how to put your arm around her?"

I could see the members of the jury beginning to shift in their seats and show some signs of finding Rhinelander's protestation of innocence far-fetched; and I sensed they were beginning to feel a bit exasperated by all this lawyerly maneuvering on my part.

Time to move on, I thought. *Let's get to the dirt!*

"Yes."

"How about . . . did you know how to kiss a girl?"

"Yes."

"There you have it. I don't know as there is much else to do. I am talking about *decent love*, Mr. Rhinelander. What about *indecent love?*" I asked and shot a look at the jury. "*Obscene and vulgar love.* Did you know about those things as well?"

"*No! I did not.*" Rhinelander insisted.

"No, you say? *You did not?* That is your testimony?"

I returned to the defendant's table and retrieved a letter, held it aloft. "I have here a letter from you, several letters, and yet that is your testimony? *That you knew nothing of indecent love?*"

I let the question hang in the silence from the witness stand.

"Very well," I continued. "*We shall get back to that.* Because, I also have letters, Mr. Rhinelander, *your letters.* Your *love letters* to Alice: I should say, *your filthy sex letters!* I *will read your letters* as well."

"Judge," Mr. Mills protested, "if counsel for the defendant intends to enter the letters, let the letters speak for themselves."

"*Oh*, that's what you want, *is it? You shall get it!* But first, I would ask for the judge to excuse the ladies from the courtroom, as well as any youngsters. *For this evidence is most disgusting, most inappropriate for ladies or young people to be exposed to.*"

I leered at plaintiff's counsel to give them some inkling of what they were asking me to do to their client, then I turned back to the witness.

"First, let me be sure, and let the jury be sure, as we get ready to hear your letters, sir: you claim you knew those things, the decent things, and how to do them when you met Alice, correct?"

Rhinelander made no answer. I am sure my mention of his letters, and in particular the obscene sex acts he described in his letters, must have had his mind in an awful turmoil. He was sweating. *Letters indeed!* Why, this had Rhinelander in a panic; and my repeated reference to the letters had the jury, the spectators, the press, and all the thousands following the trial, and even aloof Philip Rhinelander as the head of the esteemed clan—*all were suspended on tenterhooks awaiting revelation of the smut in Leonard's letters; which is exactly where I wanted them!*

At the plaintiff's table, Jacobs and local counsel were in heated, whispered conference.

"Do you hesitate, Mr. Rhinelander? And do you find yourself tongue-tied now at last because you feel your case slipping out from under you?" I said, and watched the Rhinelander lawyers snap to attention.

"I dare say, now that we have done away with the preposterous notion that you are an imbecile; and now that we see that you are not a complete innocent. Tell me, sir, did you know how to buy . . . rubbers, I think there was some mention of rubbers . . . and, perhaps now there is even more concern, given mention of your letters, and what you describe as *decent love?* We shall see. They are your letters, are they not, sir?"

Rhinelander turned a deeper shade of red and shook his head.

"I . . . I . . . I . . . don't . . . I heard about them, about rubbers . . . from the boys at boarding school."

"Yes, of course you did. Boarding school. That's where all you fine fellows learn of such things, *is it?* . . . Never mind. We'll get back to that, and to what you knew of *indecent love* when we read *your letters to Alice,*" I averred ominously and gave Rhinelander a moment or two to think about that and to perhaps further pique the jury's curiosity.

Letters? From Rhinelander, yes! Pornographic letters! Now I had the whole room—indeed, the whole universe of followers to the case—wondering what might be in those letters. Only the witness, and the defendant, dear Alice—who was also well aware of the content of Rhinelander's letters—the young lovers were in no haste to have the letters read in public. Hence I was holding back; I hoped to use the threat of the letters to pressure Rhinelander Senior into dropping the lawsuit.

"Your Honor," Mr. Mills protested, "is counsel going to enter the letters into evidence or merely—"

"*Oh, don't worry, sir, you want the letters in?*" I scoffed. "Fine. We shall enter the letters. You want filth? We will give you filth . . . but coming . . . And the ladies, the good ladies of Westchester County and beyond who have come here to hear a decent trial, dear ladies; oh, I blush even to think of what they will hear! But it was not I, *oh, no!* And not Alice Rhinelander who insisted on dragging these letters into this courtroom and subjecting the jury and spectators to *this vile filth!*"

Here I turned and glared at Leon Jacobs to remind the jury how Alice's letters were obtained, and at whose initiative these obscene documents would be entered into evidence. Jacobs noticeably squirmed in his chair; or so it seemed to me. I don't believe Jacobs knew, or had any clear idea of exactly, what was in Leonard's letters.

Jacobs called for a sidebar.

"Your Honor," the attorney protested, "Mr. Davis has not offered the letters in discovery—"

"Just a moment. I beg to differ, sir. You started all this with Alice's letters. I am merely following your lead. And the letters, copies of Rhinelander's letters, were delivered to your offices."

"I was not made aware that you intended to enter them as evidence."

"Then what did you think I was going to do with them? Publish them as pornography? I trust you are aware, sir, these letters are *extremely graphic.* They detail acts of . . . well, *we shall see.*"

"No, *we shall not see!* I won't allow—" Jacobs blustered.

"What did you say? *You won't allow it?* And since when were you elevated to the bench to adjudicate this proceeding?"

"I, I, I . . ." Jacobs appeared to have suddenly been infected by his client's speech impediment.

"That's enough," the judge declared. "Mr. Davis, do you intend to submit the letters in evidence?"

"*Oh, surely!* Yes. I believe I must, Your Honor. I hadn't planned to. But given how Mr. Jacobs has prosecuted his lawsuit, Alice Rhinelander as well has letters written to her and sent through the Postal Service to the plaintiff; copies of which were delivered to Mr. Jacobs—"

"I have not had time to review the letters, Your Honor. I must ask—"

His Honor inquired, "But you did receive them?"

"I assume so, if they were sent. Please bear with me. I am working out of hotel rooms. Were they sent to my offices in Manhattan?" Jacobs asked.

"To your offices in Manhattan, and with copies delivered by hand to your hotel, and also to local counsel's offices. You are still at the hotel here in town?"

"Well, we are back and forth."

Again I was reminded of Jacobs's poor preparation. Mr. Mills hadn't said a word.

"Mr. Mills," I asked, "did you not receive the packet of letters?"

"I did, yes, but I have not had an opportunity to review them."

The judge said, "I suggest you do so at once—if, indeed, counsel for the defense is in fact going to submit the letters in evidence. The court will also need to review the letters you intend to submit."

All three of the men looked at me as if to say: *Are you really going to bring this sort of evidence into a public trial?* Again, had any one of them spoke what they were thinking, I would have answered: *What do you expect? Am I a responsible lawyer defending my client, or a pushover? Come, gentlemen, you know me better than that. I am here to win!*

"Now," Judge Morschauser declared, "let's get on with it."

I returned to the defense table and then addressed the witness.

"I beg your pardon, sir. The letters, the letters . . ." I muttered. "Now, getting back to where we were. I believe you were telling the jury about your making love to Alice. You spoke of holding her hand. What induced you to hold Alice's hand and put your arm around her?"

Rhinelander was still flustered and appeared to have recovered barely any measure of equanimity during the brief sidebar. "I liked her. I was attracted," he said.

I was not about to let him off the hook.

"You say that you got a thrill from it, did you? But you didn't have any thought then of real love? Were you just out to take advantage of this girl? To drive her around in your expensive car, to put your arm around her, and to kiss her *and whatever else* all just to have some fun? Was that what you were about, sir? Were you imitating your friend Kreitler, the married electrician, your friend from the Orchards School? You fellows out picking up girls to take advantage of them? Is that the sort of man you are, Mr. Kip Rhinelander? A cad like Mr. Kreitler? That doesn't seem so innocent to me. And certainly not gentlemanly. Not in keeping with your family name, your supposed standards and background. *Does it to you?*"

"Maybe, in the beginning I was, but . . . I soon felt . . . I was soon in love with Alice. *I told her I loved her.*"

"Indeed you did. You spoke of your love to Alice, over and over again, and you wrote to her of your love in your letters. And in your phone calls with Alice you told her of your love. You were in love with Alice, and you were pleased to have her know of your love. And there we have done away with yet *another of the unfounded accusations in your suit.* We have done away with *the utterly false notion* that you were *tricked* into marrying Alice, *haven't we, sir?* You just told us you loved Alice! *You loved the woman you married!*"

I turned and faced the jury, and then the spectators in the gallery; I raised my hands as if to say, "What else do we need to know?" And I nodded as if to confirm the witness's statement.

"I don't know what we are doing here, in this courtroom, at this trial," I said. "You told Alice of your love for her. You gladly accepted the love she felt for you in return; but then *why, why are we here?* Why did you leave Alice? Can you explain that, Mr. Rhinelander? And why are you now seeking to annul your marriage, to do away with your bride, whom you profess to have loved? Because, *what?* What changed? Unless you were lying; or is it because of *your father?* Because *your father insists* that you rid yourself of this girl and hence free the Rhinelander family of any taint of her mixed blood? *Because, as a woman of color, she doesn't measure up to the exalted Rhinelander family standards! Is that the real cause of this lawsuit, sir?*" I said, and I let that sink in for all to consider: the real motive and force behind Philip Rhinelander's efforts to annul his son's marriage.

"*Of course it is!* Your motives have nothing to do with Alice's color, or you wouldn't have courted her and married her in the first place. *You knew damn well she has mixed blood.* That's the truth, isn't it? *You knew all along Alice has Black blood in her veins, didn't you?* You were well aware from the very beginning, having met her father, having met and played cards with her brother-in-law. And, of course, Alice *never denied* she was of mixed blood—did she? *And the fact she is of mixed race made absolutely no difference to you; isn't that so, sir?*"

"Your Honor. Once again, counsel is testifying—" Mills objected.

"*No, it's not!*" Rhinelander blurted out. "*That is where I drew the line!* When I knew she . . . when I was *convinced* that she has *Black blood*."

I shook my head and gave the jurors a look of dumbfounded incredulity. "Oh, please, really, sir? *Really?* Still clinging to that lie, are you? Do you expect the men of this jury to believe you? Do you think that they are brain-tied nitwits, such as we were asked to believe *you* are? You expect them to believe that even after you married Alice, or after you first had intercourse with her, and when you lived with her and her family in the Joneses' home, when you were together with Alice as man and wife, and had *sexual intercourse* and, more that we shall see, base intimacies with her on any number of occasions that it *never dawned on your poor brain-tied comprehension that the girl is part Black?*"

I picked up one of Rhinelander's love letters, looked at it, sneered as if in disgust, and then put it back down. *Stage direction*, I thought. *Speaking to the jury without words.*

"And when you . . . well, *we'll get to that* . . ." I said as a threat.

"Mr. Kip Rhinelander, do you really expect the good men of this jury to believe that it was not until Mr. Jacobs here, *your father's lawyer!*"—and I turned and pointed at Jacobs, who gave every impression of wishing he were anywhere but where he was—"when this man, Mr. Leon Jacobs—let us not forget who he was working for, and who he *still works for, your father, Philip Rhinelander*—when Mr. Jacobs showed up at the Joneses' home and spirited you away under false pretenses, then and only then, as you stood in a subway tube in New York City with Mr. Jacobs and the other fellow, do you mean to tell us that *it was only then that you became convinced that Alice has some Black blood?* That is what you want the gentlemen of this jury to believe, and to base their verdict upon?"

Rhinelander did not answer. I stood for a moment with a

perplexed expression, then I let out a deep sigh and shook my head ruefully. "You have no answer. I'm sorry, I can't accept what you have testified to. Nor can the court. That, sir, is ludicrous," I said and then turned to the judge.

"Your Honor, it is not my choice as counsel for the defendant to subject the jurors and this court to such filth; but I feel I have no alternative. As the plaintiff has entered into evidence letters written by the defendant, so now Alice Rhinelander is compelled, and I am wont in her defense to enter into evidence letters written by the plaintiff, Leonard Kip Rhinelander, and mailed to his wife through the US Postal Service, postmarked and dated, addressed to Alice Rhinelander.

"As I stated earlier, I do this most reluctantly. I have no wish to sling more filth in this courtroom. I am not attempting to titillate or shock the men on this jury, or to subject the good people of Westchester County, as well as all those who may be reading of this trial wherever they may be, to such . . . *such disgusting filth.* But, Your Honor, and ladies and gentlemen in the gallery: *the defendant and his counsel leave me no alternative.*"

I turned, went to the table, picked up a letter, then put it down.

"Mr. Davis," Judge Morschauser declared, "the court and counsel for the plaintiff have asked for time to review whatever letters you intend—"

"Yes, Your Honor. And, as I explained, copies of the letters have been delivered both to plaintiff's lead counsel, as well as his local attorney. And Your Honor's clerk has also received copies. Now, may I proceed?"

I took out my pocket watch and looked at it, then said, "Or, if it pleases the court, given the hour, might we take a brief recess before we begin with this . . . *unsavory business* and give the court and opposing counsel an opportunity to review the evidence, what the court will see, that the letters of the plaintiff contain . . . what is most vile and should not be uttered in the presence of children or proper women."

There was a murmur of consternation in the courtroom. Journalists whispered among themselves, and some got up and left to file their stories.

The letters! Rhinelander's letters to Alice! What did they contain? Everyone wanted to know.

With that I returned to the defense table and placed the letter on a stack of letters from among our papers and said, "Your Honor, may I forewarn the court, and in particular the ladies in attendance, the letters I am . . . as I say, *reluctantly* . . . as it were, *forced* to enter into evidence, written by this plaintiff, Mr. Leonard Kip Rhinelander, postmarked and delivered to his wife, Alice, through the US mail—which may also constitute a crime, now that I think of it, given their content—*these letters are so disgusting*, Your Honor, the ladies, and certainly the young people in the gallery, with all respect to their decency, *they should not be subjected to such filth.*"

* * *

A recess was called. There was talk of closing the proceedings to the public, and near pandemonium broke out when the bailiffs attempted to clear the courtroom, with vocal protests from some of the ladies who were directed to leave—in particular a couple of Manhattan women who were assigned to cover the trial and had produced valid press credentials. They insisted on staying, invoking their status as representatives of a free press, and finally were allowed to remain only after threatening legal action and having been reminded once more by Judge Morschauser that they were cautioned as to what they were about to hear, and that it was shocking; that what they were about to be subjected to was particularly obscene, even depraved; and that the court had afforded them every opportunity to absent themselves prior to any reading of the plaintiff's letters.

With that, the judge excused the jury, and court was adjourned for what was meant to be half an hour. Rhinelander was allowed to step down from the witness stand. He looked utterly depleted and scared. I won't say that the young sheik slunk from the courtroom, not exactly; but clearly the haughty strut to his gate was no longer apparent. As he walked past Alice, Rhinelander afforded her only a chagrined glance as apology for the embarrassment and pain he had brought upon the girl whose love he had rejected and whose honor he had so tarnished; but at least he did look at her. Some of the ladies watched him with disgust tinged with fascination.

There was a literal crush at the doorway as the reporters made to rush from the room to file their reports. Outside the courthouse the crowd was in tumult. Deputies from the sheriff's department had to push through the throng to give us exit. It seems the news that Rhinelander's letters were to be read in open court had already reached the public. I took the opportunity to suggest to Mrs. Jones that she might choose to forgo the afternoon session given the soon-to-be-revealed content of Rhinelander's epistles to her daughter. But the Joneses are a hearty lot and not given to shrink away from the baser aspects of life. They had sat through the disgusting insults directed toward them from Rhinelander's counsel in his opening; now I felt both parents were obliged to see the tables turned. I for one was committed to extracting every bit of discomfort, rude embarrassment, emotional pain, and mortification as I possibly could not only from the Rhinelander boy, but also from his lawyers, and even from his absent father, whom I knew would cringe and then become furious and scandalized by the public revelations of his son's depravity; as well he would wish he'd never set in motion the lawsuit that was bringing such dishonor to the entire Rhinelander family.

It appeared that only the defendant herself, yes, Alice was alone in not wishing to have the letters read in open court in an effort to hurt and humiliate the man who, at the insistence of his father, was doing all within his and the Rhinelander family's considerable power to convict and to defame her and her family. But as I had told Alice and reminded her repeatedly: it had to be done. When appraised within the context of the embarrassment to be felt by Alice, as noted and discussed with the defendant and her family on several occasions; and when considered in light of Rhinelander's accusations and misrepresentations as to the facts of the case, the plaintiff's letters—if in fact they were to come in—his words to Alice were to be our best evidence of the actual guilty party as to accusations of fraud; and therefore I was hardly above using Rhinelander's letters as threats to destroy the plaintiff's case. Again, I was merely following the game plan introduced by my opponents.

All this preliminary posturing with regard to the letters was my way of setting the stage. So much of being an effective trial lawyer comes with having a flair for the dramatic. I have been criticized for how I handled the Rhinelander case—particularly by some lady journalists who wrote about the trial. Perhaps I did take the defense too far, as may become apparent. I'll let posterity judge my actions based upon the outcome.

The truth is, as always when given a suit like this to defend (Was there ever another case like Rhinelander? No, not for me, not given the issues and their relevance to race and class relations in our nation; and hence, given the level of the conflict, and certainly not with regard to the kinds of revelations that would take place at this trial.), I was determined to win at any cost, though not for my own sake. I would be paid my fees win or lose. In fact, I stood to gain more as to monetary reward if Alice were to take a handsome settlement. Nor was I striving for the glory of victory because, as I have noted, there was no real upside for my client, no good outcome for Alice; only the better of two unfortunate and painful results for the rejected bride: there were only degrees of loss. Clearly it was never about the money for Alice, upon which my fee might be determined, or she would have taken the settlement offer or even demanded more, which Rhinelander had intimated he would gladly have agreed to pay—indeed, we were about to hear just how eager Rhinelander was to settle now that the news of Leonard's letters possibly coming into evidence was known.

I am now aware that in fact Rhinelander's counsel had been of the belief all along that the case would never proceed to trial; Mills admitted as much. Even as they amassed their trove of evidence as to Alice's mixed blood, it was done to convince us that our defense was futile. They misjudged Alice, misjudged her resolve as well as my intentions and my strategy in how to defend Alice; and thus they were never prepared to fight their case, particularly when we admitted Alice had mixed blood. The Rhinelander attorneys were loath to come to terms with the fact that they had no case, for they never believed there would be a need to prove their claims. They made a fatal tactical error. That to me is the only way to understand how a lawyer as thorough and skilled as I knew Mills to be could have allowed the case to proceed to trial with what was clearly evidence based solely on obvious and transparent lies—lies that the jury would be made to see were lies with their own eyes. I believe that Isaac Mills and Leon Jacobs misjudged the tenor of the sentiment aroused by the Rhinelander prosecution. *Such arrogance!* They assumed the public, and hence the jury, would be on Rhinelander's side and perceive Alice as a devious mulatto temptress intent on infiltrating rarefied white aristocracy. *Humbug!*

It must be seen that, despite the efforts of the eugenicists and even the Klan's malevolent posturing, times were changing, even in matters of race, however slowly. There was as well a rising tide of a woman's right to proclaim her sexuality and her independence. All these factors played a significant part in the Rhinelander case.

For the defense, then, it was always a matter of bringing out the truth, of showing that there was genuine love between these two young people despite their differences and the stigmata of society. Now young Kip had admitted that he loved Alice; and so it could be seen that what happened between Alice and Leonard was as human and true as love itself and never about money; never about disparate social status; never about skin color; but always about heartfelt emotion between a man and a woman. All this, I believe we had accomplished; and that it was while disproving the fraud accusation that we would prove the truth of the deep human feelings of love that brought about the relationship and led to the marriage, and hence why it should not be cursed with an annulment.

Alice's defense was always centered on her self-respect as a woman and her truthfulness; to show that she did not in any way seek to deceive Rhinelander as to her color; and even if it meant revealing not only what was in the letters, but also what would become the most sensational exhibit of this trial, and perhaps of any trial before or since. For what would be done in Alice's defense in the pleadings, in the courtroom, and in the judge's chambers was always motivated by an overriding necessity to win at trial; and therefore to save Alice's name even at the expense of her modesty; because, were this girl to lose her case, were we to fail to prove her innocence of the fraud charges, as I made clear, and as I cannot state emphatically enough, not only would the marriage be dissolved, even abolished; and not only would Alice be denied any financial support with the annulment; but Alice would also forever forth be labeled as a conniving, lying Black jezebel who would defame not only her family, but also be seen as a traitor and an insult to all the innocent women of her father's race as well as those of her mixed color.

As a lawyer, one tries not to become overly emotionally involved in the outcome of a given case. Here, however, as Alice's advocate, and as someone who had come to have genuine feelings of love and respect for this girl and faith in her cause, I have to admit that, were we to lose, were I to fail in my duty to protect this girl from what I knew would be the result of her being found guilty of fraud, I would forever be remorseful and see myself as a failure as Alice's defender. I would have deep misgivings about my future as a lawyer to be known as the advocate who failed to win for his client, and worse fears about the future Alice faced, as well as the future we as Americans could expect regarding racial relations.

Hyperbole? Perhaps, but certainly not to me. I had to win. Alice had to win. She had to be accepted as the good and honest woman she is.

CHAPTER TWENTY-FOUR

Wreck the Boy!

When court resumed, and with a wilted Leonard Rhinelander shambling back into the courtroom to take his place on the witness stand after our brief recess, I noticed that scarcely a few ladies had joined the others and chose to quit the proceedings. Brave ladies of Westchester! They would have their curiosity satisfied and even indulged. That was not to be helped; I had my work to do, and that would mean there could be no more reserve in my cross-examination of Rhinelander. I would make good on my promise to wreck the boy. But not yet . . .

With Rhinelander squirming on the stand, I held one of his letters in my hand, and I asked, "Mr. Rhinelander, please, tell this jury: When were your acts toward Alice Rhinelander anything but the acts of a gentleman?"

"Well, I . . . I believe . . . I always behaved as a gentleman until . . . well, it would have been December 1921, I suppose . . . at that time . . . when Alice and I went to the Hotel Marie Antoinette."

"By Alice you mean Mrs. Rhinelander, who was not then your wife."

"Yes."

"Prior to the hotel stay, would you agree that Alice had acted in a ladylike fashion?"

"Yes."

"She had not sought to seduce you into intimate sexual relations?"

"No . . . she had not."

"And you, sir, let me ask you frankly, *had you attempted* to be intimate with Alice prior to the hotel stay?"

"I had not had intercourse with her prior to the hotel—"

"That is not what I asked you, sir. I must ask that you *answer the questions I pose.* Let me repeat my question. Had you *attempted* to have *sexual intercourse* with Alice before the hotel stay?"

Rhinelander made no answer.

"Is this too difficult for you, sir?" I asked and looked at the jury. "And you know, do you, you understand that these questions *would never have been asked of you,* and there would have been *no cause for you to have to embarrass and disgrace your wife like this if you hadn't dragged your wife in the gutter!* You know that, don't you? You feel that, don't you?"

Rhinelander finally managed to sputter, "N, n, n . . . no, I don't know."

"Tell us, sir, tell the gentlemen of this jury, please specify which activities—*which sex acts*—preceded the stay at the Marie Antoinette?"

Leonard managed to admit, "I . . . I felt a sex urge with Alice."

"Oh, I see, and you know, don't you, that it is normal? You know that normal males and females feel sex urges?"

"Yes, I know that. I know about sexual desire. I . . . I . . . played with my hands to act upon Alice's sex urges."

"You played with your hands to act on *Alice's sex urges*—or were those *your own sex urges?* Where, tell the jury, where did you play with your hands, sir? You do recognize, Mr. Rhinelander, *that there is no more room for modesty in this case*; you understand that—given the letters? You understand that by bringing this action against your wife, and by allowing *your lawyers* to introduce the, by comparison, tepid and innocent letters written to you by your wife—you understand that you have *thrown open the bedroom door* as it were?"

Rhinelander admitted that he understood.

"Tell the men on the jury: *Where did you play with her with your hands?*"

Rhinelander shook his head, he shrugged his shoulders, and he looked about the courtroom as if hoping to see someone who might be able to rescue him and take him away. "I, I, I . . . hmmmm, I don't know . . . the *legal name for it*," Rhinelander admitted.

"The legal name?" I acted mildly shocked, or at least surprised. "Then tell us in your own terms. There is no necessity for legal terminology."

Rhinelander finally managed to say, "The vagina, or something of that sort."

"Something of that sort indeed!" I repeated, and I shook my head in apparent bewilderment as I heard a murmur of surprised amusement from the spectators.

"And . . . and her breasts. *I fondled her breasts*," Rhinelander admitted, apparently feeling more emboldened by the spectators' response.

"I see. Hmmm . . . fondled her breasts . . ." Here I again gave the men on the jury a knowing look. "And, if you can, tell us what was your goal in, as you say, in playing with Alice in this fashion? This took place while you were in the car, with the driver, on your way into Manhattan—*yes?*"

"Yes."

"And what did you hope to accomplish by this . . . as you say, playing with Alice's . . . intimate female parts?"

I had to feign trying to hide my own embarrassment at being made to ask such questions. Truthfully, I was enjoying

Rhinelander's obvious discomfort and the effect it was having on the men in the jury.

Rhinelander offered, "I wanted to satisfy . . . I was hoping that . . . I would excite her and that she would then want to have intercourse with me . . . to satisfy my desires."

"I see. To satisfy *your desires.* But was it love then that motivated you? Or was it simply to satisfy sex desires?"

"I . . . I . . . I'm not sure."

"*Not sure!*" I exclaimed. "Well, did you love Alice?"

"I . . . I don't know."

"*You don't know?* How extraordinary! But didn't you just tell us that you loved Alice? How is it that you can't make up your mind?"

"Well, when it came to . . . to the sex, I don't know if . . . I'm not sure," Rhinelander managed to admit.

"I see, you mean you loved Alice, but you also acted upon a baser instinctual desire for sexual gratification—is that it?" I asked and then abruptly moved on without waiting for an answer; let the jury come to perceive Rhinelander's ambivalence.

"Tell us, sir, *what is the color of your wife's body?*"

Rhinelander looked stunned by the question.

"Take your time," I told him. "Think back, perhaps to the time you spent with Alice at the Marie Antoinette. You do remember that time?"

"Yes, yes, of course. I . . . I would say it is dark. But not any darker than the arms of women I have seen in Havana."

"Had you *been intimate* with these women in Havana? Had you played with their private parts?"

"*No!*" Rhinelander protested.

"But you saw Mr. Jones's color—*did you not?* Of course you did. And you can see him now; you see him seated in the gallery. And you saw your wife's body; you saw the flesh that is normally covered; you saw her naked and at close quarters—*isn't that so?* While you were with her *naked in bed* . . . Tell us, sir: Does your wife's skin color resemble her father's?"

"No," Leonard said. "I don't believe so."

"You don't believe so. . . . Well, then—"

I turned to Alice seated at the defense table. "Mrs. Rhinelander, if you would, please: hold your hands up so the men on the jury may see them."

As she did, I thanked her, and then I turned and asked Rhinelander, "Can you tell us, sir: Are your wife's hands as dark as her body?"

"Her hands . . . and her body are the same . . . same color."

"I see," I said and quickly changed subjects, going back to the earlier line of questioning. "Now, you say—and tell us, please, sir, if you will: During the drive into New York, while seated in the back of your father's curtained car, how did you go about this *playing* with your wife's . . . *private parts* to excite her and . . . what was your motive again? You wanted to convince her to stay with you in the hotel by playing with her? By arousing her desire? Is that your testimony?"

"I . . . well, yes."

"So it was *your* plan?"

Mr. Mills stood to object. "Your Honor, do we really need to—"

"Yes, we do," I interjected. "*Of course we do!* And we do so, sir, because *you*, as counsel for the plaintiff, you brought this lawsuit *based as it is upon these opprobrious accusations of fraud.* We are now *at long last* getting to the truth of the case."

"You may continue," the judge said.

"What did you do to effect your purposes, to play with Alice's vagina?"

"I . . . I might have put my hands up under her dress. I don't know."

"*You don't know?*" I sneered. "But how could you *not* know? Don't you remember?"

"Well, I . . . I was excited."

"Of course you were!" I said and heard a ripple of laughter go through the gallery and saw more than one juror crack a smile. Judge Morschauser, however, appeared discomfited by this colloquy.

"And Alice *submitted?* She *let you* put your hand under her dress and play with her vagina?"

"Well, I . . . at first . . . no. She resisted. I insisted—"

"*Insisted!*" I repeated, registering shock. "*You insisted?*"

"Well, I . . . I knew it gave her . . . pleasure, so I kept at it, in a way. . . We laughed at my . . . I was not particularly . . ." Rhinelander trailed off.

"Not particularly what?"

"Not particularly . . . *adept.* I wasn't sure what I was doing, if I were doing it right. Alice . . . well, she chastised me."

"I see," I said and gave the men on the jury a sly smile. "Do you mean because you were a beginner in all this?"

"Well, we were aware that the driver, Chidester—he kept looking in the rearview. Alice laughed and warned that we might crash if the driver couldn't stop looking in the mirror instead of at the road."

Here the spectators actually laughed, as did a few of the jurors. Rhinelander blushed and turned away. The judge reminded the gallery to remain orderly and refrain from laughing.

"Did you continue with your fondling? *Playing with Alice's vagina?*"

"I tried. Alice might remove my hand, but I would put it back up under her dress, and laugh, and cuddle her. Finally, well . . . she was aroused."

"What did you hope to accomplish with this *fondling?*"

"I expected to get her aroused. I wanted to stay with her at the hotel. I wanted to arouse her so I might . . . have intercourse with her."

I cast a quick look at the jurors and shook my head.

"So, sir, you are finally admitting to this jury that you were not so dumb or innocent as Mr. Mills has attempted to portray you: *Were you?*"

"I . . . I . . . I was . . . *infatuated* with Alice . . . at that time. But I . . . I had never had intercourse with a woman before."

"Had you brought along *the rubbers* you mentioned?" I asked in a more subdued tone, seeking to calm the witness just a bit.

"Yes," Rhinelander admitted.

"So it was *premeditated.* You admit your attempt to have intercourse with Alice was *your* idea. *You planned it ahead of time. That is important.* In pursuing your plan, did you tell Alice that you loved her?"

"I . . . I might have said it, yes."

"You *might* have said it. You're not sure? But you are sure that you had an animal lust, didn't you, Mr. Rhinelander? *Tell us!*"

"Yes," Leonard admitted.

"*Yes, you did!* And which you were attempting to satisfy, *correct?*"

"Frankly . . . I wanted to be with her."

"You accomplished it, didn't you? You aroused the girl sexually. You told her that you loved her, *told her what she wanted to hear—you lied to her* to gain Alice's consent to have sexual intercourse—*didn't you?*"

"*No!* I didn't lie. *I did love her,*" Rhinelander blurted out.

"Here we go again! *You loved her!*" I fairly shouted. "You didn't know for sure how you felt; or you loved her; you had a sexual desire—*which is it?* In any case, you weren't willing to wait and court Alice in a decent manner, to marry her, and then to have sexual intercourse with her as husband and wife, *were you?* You wanted it *that very night!* You didn't want to wait. And you were *used to getting your own way.* So you aroused Alice's sexual passions. You knew how to go about that; *didn't you?*"

"Yes," Rhinelander admitted.

I paused to let this admission register with the jury. I gave the men in the jury box a long, knowing look, nodded, and raised my eyebrows.

"Of course you did," I began again. "And now—*look what we have done!* We have *completely eliminated* any notion of you having been seduced by Alice: *Correct, sir?* We have discounted and *totally demolished* your counsel's fantasy that you were a mentally deficient innocent boy in the hands of a sexually experienced vamp who seduced you—*correct? Another of your claims out the window!*" I declared, then I abruptly changed subjects without waiting for Rhinelander to reply.

"Sir, when you first saw your wife's naked body: that is, her back, her legs, her breasts in the bed at the Hotel Marie Antoinette, when you had sexual intercourse with her, *what? Several times* over Christmas holidays? *Right at it, weren't you, Mr. Rhinelander?* And I think there was some testimony that you bathed your wife. You were most intimate with her."

I stopped again at the defense table, picked up one of Leonard's letters to Alice, looked at the letter, and appeared to be reading from it. "And you went about it *naturally?*" I said while still pretending to read.

"I . . . I . . . I'm not sure I understand," Leonard managed to say.

"Thank you for reminding me to be specific." I put down the letter and looked up at the witness. "Now, Mr. Rhinelander, this is most important: when you had sexual intercourse with Alice at the Hotel Marie Antoinette, you went about it *naturally*. That is my question."

"Yes," Rhinelander was quick to answer.

"And you say that there was nothing *unnatural* about it?"

"No!" Leonard declared and blushed again. "*Of course not!*"

He glared at me as though trying to frighten me off.

"You did *nothing* to this girl that was *indecent* save one might suppose that sexual intercourse under such circumstances—that is, without the benefit of marriage—that might be considered indecent—*did you?*"

As Leonard took a moment to wonder, and to rack his mind as to where I was going with this, I handed him one of his letters to Alice, and I asked that he identify it.

"It is a letter . . ." he said and handed it back.

"Certainly it is a letter. *Whose letter is it? To whom is it addressed?*"

"Mm, mmmm, mmmm. My letter to A, a, a, a . . ."

"Let me help you, sir. This is a letter you wrote to Alice Rhinelander, your wife, who is sitting at the defense table, *is that correct?*"

"Y . . . y . . . y . . . yes."

"Thank you." I then handed the letter to the clerk. "Let the letter be entered and marked as Defendant's Exhibit N-1."

Once the clerk had so marked the letter, I handed it to Rhinelander. "Now, sir, *please read the letter.* You may read it to yourself."

As Leonard read, he turned beet red with embarrassment.

"Sir, do you still wish to proceed with this lawsuit?" I asked. "Or would you rather concede that there is *no merit to your case?*"

Leonard cast a desperate look at his lawyers. I believe the court saw Mr. Jacobs nod.

"I do, yes . . ." Leonard said.

"Let me show you a second letter for identification and ask that it be marked—can you read that one as well? And, while you examine the letter, tell us, sir: are you a *free agent* in your own case and not under the control or, as you put it, *the orders* of your lawyers?"

"I am not under anyone's control! I, I—"

"Fine, sir. And you are quite sure you wish to proceed given—

and as I'm sure you know—*that the next step is to read your letters aloud*, the letters now in evidence. I shall *read them in open court.* I will ask that *you admit as to their contents.* Now, do you still wish to proceed, sir?"

Rhinelander appeared flummoxed. He seemed unable to answer.

Mr. Mills stood to address the court.

"Your Honor, counsel for the plaintiff would ask for a brief adjournment so that we might have an opportunity to confer with Mr. Rhinelander and respond to defense counsel's *inquiry* . . . as to the letters."

I had to try not to appear overly confident. As my learned colleague Judge Swinburne once put it to me, "A trial is like a boxing match." (Ah, yes, another of these apropos prizefight metaphors!) "You may have your opponent up against the ropes, and you may feel the knockout punch is imminent. But you never can be absolutely sure until the fight is over, your opponent knocked out, and you have a victory with the verdict. Because you must always be aware that one unexpected counterpunch to your cause and you may find yourself knocked out."

"Fine," I said and withdrew my watch from my vest pocket. "Your Honor, considering the hour, and given that Mr. Rhinelander appears he is in need of some time to confer with counsel and consider if he chooses to proceed with *the reading of his letters to his wife*; and to give the court time to review the materials we intend to submit as evidence."

Court was adjourned with two of Rhinelander's letters submitted, and to possibly be entered into evidence, but as yet unread except by defense counsel and the plaintiff.

The letters! I would skewer young Rhinelander with his own pen! And roast him upon the flames of his unbridled, indecent lust. *Poor lad!*

But first I would provoke imperious demands from the Rhinelander throne in Manhattan.

* * *

When court resumed the next day, one could count on one hand the number of ladies who had taken the Court's advice to quit the proceedings; all those in the audience under age twenty-one had been removed, although some had tried to sneak back in. It was the Roaring Twenties, after all. Women were expressing their newfound independence, and even their natural interest in sexual matters. Now, with Rhinelander back on the witness stand and looking even more flustered and uncomfortable, and everyone primed to hear what was in Leonard's letters to Alice, I decided to play out the intrigue a bit longer, draw it out, as it were, to fascinate the jurors and the journalists and spectators even more, and return, however briefly, to the question of Alice's color given what was soon to be revealed in the letters.

"Mr. Rhinelander, before we get to your letters to Alice," I said, and could hear an audible groan of exasperation from the spectators. In their minds they were shouting: *Get on with it, for God's sake! Let us hear Rhinelander's letters!* But no, I would tease them as I chose. "Let me inquire, for I'm sure the jurors would like to know, as you sit there on the witness stand and look out at the spectators, can you see Alice's father? Do you see George Jones seated in the gallery beside his wife and daughters?"

You might suppose that I was not capable of keeping the narrative of my defense on track; but that is not so. I was indulging in a practiced technique, changing topics on the verge of revelation to draw out the suspense—a device a writer of fiction might call a "cliff-hanger."

"Yes," Leonard allowed.

"Do you recall your lawyers—or your father's lawyers—do you recall that Mr. Mills said in his opening remarks to the jury that when he had occasion to see George Jones, Alice's father, when he saw Mr. Jones prior to the commencement of this trial—a statement I frankly found to be ludicrous given what I know of George Jones's position in our town as the manager of the taxi stand and someone I'm sure Mr. Mills has had occasion to meet in public—nevertheless, Mr. Mills claimed that he would *never have chosen* to expend the funds—your money, sir; or rather, your father's money—he would not have seen it necessary to spend the considerable amount disbursed in an effort to establish if Alice's father was a colored man because *just by seeing him it was apparent that Mr. Jones is in fact colored?* Do you recall that statement by your lawyer?"

"I think so. . . . I'm not sure. . . ."

"Oh, is your brain not working so well now? Have we twisted up your mind a bit with our questions? *Would you prefer to drop your case?*"

"No," Rhinelander managed to state with some assurance.

"Then, let me remind you. Mr. Mills stated that, had he actually seen George Jones prior to this proceeding, he would have had no question as to the fact that George Jones is colored. Now do you recall that?"

"I believe so."

"What about you, sir, what did you think of George Jones's color when you first met him? Could you not see that he is a colored man?"

Mr. Mills stood and objected. "I believe defense counsel has—"

"No," I interrupted. "I have not . . . not gotten to the next question, and given that we have established the plaintiff is *not color-blind*; that he is *not an idiot* or an *innocent dupe*; that he is not a *victim of an unscrupulous jezebel*, but rather a young man with a sex urge he wished to satisfy with Alice—let me ask him, plain and simple, because it is important given what we now know of the couple's—well, we'll get to that."

I turned back to face the witness. "Sir, isn't it true that you were *well aware* Alice had some Black blood when you courted her and when you had *repeated sexual intercourse* with her at the hotel? Come now, admit it, Mr. Kip; you can't deny it given what you have already admitted. You knew Alice had some Black blood, AND YOU LIKED IT, DIDN'T YOU?" I raised my voice and saw young Rhinelander startle.

"The very idea of it! Of Alice being part Negro—*that appealed to you, didn't it, sir?* It was something—*what? Special? Exotic, perhaps?* The forbidden fruit. You felt you were *a real man* with a girl like Alice, didn't you? And your father and the Rhinelander name be damned—*what? You didn't care!* Why should you? You were having a jolly good time of it—*the time of your life making love to Alice*—this lovely girl of mixed race; you loved every minute of being with her, that is: *until your father threatened to take away your inheritance!*"

"Your Honor, is there a question here? Or is Mr. Davis again taking this opportunity to testify—"

"Oh, yes, there is a question here, Your Honor," I said and turned back to Rhinelander. "And I don't know why my learned opponent cannot discern it. A very relevant question, I might add . . . Sir, Mr. Rhinelander, if you will, *tell this jury*: You *liked the fact that Alice had some Black blood*, didn't you? It intrigued you. Please answer!"

Rhinelander appeared totally flummoxed. "I, I, I, mmmmm . . ."

"Oh dear, that pesky stutter is back. Just a simple *yes or no*, Mr. Rhinelander. Come now, *did you like it?* When you looked at your wife's naked body *it aroused you . . . Yes or no.*"

Mills was still on his feet, and now shaking his head in exasperation. "Your Honor, I must protest—"

I was incredulous. "*You must protest, sir?* On what grounds?

Because you don't like where this is going? *I beg your pardon, sir.* It's a little late for that. You are *the one who brought this scandalous action* on the part of the witness and his father, Philip Rhinelander."

"Your Honor!" Mills sputtered, but I would not be thwarted.

"Just a moment! Are you not the one who allowed a *patently false* and *perjurious affidavit* to be *sworn to* and entered into evidence?"

Now Jacobs was on his feet. "Your Honor!" he blurted out.

But Mr. Mills hushed him and gestured for him to sit back down, at which point I again spoke out, now addressing my comments to counsel, and pleased to see I had them both stimulated. "Sir, I believe that, given all of the slime that you and your co-counsel have allowed to be spewed upon this young girl—*and her family, I might add*—that I am well within the limits of decorum and the purview of cross-examination to ask this witness, Leonard Kip Rhinelander, the plaintiff in this outrageous action against my client, if, in fact, he did not *know of,* and he was not *well aware of,* and he did not actually *enjoy* the fact of Alice Rhinelander's mixed race and the color of her skin as he made love to her and he had sexual intercourse with her—and more, as we shall hear—*repeatedly*; and whether it was of *no consequence to him. But in fact it excited him.*"

I turned back to the witness. "*Answer the question, Mr. Rhinelander!*"

I was practically winded from having delivered this exhortation, at which point there were audible exclamations of shock and surprise, even groans from some spectators; the jurors as well appeared stunned. I was sure I had gone too far; but then again, perhaps not far enough. Because I knew there was truth to my inquiry; and the men on the jury understood what I was alluding to; and thus there was no way forward except to continue with this line of questioning; and that we were going to go much further along into the gutter, and into the forbidden territory of interracial sex once Rhinelander's letters were in evidence.

I was interested to see that the judge, rather than admonishing me to ask questions, His Honor seemed equally enthralled with the progress of my cross-examination. And so I repeated my demand to the witness.

"Answer the question, sir. *A simple yes or no.*"

"I . . . I . . . I can't . . ."

"Of course you can't! Interesting, *what?* This question of—" I stopped and looked around the room. I didn't need to say it; everyone knew what I was referring to: Rhinelander was intrigued with Alice in part *because* she was Black. Because she was different. He wasn't the sex slave at all, yet there was something of the master-slave going on here, however subtle, however unexpressed, perhaps even *subconscious*: the white male of social prominence and the Black girl at his beck and call, at least at first; but then Alice, to protect herself, and because Rhinelander was such a weakling, and because Alice was the bolder and the smarter of the two, Alice took the upper hand and steered what may have begun on Rhinelander's part as base lust for a colored girl, a mere dalliance, and she turned it into something more substantial, something more beautiful, as it were, more righteous; and not by guile, not by sexual enslavement, but by genuine love that she hoped was to become sincere love on Rhinelander's part as well and result in marriage and even a family. Yes, little Rhinelanders of mixed blood to grow up and present themselves to his lord and master, Grandpapa Philip Rhinelander as colored grandchildren. *Here was the real threat!* And young Kip, try as he might to wriggle out of it now on the witness stand, it was obvious, as he admitted, that he may have been looking only for sex with a dark girl of lower class at first; but then, as it happened, he couldn't help himself. The boy fell deeply in love with the girl, and that is why he married her; and that is what worried and upset his father.

"Tell us the truth, sir. You didn't care—no! *In fact, you liked it*—you liked the fact that your wife was of mixed race. Is it because it enhanced your lustful purpose with her?"

"*No!* I . . . I . . . I can't say," Rhinelander managed to get out at last. "I didn't think about it, not at first, not until it was made clear to me that she was, that she had some Black blood."

"Oh, come now, sir; *please*," I said. "Here we go again, and this is so *tiresome*. This prevarication. You don't really think anyone can believe that, do you, Mr. Kip Rhinelander? Do you believe that we are all brain-tied dupes to be sold this cheap bill of goods: '*I don't know. I didn't think about it. I don't know the difference between Black and white.*' Are we back to that ridiculous notion that you are an idiot?" I asked with an audible sneer in my voice.

* * *

At this point—it was late Friday morning, December 12, and even before Rhinelander attempted to answer my question, almost as though it were timed as such—a messenger entered the courtroom and hurriedly approached Mr. Mills at the plaintiff's table.

Everyone in the courtroom was distracted as the messenger bustled forth officiously to hand Mr. Mills a letter, which the lawyer opened and quickly scanned. Then, as if he had already been made aware of the letter's contents, he stood and asked for an adjournment. "Because, Your Honor, an emergency in this case arose, and of which personally, I hadn't before the slightest intimation, I would ask that court is adjourned so that counsel might attend to this matter."

This was a statement that, to me at least, appeared patently false. Of course he knew what was in the letter he received before it came; no doubt he dictated it. The whole event smacked of being staged by counsel.

I said, "I'm sorry, Your Honor. *Now what is it?* What emergency is Mr. Mills referring to?"

Mills asked, "May we approach?"

Judge Morschauser beckoned counsel to approach the bench.

"Your Honor," Mr. Mills declared once we were at the sidebar and out of the well of the court, "Philip Rhinelander has asked—apparently he has been unable to attend, or was called out of town—but he has asked that I confer with him *posthaste.* That I must . . . that I should meet him this weekend at his home in Manhattan to discuss the progress of the trial."

"Your Honor," I said, "this is most unusual. Although I have long suspected the hidden hand of Philip Rhinelander at the controls of the plaintiff's case, and though I notice with some surprise that he has not seen fit to travel up to Westchester to attend his son's and daughter-in-law's annulment trial, I find it unusual, and I hardly think it appropriate for this court to delay the trial to accommodate Philip Rhinelander."

"It is most important, Your Honor," Mills assured the court.

"I'm certain it is," I objected. "But so is the timely procedure of this trial. Already I have been asked to suspend my cross-examination so the jury could be amused by an appearance from the entertainer Mr. Jolson. And now, once again, I am being asked to discontinue my cross-examination of the plaintiff at the convenience of his absent father."

Truthfully, I was happy to have the trial halted at this point. It would only add to the mounting anticipation on behalf of the plaintiff, and his family, his lawyers, and the suspense of all those far and wide who were following the trial as to the introduction and reading aloud of Kip's scandalous letters. I was also beginning to suspect that Rhinelander Senior might have decided to call the whole thing off for fear of what might still be revealed as to the actions of yet another wayward and degenerate Rhinelander male once Leonard's letters were made public.

"Well, seeing that it is Friday," Judge Morschauser allowed, "and that I understand the need to confer, given the course of this trial, I will adjourn until Monday morning. That should give you ample time to arrange to meet with Philip Rhinelander; should it not, Mr. Mills?"

"Yes indeed," Mills said. "Thank you, Your Honor."

Judge Morschauser promptly adjourned court and announced that the trial would resume at nine o'clock Monday morning.

* * *

The sudden and unexpected (indeed, unexplained) turn of events at such a critical point in the trial—and with the threat of Leonard's scandalous letters hanging over the case like an ominous storm cloud gathered on the horizon—this mysterious development provoked a frenzy of speculation in the press, as well as among the spectators, and the crowds gathered outside the courthouse, as to the contents of Rhinelander's letters, and with rumors circulating that the letters were so sexually explicit, so filthy, and so embarrassing to the Rhinelander family as to possibly cause Philip Rhinelander—who was now recognized as the organizer behind the lawsuit—that Rhinelander Senior would have cause to order the discontinuation of the case, with Kip Rhinelander withdrawing his suit and allowing the marriage to prevail rather than having the boy's letters made public.

Talk about a cliff-hanger! This was more than I had bargained for.

* * *

The *Times* reporter theorized that Rhinelander Senior ordered the attorneys to insist that Leonard's letters be kept out of evidence on the grounds that they were too inflammatory; or, if they were unsuccessful in having the letters disallowed, they should withdraw the lawsuit: "So that the Rhinelander scion's letters would never become part of the court record and thus be memorialized in the public domain."

Extraordinary! Even the editors of respected newspapers were speculating on the potential impact of the contents of Rhinelander's letters to Alice on the outcome of the trial. But then again, there was nothing ordinary about this case—unless, of course, you consider the very ordinary fact of love between a man and a woman.

* * *

Reporters dogged my opponent Mr. Mills all weekend; they even ambushed him as he left for the train to Manhattan on Saturday morning for his appointment with Philip Rhinelander. More journalists and photographers awaited him at the station in White Plains; they traveled on the train with him seeking to question him during the brief trip; and another gaggle of photographers and reporters were gathered at Grand Central when his train arrived in the city.

Serves him right! I thought, and I had to chuckle imagining Mills's discomfort at his sudden unwanted celebrity. Reporters as well bothered me; but I paid them no mind. I managed to dispel them with the truthful statement that I had not been advised as to what was on Rhinelander Senior's mind when he called for the meeting with his son's lawyers. However, I intimated that, due to the contents of Leonard's letters—which I certainly knew and hinted were even more scandalous than anyone could imagine, given the way Kip Rhinelander had allowed his lawyers to present him to the jury as a sexual naïf, as a shy and mentally deficient child in the hands of a Black jezebel, and how poorly Kip had conducted himself on the witness stand—it was not difficult for me to suppose what the meeting in Manhattan with Philip Rhinelander and Leonard's lawyers was meant to decide: *To proceed and allow the letters to be read into evidence; or to withdraw the lawsuit?* The Rhinelander attorneys and their clients were in a quandary equal to my own.

Secretly, I wished I might have been a fly on the wall in that Manhattan mansion to hear for myself what was discussed. On the one hand, I hoped Philip Rhinelander would decide to quit his son's case, though I knew the man's reputation as a never-say-die fighter, one who would be loath to give up until the bitter end. On the other hand, I agreed with Judge Swinburne that we had our adversaries exactly where we wanted them; that victory for Alice was a probable if not definite result. Certainly I counted more than half of the jurors apparently disgusted with Kip and enamored of Alice. Yet I was aware that there were other witnesses still to be called by the plaintiff; and who could be sure how their evidence might sway the jury? I was also cognizant of the fact that one or two convincing jurors—dominant personalities who might be repelled by the idea of a Black woman in a marriage with a white aristocrat, and with the vision of little mixed-blood Rhinelanders running around the streets of Westchester and Manhattan—how such jurors might hold out and persuade the others to vote against Alice in hopes of preserving the purity of the white race; or, at minimum, cause the case to result in a hung jury and mistrial.

Should the case proceed, I knew there was still something else that I needed to do—something more than reading Leonard's filthy letters; something more than destroying the boy on the witness stand; something more than just testimony. Something dramatic had to be done to be sure to convince even the most reluctant jurors, and to move them at some deeper level of the male psyche below reason, below even surface emotion; and some evidence that would strike at and resonate at a deeper hidden level of desire and thus urge these men to vote to acquit Alice.

* * *

Would we call Alice to the witness stand? Speculation teemed. At this stage, I wasn't sure. Charming as I found the girl to be, and persuasive, and remarkably composed, I could as well perceive that there were men on the jury who also found Alice attractive despite their prejudices—indeed, almost too attractive—and who might be persuaded to reject her for want of having her, out of spite or jealousy, as it were, if her performance on the witness stand should upset them. Besides, I had to take into account that she might break down emotionally under what I knew would be a vicious and shameful cross-examination by Mr. Mills; he was famous for such displays of the lawyer's skill. I didn't want Alice to have to endure that, nor to give Mills the opportunity to show off his talents. No, I thought it better to have our Alice remain the silent muse, the quietly weeping half-Black girl left in the lurch to defend herself with her dignified silence against the prominent, mean-spirited, rich, and imperious Rhinelander clan; to show her at once under assault and too distraught even to speak on her own behalf, much as I knew this was image alone. Emotional, yes; hurt, by all means; mortified, of course; but defeated, no, never. Alice was still as resilient and determined in the heat of battle as any man I'd ever known. Indeed, when compared to her aristocratic husband's blubbering appearance,

Alice was superior in her silent impressions made upon the jury, and I wanted nothing to diminish her dignified, quiet presence.

Alice's sense of herself as a woman was on trial here, and that might best be presented in appearance alone, in her physical being; and in seeing how she bore up every day under the terrible stress of the trial; how she sat quietly absorbing the disgrace, the insults, and yet never let it detract from her reserve and her grace, her good manners, her punctuality, and her elegant poise as well as her understated style of dress. Alice was showing herself as the aristocrat, the image of subtle feminine beauty and power despite her mixed blood and lowly social status; I wanted nothing to take away from that sense of her person. To put Alice on the witness stand and expose her to the insults I knew Mills would assault her with could well destroy her equanimity and expose the raw nerve of her devastating love for her lost husband.

I left it open, however; I wouldn't decide for certain if I should call Alice to the witness stand, not right away, not until the time came. Better to keep my opponents wondering.

And besides, I thought I had a better idea.

* * *

Ah, the internal dialogue of the defense attorney when faced with the question of whether to put the client—indeed, the accused—on the witness stand! How my mind was preoccupied with such questions and deep musings all weekend as I wondered about the meeting in New York at the Rhinelander mansion. I knew there was more to do. One could never depend on a jury to find its verdict based on the facts in evidence rather than to vote according to the emotions aroused by that evidence, or by the personal feelings toward the litigants and their witnesses. I wanted the jurors to feel sympathy for Alice without hearing from her, and yet even as they believed they were voting based on the evidence, I wanted them to vote for Alice to win, and for the Rhinelanders to be defeated, to be disgraced forever for having brought the suit against the girl based as well on emotion. Any worthy trial lawyer understands that evidence, once it is examined by the jurors in their deliberations, will also be judged according to the feelings it arouses.

When the reporters asked to know what was in Leonard's letters, I told them that they would have to wait to see if the court would allow them to be read and so become part of the official record, or otherwise be kept private. I let it be known that Kip's letters were far more salacious than any written by Alice and read aloud so far in court. I shook my head and said I couldn't imagine why Kip's counsel had ventured down this path of dueling love letters in the first place, knowing that the weapons in our arsenal were far more powerful than the tender musings of the defendant.

* * *

As it was, we may never know all of what was discussed between Rhinelander Senior and Mr. Mills during that hastily called summit conference over the weekend at the height of the Rhinelander trial. Apparently even young Kip himself was not in attendance at the meeting; my informants told me that he remained sequestered in his hotel rooms at the Gramatan in Bronxville all weekend. I can report that Jacobs called me early Sunday morning as I was headed out to church, and with plans to meet Alice after the service, and the attorney asked me once again to "name my price" with regard to a negotiated settlement.

There were even rumors of threats that I would be ruined by Philip Rhinelander if I allowed Alice to proceed with her defense and to have Leonard's letters read into the record in open court. I personally am aware of no such threats, certainly Jacobs never even alluded to them, although I do know that there was some extra-legal attempt on behalf of someone claiming to have authority to contact Alice and members of her family and to make similar offers and threats. Who this was exactly, we were never able to determine, although it was believed that it came from high-level members of the Ku Klux Klan, grand dragons, and such. We do know for certain that the Klan was active in the area all during the trial.

Alice and the Jones family were kept under guard provided by the court due to these threats and to the continued presence of the Klan in and around our village. Our once quiet town of New Rochelle had come to resemble an armed camp. As more Klansmen and members of other even more extreme racist groups, something called the Army of God, came to protest the scandalous marriage, so the police presence was intensified, with state troopers, local police, federal marshals, and National Guardsmen on hand to help keep order and avoid riots.

There were even some instances of fistfights, of stores being broken in to and looted, and more threats delivered to the Jones home. Except for her brief foray out to Sunday services, Alice was made to stay indoors until Monday morning, when her presence was required in court. I asked for, and she was given, a police escort to and from the courthouse.

Leonard Rhinelander was in hiding all weekend, said to be in New York in conference with his father and the lawyers, although we believe he never left his rooms at the Gramatan. As well, the reporters noted that Leonard was not seen in Manhattan either going to or coming from the Rhinelander mansion with Mr. Jacobs and the other lawyers. Reporters camped outside his hotel, but the harried and mysterious plaintiff appeared to have decamped, retreated to take cover in parts unknown; or he came and went in the dead of night.

For her part, Alice still refused to discuss a settlement, even when I conveyed the refrain that we could "name our price."

"Oh, for God's sake! I'm insulted," she told me when I visited her Sunday after church for tea in her parents' home.

"Don't they see, Mr. Davis? Isn't it enough how they have insulted me already? Must they continue? Can't they understand that *I don't want their money?!* I never did! *I want my husband*; I want Len. I wish I could speak to Philip Rhinelander myself and tell him how I feel."

There was a novel idea! Leave it to Alice to conceive such a plan. But why not? I called Leon Jacobs myself and proposed it. "Alice Rhinelander," I told him, "while she advised me to refuse any amount of settlement, she asked me to request a meeting between her and her father-in-law."

"*What?*" Jacobs fairly squeaked with astonishment. "The woman wants to meet Philip Rhinelander?" The lawyer was astounded by the suggestion.

"The woman, yes, *his daughter-in-law* would like that very much," I said. "Is that so preposterous?"

"Quite impossible," Jacobs responded.

"How do you know if you don't ask?"

"Mr. Davis," Jacobs snapped in a tone that insinuated I must be a fool to even suggest such a meeting, "certainly you understand: Mr. Rhinelander refuses to accept the legitimacy of this marriage. He will not agree to meet the woman whom he believes is responsible for his son's disgraceful downfall. Leonard, under the circumstances, is the only male heir Philip Rhinelander has to carry on his name, his birthright, and the family business. He does not wish that the Rhinelander name be carried on by a . . . *a woman of impure blood.* He is also of the opinion that his son as well wishes the marriage to be . . . *ended* . . . come what may."

I attempted to speak, but Jacobs cut me off.

"However, be that as it may, I would ask that you in good conscience, and given that you are a respectable member of the bar and a man of good reputation—I would ask that you *desist in your* . . . in your stated stewardship of your client's case by bringing in . . . by submitting, and having read in open court letters of . . . well, as you know, letters that are *extremely lurid*, good only perhaps for their *sensational value*, and letters that would inevitably do irreparable harm to my client's name, as through his son's errant ways, and that are of *no real evidentiary merit*—"

"Just a moment, sir. I beg to differ." Now I interrupted Jacobs's bombast, which I found so tedious.

I could see there would be no meeting of the Rhinelander *paterfamilias* with the woman his son had chosen as his bride; nor, it appeared, any meeting of the minds as to the continued mutual generalship of the litigation—certainly not on my part, given where we had arrived in the course of the trial. I could not back down now. I could not retreat and be of good conscience that as Alice's defender I had done all within my legal powers to win the case despite the disgrace and scandal that would necessarily result from pursuing such a course.

Fine, so be it, I thought. I was not surprised. But I was hardly ready to allow Jacobs on behalf of Rhinelander Senior to accuse me of scandalmongering or underhanded trial tactics given that his side had initiated the submission of personal letters into evidence; and, I might say, behaved most dishonorably in their treatment of the Jones family.

"Please keep in mind," I reminded Jacobs, "and convey to your client and to his father; please explain, in case he is not aware, that it was *your decision* as his son's counsel to bring this lawsuit; and furthermore, it was *your plan* to then stoop to the level of such tactics as to enter into evidence *personal letters, intimate love letters* written by my client. You began this business of reading private letters, Mr. Jacobs. What did you suppose would happen? What did you expect me to do to defend my client? Oh, of course, I understand: you and your client expected Alice to take the money and run and hide from her shame. Well, now you know that is not possible. I would hope, Mr. Jacobs, that you and your client, Philip Rhinelander, that you are coming to appreciate that the woman Kip chose as his wife is a person of integrity. It is she, and not I, who has steadfastly refused to accept any offer to dissolve the marriage. And by now I would also think that you might understand that Mrs. Rhinelander and myself and co-counsel are not about to be intimidated, threatened, or scared off. The letters—Leonard's letters—unless you decide to put an end to the trial by withdrawing the lawsuit, and thus allow the marriage to stand—otherwise, if we are to continue the litigation, then Leonard Rhinelander's letters to his wife—shocking and disgraceful as they may be—*will be submitted.* And, if Judge Morschauser allows, the Rhinelander boy's letters *will be read in open court.* And they will become *part of the public record . . . come what may!*"

Jacobs said, "As you wish," and hung up.

* * *

Suddenly, over that weekend, as I had always suspected it might, *Rhinelander v. Rhinelander* was revealed to be not so much a case about a marriage or simply about race and class anymore. It was now clearly a case about the taboo of interracial sex.

"Do we really need to do this?" Alice asked me when we met at my office over the weekend. "I find it all so . . . *humiliating.*"

"Of course you do. And as I have repeatedly reminded you: expect it to get worse," I told her. I was beginning to get a bit perturbed with all these second thoughts regarding my stewardship of Alice's defense given that I was following her orders. "And, be prepared, as I have reminded you and your family several times: it may have to get *much* worse before it's over. Rhinelander refuses to meet you; he refuses to believe your marriage has any validity whatsoever. He maintains that you are so far beneath the Rhinelander epitome of social class and distinction that you are *unacceptable* to hold their family name. *To hell with him!* In your defense, young lady, as your lawyer, I intend to prove this is naught but rubbish. You have entrusted me with the management and presentation of your defense," I counseled, and I assumed a far more conciliatory tone while I took hold of her lovely, soft hands in mine. I kissed her delicate fingertips, clearly trespassing beyond the boundaries of my role as her attorney.

"Please, Alice, do keep in mind what we know: that Leonard's father's lawyers not only brought this suit, but dictated how it will be fought according to their tactics of assault on your intentions, your honesty, and your character; they have accused your family of conspiring to take advantage of an innocent boy ensnared in a relationship with a devious and greedy Black girl. *No! We cannot let them prevail! Hell, no!*

"Excuse me for cursing on the Sabbath; but, as I have explained over and over, dear girl, *this must not happen.* And it is my obligation as your attorney to do what I deem necessary to protect not only your rights as a married woman who has been vilified by a man who has proven to be most—well, let me say it again: Leonard is compromised; he is at odds with himself in his affections for you. He is not a free man; never has been. We know that Leonard is under the complete control of his father, whose chief aim is to prevent any perceived disgrace to come upon the family name even if that means utterly disgracing and essentially criminalizing your name and that of your family, labeling you, and libeling you all as conspirators in a fraud to extort money from the

Rhinelander fortune. *That is their ultimate objective.* You do see that, don't you, Alice? This is not just an effort to end your marriage. The marriage is doomed; we understand that. Now, what they—what the Rhinelanders are about now is *ruining you* and *ruining your family.* They will not be satisfied; it won't end here even if they were to win the case. They will do all within their considerable power to have you and your family driven from Westchester, perhaps driven from New York State, to contain what for them has become an unacceptable scandal for a family that was hitherto so highly regarded in these environs.

"They believe they must utterly crush you by having you revealed to the public as a liar and a fraud, or so they—specifically, Philip Rhinelander—believes that is the only way for him to save his family's name. That leaves us no alternative: *we must fight.* As I see it we must seek to turn the tables on them and destroy their cause at whatever cost, and exonerate you and your family in the process. And that means using Leonard's own words, and his own behavior to disprove his allegations against you.

"I'm not happy having to proceed along these lines, believe me; and I certainly understand how hurtful it is for you to have these letters read in public; but you do see how it is having its effect. Philip Rhinelander—we don't know, but my belief is that he's deeply concerned. He may yet choose to call off his lawyers and ask them to withdraw the suit once he realizes that he cannot keep Leonard's letters out. I expect that is, as he sees it, his only way for them to protect the family name from what he must know is a worse scandal than any he might imagine as the result of . . . of allowing the marriage to continue.

"*Such stubborn pride!* Good Lord! To not even agree to meet you—why, the man chooses to bring this disgrace upon his family himself. What sort of man does that? And out of what twisted and arrogant sense of family pride and honor? It's dismaying."

"I know," Alice said. "I don't understand it, and it is so hurtful. And why Len . . ." She let out a deep sigh. "Oh, it's . . . you know, Mr. Davis—remember the note he sent, telling me to fight? Len doesn't want this."

"That, of course, is our object here, my dear: to reveal Philip Rhinelander as the culprit, the proud and hateful force of racism, classism, snobbery, and prejudice who has chosen to ruin the happiness afforded his son and his daughter-in-law in this union to protect his family name. *To hell with that!* Here I am cursing again. Lord forgive me! And—I hasten to say this—since, as I believe you know, Leonard is not now and perhaps never will be a free agent in this case, or in his marriage to you, my dear girl. There is no happy ending, Alice, no, no . . . I'm sorry to have to say it, but you know it as well as I—because you know that Leonard's father has made it clear he will not allow his son's happiness if it involves marriage to you. He will not accept you as Leonard's wife. Finished. End of story *or so he believes.* He is determined not to allow you to become a member of the Rhinelander family even though you already are legally a Rhinelander. You will always be a Rhinelander—*unless this annulment succeeds.* Now, and so there you have it: the letters are our best proof of Leonard's true feelings and intentions.

"I must remind you, Alice: you, and you alone, chose to fight this case. You will recall that I advised you more than once that perhaps you would be better off to accept the settlement and avoid what I knew would be a traumatic experience. You, however, steadfastly declined the settlement offers and insisted you wished to defend your good name. I support that decision now wholeheartedly. I believe in your decision. And I do not want to see Rhinelander win. I do not want to see you lose, and then to have the Rhinelanders succeed in crushing you. I do not want to allow them to do this to you and to your family. And so, what we have, and since they have opened the way for this, we as well have letters. We have Leonard's letters. We have irrefutable evidence in our favor. And I have no doubt that Leonard, his lawyers, and now his father, *know it.* I'm certain that is the purpose of this hastily called conference. They may well decide to withdraw their lawsuit if they can't prevent Leonard's letters from being read in open court."

"Oh, dear God—*really?* Is there no other way?" Alice lamented, tears beginning to well in her remarkable eyes. "It's all so . . . *horrid.*"

"No, I'm afraid not; there is no other way, not if we hope to win. If they choose to go forward, we must not back down now. We must proceed to destroy their case with Leonard's own words. You have the rest of your young life to think about, Alice, and what will become of you if this . . . if the Rhinelander case against you succeeds. It will not be pleasant either way; we know that. But losing, being made to accept their utter rejection and nullification of your marriage to Leonard; and of your good name and reputation; *being found guilty of fraud! Good Lord!* And all that might entail and do to harm you, and to further inflame the passions of racism and social prejudice against you and your family—*no!* That is not an outcome I as your advocate will allow without a vigorous and tenacious defense—a fight to the bitter end *however nasty it might be.*"

Even as I said this, in the back of my mind I heard the words *But what if we lose?* I had to push away such thoughts.

"That, dear girl, is why you engaged me as your attorney. I cannot in good conscience and in keeping with the vows I have taken as a member of the bar who has been engaged to represent you and your cause to the best of my ability, I cannot allow this: I cannot allow their fraud to succeed and the Rhinelander deception and mockery of your good name to win. *No!* And thereby ruin you and your family. You have chosen this course, and so we must fight them *tooth and nail*, as it were, and with every fiber of our beings, and every weapon at our disposal."

I smiled and gave Alice a hug as much to reassure myself as to comfort her. She looked up at me, smiled, and said, "Yes. Yes, of course we must. You are right, Mr. Davis. And we will win!"

And with that heartfelt vote of confidence, I took my leave.

* * *

As I walked home that evening, I considered how the Rhinelander annulment suit had, more than any other case I had prosecuted or defended in my long career at the bar, how *Rhinelander v. Rhinelander* had come to represent for me the crucible of the lawyer's calling—that is, that juncture at which the client's apparent best interests were seemingly at odds with the advocate's desire to defend against the claims.

By any reasonable assessment, and I knew this from the beginning: Alice should have taken the settlement. It was a lot of money, more money than she otherwise would have seen in her entire life: $250,000 was the final amount proffered; I suspect Rhinelander probably would have gone higher if pressed. Was victory a possibility given what I knew of the profound dread of interracial marriage that lived in the hearts of most white men? I had to convince the jurymen that, even if they were to exonerate Alice, the marriage would not—indeed, it *could* not—survive.

Was it worth it then to win at any cost?

CHAPTER TWENTY-FIVE

Sunday, December 14, 1924

Dear old friend,

Hello again. Yes, it's me, the famous defendant in *Rhinelander v. Rhinelander!* And here I thought I was simply to be Mrs. Leonard Rhinelander. Who could guess that to marry Len would be considered a crime? I'm a criminal? People treat me like I am. Isn't it enough that I lost the man I love? And now that I admitted I have some Black blood—which everyone already knew in any case—now they won't even allow me into a few of the places in town! Because now I'm a Negress, and a criminal!

They call me a Black vamp—whatever that is supposed to mean. I've seen horrible pictures of vicious females called vamps—women vampires who suck the blood out of their male victims: that is what they say I am. They say I drove Len crazy with sex. How crazy is that? Wait till they hear Len's letters! This is so embarrassing!

Mr. Davis was here today. Actually, he just left a short while ago. I do like Mr. Davis, and I trust him. I know he's a very good lawyer, but I'm not always certain that what he wishes to do in defending me is necessary. Of course, you could say—what do I know? How do I have any idea how to win a trial? Mr. Davis has won a lot of trials for some very big people who had done much worse things than what I am accused of. What worries me is how he seems to want to hurt Len. I don't agree with that. Whatever happens, that is not my way of doing things, to try to hurt someone else to ease my pain or win my case. Losing Len is already so painful to me that I will feel no better by hurting him.

Of course I want to win. As Mr. Davis makes clear, to lose this case would be horrible: a disaster! I've been all over this with my family; with everyone telling me I should accept the money and be done with it—not everyone, certainly not Father. He's always been on my side from the moment I chose to fight when I saw Len's note telling me to get a lawyer and fight. So that's what I'm doing. I still believe Len has some plan.

At first I didn't understand Mr. Davis advising me to admit I had Black blood. In the first place, we never looked at it that way. Father is from the West Indies. He doesn't have African blood. We are not Negroes. And we are not ashamed of who we are in any case. We wouldn't be ashamed of who were even if we were Negroes. Robert Brooks is a Negro, and he was accepted as part of this family. And when I understood how they—how Len's lawyers—were going to such lengths to prove I have colored blood, well, why deny it? It's obvious. Mr. Davis, of course, was right, much as it may have seemed wrong to me at the time. I'm sure he's right about Len's letters too. They are certainly a lot worse than mine! I mean, not worse—but . . . well, much more embarrassing.

Now Mr. Davis is going to read Len's letters to me in court! O my God! The whole world will hear what Len wrote! There does not seem to be any end to the embarrassment and the upset. God, how I wish this trial was over! And Len and I could just go back to the way it was before all this happened. I do miss him so.

There is a part of me, a nasty, sick part of me that actually enjoys it—the trial, that is. Yes! I know that sounds crazy, but I can't help it. It's because I know I am in the right, and as though, as I sit there in court listening to all those terrible things they say about me—how I seduced Len, how I used my sexual desire to make Len lose his mind so he would marry me, how I had my whole family in on the plot to trick the Rhinelander family—there is another me, or another part of me, and even while I'm crying, that other part of me is laughing and saying to me, *These people are all out of their minds! Do they actually believe this nonsense?* Then I worry that I'm losing my mind. How could I find this amusing? I'll tell you how—because it's so crazy! Because I know I'm not guilty of anything but falling in love. All the rest of it is just a kind of madness. Either I'm crazy or everyone else is crazy! That's what makes me feel like laughing inside even when I'm crying. When I told Father about this, I had the nicest talk with him the other evening after everyone left. He's my strength, George Jones. He understands me and what I'm going through. He's been going through this all his life. You can't do this; you can't do that because of the color of your skin. Well, he showed them all they were wrong. He accomplished everything he set out to do. He married Mother. He brought us to this country. When I told him how I felt like laughing sometimes, you know what Father did? He laughed! We both laughed! He hugged me, and we laughed. “Don’t worry, child,” he said. “It’s of no consequence what they say. God knows your heart.”

I suppose the rest of the family thinks Father and I are both mad. But I would rather that the whole world thought me crazy than to have them believe I lied about my color and deceived Leonard into marrying me so as to get at the Rhinelander name and their money. That would mean denying who my father is. No! That is not how Alice Jones Rhinelander chooses to live her life.

Oh, well, I must try to get some rest. Tomorrow it begins all over again!

CHAPTER TWENTY-SIX

Patricide

If I had followed through with my fantasy of killing my father, of bludgeoning Philip to death with a candlestick holder, I could not have committed a more heinous crime than what I have managed to do first with my marriage, and now with my letters to Alice possibly becoming public. That my letters are to be read in court, which by the time they gathered at our home in Manhattan with the lawyers—Leon Jacobs, Mr. Mills, and another man I'd never met who was said to be a law professor from Harvard University Law School and an expert on matrimonial law—by then the consensus seemed to be that there was no way around it, no legal way to keep my letters from coming in.

The lawyers had prepared and submitted a motion to the court arguing that the letters were so "inflammatory" and that they would be so "prejudicial against the plaintiff" that the judge should not allow them in; but Judge Morschauser ruled against them. The lawyers then submitted an emergency brief to the Court of Appeals, asking them to overrule Judge Morschauser. The Court of Appeals ruled that, as we had submitted Alice's letters in an obvious effort to denigrate her character, we had no claim of prejudice against the other side even if the letters they wished to submit and have read were considerably more damaging. Father instructed Mr. Jacobs to call Alice's lawyer, Mr. Davis; but that as well produced no result. The letters—my letters—are to come in; at least as of right now. There is nothing we can do to prevent it short of withdrawing the lawsuit.

How I wish they would withdraw the suit and let my marriage be!

But no! So—*fine!* Let the letters come in. I don't care anymore; it serves them all right. And Alice's lawyer will have a time of it exposing my—whatever—my degradation? I don't care because nothing anyone can do to me is as hurtful as losing my wife. Father wants to destroy my marriage to Alice; well, let's see how that turns out for him and his holy Rhinelander name and reputation.

It's true! I could have murdered Philip and it would have been a lot easier on him and the family. In a way I suppose that is what I have done—or I will have done, once the letters come in. I will have disgraced and forever dishonored the Rhinelander name. Well, I warned them. I urged them not to go through with this lawsuit once it became apparent that Alice would never back down—as, of course, I had hoped and urged her to fight. Father has not bothered to attend the trial. Well, good for him. All his and his lawyers' advice to me, their brilliant tactics and strategies: look where it's got us! Now let him try to hide from the embarrassment my letters will bring to his beloved Rhinelander name.

There was a lengthy discussion with the lawyers to the effect that perhaps we should withdraw the lawsuit to prevent the letters from being read; this, of course, was my preference, though I said nothing. It does no good for me to express an opinion in any case. They ignore anything I have to say. Mr. Mills was in favor of this alternative; he argued that the trial was not going particularly well for our side in any case. Father bristled at the suggestion. "*Quit?*" he said. "*Give in?*" It is anathema to him as a Rhinelander. He said he would "rather go down fighting than to give in." All the lawyers agreed that there would be an appeal of the verdict in White Plains and that if in fact we were to lose at trial, we might stand a better chance of winning on appeal. Mills and Jacobs both expressed feelings of bias against our side by Judge Morschauser, although I haven't seen it; he seems like a fair man to me.

They were concerned with the makeup of the jury; and they are somewhat in awe of how Mr. Davis has been able to control the trial thus far, and even to seemingly manage the mood in and around the courthouse which, all seemed to agree, that with the exception of the racist outside agitators, most of the observers and even the news reporters have taken Alice's side. I'm made to be the villain in all this. Good. I told them it was a bad idea to begin with. But no one listens to me. That is the most extraordinary aspect of this entire fiasco. No one seems to give a damn what I think. The fact that I love Alice, and that I married her knowing full well she has some Black blood from her father's side, I am expected to lie about all that. Of course I knew that! I am not the idiot they wish to portray me as. The only idiotic thing about all of this on my part is that I go along with it. *Why?* O God, how I wish I had an answer to that question. The best I can come up with is that I am afraid—afraid of Father's wrath, yes, afraid of how he would make my life with Alice into a misery for us both and afraid of how it would hurt my mother's memory.

So why did I marry Alice in the first place? Because I love her, and I wanted to make her happy. I thought people might just let us be. What a fool I was to think my father would accept Alice.

Surely I had to know Philip would never allow me to be happy with Alice. Instead I have made us both miserable.

The lawyers agree our best hope is when the case goes to the jury, that the issue of race prejudice will be "our trump card," as Mr. Mills is fond of saying. He believes it will all come down to the fact that twelve white men will be strongly disinclined to rule in favor of forcing a white man of my background to stay in a marriage to an admitted Negress. After they hear my letters to Alice, there's no way of knowing what a jury might do. Once those men—and all who are following the trial here, there, and everywhere—once they hear my letters to Alice, God only knows how they might react. I may be tarred and feathered and run out of town.

Ah, my girl, my Alice—how I miss her warm words of love, her tender touch, and how I hate myself for allowing this to come of the one thing in my life that made me feel like a good person. And now it's—what? A scandal that is upsetting my whole family and Alice's family as well. And it's all my fault. Once again I am horribly comfortable in my own abject misery, in my low opinion of Leonard Kip Rhinelander. I am living up to all my father's worst expectations of me as his son.

And for that, I cry and I pray to my mother's soul for forgiveness.

PART THREE

DUSKY SKIN

CHAPTER TWENTY-SEVEN

A Kiss upon Lips That Never Smile

With trial set to resume Monday morning, December 15, the deputy sheriffs opened the doors to the courthouse at nine o'clock, and the courtroom quickly filled to capacity. On the judge's orders, children under twenty-one, and women who were not accredited journalists or accompanied by their husbands, were refused entry; still several adventurous women were able to find their way into the courtroom. More than two hundred would-be spectators of both genders had to content themselves to wait for word on the progress of the trial while standing outside in the chill fall air.

Kip Rhinelander entered accompanied by his pair of bodyguards. Instead of resuming his place on the witness stand, he took a seat beside his attorneys at the plaintiff's table.

Once the jury was brought in and seated, Isaac Mills stood and addressed the court.

"If Your Honor please," Mills began, "before we continue with the testimony, I crave leave to make a statement of explanation."

I stood and objected that I had been given no notice as to the content of Mills's statement; to which Mills angrily responded, "I decline to inform him of the contents any more than he allowed me to read the letters when he marked them for identification!"

Ah-ha! The letters. We were off to a good start. Judge Morschauser allowed Mr. Mills to proceed.

"Your Honor, first I feel I must explain *why* I requested an adjournment on Friday—" Mills began.

"Your Honor," I interrupted, "that is not necessary. We know why—"

"No, you don't, sir!" Mills protested. "Or perhaps *you* do. However, I wish to explain for the sake of the jury and for the record. Now, twice, Mr. Davis—*twice* you handed the witness, Leonard Rhinelander letters that you then asked him to read for identification. And, rather than reading the letters for the jury, you proceeded to ask Mr. Rhinelander if he still wished to proceed with his case."

Mr. Mills turned to address the judge. "Your Honor, that was a deliberate *threat* to the plaintiff that unless he discontinued this action, the letters, which would disgrace and embarrass him, would be spread upon the record and made public. We ask that the court preclude the defense from entering the—"

I sprang from my chair.

"Just a moment, sir! This is the most improper statement I have heard from a lawyer in a lawsuit made for just one purpose: in a desperate attempt to keep the plaintiff's letters from being read!"

"That is not correct, sir," Mills declared. "After I read the letters, I thought it my duty to give the persons who are interested in this young man, or who by nature ought to be, an opportunity—"

"I beg of the court," I cut Mills off, "is there any evidence before Your Honor as to that? I do not care what Mr. Mills says."

Mills fumed. "Your Honor, I wish you would admonish this man and order him to stop interrupting me! He has been ruled against."

"What ruling? I know of no ruling—"

Judge Morschauser intervened. "Gentlemen, please, let us proceed. Mr. Mills, sir, I expect that you will keep your comments within proper bounds, as I do not wish for this proceeding to result in a mistrial."

"Of course, Your Honor," Mills replied. "I would only wish to make clear that when Your Honor adjourned the trial on Friday, the question arose as to whether it could continue."

Mr. Mills clenched his fists, raised his arms like a prizefighter in a dramatic gesture, and loudly proclaimed: "My answer to his threat is that I *defy him* and I *dare him to do his worst! We proceed with this trial!*"

Bravo! I thought. *You asked for it!*

Whereupon Mr. Mills turned to young Kip and instructed his baffled client, "Mr. Rhinelander, please take the witness stand!"

With Leonard perched uncomfortably on the stand, to continue my cross-examination, I handed the witness a photograph of himself in bed, which was taken during the couple's assignation at the Hotel Marie Antoinette, and I asked, "Do you recognize this photograph, sir?"

"I . . . believe so, yes."

"That is you, in the bed; is it not?"

"It is," Leonard asserted.

"When this photograph was taken, you were in bed at the Hotel Marie Antoinette in Manhattan; is that correct?"

"Yes."

"Was the defendant, your wife, Alice, with you?"

"Yes; we were together."

"Sir, if you would, *please tell us*: Is there some part of your anatomy showing in that photograph, down near your waistline?"

Leonard looked at the photograph, blushed, and said, "No. I don't think so."

"You don't think so?"

Of course there was! *It was his penis!* I took a magnifying glass from my pocket, and handed it to the witness.

"Look again, sir—there." And I pointed. "Aren't your *private organs* showing there?"

This question provoked a few loud guffaws and muffled titters from the gallery as well as several smiles from the jurors. A magnifying glass! To view the man's privates, no less. I had my visual aids at the ready.

"No!" young Kip insisted.

"No?" I took the photograph and the magnifying glass and handed them to the jury foreman. "Well, let's let the jurors decide for themselves."

Judge Morschauser chose this opportunity to inquire, "Mr. Davis, do you still intend to read the letters you have marked for identification?"

"Yes, Judge. I will read, but not without adequate warning."

His Honor then addressed the spectators in the gallery. "I want to give every woman still present a chance to leave this room," he warned. "I am familiar with the contents of the letters. And I must tell you that I would not want to stay if I were a woman. As we proceed, the letters in question could be read at any time. If I were a woman, I repeat, *I would not want to stay in this courtroom as a spectator,* not in any capacity—unless my presence is required by the court. Now, I see that the young people have been removed; that is as it should be."

His Honor assumed a grim facial expression and brought an imperious tone to his voice as he declared, "To you ladies who insist on remaining, I remind you that *you do so at peril to your dignity.*"

"Thank you, Your Honor," I said and waited. However, none of the few curious ladies still present—in addition to the three women reporters—chose this opportunity to quit the proceedings. I repeat: brave ladies of Westchester!

"Mr. Rhinelander," I continued, "if I may ask you to remember, did you tell this jury—I believe it was sometime last week, before we took an adjournment—did you tell these men that your relations; your *sexual practices* with Alice Rhinelander—were always *natural?*"

"I did, yes," Rhinelander asserted.

"And *you still maintain that position today?* As you sit here, sir, under oath, do *you still profess that your relations* with Alice Rhinelander were *decent* and *normal?* Nothing *degenerate* or *perverted* at all?"

Rhinelander flushed and began to sweat. He twitched nervously. Before he could respond, I continued, now addressing the court.

"Your Honor, it seems the witness is unable to answer. Perhaps I can help. Counsel for Mrs. Rhinelander here offers *Defendant's Exhibit S* into evidence." I handed copies of the letter to Mr. Mills and to Judge Morschauser. "I will now read the letter."

"Just a moment, sir!" the judge announced to cut me off and halt the reading. "*This letter ought not to be heard by women!*" he emphasized. "Everybody that hasn't any business in this courtroom will leave, *in the shape of a woman.* We will now take a ten-minute recess. When I come back, *no women will be allowed in the room!*"

There ensued a commotion of complaints and protestations of male chauvinism and sexism that echoed the words of prominent ladies who had been voicing and publishing articles and treatises on the subject of women's rights. The dispute continued outside the courtroom and, no doubt, in parts far from the courthouse in White Plains, New York.

However His Honor, Judge Morschauser, remained adamant.

* * *

So it went. The judge was to have his way. He required the now several women writing about the case for legitimate publications to again produce their press credentials. The sheriffs' deputies then removed any recalcitrant women who did not have valid press assignments to report on the case. Alice stayed in the courtroom, but her mother and sisters joined the displaced ladies in the hallway outside. The hallway was quickly crowded with angry women and anxious men trying to push their way past the sheriff's deputies to take those seats vacated by the women ordered to leave. There were so many resentful, noisily complaining women voicing their anger that the judge's order had been discriminatory that deputies with clubs were called in to force them down the stairs and outside the building. Again there was a mood of riot in the air in and around our county courthouse.

While in the courtroom, as a prelude, in effect to warm the jury up for the truly scandalous letters yet to come, I chose to read a letter from Leonard to Alice dated July 18, 1922, in which the young sexual adventurer wrote:

> Last night, sweetheart, after writing three full pages to you, I undressed and scrambled into my bed, but not to go to sleep. No, baby, do you know what I did? Something that you do when my letters arrive at night. Yes, love one, I took every one of your notes that I received at general delivery and read them while lying on the bed . . . when you mention the time we were in bed together at the "Marie Antoinette," something that belonged to me acted the way it usually did whenever I am with you, darling, and it just longed for the touch of your passionate little fingers, which have so often made me very, very happy. You know, don't you, old scout, what that "*something*" is and how it acted when you began acting naughty!! Oh! Sweetheart, many, many nights when I lay in my bed and think about my darling girl it acts the very same way, and longs for your warm body to crawl

upon me, take it in your soft, smooth hands, then work it up very slowly between your open legs!!!! God! Alice, can you imagine me reading your tempting notes in bed last night; and the way I must have felt and how that "*something*" which belongs to me acted! Baby love, do you remember when we were in bed together how I used to ask you to do it for me, because I couldn't manage it myself? You always were able to make both of us happy, weren't you, darling?

Yes, honeybunch, I loved for you to crawl upon me and do it all yourself, because you never failed, you knew how, didn't you, sweetheart? Am I tempting you and does it bring back memories of past days?

Oh, Alice, love, be good, dear child, because I want you in the days to come and remember to keep our secret locked safely in your heart.

"Sir, Mr. Rhinelander," I inquired of the now thoroughly embarrassed and visibly sweating witness, "can you tell us: Did you love Alice when you wrote this letter to her? What were your intentions?"

Leonard replied, "I did, yes."

"You did. I see. You loved Alice. You weren't trying to arouse her sexual feelings to tempt her with thoughts of sex, then, were you?"

"No, I was not."

"You didn't think that it might tempt this girl—writing about that *something*, which I assume was your private male organ—acting the way it did when she was nearby?"

"I did not, no; that was not my intention."

"That *something* you refer to—was it in fact your private organ?"

"I . . . I . . . I . . ." Leonard couldn't spit it out.

"That's all right; I believe *we know what it is.* It's your male organ, is it not?"

Young Kip blushed deep crimson at the mention of his penis: Who could blame the boy? We were in court, after all, and with a room full of spectators; quite a few still ladies. These words were all going down in the record, and many of them would be recounted in sensational newspaper stories by the next day. To say I was having a jolly time of it embarrassing the naughty young aristocrat is only partly true; for I knew, and all could see, how it was affecting his bride.

I reached for another of Kip's letters and asked, "Now, sir, when I read this next letter, I would ask you to consider if you wrote it to entertain Alice, or to provide pleasant sensations for yourself—"

Before I had finished my question and begun to read, Rhinelander blurted out, "I wrote it to show my being true to Alice! *Don't try to make it something it was not!* I had no other outlet to relieve my emotions except by my letters, and in them I put my very heart and soul. I have a clear conscience. I gave my word of honor to Alice of being true."

"That's commendable, sir," I congratulated the boy. "I am sure we all applaud you for that. However, these letters, well, they are . . . would you . . . *heart and soul.* Interesting you put it that way. I would venture it was *something more* you put into these letters. How—let me ask you, Mr. Kip—how would you describe these letters you wrote to Alice? Besides their being laments from your *heart and soul.* Would you say—could you admit that they are what is commonly referred to as *smut?* Or, more properly known as *pornography?* Is that an accurate description of the contents of your letters to this girl? Recalling, of course, that you were new to all this . . . *behavior.* Or have we dispensed of that idea as well?"

"*No!*" Rhinelander insisted. "They are love letters."

"They are *love letters*, you say. Therefore you are telling the men of the jury that you wrote these letters to Alice out of love, and because this is how you wished to express your love. *Is that correct?*"

Rhinelander made no reply.

"Perhaps the next letter will enlighten you as to your intentions when you wrote it. We will get to that. I think you know what this letter contains. We will let the jury decide. I ask you to recall your previous testimony where you stated that you did not engage in any sexual activity that could be considered *unnatural* or *perverted*. Do you recall saying that?"

Rhinelander appeared unable to answer. I asked, "Would you like to have the court reporter read the record back to you, sir?"

I was concerned that the first letter I read might support Mr. Mills's characterization of Rhinelander as an inexperienced boy in the hands of a sexually adept woman who had captivated him with her wanton ways. The letter I was poised to read next would go a long way to dispel that idea.

Rhinelander managed to say, "I suppose I do agree. One might consider this *smut*."

"I see, very good. Now . . . *let us move on*."

To His Honor, the court reporter, the jury, and the spectators still in the room, I announced, "I will now read from *Defendant's Exhibit M-1*, a letter written by the plaintiff, Leonard Kip Rhinelander, to Alice Rhinelander, and dated June 6, 1922."

> It makes me feel so happy, darling, when I hear from you and especially when you write about how you used to caress me and make me feel as though I were in heaven. Oh! Alice, dear, you certainly did tempt me when you told me the way you used to crawl upon me and lay upon my stomach. Do you ever think, when you are lying in bed at night, how I used to love to make you passionate with my warm lips and the way I did it? Do you ever long for my lips? Yes, love,

> my warm lips and tongue, which have often made you very, very happy. You said you liked my ways, didn't you, dear? Well, sweetheart, I just love your little ways too. They are all so gentle and have a manner all their own.
>
> Do you remember, honeybunch, how I used to put my head between your legs and how I used to caress you with my lips and tongue? You loved to have me do that, didn't you, old scout? Can't you feel me, darling, as I am talking to you, trying to recall past days when we were in bed together? Oh, I often think when I used to lift up your nightgown and crawl down to the foot of the bed, so I could be right under you. "Please, dear, *come*." Do you recall how I asked you to do that? Oh, blessed child, when my lips and tongue were making you so happy you used to say to me, "Oh, Len! Oh, Len!" You were in heaven, dear, because your old faithful, true boy was with you. Love one, you asked me to write an interesting letter like you sent me, so I have tried my best. Have I tempted you, sweetheart, and have I made you imagine I am right next to you?

I put down the letter and scowled at the witness. "Sir, did you write those words to this woman, to Alice Rhinelander?" I asked in a loud voice to be heard over utterances of shock and exclamations of astonishment issuing from those members of the audience still present. I noticed several men of the jury shake their heads and look away in disgust.

Old faithful, true boy Rhinelander on the witness stand flushed; and then, to my surprise, he shrugged, and, I do believe, *he smiled!*

What? Yes, the boy appeared amused!

Judge Morschauser looked down from the bench and said, "Answer the question, Mr. Rhinelander."

And then, to the gallery, the judge said, "Quiet, please! *Order!*

This is unseemly enough without undue commotion in the courtroom!"

"Are those *your words*, Mr. Rhinelander?" I asked again when Kip appeared stymied. "Did you write this, this—well, again, we will let the jury decide what to make of these words, these *things* you wrote of to your wife. My question is—I want to hear you acknowledge it—did you write this? These words are in fact from a letter written by you, are they not?"

If I had expected Rhinelander to be embarrassed, the boy surprised me yet again. He nearly appeared proud of himself. He looked around the room, he gazed at the men in the jury with a look that bordered on smug self-satisfaction as if to say, *See, fellows, I'm no shirker when it comes to pleasuring a lady. Don't you all wish you could have gone there—to kiss the lips that never smile?*

"Yes," Rhinelander admitted and he gloated with a look that seemed to say, *There, top that!*

If nothing else, the boy was unpredictable. I must say these were my impressions, and those shared by my co-counsel; others present in the courtroom may have interpreted Kip's response to having his letter and others read in open court differently. I suspect his lawyers had counseled him to own up to the evidence—at least by his demeanor—as something of an accomplishment, since there was no way around it, and not to let it further injure him and his case in the eyes of the jury; this may have been the only way to respond under these circumstances. Or perhaps it was in fact the boy's true nature at last exposed of all pretense to upper-class moral superiority. And yet there could be no question this letter and others severely undermined the Rhinelander lawyers' claim that the boy was unworldly in matters of sex.

"Did you love this girl, Alice, your wife, when you wrote this . . . *stuff?*" I asked him.

"Yes," Kip admitted.

"Did you intend to marry her?"

"I had visions of it, yes."

"*Visions?* Did you mean *to tempt her* when you wrote of such things?"

Leonard again appeared to smile when he said, "I wrote to make it interesting."

"*Interesting!* Were you also attempting to arouse Alice?"

"I believe I was," Kip admitted.

"Let me ask: Did you ever get a letter like this from your wife?"

"No," Leonard said. "I think not."

"Thank you. I as well think you did not. You knew, you were aware this—what you wrote about—you are aware that what you describe, this . . . behavior was *the vilest kind of smut—what?* And, as you sit here now before this jury, you know that your earlier statement about the *unnatural sex acts* you performed: You know that is not true?"

"Yes," Leonard admitted without appearing upset or embarrassed.

"And you were trying to excite her?"

"At her request I was."

"*What?*" I demanded, my voice rising. "*At her request?* Do you mean to say that Alice *requested you to write this smut?* Sir, I implore you: *Let me have one letter showing a request from Alice for this sort of letter!*"

Rhinelander was at last beginning to lose composure. Of all the statements he had made, I found this the most loathsome. He no longer appeared pleased with himself. He began to twist in his seat, his stammer abruptly returned, and he looked as though he were ready to get up and flee from the room. One moment he was proud of his depravity; the next he was ready to run and hide.

"Did you mean the things you wrote in the last letter?"

"I, I, I . . . I did, yes."

"And did you . . . *did you do the things* you wrote?"

After some more stammering and looking about as though for someone to help him, Kip managed a tentative, "Yes." And then a more forceful, "Yes, I did!"

"You were bringing some kind of sex delight to this girl without the use of your own natural organs?"

Rhinelander replied, "Yes."

"Using your tongue?"

"Yes."

"And your lips?"

"Yes!"

"And you are telling the men of this jury that you hadn't the slightest suspicion, in doing that to this girl that it was *an unnatural thing?*"

"I did not, no," Rhinelander answered. "It seemed natural to me."

This response provoked muted cries and gasps from some of the spectators, and hoots and guffaws from others. Rhinelander looked about the room—and again he smiled! Who could understand this lad? He seemed to want nothing more than to amuse the spectators with evidence of his depravity! He wanted to be liked for being a sex pervert!

I leaned in closer and asked, "Have you any suspicion about it now?"

There was some commotion at the rear of the courtroom as the doors opened and several ladies managed to barge their way back into the room.

Rhinelander looked directly back at me; he glared at me without the slightest trace of shame. "No," he said and smirked. "I have no suspicion. *Do you?*"

I shook my head in disbelief, realizing I had pushed him too far, and that now he was ready to take a combative stance against my questioning, feeling he was engendering some sort of fellow feeling from at least some of the men of the jury, and as a last resort to keep what remained of his pride. In hindsight I see I would have been wise to quit this line of questioning while I was ahead.

"Sir, Mr. Rhinelander, you still tell this jury that you think that what you describe doing to this young girl—with your tongue, as you write, and your lips—that it is a natural thing to do? *Is that it?*"

Leonard smirked and said, "As far as I know."

Which remark brought peals of laughter from the men in the gallery and in the jury box.

"ORDER!" His Honor demanded.

I gave Rhinelander and the jury an incredulous look. "*Still?* As far as you know *now?* You don't know any better *now*, as you sit here?" I pressed him.

Kip shrugged his shoulders and answered, "No, I don't."

I couldn't believe what I was hearing from this young man; but I should have seen it coming. Often in the heat of cross-examination one can lose perspective and keep at an issue or line of questioning until it begins to work against the interrogator and his purpose; hence, I adjusted my tactic.

"Sir, your own lawyer attempted to portray you as a slightly retarded boy who had virtually no sexual experience before meeting Alice. I believe he said of you that you were a young man upon whom 'no girl had ever smiled before.' Now here you are telling this jury that you . . . that you performed *this unnatural sex act*—call it what it is: *cunnilingus!* You performed *cunnilingus* upon this girl! And yet you wish this jury to believe that you have no understanding that what you were doing is unnatural? And that you haven't heard since then, since you admitted doing this thing, that it is *an unnatural thing? A depraved sex act?* Where did you learn of this vile thing?"

Rhinelander looked back at me with what I can only say was

a glint of amusement in his eyes and said, "No, sir, I have not, and I do not. I didn't learn of it anywhere. It just came *naturally*."

There were loud sounds of shock and hoots of amusement from the gallery. The men in the jury box shifted uncomfortably; some shook their heads with dismay. Others appeared amused.

"What? *Natural?* I beg to differ. Are you aware, sir, do you know that there are *statutes*, there are *laws* written in the criminal code of New York in an entire section on Crime Against Nature that define such activity as *sodomy*, a criminal act, and that provide for up to *twenty years' imprisonment for a conviction?*"

Mr. Mills stood to object. "Your Honor, I must take exception to this entire line of questioning as irrelevant and outside the scope of this proceeding. Mr. Rhinelander has not been charged with any crime. We are not here to determine the lawful or illegal activity of Mr. Rhinelander—"

"I beg your pardon," I said and cut Mills off. "Indeed we are here to determine the legality of this marriage, and as such, the activities between the husband and wife, which counsel has attempted to portray in a manner as to characterize the defendant, Alice Rhinelander, as a sexually aggressive female vamp; and the plaintiff, Leonard Kip Rhinelander, as a naive boy with no experience in sexual activity. Yet we now have in evidence letters written by Mr. Rhinelander describing sex acts that are—well, vile, unnatural, *and illegal.* And we have heard his testimony; we heard him tell the jury just now that he finds nothing unnatural in these things he did to his wife. We have heard in Mr. Rhinelander's own words in letters to his wife of the filthy and debased sex acts he performed upon this girl, his wife, whom he now seeks to condemn as the perpetrator of a fraud upon himself as a man his lawyers have portrayed as an idiot and unworldly in matters of sex. This, I believe, is most pertinent evidence to *disprove this false characterization* of the plaintiff by showing who in fact—the witness, Leonard Kip Rhinelander—was the instigator of unnatural and in fact illegal sexual activity—"

"That is enough; the letter is in evidence," Judge Morschauser ruled. "It speaks for itself as to the plaintiff's intentions, his sophistication, or understanding as to the matters written in the letters. The jury will have an opportunity to review the letters in evidence and to make their own determination as to the intent and the character of the author of the letters. Therefore it is proper for counsel to inquire on cross-examination as to what the plaintiff knew or did not know with regard to the social and legal interpretations of the acts he describes. I would add, however, Mr. Davis, that I believe the point has been made and that you should move on."

"Thank you, Your Honor. Indeed, I will move on."

* * *

But where to go from here? *Cunnilingus indeed!* Described in vivid detail by the Rhinelander boy in his letter, and owned up to on the witness stand as though it were some sort of bold and commendable lovemaking technique he had perfected. Was there any depth of depravity to which Kip Rhinelander had not readily stooped? One might wonder if, while he was down there rooting around with his warm lips and tongue between Alice's legs like some sort of animal if he had not managed to stray around the bend to that other darker orifice. If ever there was a flagrant example of the moral degeneracy of the aristocratic class exhibited before a judge and jury in a legal proceeding—and hence the world—here was Kip Rhinelander looking self-satisfied on the witness stand for all to see; and who, to my astonishment, appeared to sit up straight in the chair and stiffen with pride as though this were his shining moment.

(It would be reported, though I have no idea upon what basis of fact, that for weeks following the conclusion of the Rhinelander trial, Kip received a number of letters from young ladies, often accompanied by photographs, and with offers of romance.)

* * *

The other letters I read into evidence—and there were parts in all of them that were if not equally shocking certainly pornographic, with Kip making reference to his penis time and again, with it jumping and stirring and becoming erect at the memory of ravishing Alice in ways and in positions he had read about in his book of some Indian sex religion; and his relieving himself in her absence—these letters proved, if nothing else, that Rhinelander was familiar with, and that he knew at close inspection, every orifice, every nook and hidden cranny of his bride's body with his eyes, his mouth, his lips, and his tongue, and that he would surely have discovered in his explorations clear indications that the girl was not totally of pure white blood.

"And all this time," I asked, "all the while that you were engaging in this *unnatural*—although you claim it to be natural—all this time it never occurred to you that your wife was not of pure white blood? You still wish the men of this jury to believe you, sir, when you say that, given what you have now admitted, and claimed to be quite natural, given this: that even as you were engaged in this activity with your wife, it still did not appear obvious to you that she has some Black blood?"

"No, I did not. I believed her when she told me she was white."

Now I was angry. I felt there was no reason for me to continue my cross-examination. Where could one hope to go from such revelations? I did ask that one outstanding question, however, as delicately as I could.

"Sir, Mr. Rhinelander, are you telling the gentlemen of this jury, and do you expect them to believe that as you were . . . thus engaged in—I don't think there is any other way of asking it—*of licking your wife's vagina*, as you put it in the letter, with your head between her legs—that even then you were unable to perceive that Alice was not of pure Anglo-Saxon white blood . . . given the texture of her pubic hair?"

Rhinelander surprised me once again and provoked an outburst of loud laughter from the audience when he answered, "At that time, I wasn't thinking about it."

A great answer! An inspired response!

"Of course not!" I shot back at the witness. "You were otherwise occupied. Why think about it? *It was obvious, was it not?* You hadn't visited there, between your wife's legs, expecting to find the soft down of a pure white girl—*what?*"

"I wasn't sure what I would find."

More laughter! More cries of surprise.

Judge Morschauser called for order in the court.

"But you knew, that is, once you went down there and began licking, you knew, didn't you, sir? There could be no mistake, could there? Alice, you had to know then—*in fact you already knew quite well*, didn't you, Mr. Rhinelander?" I shouted angrily. "*All this is nonsense* because *you knew* Alice was a girl whose blood had been tainted with the tar brush, *didn't you, sir?* There was no question in your mind—which we have shown to be sound and not that of an imbecile, as your attorneys would have the jury believe—you knew Alice was of mixed race then, when *you were licking her vagina*. You're no sexual neophyte, as your lawyers want this jury to believe. *That's all lies*. You are in fact a man with no conscience, no moral guideposts; and you knew Alice had mixed blood through every moment of your seduction and . . . and . . . your ravishing of the girl. You knew it when you met her family. You knew it when you met and spent considerable time with Robert Brooks,

Alice's brother-in-law, and his daughter, Roberta. You knew it when you were living in your wife's, the Joneses' family home *before and after* it had been revealed in the newspapers. And you know it now as you sit there in the midst of your false evidence against your wife in this despicable lawsuit—*do you not, sir?* You know in your mind and your heart and soul, as you put it, that this lawsuit, instigated by your imperious father, Philip Rhinelander, and executed by these men, Leon Jacobs and my colleague Mr. Mills, you know this is an action brought against this girl, your wife, who betrothed herself, gave her love and devotion to you, you know that it is *based upon nothing but false claims, lies*, and *gross misrepresentations*. Do you still wish to proceed with your lawsuit, Mr. Rhinelander?"

Mills was on his feet. "Your Honor! Please, is Mr. Davis cross-examining the plaintiff, or is he summing up? He is badgering the witness! May I remind Mr. Davis and the court that counsel for the plaintiff has given *no indication whatsoever* that Mr. Rhinelander has any wish or intention to withdraw the lawsuit!"

"Fine. Then let us move on," I said and turned back to the witness.

"Sir, Mr. Rhinelander, as you look at your wife, Alice Rhinelander, as you look at this young woman—how would you describe her color?"

Without actually looking at Alice, Kip replied, "Dark. She is dark. But no darker than women I had seen in Havana—"

"*Havana?* Excuse me, sir. We are not talking about women you may have seen in Havana. You weren't married to them, I suppose. We are talking about *your wife*, with whom you lived in close physical contact and, as the jury has heard, with whom you engaged in the most intimate, *unnatural*, and . . . well, *telling* sexual acts."

I turned to Alice. She knew what was coming; I had discussed it with her, and with her mother and her father, George Jones.

No one was happy with the prospect I had proposed—that of displaying Alice's body as an exhibit in the proceeding—least of all me, for I knew how I would be roundly condemned for having further disgraced and degraded the girl in a scene reminiscent of the slave trader's auction block with Alice's body exposed and her considered as an object and not as a person, not as a young woman with human feelings.

Alice and her parents had asked if this display might not be unnecessary; of course it might be too much for the girl to bear. Even my co-counsel advised that I might be taking the defendant's evidence too far. But I knew—or I believe I knew—as the lawyer trying the case; and as the chief litigator who had been carefully observing the men on the jury at every stage in the proceedings; and as the one who was best able to gauge their reactions to the testimony; and as the authority charged with ultimate responsibility for Alice's defense: I knew that if Alice were to lose and to be convicted of fraud, as her defender, I would be the party deemed responsible. I had become convinced that to utterly win over the men in the jury, it was necessary to let them see with their own eyes *real evidence* of what was apparent to Leonard Kip Rhinelander when he made love to this young girl before he married her and after she had become his wife.

"Mrs. Rhinelander," I said, turning to Alice, "with your permission," then I turned to the judge, "and with Your Honor's accordance, I would ask now that the courtroom be cleared not only of the women, but of all spectators, anyone who does not have business before this court to depart from the courtroom, and let the courtroom be closed so that only the men on the jury; the court clerk; the stenographer and bailiffs; the parties to the proceeding; and Alice's mother, Elizabeth Jones, be permitted to remain. At which time I will ask the defendant, Alice Rhinelander, to display her legs and torso for the members of the jury to prove that her race is *in fact obvious* and *clearly discernible* in her physical appearance."

There were exclamations of dismay and muted outrage from the spectators. *What?* The girl would be made to strip before the jury? Even the men in the jury box appeared stunned by this suggestion—however, I will venture to guess that more than a few of them were intrigued by the prospect of viewing Alice's naked body for themselves; to see with their eyes what Rhinelander saw when he made love to his wife. That surely would be conclusive and irrefutable evidence of the girl's mixed race.

Mr. Mills objected vehemently. "Your Honor, I do not want a demonstration of a naked body at this trial! Already there has been far too much inflammatory testimony introduced by defense counsel—"

"It will not be entirely naked," I interrupted. "But, for the benefit of the plaintiff, Mr. Kip Rhinelander, who seems to be unable to perceive what is quite obvious to others, and so that the men of this jury may decide whether Rhinelander was deceived by his wife as to her color, which is the crux of the matter in this lawsuit; or if Mr. Rhinelander and his lawyers are attempting to deceive this court and jury with their claim that young Kip was unable to discern his wife's skin color and mixed race: I believe that *the actual evidence of Mrs. Rhinelander's body* is obvious and of the utmost relevance and importance to this jury so that they may be allowed to come to a verdict based upon *what they are able to see with their own eyesight* while looking at Mrs. Rhinelander's body."

Judge Morschauser agreed. He ruled that displaying Alice's body to the jury was "proper and important" because, in his words, "it must be shown in this sort of case."

"Thank you," I said. "May I suggest that, rather than conducting this procedure in open court, perhaps it would serve our purposes better if we withdrew to Your Honor's chambers . . . for the demonstration."

"Very well," the judge concurred.

I had the impression His Honor was enjoying this; we were breaking new ground in a trial that was already infamous; and I suspect that Judge Morschauser himself was intrigued by the prospect of seeing Alice naked.

"And whose presence would you request in chambers besides the witness, Mrs. Rhinelander, the jury, and counsel?" the judge asked with a trace of amusement.

But Mr. Mills interrupted. "I am sorry, Judge Morschauser, I beg your indulgence. For the record, and on behalf of the People of New York, I must again object *strenuously* to this indecent procedure. This is unheard of—an affront to the dignity of this court. You go through the farce of exposing her body and asking him if she is the girl! What a ridiculous thing that is! Is there any possible question about it? The witness, Mr. Rhinelander, has been asked to look at her and identify her as his wife a dozen times in court. It is an indecent proceeding, Your Honor."

"Oh, please, sir," I said with a slight intonation of ridicule, "we will endeavor not to offend your delicate sensibilities, Mr. Mills. This will be a decidedly decent demonstration for counsel's sake, for the members of the jury, and in deference to Mrs. Rhinelander's modesty. Clearly, sir, I will not ask that the witness identify his wife; we've done that. I will ask Alice Rhinelander to expose—and I shall ask the men of the jury to look upon the defendant's body from the waist up, as well as her lower limbs—"

"Fine, sir!" Mills barked. "What else is there . . . *her feet?* You've described her entire body!"

There were peals of laughter in the courtroom with this outburst; even I could not suppress a chuckle. Alice, however, was not laughing; and I felt badly for making fun of what was for her a most disgraceful and embarrassing episode. But it could not be helped, not if we were going to achieve our goal of utterly defeating the Rhinelander lawsuit.

Mills went on. "Of course, Mr. Rhinelander is able to identify this woman as his wife. He has admitted he saw her naked at the hotel."

"Your Honor, as I'm certain my learned colleague understands, that is not the issue I wish to demonstrate with this evidence. The question is: Could Mr. Rhinelander, upon seeing his wife's naked body—those parts of his wife's body not readily apparent as to the jury—could Rhinelander possibly have failed to know that she is of mixed race? *That is the issue before the jury*, and that is the question to be addressed for the jury with this *display*; the jurors will be allowed to see in private what they are not able to see of the defendant, when she is fully clothed, as in open court."

It was clear Rhinelander's lawyers did not wish for this evidence, as it were, to be allowed in; and yet they struggled to come up with justifiable grounds to keep it out.

Mr. Mills asked for a sidebar. "Your Honor," he began, "Mr. Davis is in the middle of his cross-examination of the plaintiff. We are at a critical point in the examination of our chief witness. Furthermore, we have not finished presenting Mr. Rhinelander's case. I still have additional witnesses I plan to call. This is highly irregular, at this point in the trial, with the plaintiff's case still in progress, for Mr. Davis to ask to present his own witness, the defendant, to testify in her own behalf—"

"No, Your Honor, I beg the court's pardon," I interrupted. "That is not what I am asking. On the contrary; I am offering Mrs. Rhinelander's *physical* appearance, that is to say, her body, to be entered as *real evidence* of her obvious mixed race; offering such *real evidence* as allowed under the rules; which is, and here I quote the rule: 'evidence acquired directly by the court or jury themselves, through the medium of their own senses, by the inspection of the subject matter itself.' Now, in this instance, the defense is offering the *defendant's physical body* as such *real evidence*, which, I'm sure Your Honor will agree, may be entered at any time to allow for the tribunal's own view of a thing shown to it.

"With the court's permission, Mrs. Rhinelander will appear and offer the proof of her *physical body* as real evidence for the jury to consider. She will not be asked to testify; I will not ask her any questions, as I'm aware that is not allowed in a presentation such as this of real evidence. Only various parts of her body will be exhibited to the men on the jury with limited colloquy; and, as such real evidence, it is to be entitled to the greatest weight by the decider of facts when the jury is asked to assess the value of the evidence introduced by both sides."

Judge Morschauser agreed; His Honor ruled, "As there is no evidence of what her condition is to the eye; that is to say, it is not readily apparent whether the defendant is dark or light, for that limited purpose, as submitted as real evidence, I will allow counsel to make profert of the plaintiff's body that it may be received in evidence."

I reminded His Honor that Rhinelander as well was needed to be present during the viewing.

"Certainly," the judge agreed. "Mr. Rhinelander, please step down from the witness stand and accompany your lawyers to my chambers. Let it be noted that the witness is still under oath."

Alice wept quietly as her mother, Elizabeth Jones, led her from the courtroom and into the judge's chambers. I followed, as did the witness, the plaintiff, Kip Rhinelander; his three lawyers; and my co-counsel.

It soon became apparent that the judge's chambers would not accommodate the witness, the jury, Judge Morschauser, all the attorneys, and others deemed essential to the display and submission of Alice's body in evidence; thus the judge asked to have the procedure relocated once again, this time to the jury room.

Alice was shown to a side room where she undressed; she then covered her body with her overcoat. With the men of the jury present; with Kip and his lawyers; my co-counsel, Judge Swinburne; His Honor; the court clerk and stenographer in attendance; Mrs. Jones led her weeping, distraught daughter back into the jury room. I begged Alice's forgiveness for the blatantly disrespectful spectacle of being asked to expose her body before a roomful of men who were sitting in judgment of her.

"I am very sorry, Mrs. Rhinelander," I began. "I am most apologetic to have to ask you this. But now, for the benefit of the jury, would you please *let down the coat* . . . that's it . . . and now, if you would, please stand before the men of this jury. . . . Yes, that's right. . . . Now, *let the coat down* . . . just a bit more . . . *so that the upper portion of your body, as far down as your breasts* is exposed and visible to the members of the jury."

Alice, still in tears, complied. The twelve men all gazed upon Alice's naked upper body: her back, shoulders, and her breasts. It was apparent—if Alice's face, her arms, and her hands may have been seen as dark due to exposure to the sun—the parts of her upper body normally covered with clothing were obviously those of a woman who had Black blood in her veins; there could be no doubt in anyone's mind who saw her naked that she was not of the pure white race. She had lovely skin: a rich, swarthy brown color, and smooth; but it was clearly skin with pigmentation of a decidedly mixed-race person, and not that of a pure white Anglo-Saxon girl; and no one with functioning eyesight could deduce otherwise.

"Thank you, Mrs. Rhinelander," I continued. "And now,

would you be so good as to raise up the coat . . . as high—that's it, very good. You can lift it up to your waist so that the men on the jury can view your upper legs, to just above your knees. . . . *Fine. Just so . . .*"

Again, Alice did as she was asked, one could say almost gracefully, seductively, even if done while weeping with shame; and all eyes were upon her. She lifted up the hem of her coat; we saw her firm, shapely thighs and just the start of the round curve of her buttocks. *Oh, no! Those buttocks! Could there be any question?* The skin tone was one thing, and the shape of her buttocks quite another. I noticed most of the jurors gazed at her curiously, attentively (wantonly? lasciviously?). I could only surmise based upon my own impressions and reaction. The girl was lovely with her clothes on, more beautiful yet naked. These gentlemen had most likely never before had occasion to view the body of a mixed-race girl; nor had I. My God, what dark feminine beauty! Only a couple of the older gentlemen gave her a quick look and then turned away, as if to save her some of the humiliation, or to thwart whatever suppressed fascination they may have felt and wished to avoid given their age.

Fraud you say, Kip Rhinelander? Where is the fraud? Why, Alice's skin is not fraudulent. Here is her naked body—the *real evidence.* Not conjecture. Not opinion. Not supposition. *Here is the proof.* And let this display prove as well how our nation is guilty of fraud, how we lied about freedom and justice for all. Now we would condemn a girl for loving her man. Why? Because of what no one with eyesight could deny. Even if Alice had told Rhinelander that she was of pure white blood, which we know she never did, still her flesh, her dusky skin, said otherwise: Rhinelander is the liar; what Alice's body revealed could not be denied. The men on the jury must vote in favor of Alice, or they would acquire Rhinelander's guilt.

* * *

Yes, of course the poor girl was upset at having to stand naked before the jury. People may ask how I could have put her through such a humiliating display. Well, I'll explain, in time, and with the facts. After the disrobing, once she was dressed, Alice had to be removed from the jury room in a state of emotional collapse, as much a result of the disrobing as of the accumulated shame and stress of the trial itself.

Accompanied by her mother and sisters, she was taken from the courthouse in tears, her whole being racked with sobs. She had to be carried from the building by her father, and she was protected as Mr. Jones and two court officers fought their way through the frantic crowd outside held at bay by the army of policemen and sheriff's deputies. The men pushed and shoved to get close to Alice, as if to make their own judgment as to her race and her beauty. Alice would not return to court for the remainder of the day; in fact, none of the Jones family was present during the afternoon session.

* * *

With an outwardly stoic Rhinelander back on the witness stand (I had to ask myself, *Has this man no human feelings? Does he not care what he is putting his wife through? Or is it all sublimated? Turned from humiliation into cockiness?*) the court was brought to order over desperate objections from Mr. Mills. He asked that the entire disrobing episode be declared unseemly; that it be stricken from the record; and that the jury be instructed to ignore it, all of which Judge Morschauser angrily denied.

"I have ruled!" the judge declared. "I allowed it, and I still allow it. Now—move along!"

I was given permission to continue my cross-examination of the plaintiff. Once again, and over more objections from Rhinelander's lawyers, who were now quite obviously in a panic as feeling their case failing, I began a series of questions related to what the witness and the jury had just observed in the jury room.

"Mr. Rhinelander," I began, "you have now had an opportunity to view portions of your wife's body, correct?"

"Yes," Rhinelander agreed, and made an effort to appear bored.

Alice, her mother, and her father still had not returned to the courtroom.

"Very well, sir. And now, please tell the men of this jury—who also viewed your wife's body—is your wife's skin the same shade now as when you first saw her naked body in the Hotel Marie Antoinette? And when you bathed her? When you . . . well, we won't revisit that subject, but I'm certain you understand what I refer to. Tell us: Is your *wife's skin color the same now* as it was when you first saw . . . *these parts of her body exposed?* When you first seduced her and saw her naked?"

"I . . . well, I—"

"Just answer the question, sir! Yes or no?"

"Yes," Kip admitted.

"Well," I said, "fine. Thank you, sir, for clearing that up. And you have admitted that your eyesight is good, correct?"

"Yes."

"You can see color. You are able to perceive *Black and white, brown and tan, green and red*—you still assure the men on the jury that you are not color-blind, correct? Nothing has changed there—*what?*"

"Yes," Rhinelander agreed.

"Yes, you are not color-blind. Thank you. Very good, sir. So we may understand that you have no difficulty seeing and discerning colors, correct? And with all of that understood, please,

I pray, and now, if you will, *tell this jury*, Mr. Rhinelander . . . *what color is your wife's body?*"

"I, I, I . . . Well, seeing it now, as you say, I find her *dark*—"

"Darker than she was when you saw her naked in the Marie Antoinette? Darker than when you bathed her?"

"I don't know. I can't be sure," Rhinelander stammered and looked at his feet.

"But you told us your eyesight is fine, no difficulty seeing colors. You said your mind as well is functioning normally. *Yet you still wish the men of this jury to believe that you were not aware your wife has colored skin?* How can that be? We saw her body just moments ago. We could see it plainly. And I think you should admit it, and please *tell us the truth*—for once in this trial, for once in this entire lawsuit, perhaps even *for once in your life*—please, Mr. Rhinelander, admit that *you knew all along* as you made love to your wife at the Marie Antoinette, you knew, because you saw what we have just observed, that your wife, that Alice Rhinelander, has an obvious mix of white *and* Black blood. You knew it because you could see it when you saw her naked in bed at the Marie Antoinette *before you married her.* Isn't it true: you could see with your eyes what the men on the jury—and you, sir—what we just saw in the jury room when you looked at your wife's naked body! *There was no question in your mind before you married Alice as to her mixed race just as there is no question now—correct?* You knew all along that Alice has Black blood! And, admit it, sir, as you admitted to Barbara Reynolds, the newspaper writer for the *New Rochelle Standard Star*, who interviewed you when the news of your wife's racial taint was first reported; you told Miss Reynolds then that you knew Alice has some Black blood in her veins given that her father, George Jones, is a colored man. But as you told Miss Reynolds, *it made no difference to you*, because you *loved Alice* and you married her *knowing of her mixed race*; didn't you, sir? Please admit the truth before this jury *that you were aware of Alice's mixed blood*, but that it was *of no significance to you*; it mattered not at all to you; *in fact, you liked it*; it intrigued you and excited you; you were fine with Alice's racial mix, and you loved your wife until—*what? Until your father, until Philip Rhinelander, found out* that you had married Alice, a girl of mixed race and well below the Rhinelander social standing; and then *he, your father, determined that the marriage was not acceptable*, and he *demanded* that your marriage to this girl be *terminated. Isn't that so, sir?* Isn't that *the truth of what happened* and why we are here in this courtroom, because your father *ordered this man*"—I turned and pointed at Leon Jacobs—"your father, Philip Rhinelander, ordered Mr. Jacobs to take you away from Alice, to remove you from your bride, take you away from the woman you married, the woman you have told us *you loved*; took you away, and in the company, under the guardianship *of this man*, Mr. Leon Jacobs, your father's factotum and alleged attorney—"

"Your Honor!" Jacobs leaped to his feet.

"Oh, sit down, sir! You'll have your chance," I said, provoking chortles from the gallery. I swung around to face the witness.

"*Tell us the truth, Mr. Rhinelander!* It was *only then*, when your father, when Philip Rhinelander *threatened to cut you off from your inheritance if you insisted upon continuing what was to him an unacceptable marriage*; it was then, as you were afraid of losing your claim to the Rhinelander wealth, that *forced you to reject your bride* on the *false claim* she deceived you as to her color? *Isn't it true, sir*: your father's money, his threats of your being severed from the family fortune: *that is what made you decide to accuse Alice of deceiving you?*"

"*No!*" Rhinelander managed to blurt out with some conviction, although it was hardly convincing. "I may have suspected, but . . ." His face flushed and here he lost confidence. "That is, when I looked at her, and when she told me she was of pure white blood, I believed her. I . . . I loved her, and I wanted so to believe her. I . . . I . . . I just couldn't believe it until . . . until it was out, until the truth was known."

"*The truth?*" I demanded. "*Whose truth?* You, sir, when you looked at your wife, Alice, when you saw her naked as the men of this jury just did, when you looked at Alice's body: *What did you see?* There is all the truth anyone needs to know that your wife has some colored blood. You have just looked at her with the men of this jury; you looked at her body, those parts of her body not normally exposed, and you have seen, as have the men of the jury, you have seen her body, and recognized that her skin is that of a mixed-race girl: Is it not? *Tell us!* Tell us, as you say—*the truth!*"

Rhinelander made no answer.

I sighed and shook my head. I knew I had him fully exposed as a liar to the men on the jury as well as to anyone else following the trial.

"I see, nothing to say, aye, Mr. Kip? *You knew your wife's father!* And you played cards with her *brother-in-law!* Please, this is all so tedious, so transparent. *Where is the truth?* Because, what you are saying then, if you persist in denying what we all know is true, what I take it you wish this jury to understand about you, sir, as to your character, Kip Rhinelander, what you want the world to know about you is that, in essence, the truth is that although you knew your wife had mixed blood, *you have no mind of your own!* You have no *perception of reality* that is not *dictated to you by others*, whether by your father, your father's lawyers, or your reading of the newspapers. So if I am to understand it, what you are telling the men of this jury, and indeed the world—is that *you are nothing, sir . . . and not really a man at all, Kip Rhinelander, certainly not a gentleman!* No, not when it comes to taking responsibility for your actions!

"In fact, isn't it true, sir, that, as you sit there on the witness stand—" Here I stopped and looked directly at the jury. I shook my head in apparent dismay, and then turned back to face the witness and loudly declared, "Isn't it true, Kip Rhinelander, that *your father*, the high and mighty Philip Rhinelander, who does not lower himself to attend this trial *of his son* and his *daughter-in-law*, isn't it true that your father *rules your every thought*, your *every action*; and that, as you sit there before this court giving this testimony *as your father and your father's lawyers have directed you, and ordered you*, is it not true that you, sir, Kip Rhinelander, *YOU ARE NOTHING MORE THAN AN EMPTY SUIT!*"

"NO!" Rhinelander bristled and flushed with anger. "*You're wrong!*"

"That's all right, sir," I cut him off. "I believe we've heard enough."

And then to the judge I announced, "I have no further questions for this witness at this time, Your Honor."

* * *

The court was in a bit of turmoil; more than a bit, actually; it was a hubbub. Judge Morschauser called for order, and then he announced a brief adjournment and asked to see counsel in his chambers before Mr. Mills would conduct his redirect. We withdrew.

During a conference with the judge and Mr. Mills, when queried by His Honor, I said I had no other letters I expected to enter into evidence unless to rebut something the plaintiff might state during his redirect.

"Thank goodness for that," said the judge. "And any more *displays?*"

"No, Your Honor. Nothing more."

Therefore it was decided to permit the ladies and young people back into the courtroom, as they were clamoring and causing a bit of a disturbance in the hallways and in the square outside the courthouse.

It was an uncomfortable conference. Mr. Mills, His Honor, the other lawyers, and I all felt oddly enervated and bemused by Kip's stunning appearance on the witness stand, and more so by the emotionally fraught disrobing of the defendant. I was seen as the instigator of unwanted sensationalism. We were all aware that nothing like this had ever taken place in a court of law before, and even I wondered at the propriety of such a display: Would this evidence withstand appellate review? Of course, in a trial where the plaintiff had been cross-examined regarding his testimony as to having readily performed cunnilingus on his wife, what could be more shocking to the court if not to the witness himself? Indeed, the Rhinelander trial appeared to have broken new ground in the practice of family law. It was a cruel farce, and a blatant display of class and race arrogance turned on its head.

Mr. Mills and Leon Jacobs were both obviously distressed by the rapidly deteriorating progress of their case. Though they weren't ready to admit it, they knew that Rhinelander's appearance on the witness stand had been a major setback. Once again, I was reminded that they had never planned for a trial; never devised a sensible trial strategy; never considered what a poor witness the plaintiff might prove to be; and always assumed that Alice would accept the settlement and quit the marriage.

Judge Morschauser was rightly concerned about the looming possibility of a mistrial, and so in the meeting in chambers he admonished counsel to make every attempt to bring the case to an acceptable and judicious conclusion. We discussed additional witnesses to be called, the possibility of Alice testifying, which (though I didn't say so, wishing to let them believe the option was still open) asking this of Alice was doubtful, given her emotional state after the disrobing. I felt what we accomplished in the jury room was more than I could possibly hope to achieve with Alice on the witness stand; nor was I comfortable with the prospect of subjecting her to what would surely be a vicious and distressful cross-examination by Mr. Mills. No, I had resolved in my mind not to call Alice unless there was some as yet unforeseen event in the course of the trial that could only be cured by testimony from the defendant.

We returned to the courtroom with the firm commitment to bring the trial to an expeditious and decorous conclusion so that the jury might have the case by week's end. With the defendant and her family still absent, and given the lateness of the hour, Judge Morschauser adjourned proceedings for the remainder of the day.

* * *

There was an even larger and more eager crush of reporters and photographers to make one's way through before being assaulted by the crowd of spectators in the street, an unruly mob that had continued to grow and become more clamorous with each passing day of the trial and that had become even more unsettled as the trial's end drew near. Alice and her family had to be removed surreptitiously through a rear exit and delivered straight into a waiting car provided by Rhinelander. Rhinelander as well was mobbed, although he arrived and exited in the company of his phalanx of bodyguards, who charged through the crowd like football linemen on the gridiron.

In discussing the trial with my colleagues in our offices later in the day, I said that, on balance, I believed that Kip Rhinelander's questionable testimony, and in particular the display of Alice's body, had brought about a decidedly positive turn in the trial for our side given the evidence in rebuttal to the plaintiff's case;

that young Kip's performance on the witness stand had been dubious at best; and that we had virtually proved the defendant not guilty of any sort of fraud. Yet, with all that, I admitted to the feeling we all held that there had been something else, some facet of Rhinelander's appearance, that might have been curiously disarming in his demeanor on the witness stand: yes, he was pitiable, and that bothered me. I worried that it might be seen to work against us by evoking sympathy for the boy; that is to say, one could not help feeling compassion for a weakling who was so obviously under the strict rule of his rich and powerful father. And yet here was a young man who had shown the desire and the will to strike out on his own in defiance of his class, his race, and everything he was meant to become and acquire as the heir apparent of the Rhinelander name and family fortune, and to distinguish himself first by falling head over heels in love with Alice, a girl so obviously unacceptable to his father, and then by marrying her. These in themselves made for a romantic tragedy with Kip as the reluctant hero, and the possible costar of the melodrama. Then there was the whole dreadful childhood trauma brought about by young Kip's mother's death, and how that had affected the lad, leaving him emotionally vulnerable perhaps to an older, more experienced, and more confident woman who gave him comfort and emotional solace. I was concerned that the jury as well may have felt sympathy for Rhinelander and his lovelorn quandary: forbidden the bride he so clearly loved. One needed to foist the blame for the lawsuit away from young Kip and onto his father.

In addition to this, and given how complicated I found Kip to be, one could sense some new mood, and with it a change in behavior that seemed to have come gradually to animate the boy while he occupied the witness stand; indeed, as though he were proud of himself; as though, perhaps, one might perceive that he is not totally under the thumb of his father after all, certainly not when it came to his sexual adventurousness and prowess. And that was it: I understood the very divided nature of young Kip Rhinelander! He was two men: the real man who loved Alice, the free-spirited and open-minded modern young man who loved jazz music, who never saw race or class; and the Rhinelander scion who was brought up to believe that he was superior because of who his family is, and who lived under the controlling presence of his father, of his family name, of the name and social prominence of his dead mother, and all that meant to elite New York society and to the world beyond Kip's influence—a world that had so long dominated him, and a world that he was expected to answer to when it came to whom he chose to wed.

It was that simple and yet that complicated: Kip was not and could never be free to live as the man he wanted to be because the world from which he came would not allow it. That world—the world his father's and his mother's families had helped to shape, and then had come to occupy, that of the very highest of white New York aristocratic society—that was a force to be reckoned with, as personified by the mad crush of reporters feeding the hungry maw of the public's fascination with the lives of the rich and well born. Kip was blessed and cursed with his birthright. To be the hero of his own tragedy, he would have to renounce his birthright, become nothing or no one special, and then to reinvent himself as a man.

Now, with these revelations of his prowess as an adventurous lover—indeed, as the undaunted lover of a beautiful young Black girl—and with his obscene and yet adoring letters, Kip had become something of a rogue iconoclast beloved by the younger generation. By taking up the role of the modern sheik whose behavior was a rebellion against the staid mores of previous generations as well as an affront to his family name; and as one who was forbidden to be himself by familial and social pressures and responsibilities, yet with his defiance, Kip gained in esteem. He drove about in his flashy new automobile and picked up common dark-skinned girls. He and his friends carried flasks of bootleg gin. He took rooms at Manhattan hotels with his lover under assumed names and engaged in an orgy of forbidden premarital sex. He boldly married a pretty girl of dubious race and of decidedly lower social class. He was a proud sex deviate who wrote obscene letters to excite his young bride. He may have been an affront to everything his father hoped the Rhinelander and Kip families stood for, and an even worse example of and participant in the racial mixing and mongrelization that appalled and terrified the eugenicists. However, to the young flappers and sheiks following the case as though the future of what was morally acceptable social behavior hung in the scales of justice, Leonard Kip Rhinelander had become a paragon of the emerging less stringent morality in these young and Roaring Twenties.

Earlier in the day, as I left the judge's chambers and returned to the courtroom, I had become aware that the witness saw his appearance on the stand as a liberating performance; and I gathered that Kip was gaining the sympathy of an audience—perhaps not the jury, but the younger members of the huge crowd assembled outside the courthouse; and, by extension, young people and freethinkers following the trial all over the world. The very foundations of morality and sexuality were under attack in the trial of *Rhinelander v. Rhinelander*, as though Kip stood for a new open-mindedness in matters of race, class, and sex that challenged and terrified his father's generation and to which they would bring whatever force was deemed necessary to try to crush.

The tragedy, of course—as I saw it, in any case—was that Kip lacked the self-confidence, the individuality, the force of personality, and a unified strength of character one might suppose was needed to carry off and measure up to this emerging personification of him as heroic, the opposite of how his lawyers had portrayed the boy to the jury at the outset of trial, and who now was perceived as a free-thinker who saw no harm in crossing racial and class lines when it meant courting the girl he loved; and one who would admit that he found cunnilingus "natural."

I would need to reveal this emerging perception of the plaintiff as bogus and show the jury the reality that Kip was a mere poseur in his new role; an actor playing a part; a faker; and as false a man as his dubious lawsuit against the only real person of any integrity in the matter before the court: his loving wife, Alice, the girl he allowed his father and his father's lawyers to attempt to crush and defame. Alice, after all, with all her humility, it was she who stood naked before the jury, the bride who made an exhibit of her body to defend her name while Kip Rhinelander stayed hidden behind his spectacles, his three-piece suit, his conceit, and the social wall set up by the Rhinelander family name and fortune to separate him from the rabble.

My guess, and I may never know the truth of this, but I believe that in the end Rhinelander's lack of resolve all came down to the question of money, as so much in this material life inevitably does. Rhinelander may have been naive, but he was no fool. Seeing what had become of his disgraced and exiled uncle, Kip was loath to give up the family millions and become a persona non grata in society. He had seen how being cut off from the family name and fortune, and their high status in the best circles of New York's social milieu, had resulted in his uncle's banishment, his fall from grace with his own family, and his disreputable end. Kip had no heart for that fate; although, I believe, had he thought about it, he would have realized that to win against his wife was no better result. This trial already had brought more scandal to the family than his uncle's marital misadventures ever could; and Rhinelander would lose the woman he loved as well as his standing in society regardless of the jury's verdict.

For her part, when I asked Alice what she thought of Kip's lack of resolve to live up to his daring love for her, she had a different idea. Alice believed that Rhinelander Senior had dissuaded the boy from following his true love not simply with the threat of disinheritance; but, more importantly, he put the fear of such a union in the lad by invoking the ghost of his mother. Alice said that whenever the subject of Kip's dead mother had come up between them, though Rhinelander said he believed his mother would have wanted to love Alice, she would be reminded that the prospect of their marriage resulting in mixed-race children being brought into the world would have horrified the Kips and scandalized his mother's family no less than it terrified the Rhinelanders. It was unacceptable. Society wouldn't allow it. Alice, Leonard intimated, might have been perceived as acceptable as a mistress, but not permissible as a bride, not worthy to be the mother of mixed-race children poised to inherit the Rhinelander and Kip names, their social status, and business empire.

So, in fact, it did indeed all come down to money and class—which, in America, at least in these changing times of social mobility, is often conflated to mean the same thing. Kip could never be his own man and a Rhinelander and a Kip and retain the social access afforded the family name, their place in the world, and their millions; not with a partially Black wife as the mother of his offspring, for then those descendants of the noble Rhinelander and Kip names would also be Black.

* * *

On redirect the next morning, with Alice and her family back in the courtroom, Mr. Mills asked Rhinelander many of the same now tired and discredited questions that had been posed at the outset of the boy's testimony, and the lawyer rehashed them in a weak attempt to resurrect the characterization of his witness as a naive boy who was easily manipulated by a sexually aggressive, older Black female vamp.

"Tell us, Mr. Rhinelander, why did you do *that thing* to this woman as described in your letter read by defense counsel: What was it that made you wish to do it . . . to her?"

"Be . . . be . . . be . . ." Rhinelander sputtered and blushed. "I think . . . I did it because she asked me to do it."

Oh, please! This really was too much. Rhinelander was rapidly losing ground even in his new role, for I believe this testimony not only fell flat but actually further discredited the witness, and was hardly convincing to jurors who had heard all of Rhinelander's admissions on cross-examination, and who had heard me read from several other of his obscene and degrading sex letters. No, the men in the jury weren't going to accept this—what, the girl *made* him do these things to her! Please, grow some gonads. Kip had described in smutty detail how he enjoyed pleasuring the girl. Now he wished to say it was all her idea. I saw several jurors appeared put off by the question, and even more so by the weak and despicable answer.

During his final time on the witness stand, while during my re-cross-examination, Rhinelander himself gave the impression that he was uncomfortable with the image his lawyer sought to convey, realizing, as I'm sure he did, no one would believe him to be an innocent boy duped and manipulated by a clever Black woman into believing she was white, cajoling him into performing lewd oral sex acts upon her, and then coercing him into marrying her. Kip had appeared proud of himself as a man who dared love a Black girl and to love her well; and his lawyer's last-ditch attempt to prove Alice the aggressor was weak indeed.

As if he had also realized this tact was not working, before dismissing his witness, Mills attempted another line of questions to prove the ambiguity of Alice's color.

"Now, Mr. Rhinelander, one last point I wish to clear up. You remember the day you applied for the marriage license, don't you? What you said about the clerk who interviewed you and Alice?"

"Yes."

"Did the man—the clerk in the mayor's office—did he inquire of either of you if you were white or colored?"

Leonard shook his head and said, "No, he did not."

"Do you mean he just put it down himself, based on his observation?"

"Yes."

Mr. Mills told the court that he was finished with this witness. I said I had only one further question. "Sir," I said, "with regard to the clerk in the mayor's office." By now I believe everyone guessed what was coming.

"When this man observed you and Alice, and as he filled out the marriage license application, I assume you were *both fully dressed, correct?* You and your wife weren't naked, *were you?*"

When the laughter died down, the judge excused Rhinelander.

With that, Kip wiped his brow and stood from the witness chair looking for all the world like a man who had been through the ringer. One could sense that not only the witness, but the room itself, the spectators and jurors, and even the judge, and certainly counsel for both sides seemed to join in a collective sigh of relief. The testimony and evidence may have been titillating to the public following the trial from afar; but it had been shocking not only for the court and the gallery but also for the witness and for the defendant, Alice, who had just returned to the courtroom looking frail and overwrought. I was increasingly concerned for Alice's physical and emotional well-being. She had informed us that she wished to return to the courtroom. My brutal cross-examination of young Kip as well as the revelations included in his letters had been exhausting for Alice, and I think we were all relieved to see this portion of the trial finally ended.

As Rhinelander stepped down from the witness stand and made ready to depart from the courtroom, while choosing not to resume his place at the plaintiff's table for the remainder of the session, instead making his way toward the exit, I anticipated that he would leave the room with some measure of his haughty strut, given how he had seemed to enjoy the scandalous role he played; and that he would again refuse to acknowledge his bride. I won't say that the boy swaggered as he left; no, that would be overstating it; but he certainly left the courtroom with more confidence, more verve in his step than he had entered; the pompous strut had become a self-possessed manly gait, which struck me as proof that he believed in the success of his performance in his new role as a modern chap with an open mind.

And then, even more unexpectedly, when Kip passed by Alice at the defense table, whereas I assumed that he would not dare to give her a second look; or that he would be too chagrined to glance at her—*no!* Again, the boy surprised me—and Alice, I dare say. For, not only did he look at Alice, but also he gazed at her steadily and *with a warm smile!* Yes, there was no mistaking it: Kip looked at Alice and he smiled. He looked at her with kindness and compassion, one might even say with genuine love in his eyes and his warm facial expression. There was no doubt, not in my mind, nor I daresay in Alice's: the boy smiled at her with a look that spoke of the enduring love he felt in his heart for his girl and his wife. Alice, for her part, winced with tenderness.

For the life of me, at that moment, I couldn't understand this man; he was such a paradox, a human enigma. What might have caused Rhinelander to believe that his appearance on the witness stand had been anything but a complete catastrophe for his case and an ignominious insult to his bride? That he had accomplished nothing but to disgrace himself and his wife? So why was the boy smiling? Was it because he took pride in being seen as a moral and social interloper? There had to be more to it.

And then, as the jury was dismissed for the day, and as I gathered my papers and made ready to leave, I suddenly had an insight. I had to sit back down and think it through when I realized—*too late!*—the importance of my thought. Of course. Now I understood Rhinelander's strategy—not his lawyer's, but the boy's goal, and what Alice had been trying to tell me all along: Leonard wants to lose his lawsuit. He does not want to win and thus ruin Alice because, through it all, the boy still loves her. I could have kicked myself for not realizing this earlier; for not listening to Alice; and for not asking Kip while I had him on the stand if he did not in fact still love his wife with the same love he had admitted having for the girl during the time they were together; and, therefore, if it were not in his heart to see his wife exonerated of the charge of fraud.

Could there be any question? Surely he would not have been able to deny it; and yet such admission would clearly nullify his case. Rhinelander might lie and deny he was aware of the taint in her blood; or perhaps, as he intimated, he never bothered about it; but to deny that he loved Alice regardless of the color of her skin—no, not possible. He could not deny his love if I had pressed him and deftly questioned him as to his motives and to his deepest emotions—he could not have denied how he loved Alice still even acknowledging her mixed race.

How obtuse of me not to have suspected this sooner, and not to have altered the course of my defense. How dull of me not to have listened to Alice. Rhinelander had purposely thrown the case; but he had done it in such a way that it was not obvious to the jury; not apparent to his lawyers; hidden even from the judge; revealed solely to Alice and to me when we were given an opportunity to understand his true feelings, which Alice knew all along, but that I only understood when I saw him smile at Alice with love in his eyes as he passed her by and exited the courtroom.

What a fool I had been not to see this from the very beginning. Yes, certainly, and Alice knew it; she pleaded with me not to be so hard on Rhinelander because she felt in her heart that there was still love there. Only I, in my superior attitude and arrogant belief that as her lawyer I knew best how to defend her cause, when in truth I had missed the most important fact as it were, right there from the very beginning in Rhinelander's note to Alice proclaiming his love, urging her not to accept the annulment, and to fight the case: obviously he wanted to lose. He intended to lose. And I hadn't given the note proper credence, and then reorganized my defense in an entirely different manner; based not on anger and aggression and hate; no, but based rather on thwarted love, on the innocent and beautiful love of two young people that had been perverted by racism and class disdain, though not on behalf of young Kip, who showed no such prejudice; but instigated by his overbearing father, undergirded by social and class arrogance, and fraught with white America's fear of mixing the races.

The boy wanted Alice to win. Of course he did! There was no other explanation. How could I have missed it?

* * *

Mr. Mills announced that the plaintiff had concluded his case.

I stood and addressed the judge. "Your Honor, on behalf of the defendant, Mrs. Alice Beatrice Jones Rhinelander, counsel hereby moves the court to dismiss the suit against Mrs. Rhinelander. We do so, Your Honor, on grounds that the plaintiff *has failed to prove a single allegation of fraud by this defendant.* The accusations of fraud, whether by active or passive deceit, are utterly without merit, Your Honor, and therefore they should not need to be decided by a jury."

Judge Morschauser replied that, on the contrary, he had decided to allow the revised complaint as requested by plaintiff's counsel; and he denied my motion to dismiss the lawsuit, determining that there was ample evidence to allow the jury to decide the merits of the allegations as to whether in fact Rhinelander's lawyers had proved their case.

"You will have an opportunity to present your defense against the charges," the judge said, and I had an unhappy feeling of foreboding given what I believed the judge's sentiments to be, and knowing only too well how a judge not only rules his court but also has tremendous sway with the jury. So much for his stated wish to avoid a mistrial.

With that, court was adjourned for the day, while the legal issues were briefed and decided by His Honor.

* * *

The newspapers, my colleagues, the courtroom buffs, and nearly everyone I chanced to encounter after the Rhinelander boy's appearance on the witness stand, and in my social comings and goings with family and friends, as well as colleagues and avid followers of the trial whom I chanced to meet in the street—nearly everyone saw fit to congratulate me on what was said to be a masterful example of the trial lawyer's art in cross-examination. Conversely, I was also strenuously criticized and condemned by journalists, feminists, and so-called legal experts in the newspapers and barrooms and at dinner tables, with my detractors hailing from throughout the populace both during and following the trial for what was seen by a good many as a sordid, irresponsible, and sensationalistic display in having Alice disrobe and expose her body before the all-male jury. The *New York Evening Graphic* tabloid newspaper published a shocking composite photograph of a woman meant to be Alice standing half nude before a panel of men ogling her; and beneath the picture the printed caption: "Alice Disrobes in Court to Keep Her Husband."

The supposed affront to the girl's humility caused me no end of disapprobation; and yet, at the same time, acclaim by others: those experienced trial lawyers I counted as my colleagues who understood what we were faced with in litigating against the Rhinelander name and their fortune. These professionals recognized the display of Alice's body as a stroke of brilliant legal strategy, and they congratulated me for my having had the gall to challenge Rhinelander and his lawyers with so shocking and obvious a display of real evidence in a trial that was replete with nothing but uncorroborated witness testimony. Rhinelander may profess what he will: "I didn't know, or I was too blinded by love and delirious with lust to see the color of Alice's flesh." But when confronted with the actual physical evidence, he may want to say he couldn't discern her color; but, look at her, sir! Look at her, good men of the jury. See her dark skin even as she is displayed before you twelve men who must determine her fate, and to reveal the Rhinelander lie with her exposed body.

Again, be that as it may, and despite what was seen as a brilliant defense, I must admit that I felt only an empty sense of complete and utter failure as Alice's advocate for having refused to listen to my client and adhere to her wishes, and in having failed to understand the true meaning behind Rhinelander's note to his wife urging her to fight the case; and, finally, in having completely misjudged Kip Rhinelander's character and the sincerity of his feelings for Alice until the moment I watched him leave the courtroom. Only then did I come to understand that Rhinelander was doing all within his power to make sure Alice would win even while he made it appear that he was out to destroy her. What a conundrum the man was!

Really? Was this true? Was Rhinelander actually that clever to knowingly forfeit his case while appearing to defend himself? Yes, I believed he was; but effecting it, as I reasoned, most subtly, without any indication that was what he was about until the penultimate moment, when it could only be seen by his wife and by me as he left the stage, as he made his subtle and yet famous exit with that knowing smile, that heartfelt look that said, "There, my girl: victory is yours."

And yet I couldn't be sure; who could know what lurked in that boy's divided psyche and turbulent heart? Perhaps Rhinelander himself did not know his true designs. I believed we still needed to defeat the lawsuit of our own accord and on our terms. A mistake at this crucial stage in the proceeding with the onus shifting to the defense could mean losing whatever persuasion we may have gained with the jury up to this point.

* * *

As it turned out, we may never know the truth of young Rhinelander's feelings or his hidden intentions, if in fact there were any. Leonard—or Kip, as he seemed to like to be called—gave no interviews to the press during the trial, and he gave only a few comments to one reporter before he virtually disappeared from public life after the trial and verdict.

Still, it must be remembered that, given where we stood at the conclusion of Rhinelander's evidence against his wife, with Leonard's name on the filing as the initiator of the lawsuit, and no matter the force of the evidence of Alice's body before the jury, I for one remained cognizant of the issues involved. Trying to persuade twelve men of different age and experience in an all-white jury, and each man on the jury with his own ideas and opinions as to the contentious issues and conflicting testimony before them to be considered; and then to bring them all to see and weigh only the facts presented in evidence by both sides in the case without prejudice, without personal animosity, no matter how scandalous; to ask them to put aside their personal beliefs about race and their feelings about interracial sex and marriage; and then to judge their interpretation of the evidence presented at trial in the same way or at least in concert with their fellows on the jury; and finally, to reach a verdict exonerating the defendant: that, I was fully aware, is indeed a prodigious and daunting challenge. Yes, the evidence was in our favor; but a jury is a curious animal, an anomalous, and unpredictable body with as many heads and opinions as personalities. One could never be sure how a jury would rule. That is why I wanted to give them something real—the defendant's physical appearance—to ponder.

There is a school of thought in trial tactics that adheres to the premise that if your opponent's case is so obviously flawed, or when the weight of the evidence is clearly in your favor when opposing counsel rests, one might be prudent to decide against putting on a defense at all. The jury may be made to see that the plaintiff's case is so flawed there is no need to defend against it.

And it is always risky to expose the weaknesses of your case, and to display your witnesses to the jury while subjecting them to the rigors of cross-examination while intending to prove their evidence truthful and accurate. I understand this reasoning; at times I have employed this tactic. Our side considered resting after Mills completed Rhinelander's case. However, in most trials I have come to believe that, no matter how flawed the prosecution's or the plaintiff's case may be, a jury wants to hear from the other side; they want to judge the defendant and his or her evidence—if not in the defendant's actual testimony, then in the presentation of witnesses who have real evidence of value as to the issues to be decided.

While Rhinelander's appearance on the witness stand may have been seen as a setback for his lawsuit even as it made him something of a celebrity lover sought after by sex-starved females; and as his behavior might be imitated or emulated by enterprising gadabouts; those alone were no guarantees of victory for Alice. She might yet be perceived as the lascivious Negro temptress who unleashed a randy young Lothario upon the innocent young ladies of white upper-class New York society. The defense team would still need to marshal our evidence, and to bring a clear and believable defense to bear against the underlying issues of the Rhinelander lawsuit: racism, class prejudice, and the bugaboo of interracial sex—if Alice were to be totally vindicated.

* * *

The following morning, once Judge Morschauser had settled upon the bench, but before the jury had been brought in, Isaac Mills stood and asked the court's permission to amend Rhinelander's complaint. *Not again!* I thought.

"Your Honor," Mills began, "the plaintiff asks of the court

leave to file a revised complaint; to enter a new complaint charging the defendant, Alice Jones, with *failing to inform* her husband before their marriage of what she has now *admitted*, through counsel: *that she does in fact have Black blood in her veins.* Had counsel for the plaintiff been advised prior to trial of this admission, we would have proceeded to trial in an entirely different manner, filing a complaint alleging a case of *negative fraud.* In failing to inform her husband of her racial taint *before the marriage* the defendant intentionally deceived Mr. Rhinelander as to the purity of her blood. Under the law, such deceit is proof of *negative fraud.*"

I stood and shook my head in disbelief. Much as I was aware that the impact of this late attempt to revise their complaint could only be perceived by the court as a last-ditch effort on behalf of Rhinelander's lawyers to save a lawsuit they knew was in deep trouble; nevertheless, I wished to avoid what would be a costly upset to our side if the judge granted the request. The law when an amended complaint is allowed at this stage in the proceeding would require the removal of one juror; then call for a special session of the court; and, finally, what Judge Morschauser had warned counsel to avoid: declaration of a mistrial.

"Your Honor, I am flabbergasted by this late and *obvious* effort on behalf of the plaintiff to shore up a rapidly sinking cause by *disrupting* the proceeding as it is nearly ready to go to the jury. First they say Mrs. Rhinelander said *too much* in claiming she was white; now they claim she deceived the boy *by saying nothing.* Well, *which is it?* In asking to amend the complaint at this late date counsel for the plaintiff is guilty of *laxity* if not *irresponsibility.* Your Honor has asked that exactly this sort of upset to the conclusion of this trial be *avoided at all cost.*"

Judge Morschauser said he would reserve his decision. He

ordered the trial was to proceed while he reviewed submissions from the parties. Given how His Honor had urged counsel to do all within limits to avoid a mistrial, it seemed apparent how he would rule; indeed I believed I could read his decision on his perturbed countenance. However, I would be surprised. The unseen influence of the Rhinelander name still held sway in Judge Morschauser's court.

* * *

With the courtroom again filled to overflowing with spectators of all ages and both genders, and more distressed avid followers of the trial refused admittance and loitering noisily outside, once the jury was brought in and seated, and as I was poised to call my first witness, Mr. Mills announced that he had two additional witnesses he wished to call: a Mr. Joseph and Mrs. Miriam Rich, who were proprietors of a furniture store in New Rochelle, and erstwhile friends of Alice.

The Riches made an unpleasant impression on nearly everyone. Miriam Rich was a portly, self-important social-climbing busybody with an abrasive voice; her husband, Joseph Rich, appeared as a henpecked milquetoast. Mrs. Rich claimed she was appalled when Alice was described as a "Negress" in news reports. She told the jury she had intended to testify on behalf of Alice, as to her good character; and that "Alice was a charming white girl." She changed her mind and offered to testify for the plaintiff when she learned Alice had deceived her as to her race. "She said she was of Spanish descent. She explained her dark color as being due to her Spanish blood," the lady averred.

I relished my opportunity on cross-examination to reveal this couple's true colors if not Alice's.

"You knew Alice quite well. *You were friends.* You and your husband had accompanied Alice and her husband, Leonard Rhinelander, to Manhattan to a night out at the theater and then to dinner. *Who paid for that outing, Mrs. Rich? Did your husband pay?*"

"Well, no . . . We were invited."

"Who invited you?"

"Alice."

"Alice, *your friend.* Alice invited you out of friendship—*what?* The young couple spent a considerable sum of money in your store—*yes?*"

"It was Mr. Rhinelander who spent—"

"*Of course it was!* You knew that they planned to marry. And *Alice paid* for your evening out to dinner and the theater—didn't she?"

Mrs. Rich was mute. I could see that even the judge disliked the witness as he ordered, "The witness will answer counsel's questions."

"Mr. Rhinelander paid."

"You befriended Alice so that you could get in with Mr. Rhinelander, who also paid *several hundred dollars* for furniture purchased from you and your husband—*didn't you? Isn't that so, madam?*"

"No."

"You were happy to take Alice's money—"

"Her husband's—"

"Her husband's, *yes!* It was Alice who brought her husband to your store. Alice who invited you and your husband to join her and Mr. Rhinelander on a night out in Manhattan. They paid for theater tickets, paid for dinner. For the car. So I can understand: *What has changed?*"

Before she answered, I asked, "Do you like Alice, Mrs. Rich?"

"I did, very much. She had lovely manners, and I thought she was a beautiful Spanish girl."

I gave her a surprised expression. "*A Spanish girl?* Well, have you ever seen a Spanish woman?"

Mrs. Rich appeared flustered by the question. She managed after a moment to say that she had seen Spanish women, "on the stage. I thought Alice was even more beautiful than they were. I felt sorry for her because she said she was so dark the millionaires would not have her."

This observation, along with my raised eyebrows as I turned to regard the millionaire plaintiff, brought murmurs of amusement from the gallery.

"And now?" I asked. "Do you like Alice now?"

"*No!*" the lady snapped.

"Why? *Do you hate her?*"

"I never hate anyone," she snarled with anger and animosity.

"That's so good of you," I sneered. "But, you *dislike* Alice now?"

"*Yes!*" came a nasty squawk.

"Since when has this new attitude toward Alice taken over?"

"Since about four weeks ago. I dislike Alice because she deceived me as to her, whatever was her true; *her race.* Now the whole of Mount Vernon had a good laugh at me, and my husband too, for believing her."

"Tell me, Mrs. Rich, before this trial, had you ever seen Alice's father, George Jones? And her brother-in-law, Robert Brooks? Do you see him now, seated in the gallery?"

"I . . . I may have," she answered.

"*You may have seen Mr. Jones.* You mean, *when you were invited as a guest in the Joneses' home?* When you had dinner at a dinner party in their home? Do you mean you may have *noticed* George Jones and Robert Brooks are *both men of colored blood?*"

"Mr. Jones spoke with an English accent. He dropped his h's and said his 'appy 'ome had been broken up by the news. I thought he was English, not colored."

This statement brought about laughter from the gallery and smiles from some of the jurors. Judge Morschauser again admonished the spectators to refrain from laughter.

"And Mr. Brooks, Emily's husband. He doesn't speak with an English accent, does he? Might you have been able to see he is a colored man?"

"I don't know him. *I never saw him,*" the lady claimed

"*What?* You never saw Mr. Brooks? You don't recall telling the jury that Mr. Brooks accompanied Alice to your store and helped to arrange delivery of the items Alice purchased? Which delivery never took place, I might add, as you and your husband *clung to the items* when you knew there was difficulty in the marriage. Mr. Brooks and his wife, Alice's sister, were living in the Joneses' home. And yet you are testifying—and I feel I must remind you, madam, that you do so under oath. Now, madam, do you still wish to testify *that you never saw* Mr. Brooks? You *never noticed the man is a Negro?* Or perhaps you saw him but you failed to *notice* him." I accused the witness to insinuate that she might be inclined to see only what she wished to see—as one might suppose of so many of us when it came to matters of race.

* * *

Mr. Rich took the stand as his wife slunk away obviously chagrined by her unsavory appearance. Mr. Rich struck me as painfully uncomfortable. His testimony was even worse for the plaintiff's case than that of his wife, whom he complained had put him up to testifying against his will. Rich said he was happy to take Rhinelander's money and never gave much thought as to Alice's color, "until it was all over the news that she has Negro blood." Now, he said, he too was angry with Alice.

"Not so angry as to give her money back, were you, sir?"

"I didn't think of it," Rich said. "She never asked for the money."

"The furniture and other items the Rhinelander couple purchased; those items were never delivered—is that correct?"

"Yes . . . I mean no, they were never delivered."

"And when you were approached by the Rhinelanders' lawyer, Mr. Jacobs, hadn't he taken possession of all the furniture and the other items Alice and her husband purchased from you? And didn't Mr. Jacobs threaten to return them and ask for the Rhinelanders' money back? Did you think of giving them their money back then?"

"He told me that we wouldn't need to take the items back—"

"You mean, *if you agreed to testify?*"

"I suppose," Rich admitted.

"I ask you to look at the defendant, Mrs. Rhinelander. You see her there, seated beside my co-counsel, Judge Swinburne—*yes?*"

"I do, yes."

"Can you tell us, is your eyesight good, sir?"

"Yes."

"You can see colors, can you?"

"I can, yes," Rich asserted.

"Very good, sir. Now, as you look at Mrs. Rhinelander, tell us what you see. How does Mrs. Rhinelander appear to you, as to her color?"

"Dark," Mr. Rich answered.

"*Dark*, I see. And when you went to New York with her and dined in a restaurant with Alice and Rhinelander, how did she appear to you then?"

"Well, I could see that she was dark then as well. But she is darker today than she was then."

This statement brought about a loud burst of laughter from the audience. Judge Morschauser banged his gavel and demanded order. "I will have to clear the court unless you stop your giggling. I am giving you fair warning," His Honor commanded. "If this happens once more, out you go! This is a courtroom, not an amusement hall."

Both Riches impressed me, and I believe the men on the jury, as opportunists who befriended Alice to get in well with young Rhinelander so they could sell the couple at top dollar the complete furnishings for the apartment they were never to occupy; and then, as I pointed out, never deliver the items while keeping the money. Now they had become shills for Philip Rhinelander's attorney.

For the purposes of what Rhinelander's counsel had hoped to achieve with this rather despicable couple, however, clearly it backfired. I chastised them both for having turned against Alice, a former friend and good customer; a good and honest girl who bore them no malice; and for what? Notoriety? To come up on the stand in this now famous case so as to advertise their furniture store while denigrating Alice? To appease the Rhinelanders? They would have been better off to stay home.

"*What,*" I asked Mr. Rich, "please tell us, sir: What has this young woman—Alice Rhinelander—what has Alice ever done to you and your wife beside befriend you, spend money in your store, and invite you to a night out in Manhattan? You claim she deceived you as to her mixed race? Surely Mr. Rich, you and your wife—like the plaintiff, Kip Rhinelander—*you both have eyes and you can see.* You see Mrs. Rhinelander in this court, and you saw her then. Why is it that you couldn't discern then what you can see now? Is it because you were only able to see the green color of the Rhinelanders' money?

"Why," I turned to the jury, "I must say: *with friends like you and your wife, one needs no enemies.*"

* * *

At last, after nearly two and a half weeks of testimony, and with the Christmas and New Year holidays close upon us, plaintiff rested their case. Halfway through trial, I began to present Alice's defense. I hoped to give the case to the jury before the Christmas holidays.

It was anticipated that I would call Alice—that is, by those writing of the case in the press, by the spectators, and perhaps by the jury; and though we may have allowed that impression, my intention was never to put Alice on the witness stand. Alice was not present in court on the day I stood to begin her defense. I explained to the judge that she was not able to come to court "due to the extreme emotional distress" she had been made to endure during the plaintiff's testimony, and as she experienced what I described as "a complete emotional breakdown, and she is in dire need of rest and recuperation."

As Alice's first witness I chose to call Barbara Reynolds, an attractive, well-spoken young news reporter for the *New Rochelle Standard Star,* who proved a critical witness. Once Miss Reynolds had taken the oath and identified herself as a reporter whose principal beat was the Westchester County Courthouse, I asked if she knew the plaintiff, Leonard Rhinelander. Miss Reynolds said she did; that she had met him on November 13, 1924, while assigned to report on the marriage of Rhinelander to a local girl.

"How did you hear of the marriage?" I asked.

"Well, it had been reported, the beat reporter who covers City Hall and the mayor's office reported that the Rhinelanders had taken out a marriage license and been married by the mayor. Given the prominence of the Rhinelander family in society, and their influence in the community, this was certainly a newsworthy story. Everyone wanted to know who the bride was. I went to the clerk's office and asked to see the marriage license. When I saw who Mr. Rhinelander had married, Alice Jones, a local girl, I set out to discover as much as I could about his bride."

"Can you tell us where and under what circumstances you met the plaintiff, Mr. Leonard Rhinelander?"

"I was waiting outside his . . . outside the Joneses' home in New Rochelle. I hoped to get an interview with one of the family, when Mr. Rhinelander came along. The first question I fired at him was, 'Mr. Rhinelander?' to make certain I had the right man, though I recognized him right away. When he confirmed he was who I believed him to be, I got right to the question everyone wanted asked and answered. I said, 'Is it true that you have married Alice Jones, the daughter of a colored man?'"

"What did Mr. Rhinelander say?" I asked the witness.

"He admitted it. He said, *yes*."

"He said he knew his bride's father was colored?" I confirmed.

"Yes. I was impressed that Mr. Rhinelander was so forthcoming. I certainly knew who the Rhinelanders are and of their position in New York society; by this time everyone knew. I asked Mr. Rhinelander if his family were still alive—which, of course I knew that they were; or, at least his father, Philip Rhinelander, was very much alive. Leonard said his mother had passed, which I knew . . . how she had died in that tragic fire."

I nodded, shook my head, and agreed. "Yes, a tragedy . . . Now then, what was your next question to Mr. Rhinelander, if you can recall?"

"I said, 'Does your father know that your wife's father is colored?'"

"What did Mr. Rhinelander answer?"

"He said no, his father did not know. He was obviously concerned. So my next question was: 'Well, if your father knew your wife's father is colored, would it make a difference?'"

"And what did Mr. Rhinelander say in response to that question?"

"He said, 'Yes; it means my wife's happiness and mine.' He seemed quite perturbed."

"Go on," I urged the witness.

"I asked how he intended to break the news to his father. He said he had devised a plan; and he asked that I withhold my story until after he had managed his explanation to his father—which, of course, was impossible. The story was already out; it had been reported—although not in much detail, just that Rhinelander had married. And soon reporters from all over the state, from all over the country were flocking to New Rochelle and looking high and low for Mr. Rhinelander or for his bride, Alice; and reporting that Mrs. Rhinelander was colored."

"So, as of this date—you are sure the date is November thirteenth?"

"Yes, I am sure of the date because that is the day I filed the story."

"When you asked Mr. Rhinelander—that is, when he said he was *aware his wife's father is a Black man*—did you ask how he felt about having married *a woman who had Black blood?*"

"Not in so many words, no. I did ask him why, or how he happened to marry Alice, since, as he admitted that he knew she had a Black father, and he knew it would upset *his* father."

"What did Leonard Rhinelander say in answer to that question?"

"Well, he was quite frank. He said that it couldn't be helped because he didn't care one way or the other if she had some Black blood. He said he married Alice because he loved her. His exact words were: 'I married the woman I love.'"

"He—Leonard Rhinelander—said that: '*I married the woman I love.*' You're quite sure that is what he said?"

"Yes, I'm positive. I put it in my story."

"Thank you, Miss Reynolds," I said and turned to Mr. Mills. "Your witness."

This was crucial testimony from an obviously unbiased source—indeed, a journalist with no axe to grind for either side. Miss Reynolds confirmed that Leonard was aware of Mr. Jones's color, and that he was still living in the Jones home knowing the race of Alice's father, aware Alice had Black blood, and what that would mean to Leonard's father if he were to find out—which, I must say, showed just how unworldly the boy was; or perhaps he was in denial to think that his father would not discover the truth about his marriage, and his wife's father's color, when by now the whole world was about to know of the marriage.

Even more germane to our argument, Rhinelander told Miss Reynolds that he didn't care that Alice was the daughter of a colored man. Clearly, at least at that point in the marriage, Leonard was happy with his bride, and he had no intention of ending the marriage.

Extraordinary naïveté! For the boy to think that his father would countenance such an infamous marriage, why, Leonard must have been living in a bubble; but that bubble was about to burst.

Mr. Mills's cross-examination of Barbara Reynolds was brief and pointless, merely pro forma; if anything it confirmed what she said on direct. She proved a most reliable reporter by actually producing her notes when Mills asked if she had made notes, which I neglected to ask, and which confirmed the date of the interview. I gave Mills a curious look that implied he'd have been better off to forgo any questions for this witness, as all he'd managed was to remind the jury of how damaging her testimony was to his case.

* * *

And then, as if to rub it in, almost on a whim as emboldened by how our case was progressing, feeling momentum gaining in our favor, and without much planning, taking what most lawyers would see as a risky step without thorough preparation, I turned and called Leonard's Manhattan attorney, Mr. Leon Jacobs, to the witness stand.

Jacobs gave me a murderous scowl; he had no desire to be examined, and I had neglected to warn him of my plan. There was readily apparent animosity between Mr. Jacobs and myself before his appearance as a witness, a good deal of which was manufactured for the benefit of the jury; but there was certainly more than a grain of truth to the disdain I held for this man as a brother at the bar.

As I've stated, there is a marked difference between a conscientious advocate and a spineless lackey, in which latter category I believe Jacobs belongs. A lawyer has to have some moral integrity; he must have some sense of right and wrong that is maintained as a fundamental tenet from which he will argue and fight for his client; or he is merely a whore and a shill who will do and say anything for a fee in hopes to win his client's favor even if he knows the cause is false and destined to fail. I will state here in this record that, in all honesty, had I believed that Alice knowingly and intentionally deceived young Kip; that she lied to him about her racial makeup; that she tricked him into marrying her while professing that she was of pure white blood; that she had done so merely for pecuniary advantage; and that her whole family had conspired and was in on the game to fleece the Rhinelanders of their millions by urging Alice to seduce and entrap the boy in marriage: had I truly believed any or all of that

I would have counseled her to take the settlement, and I would have refused to defend her case at trial.

As I was aware, on the surface it looked like Alice's defense was a lost cause. We could prevail only by admitting she had some Black blood and to assert that Rhinelander certainly knew it when he married her; that might win the case, but such an admission would surely only serve to eliminate any hope of saving the marriage. I'm not sure Alice ever fully accepted this result.

What I believed at the time of trial, and what I wanted the men on the jury to come to believe, is that this young couple did in fact fall in love—real, genuine love for one another regardless of class and skin color—and that they did so both fully aware of their differences; but they were still in love, plain and simple—although, as we have seen, hardly simple and acceptable to much of the rest of the world. And, as they were in love, they saw no color; they saw no class difference; they saw only each other as lovers. They felt no prejudice, no disdain. They only felt love.

And yet I wanted the men on the jury to understand that, as important as all this was—at least to me, and to the bride and groom—it was beside the point. Whatever personal feelings the men on the jury might have regarding love and marriage between the races was irrelevant; it must not be factored into their deliberations. They need only consider the facts of the alleged fraud. And as to that question, Barbara Reynolds's testimony was crucial; it had done a great deal to establish Rhinelander's state of mind and what he knew of Alice's racial makeup *before* he married her. Now I needed to show how and why all that had changed.

I wasted no time letting the jury know just what I felt about the obsequious attorney from Manhattan, Mr. Leon Jacobs. After he identified himself, I asked with barely suppressed scorn, "Sir, please tell us, how long have you been a practicing lawyer?"

Jacobs answered, "Since 1907."

"Whose office are you in?"

"I am all alone."

"Oh, I see, a solo practitioner, aye? But . . . *whom* are you *associated* with? By that I mean to say, what is the nature of your practice?"

"I am associated with myself," Jacobs snapped.

"*Ah-ha!* Well, very good. Most important that a lawyer be associated with himself—*what?* We wouldn't want you to be *disassociated* from yourself, would we? That, they say, is a sign of insanity."

Which comment brought the first of several bursts of laughter from the gallery, and more angry threats from His Honor to expel anyone who was unable to contain his or her mirth.

"But, tell us, Mr. Jacobs: Are you alone . . . in your office? I ask because, well, you obviously have much to do with the Rhinelander family, and the Rhinelander Real Estate Company, *no?* To say nothing of handling young Kip's affairs as well.

"I am sure the jurors will recall how *deeply involved* you have been in this fellow's case, and the concerted attempt by you at Philip Rhinelander's behest *to destroy his son's marriage to Alice Rhinelander*, Mr. Rhinelander Senior who still has not bothered to grant us the honor of his appearance in this courtroom at the trial *he initiated* on behalf of his remaining son—"

"Your Honor," Mills objected. "Once again, counsel is testifying. Can we please have a question of the witness?"

"*Of course you may.* Excuse me, Your Honor. It's just that, well, when questioning a fellow lawyer, one likes to be precise."

"You may continue, Mr. Davis."

"Thank you, Your Honor. Now, Mr. Jacobs, you are the *principal actor* on behalf of Philip Rhinelander's *relentless efforts* to destroy the marriage of these two young people, *correct?* You, sir, are, so to speak, Philip Rhinelander's general in the field; *are you not?* Mr. Rhinelander Senior's principal factotum out running around all over hill and dale, and even down into the bowels of the city's train stations to get the boy away from his wife and have him sign *falsified documents* that *you provided?*"

Jacobs turned deep red and blurted out, "*No, sir, I am not!* And I resent that term, which you have used countless times in an effort to disparage me and my service to the Rhinelanders."

"Which term is that, sir?"

Jacobs sputtered, "*Factotum!* I am no such thing. I am an attorney, a member of the bar in good standing, who is representing my client."

"I see . . . You mean, Mr. Philip Rhinelander?"

Here Jacobs mistakenly admitted, "Yes." And then, to clean it up, he added, "As well, I am retained to represent the plaintiff, Mr. Leonard Rhinelander, of which you, sir, are well aware."

"That may be so," I said, "but we are trying this case for the sake of the men on this jury, not for my edification. And I'm sure that the jurors would like to know who is actually behind the, as I say, *the relentless efforts to destroy the marriage* of these two young people. Tell me, if you can, sir: *Why are we here?* Who put you up to this?"

"You know very well why we are here—"

"Please, Mr. Jacobs, as a lawyer, you know the questions I ask and the answers I hope to elicit from you are not for my personal edification but rather for the benefit of the men who will decide the verdict in this case—the men you see seated in the jury box. As a lawyer surely you understand this. Now I will ask again: *Why are we here?* Why has your client—and let's be clear, you work for Philip Rhinelander, not for the boy, not for Kip, who has no money of his own. Philip Rhinelander is paying you to represent his son; Philip Rhinelander paid you along with your henchmen to steal his son away from his bride and bring this scandalous lawsuit; *isn't that so, Mr. Jacobs?* So, tell us, why has Philip Rhinelander stayed aloft in his high ivory tower from which he chooses not to descend and lower himself by rubbing shoulders with us common folk—"

Mills was on his feet. Now his face was turning red. "Your Honor! *Here we go again!* Counsel is testifying. Must we listen to this superfluous verbiage the intent of which is to prejudice the men of the jury?"

Judge Morschauser agreed, though I could tell by the glint in His Honor's eye that he was enjoying seeing this Manhattan lawyer roasted by a local boy. "Mr. Davis, please ask questions and refrain from delivering soliloquies," the judge said. "We are aware that you are a gifted and highly esteemed orator."

"Thank you, Your Honor. I appreciate your words. I am doing my best. But, as you know, I am examining a lawyer, one who is well adept at obfuscating facts with fancy rhetoric."

I turned abruptly back to Jacobs and demanded, "Tell us, sir, in plain and simple language: *Why are we here?* Who is behind this case? Whom do you represent in this despicable action? *Tell us, Mr. Jacobs!*" I shouted.

"The plaintiff!" Jacobs shouted back.

"Is that all? Tell us, *who else do you represent?*"

"I represent the estate of Philip Rhinelander, the estate of William Rhinelander, the estate of T. Oakley Rhinelander, the estate of Philip Rhinelander the second; the Atlantic Mortgage Company, the estate of Cornelia B. Kip, and several other real estate companies."

"Very good, sir. That is an impressive client list indeed. Don't these companies all belong to the Rhinelanders?"

Jacobs said, "Well . . . certainly they are interested in them all."

"You mean, certainly Philip Rhinelander, the mysterious

presence behind this case, the plaintiff's absent father is interested in them all."

"Yes; he is a principal."

"So you work for him?"

"And other members of the family. For Leonard Rhinelander in this proceeding."

"I see. All that must make for a very busy practice indeed, representing those many companies. And yet, sir, tell us: How is it that you still found time to run up to New Rochelle and spirit young Kip Rhinelander away from his bride? And then to accompany the lad, one might even say *keep him under wraps*, shuttle him from boardinghouse to hotel rooms, from one city to another, to our nation's capital for some unknown reason, and then drag him down into train stations under the streets of New York City to sign annulment papers that were—well, that we *now know contained fabrications! Lies! In a train station?* Why not in your offices? You do have offices, I'm sure. Were you hiding? Was this some sort of *clandestine activity* that had to be done in a secret place? You will admit, it is a most extraordinary venue and a most unusual way to conduct the business of a law firm, *is it not, sir?*"

"You Honor—" Mills stood to object. "Counsel is harassing the witness! Are these questions or statements?"

"Just a moment!" I snapped at Mr. Mills. "This is my witness! I'll get to you!" Then back to Jacobs, I said, "Sir, you, as a licensed attorney in the State of New York, surely you must be aware of *the laws against* what was done in this case. Not only the laws, but also *the oath you took* as a member of the bar. Well, in case you forgot, given your busy practice representing the Rhinelander empire: *It is perjury, sir!* And *suborning perjury!* Drawing up *legal documents* that are based on *false allegations*; compelling your client to sign and swear to a legal document that was and is *replete with falsehoods and out-and-out untruths.* You knew, didn't you, sir, *you knew that what you were doing, and what you were asking*—or actually *ordering*, as Mr. Kip has said—*ordering this man*, the plaintiff, to sign and swear to *falsified legal documents* in a train station—perhaps that is why you chose to conduct your business underground, as it were—because you *were only too well aware that the complaint in this matter is filled with lies*, and you knew that you were *breaking the laws of New York* by composing this document and ordering your client's son to swear to its truthfulness and sign it—*didn't you?*" I demanded.

Jacobs remained remarkably unperturbed. Mr. Mills as well remained seated and apparently thought better of objecting again only to have the judge find the question acceptable. It was clear that Jacobs and Mills had prepared themselves for this attack. Jacobs looked up at me with a complacent expression, the slightest mocking squint to his gaze, and said, "I was engaged by and operating under the instructions of my client, Mr. Philip Rhinelander, and Mr. Mills."

"*What?*" I practically bellowed and caused the witness to flinch. "*Mr. Mills, you say?* This man, who is also engaged as counsel for the plaintiff? And who is also a licensed attorney in this state—indeed, a former judge, and therefore subject to the rules. You say *he* instructed you *to compose and file false documents!*"

I turned to the judge. "Your Honor, I am stunned. *This is an outrage!* I . . . I . . . well, I don't know what to say. I feel compelled and, under the circumstances, I believe my only recourse is to renew my motion to have Your Honor dismiss the case."

"So noted. *Denied. Proceed,*" Judge Morschauser ordered.

Though hardly surprised by the ruling, I shook my head in apparent dismay, turned back to Mr. Jacobs, and said, "That is all I need to know; and, I'm sure, *all the jury needs to know* as well."

To the court I said, "I have no further questions for this . . . *witness.*"

* * *

As if the vivid testimony about cunnilingus; and then the dramatic and excruciating spectacle of disrobing Alice, and the display of the girl's naked body before the all-male jury; as if that had not been enough; we now had a licensed lawyer on the witness stand representing the plaintiff and admitting that he had written and filed a document—several documents—with the court on behalf of the plaintiff knowing that these papers contained lies he had composed at the behest of none other than his employer, Philip Rhinelander, and with instructions from co-counsel.

Good Lord! All this—in my mind, and in the opinion of a number of legal experts who commented on the case after it was decided—why, this alone should have resulted in the court ordering that the case be dismissed. Judge Morschauser, however, was not wont to do so no matter how egregious Jacobs's management of the case appeared, no matter what Jacobs and Mr. Mills had conspired to do to win their verdict. Judge Morschauser, no doubt aware of the huge and unprecedented international publicity the case had generated, and not wishing to be seen as a judge who allowed the trial to get out of control with lawyers running amok under his auspices, His Honor was determined to stick it out to the bitter end, come what may. And, I must say, though I admired Judge Morschauser for having such firm resolve, I knew that he did so only because of the prominence of the plaintiff's family, the Rhinelander name and fortune, knowing, as I am sure His Honor did, just how ugly Philip Rhinelander could make it for anyone in public life in and around our city who should defy him.

As Alice's defense team, given how the trial had progressed to this point, with the plaintiff's case rapidly losing credibility, should we win, the last thing we wanted was to have the case overturned on appeal, then to have to try the lawsuit all over again, with the case then brought under new allegations and with better preparation on behalf of the plaintiff. Certainly, I understood that should the jury vote in favor of an annulment, Judge Morschauser was content to let the appellate courts sort it out. More than anything, His Honor wanted the trial to end in a verdict so as to get him out from under the unrelenting public attention and scrutiny *Rhinelander v. Rhinelander* had engendered. And he was not the only one: I as well was anxious to have the case end in a verdict.

Jacobs's testimony was devastating for the plaintiff; I believed that there was no other way to look at it. Rhinelander Senior *ordered* his lawyer to compose and file a *false claim!* Mind-boggling. And here it was again: the image of Rhinelander Senior off somewhere in his aerie, an angry demigod above not only the hoi polloi of us common folk down here on Earth, but also above the law, attempting to crush the girl his son had married by ordering his minions to break the law. Philip Rhinelander is the one who should have been on trial here and not his rejected daughter-in-law. The sins of the father indeed! Ah, but how the rich flaunt the law and do what they will with barely any repercussions and certainly no remorse—as if it were their divine right.

One thing I knew: my jury was virtually eating this testimony up. Rhinelander would be hard pressed to pull one over on these simple men.

* * *

Anticlimactic as it might appear given what we had just witnessed, and feeling that the jury could use some relief from the intensity of the drama, once Jacobs stepped down, I called as our next witness Alice's quite obviously Black brother-in-law, Robert Brooks. Brooks took the stand, identified himself, and then gave the jury a fine grin. Here at last was a witness in this trial that everyone could agree was undoubtedly a Negro.

Brooks was well spoken, nattily dressed, and, one could see, quite comfortable on the witness stand. He smiled often, exposing a mouth full of gleaming white teeth. I thought back to the appearance of Mr. Jolson on the stand; here was the real article!

First, I established that Brooks had met Kip in September 1921, while Brooks was living in the Jones home with his wife, Alice's sister Emily, and their baby girl, Roberta; which date, I reminded the jury, was well before Rhinelander had testified that they met.

"How were you introduced to the plaintiff?" I asked.

"By Mrs. Rhinelander, by Alice. She said, 'Leonard, this is my brother-in-law Mr. Brooks.'"

"Were they married at that time?"

"No. They were courting."

"Very good, sir. And, if you can recall, how often did you have occasion to meet Mr. Kip Rhinelander . . . after that first meeting?"

"Well, quite often after that, actually. Leonard—I called him Len, not Kip; he said he didn't like to be called Kip. We met nearly every evening. Sometimes at the Joneses' home, but also Len would come to our home and join in with my friends to play cards."

"These friends, were they also Black men?"

"All my friends are colored."

"And can you tell us: Did Mr. Rhinelander ever object to your color? Or to the color of your friends?"

"No, not at all. He was very friendly. We got on well. Len was especially fond of our daughter, Roberta. He brought her presents; he sat her on his lap. I could see that Len loved children."

"Thank you. . . . Oh, sir, what, may I ask, is your occupation?"

"I work in a private home . . . as a butler."

"I see . . . and Mr. Rhinelander, did he appear in any way—that is, did Mr. Rhinelander know how you are employed?"

"Yes. We talked about it."

"Did Mr. Rhinelander appear in any way . . . discomfited when he learned how you were employed?"

"You mean, did it bother him?"

"Yes; did it appear that it was discomfiting to Mr. Rhinelander? Given his status in society, to be on such friendly terms with you, given your employment as a butler; did that appear to make him uncomfortable?"

"No, not at all. We got along fine. He said he liked coming to our home because it was relaxing for him, and he was so fond of little Roberta; she called him Uncle Len. He was always bringing her things from the city, dolls or games. We had tea together. I drove Len to the train station. I looked after his car when he was away in the city."

* * *

With this testimony, court adjourned for the noon recess. After Kip's harrowing appearance on the witness stand, and the pitiable performance of his Manhattan lawyer, Leon Jacobs, with his damaging testimony that went to the very heart of the impetus behind the lawsuit, Leonard, remarkably, I must emphasize that the boy appeared for all as a new man, and far more relaxed. Again, I was dumbfounded. While this, in my mind, it bore out my belief that Kip hoped to lose his case and was pleased with how badly it was going for his side, I still found it bewildering that he didn't just stand up and order the fiasco to cease. He had the power to withdraw the lawsuit, to quit his claim of fraud against his wife; his father and his father's lawyers be damned. Alice clearly was not bearing up well. Surely the boy could see what this was doing to the girl he loved.

* * *

Alice did all she could to avoid being seen in public due to the fierce attentions of the crowds wherever and whenever she chanced to appear. It was dreadful. Trips to and from the courthouse were like escorting an infamous criminal. During breaks in the trial, I accompanied Alice to a room in the courthouse reserved for counsel; there she would take her lunch, rarely eating more than a few bites of whatever her mother would bring her. The girl was under such unrelenting nervous strain throughout the trial that her family and defense team sought to keep her from the public as much as was physically possible. Even the reporters following the case commented on how her looks had changed for the worse as the trial dragged on. She looked tired, haggard, and even more overwrought as the trial was almost in its fourth week.

On this day, while we had Mr. Brooks on the witness stand, and after Alice had suggested some questions I might ask him, once we left the room where she had picked at her lunch, and as we took the elevator back to the floor where the courtroom was located, as the elevator doors opened and we entered the hallway, Alice walked straight into her husband. They actually bumped up against one another.

Rhinelander appeared stunned. He doffed his hat while never taking his eyes off the girl who was his wife.

If eyes could talk! With the look Rhinelander gave Alice—not unlike the smile I'd seen him show her before—a secret look, his eyes filled with muted love, love that he was apparently painfully unable to express beyond a look in those pale eyes; and a sad smile that was very nearly a frown playing at the corners of his weak mouth—that look said it all. There was no denying it. The couple—perhaps both recalling the days and nights filled with love that they had spent together, the glorious time on Cape Cod when they lived as man and wife far from the madding crowd—both gazed deeply into each other's eyes. For just a brief moment I thought Kip would break down and take his bride in his arms and hold her to him to ease the pain it was obvious they both felt. *But no!* Acting instead as though he were meeting a stranger, with his hat in hand he said, "Excuse me, please."

The boy then made an awkward move to go around his wife while still unable to take his eyes away from her, and to step into the elevator. Alice gasped. She sobbed. She had to lean up against the wall to support herself and keep from collapsing.

Mrs. Jones, who was in the hallway, seeing her daughter break down, rushed forth to comfort her. The entire episode left me feeling deeply saddened. I walked into the courtroom struggling to regain my animus. Mr. Brooks having resumed his place on the stand, and with Alice still emotionally shattered from her brief encounter with the man she loved, I approached the bench along with Mr. Mills and told Judge Morschauser of the encounter, how it had affected the defendant, and that I wasn't sure how much more Alice could take before she experienced a total emotional breakdown. Therefore I asked of His Honor if, once I'd completed my examination of Mr. Brooks, court might be adjourned for the day.

"I know, Your Honor, that there is still much to do before we get to closing statements and Your Honor's charge to the jury, and that we are all tired and anxious to see this case resolved before the Christmas and New Year break. But I am also painfully aware of the emotional toll the trial is taking on Mrs. Rhinelander; and, for her benefit, as I do not wish to see her have a complete physical and mental collapse and require that the trial be halted, I ask your forbearance."

Mr. Mills said he had no objection to ending the day early; the judge agreed; and we resumed with Mr. Brooks's testimony.

"I have just a few more questions," I said to Robert Brooks, "then we'll let you go."

"Oh, I'm not going anywhere," Brooks said with his winning smile. "I'm here till the end . . . to be here for Alice."

"Thank you, sir, and I am certain that Alice thanks you as well. Now, I have only one more question. Do you recall—let me put it this way—was there ever a time that you recall when you were *not* welcome in the Joneses' home? My question is: Was there any animosity between you and Mrs. Jones; did she send you away because of your color?"

"Emily, my wife, never stayed away, but I did. I don't know whether they approved my marrying Emily; there were other issues, because of Emily's age when we married. Mr. and Mrs. Jones never showed they minded due to my being colored. Other matters concerning Emily had come up that needed to be sorted out."

"I see. But not to do with your race?"

"No."

"Thank you, sir."

Mr. Mills declined to cross-examine the witness. In keeping with my request for an early adjournment, Judge Morschauser spoke to the clerk, who announced, "All rise."

As the judge departed, the clerk said, "Court is in recess until tomorrow morning at nine o'clock."

* * *

I urged Mrs. Jones to get her girl home, give her a good strong cup of English tea, make her eat a decent meal, and get her to rest.

"Alice," I said as we left the courtroom, caught in the gawking crowds gathered in the hallway. "I know this is hard on you. I'm sorry you have to go through this. You remember how we discussed it, when you—well, my girl, when you insisted on going to trial."

I felt that it was important for me to keep Alice's spirits up as much as possible by reminding her of the challenge she had chosen to undertake. In my experience, one is not as inclined to buckle under the pressure that one takes of their own accord rather than some unwanted thing forced upon them by outside influences.

"I'm not sorry I insisted," Alice told me with firm resolve. "I still believe it is the right thing to do. Of course, I knew before we started that it would be hard, that it would be—well, isn't that why they call it a trial?"

I smiled. "Yes, dear, indeed it is."

"I'll be fine."

Alice stopped speaking and looked around as though to see if Rhinelander had found his bodyguards and departed, which apparently he had. Then she looked up at me with those dark, lustrous eyes. I was struck, looking at her, as I so often was, by the rare beauty of her eyes, those deep, dark orbs like pools or like portals one could slip into and forget about everything else. Her eyes and the way she looked back at me spoke volumes as to the depth of her character, her strength, her curiosity, and her love of life; and the love she still felt for her husband. I remember thinking, *The Rhinelander boy simply doesn't deserve such a girl as his wife.* He'd proven, at least to me, that he was not worthy of Alice; that he lacked the personal fortitude to love such a girl—which, of course, was the real reason we were here in this court. Alice and Leonard were a rare pairing indeed, not simply just their obvious social differences, which were profound, but also in how Alice seemed to be attracted to a man who was so far beneath her measure in strength of character that he was not true to himself. And, in the end, when it comes down to it, isn't that what this ambiguous time spent here on Earth is about: how we face and live up to the challenges we all accept and therefore must endure?

Alice continued, "I think I just didn't realize how it would hurt so to see Leonard like this, day in and day out, and to be in the same room with him—so close, and yet have him so, so *coldhearted*, so *distant*, as if he doesn't even know me. That hurts when what we had—*we were so close.* Of course we knew how different we were, but we loved each other so much . . . in spite of our differences, perhaps even more because of our differences. And I still love him; I always will no matter what happens to us. It just . . . it saddens me so to see him like this. I can't understand how love like we had could just . . . go away."

"I believe he still loves you," I said.

"Yes . . . Others have said so as well."

I nodded.

"Then . . . *why?*" she asked.

Alice posed the question that I believe was on everyone's mind.

CHAPTER TWENTY-EIGHT

Striptease

Dear diary,

I don't even know what day it is. I've lost all track of time. Thanksgiving came and went in a blur like everything else. The trial! It's been going on for weeks now. And, of course it's in all the newspapers: I stood naked before the men in the jury! Mr. Davis, sometimes I don't know about that man, what goes on in that mind of his! It was his idea. He asked me, he said, Alice, I would like to have you disrobe—that was the word he used; oh, you know Mr. Davis is a fine one for using all sorts of words to say something quite plain and simple. Take my clothes off and stand naked before the men on the jury! All the lawyers, the judge, fifteen or sixteen old men all standing around—or sitting, actually—and looking at my naked body! I was shocked by the idea!

I remember I said to him, "So what am I now, a burlesque dancer? A stripper?" We both laughed. That's one of several good things I will say about Mr. Davis—he has a mischievous sense of humor. I thought he was crazy—and it was not the first time I have thought this. Then I thought, *Oh, he's just a dirty old man; he wants to see me naked.* But when he explained it—how there is a difference between what he calls real evidence and testimony—that is, words from the mouths of witnesses who obviously have a tale to tell—I understood it immediately. Of course, my face is one thing, and because of my features it's confusing. People don't know when they look at me if I am white or mixed or whatever. All my life I have been faced with this question: What are you, Alice? Are you colored or are you white? As a child in school I was often teased. Some of the other children would call to me, "Eeny meeny miny moe; catch a nigger by the toe." It was horrible. Mr. Davis would say that I am both white and black, of course, and it is all in the eyes of the beholder. But definitely a lot clearer when you see those parts of my body that are usually covered by my clothes. Okay, I know that, so you want me to take my clothes off and stand there in front of twelve—no, fifteen—dirty old men! You're insane, Mr. Davis, and you are brilliant. All right, I agreed, I'll do it. I'll become, as I've heard it said and read in the newspaper stories, I will present myself nude as a piece of evidence!

Surely I was embarrassed, but in a way I didn't mind it. For one thing, I know I have a nice body.

What do I care, really? I can be an actress if need be. Mr. Davis was right; the men would get a thrill and they would also know Len was not telling the truth about what he knew before he married me.

But listen, dear diary, and you know I've written to you about this before, taking my clothes off for the jury, that was one thing, but to have Len's letters to me read out loud in court! Well, that was altogether different. The things he wrote about! And to have them read to a room full of white men! (All the women were ordered to leave the courtroom.)

No! Now, that was something that no one could have imagined happening in court. O my God, Len's letters! I felt so badly for him! Silly boy! How could you let your lawyers do this to you? And your father! Because, dear Len—it's your fault! People were horrified—or at least they pretended to be. They act like what Len and I did was something only animals do. Not so! I've talked to a few girls who all said they did it too—and they liked it! Boys like it too!

Oh, but please, to have all this come out in reading Len's letters in court! Now it's in all the newspapers, although they don't say exactly what it is, just that it is an obscene act or something like that.

Oh well, let them say what they will. We like it—both of us.

And that Mr. Davis, he really gets me sometimes. His favorite words when I ask him how something might be seen by the jury or by anyone else, for that matter, he always says the same thing, "Well, my dear, it cuts both ways."

Cuts both ways? I guess that's what happens if you're a lawyer—everything cuts both ways. Nothing is Black or white—just like me!

Poor Len. I can imagine it only cuts one way with his father—the wrong way! Well, it's all his fault, really. I have no pity for Len's father. If Philip Rhinelander hadn't forced his son to bring this case against me, none of this would ever have come out and been all over the news.

I'm sick about it. This trial is making me ill. My nerves are frayed. I can't sleep. I can't eat. I can't go out on the street without bodyguards or I will be taunted, called every ugly name, chased by boys yelling nasty things. It's horrible. My life has become unbearable. But in Mr. Davis's famous words, it cuts both ways! My father said that when we go though things like this—trials!—it only makes us stronger. And I agree with that. The more they throw at me, the more I want to stand up to them and say, Never! I will never give up my pride in who I am. This is a nasty business for sure, and I'm not talking about just being made to strip in front of a bunch of old white men—not all were old, actually. And I'm not talking about having those things Len used to like to do to me that are supposedly unnatural read about aloud in court. The nasty part is this whole business about my color based on the fact I have colored blood from my father, somehow that makes me less than acceptable to the pure white world Len is from. Why? He didn't see it. It never bothered him. Not until his father heard about it. It's wrong. I don't care what they say. They are wrong. There is no crime in my loving Len and his loving me. It was and always will be good and true no matter what they say.

CHAPTER TWENTY-NINE

The Defense Rests

Of course, yes, certainly: I heard the rumors circulating in and around the courthouse, as well as all over town, even in the city among those following the case—practically everyone! I listened to what was said during those final days of my testimony, then after I took the stand, and while Alice's lawyers put on her defense. It was rumored that I had intentionally made a poor showing; that I had done all I could without being obvious so as to let Alice win the case. It was even speculated that I conspired with Alice's attorneys to forfeit our cause.

None of this is true. It may have appeared that way to some, but the truth is that I didn't know what I was doing. I had no idea. Certainly if it had been my intention to forfeit the case by making a poor showing, I would hardly admit it. The truth is, I was afraid—afraid of how I knew Mr. Davis would make a mockery of the way my lawyers had chosen to portray me: as an idiot, as an innocent fool, an imbecile duped by a vicious Black nymphomaniac. *It made me sick!* I told them, how many times, I can't remember; I told my father; I told him with the lawyers all present: *This is nonsense. This is insulting.* I was not and am not and never will be an idiot. What I am is a man who . . . well, how to explain it? A man who was attracted to a girl I knew was different from any girl I had ever met and whom I was immediately attracted to regardless of her skin color and the humble origins of her family. *To hell with all that!* Who cares about any of that anymore? *Not me!* All I could see when I looked at Alice was a girl who gave me a thrill just to be near her, to touch her, to listen to her speak. I wanted to be with her and to be left alone to love her as I chose.

Alice's lawyer, Mr. Davis, he understands that I live in terror of my father, and for that I hate him—Philip, my father, I mean. Yes, I hate my father, and I love him. I feel sorry for him, actually. Not only for how I have disgraced him and the Rhinelander name, but because he is so stuck in the past. He doesn't see that the world is changing—or perhaps he does see it but he can't understand it.

Not so with Mr. Davis; he knows exactly what's going on. And though I was terribly afraid of him, I like him, and I like what he is doing for Alice. Having her strip and stand naked before the jury! O my God, that was a pure stroke of genius on his part. All those old geezers sitting in judgment, one look at Alice's body, there was your verdict right then and there. My letters! Now, every day I get letters from women asking me to come see them. Or from men calling me a pervert.

I know what Mr. Jacobs told me to do, and Mr. Mills. I know how I was instructed by Mr. Mills to comport myself on the witness stand as a foolish boy entrapped in a sordid love affair by an unscrupulous Black vamp. We actually rehearsed my testimony, Mr. Mills, Leon Jacobs, and I, in my hotel rooms for several hours over a few sessions before I was called to testify. None of it made sense to me; and, once I entered the courtroom and sat down on the witness stand, I was so nervous, so uncomfortable with just having to be there, and so upset with how my lawyers had forced me to defend myself—I'll get to that—and so disturbed with what all this was doing to Alice that I lost any ability to appear as my lawyers had instructed me.

It was ridiculous; and it was insulting. I was offended and sickened by the whole process; in particular by the pathetic role I was forced to play in the action against my wife. I shall never live that down as long as I live. I wake with it every day, and it hurts me still and gives me such regret.

When we practiced for my appearance, and both Jacobs and Mr. Mills grilled me with questions such as they expected Mr. Davis would ask, I was . . . I felt as if . . . Well, the truth is, I hated what they wanted me to do, how they wanted me to appear for the jury, and how they wanted me to express how I felt for Alice. It disgusted me. It was all untrue. I told them it was foolish nonsense. A stuttering nut (as Mr. Davis called me); a naive and helpless young boy seduced by a calculating Black vamp (as my lawyers sought to portray me and the girl I love); none of that was true. It was all a pack of lies. And ridiculous to think that any jury made up of even halfway intelligent men would accept such a lot of rubbish. Once Mr. Davis read my letters to the jury, any hope of my appearing as an innocent boy entrapped by an older Black girl was seen as utter nonsense.

When I walked into that courtroom and saw Alice with her lawyers, even as I tried not to look at her, knowing what it would do to me to see her suffering such pain and humiliation all on my account, I simply lost any ability to behave and answer questions as I was instructed. Mr. Davis scared the hell out of me. Once I understood how clever he is, I knew I had no hope of outsmarting him; and, as they say, pulling the wool over his eyes and the eyes of the men on the jury. When I was on the witness stand with Mr. Davis questioning me, it was excruciating. I was bound to make a fool of myself and a poor showing for our case.

So what? Our case! What case? There was no case! It certainly wasn't my case. They all knew it—my father, the lawyers, Mr. Strong, Bowers, my driver Chidester—they knew that it was a false story I was supposed to tell: seduced by Alice, deceived as to her color. Anyone could see it! So you want to make me out the fool? The dupe? Absurd and offensive. I was so angry with the way they tried to twist what Alice and I had, I thought, *Fine, let it be seen for the utter farce I always knew it would be.*

What Alice and I had, as different as we might be superficially, we had true love, happiness, glorious love making, and the promise of a life together until Philip ruined it. *The bastard! I hate him!* He got what he deserves. They all did. And to hell with them for not listening to me from the beginning. I told them their ridiculous defense was never going to work. No one ever listens to me, not even when it comes to things that only I know about—such as my feelings for Alice.

I miss Alice, I miss the love we had every day, every hour, and I despise myself for allowing my father and his lawyers to do this to her. They got what they deserve when my letters were read in court and are now infamous all over the world. Hah! Put that in your pipe and smoke it, Philip! Your son licked the vagina of a Black girl—and he enjoyed it!

So, did I want to lose the case? Yes, goddamn it, of course I wanted to lose! I never wanted to bring the lawsuit in the first place. Did I purposely try to lose the case? I suppose, given that my heart was not in it, and I made such a poor showing, one could say that I did. But the truth is I simply didn't know what I was doing. I was so upset, so angry at the pain I knew all this was causing Alice that I couldn't think straight.

I was angry with the lawyers and the whole ordeal. I was warned by Mr. Mills, and by Leon Jacobs—who, truthfully, I had come to dislike rather intensely, and I had very little regard for his abilities as a lawyer. He may have been fine for doing legal paperwork in the office with deeds and contracts and such, but he had no idea how to conduct a complicated lawsuit with a jury trial such as they forced me to bring against Alice. Their idea of how to characterize me and my relationship with Alice was absurd, the stuff of cheap fiction; innocent white boy seduced by a calculating Black vamp. *Please!* What utter nonsense.

The truth is, from the first time I saw Alice all I wanted was to be with her, and to be her man. Once I got to know her, I never wanted to part from her. Alice and the love we had is the first truly good thing that happened in my life since my mother died. I told this to my father and to his lawyers. They thought I had lost my mind; that a Black sexpot or some such nonsense had somehow bewitched me. Was the lovemaking wonderful? Oh, yes, I will tell you that it was. But that's because we really love each other, nothing to do with the color of our skin. We were happy in each other's arms. Life has been a perpetual misery for me since we were forced apart.

Jacobs told me that Mr. Davis was revered and feared as one of the most vicious and clever cross-examiners anyone had ever had the misfortune to encounter on the witness stand. Clearly, I wasn't looking forward to it. When it all came to pass, rather than intentionally giving up my case as people are insinuating, I was confronted with the truth. There it was before the jury in clear and obvious facts, and in my letters, and I was unable and unwilling to lie my way out of it. The moment I opened my mouth, I'm sure that every man on that jury knew it was all lies.

The lawyers made me tell lies. Their strategy from the beginning was to make our case all about race; how I was duped into believing Alice was a pure white Anglo-Saxon girl. *Nonsense!* How could I say that and expect anyone to believe it given how I knew Mr. Jones? And Robert Brooks? How I had made love to Alice and seen her naked body countless times? Their idea was to bet on the supposed racism of the men on the jury. They believed that they could win the case by appealing to the fear whites have of Blacks and of the mixing of the races. That and the power and prestige of the Rhinelander name.

Well, we shall see. Now that it's nearly all over, with final arguments and then the judge's instructions to the jury before they go out to deliberate, I'll tell anyone who cares to listen the real truth, which is probably quite obvious by now. I never wanted to sue Alice. I never wanted our marriage to be dissolved. I was happy with Alice as my wife, I loved her dearly, I still do, and I don't give a damn what color her skin is or who her people are. All I cared about was how we felt about each other, and it was the most wonderful feeling I have ever experienced. For my father and his lawyers to take what Alice and I had and try to turn it into something deceitful, something dirty and vile, a trick or a plan hatched by the Jones family to entrap me into marrying Alice to get at my family's money: those are all disgusting and horrible lies.

I never stopped loving Alice, and I never wanted the marriage annulled so that the poor girl would have nothing but guilt and disgrace for the rest of her life. *No!* That's not what I wanted. The guilt is mine for not standing up to my father. That is why I made sure she got my note urging her to fight the lawsuit. I suppose that I did intentionally make a poor showing of my case even if I wasn't fully aware of it at the time.

Mr. Davis knows exactly what was going on; you can't fool that man. He got to the heart of the matter in short order. I believe he knew it even before the trial started. He knew of my note to Alice. He knew from the beginning that I was not the instigator or even the . . . well, my curse: I was the pawn, the passive, reluctant wretch who allowed this travesty to be brought in my name against the woman I loved. Sickening, the whole disgusting charade. I would return to my hotel room in the evening after a day in court and feel like retching with all of the lies and false claims still festering in my mind, my heart, and my soul.

Why? How could I allow this to happen in the first place? That's the only real question in this whole matter. Why didn't I refuse when Mr. Jacobs and Mr. Strong came for me at the Hotel Marie Antoinette? And then again when I was living with Alice in the Joneses' home after we were married? *Why was I such a coward?*

I will try to explain, though I don't know if there is any real, valid explanation beyond abject cowardice. I admit that I was then, and I still am afraid of my father, physically and mentally unable to stand up to him; and, the one thing I did in my life that took any real courage, courting and loving Alice, I couldn't maintain it when faced with my father's wrath and his will. I was afraid of my father's rejection, of his hatred.

That calls for more explanation, and I'll get to it. But I also wanted to believe at the time, and against my better judgment and everything I knew about my father, in my self-hypnotized state, I kept telling myself that, if Philip would only allow me to explain how I felt about Alice; if he were capable of putting his beliefs and feelings aside to understand how good Alice made me feel about myself, and how happy we were together, I held out some vague but tantalizing hope that my father would relent and let me have the woman I loved as my wife. Let me be the man I wanted to be.

Of course, looking back on it now, I realize that I was deluding myself. One wants to believe that one can bring others to feel and understand what one feels. But no, not when that other person is Philip Rhinelander. My father is the most single-minded man I have ever met, which is no doubt why he has been so successful. He believes that the entire world should view life as he does, and that if they did, there would be no mixing of the races; no misunderstanding of class differences; no breakdown in morality; no weakening of the American spirit, as he calls this belief in white superiority and manifest destiny. He wished to impose this view of the world on everyone he knew, but in particular on his children. He never got over his brother William's straying from our family's position and the scandal his marriage caused. It shocked and horrified Father. He saw willfulness and any sign of individuality that opposed what he called "our sacrosanct Huguenot heritage" as a clear indication of insanity or, in my case, feeblemindedness. He believed that I was simply not intelligent enough, or not experienced enough in the ways of the world to understand what it meant to love and marry a girl such as Alice, what that would do to the family name, what it would ultimately mean not only for me but also for Alice, because, as he put it, she could never be accepted as "one of us."

My father harped on this: how what I had done, if I didn't stop it and denounce my wife as having defrauded me, how Alice would suffer. "Give her some money and let her go away and have a normal life!" he insisted, as though that were all it would take to appease her, to save me from ruin, and to make it all appear as though it had never happened.

"This marriage cannot and will not be made legitimate!" he bellowed when we first met after news of the marriage had been made public. "I will not have my son married to a Negress! Do you understand? Have you lost your mind, Leonard? Need I have you committed to an asylum? Son, I am ordering you: you must end this! *I* will end it! There will be no Negro offspring by the name of Rhinelander!"

It hurt me so much to hear Father say these things, although I certainly should have expected it, and I knew that Mr. Davis understood this and that he tried to make it clear to the men on the jury that it was all my father's doing, all Philip Rhinelander's plan to annul the marriage, and that I was no more than a cog in the wheel of my father's machinations. I have never been able to forgive my father for this, for forcing me to bring the lawsuit against Alice; it has forever destroyed not only my marriage, but undermined the love and respect I had for my father as well, and certainly caused me no end of disgust and self-hatred. I used to fantasize killing my father. But then I knew that the humiliation I had caused him with my letters being read in court was even worse than death for him. I will always be angry and upset and hurt, and deeply ashamed of myself for allowing Philip to compel me to seek to annul my marriage and for taking me away from Alice, the girl I loved and still love, my wife, whom my father referred to as "that nigger girl!" And for his cursing and ranting and calling on my dead mother's soul to condemn me for making Alice my wife unless I was willing to sign those papers knowing that none of what was written in the documents is true. And then to swear an oath to tell the truth, take the witness stand, and tell lie after lie. Become a perjurer. How could my father do this to me—his son?

Believe me, were it not for the fact of the Rhinelander name, we are the ones who would have been on trial for perjury.

I'll tell you how my father was able to force this trial to end my marriage. It is simple: because he never loved me. He was always ashamed of me. As much as it hurts me to say this, I know it's true: I disgust my father.

Philip Rhinelander, oh, he is such a proud man. I used to ask myself: *Proud of what?* That we are rich? That we are supposedly descendants of some royal Huguenot family bloodline? So what? Okay, dandy, all well and good. But the world is changing. Society is changing. America is changing. What good are we doing the world? Oh, I know, there are the charities, the donations given in the family name. But what do we really stand for? Prejudice . . . class superiority. That's all nonsense.

I want to believe that my mother, that Adelaide, would have embraced my marriage to Alice. She would have understood what it means to love someone. My father rejected it because—sometimes I think he clung to the outmoded beliefs about class and race just to spite my mother's memory and the Kips who, though easily as well bred, perhaps even more distinguished than my father's family, but who nevertheless at times struck Father as too forward-thinking, too modern.

Now, when I consider how Philip felt about me, clearly I frustrated him, and I worried him. From the time I was a little boy, with my stutter, and with my . . . I don't want to say effeminate mannerisms, because I wasn't really a girly boy, but with my lack of interest in the same kinds of manly pursuits my father and my older brothers enjoyed: football and fencing and those activities they thought of as proper pursuits for boys and men. I was aware that I let my father down, that I didn't live up to the Rhinelander ideal of what a young man should be.

That's why he sent me away to that school, the Orchards, and that's why he never came to visit me while I was there. Interesting that by sending me to the Orchards, that was how it all came to pass: my meeting Karl Kreitler, our driving down to New Rochelle to pick up local girls, and then meeting the Jones girls, and falling in love with Alice. It never would have happened if my father hadn't insisted on sending me to the Orchards. *Hah! It is all his fault!* He wanted me out of the way because I was an embarrassment to him, and he would have been happy to keep me somewhere else, anywhere else—that is, until I married Alice; then he could no longer ignore me or try to buy me off with gifts and an allowance. Oh, he tried, certainly he and his men, Mr. Jacobs, Mr. Bowers, Mr. Strong, even the chauffeur,

Chidester; they tried to keep me away from Alice. And they were still trying all during the trial—to disgrace her, to hurt her and her family, to bring false charges against the girl I loved, to defame her and cast her aside . . . all in my name.

Yes, it was my father, Philip Rhinelander, who simply would not accept Alice and allow me—allow us—to be happy. He put himself first; he put his own pride over his son's happiness. That made me believe what I had always suspected about my father, which I told Alice: that my father never really cared for me. Yes, I believe the truth is he was ashamed of me. I knew it; I saw it in his eyes even when I was a boy because I didn't live up to how he expected a man, a Rhinelander man, to appear and to behave in the world and in society. I was a disappointment to my father, I could see it in his eyes, I could hear it in his voice, and I could feel it even as a child. My father *didn't even try to hide it.* He stayed away from me once I was sent off to the Orchards School. And well before that, he cringed when I stuttered. He never embraced me. He drew away when I sought his love. He never told me that he loved me. I felt he would have happily given me up as his son if he had a choice. But my brothers were gone: one dead as an infant, another killed in the war, and the other married and moved away. It wasn't until I courted and then married Alice and horrified my father and scandalized the family with the prospect of Black blood infiltrating and tainting the Rhinelander line that Philip paid any attention to me. Yes, he bought me a car. He paid for the finest school, and for whatever else he believed I needed to become the man he wanted me to be. But he never put his arm around me, he never hugged me and said, "You're my boy, Leonard, my son, and I love you."

Never! When he looked at me, when Philip would take the time and look at me, what he saw, he saw me, and he saw my mother; he saw that side of my mother that always troubled him: her—for lack of a better word—humanity, which he saw as weakness. Her open-mindedness; her love of the arts, which he considered frivolous; her treatment of our servants, which he considered too familiar; the novels she read, which he considered scandalous trash; her opinions on current events, which he considered far too liberal, far too cosmopolitan, too *au courant*: That women should have the right to vote? Never, not in my father's view of the world. And all of what was happening in these times, the 1920s, which my mother—had she lived that long—I know she would have embraced and been pleased to see these changes come to pass, particularly with regard to women's rights; and, I believe, in matters of race and social class as well. My mother was ahead of her time, and her time caught up to her too soon. I know that, had she lived, I want to believe that she would never have forced me to bring the lawsuit against Alice. She would have seen it for the travesty it is, and she never would have abided Alice to suffer as she has because of what my father tried to do to her.

You know, there was always that question in my mind about the night my mother died. I know she had been drinking. I saw, not long before it happened—and I could always tell when Mother was tipsy: she slurred her words; she was overly affectionate; and she often lashed out angrily at Father. That night Father was not at home, it was just Mother and I and the servants at the vacation home in Tuxedo Park. Much as I try to recall what happened, I have blocked some parts of it from my memory. I can't even think about it now without feeling practically crippled with grief. To add to that, losing Alice, I don't know how I am to continue living. I don't know if I care to continue living. Life makes no sense to me now. It all seems pointless and sordid.

To get back to the question on everyone's mind as the plaintiff's case was finished and the defense about to start: Did I intentionally try to lose the case? Again I say no; by that I mean it wasn't premeditated, so to speak. I simply allowed it to happen. I allowed the truth to come out because I hated the whole idea of the lies that were the bases of the lawsuit, and I despised the way my attorneys sought to portray me as an idiot, a "stuttering nut," as Mr. Davis called me, a foolish, mentally deficient boy with no will and no understanding of what I was doing when I pursued a Black girl; a simpleminded boy who allowed himself to be seduced into marrying a girl he thought was white. *Ridiculous! All lies!*

My father and his men, his lawyers—his "factotums" as Mr. Davis calls them—they did everything within their power to attempt to get the men on the jury to believe these absurd lies. I simply acquiesced to what I knew was a hopeless case to keep my father from—God only knows what he would have done! Disown me? Certainly. Done everything in his considerable power to ruin Alice and me? Probably. Tried to disgrace and crush the Jones family? No doubt. That upset me. So I put up a poor showing because I hoped to keep our lawyers from ruining Alice and her family; and because I knew the lawsuit was based on lies.

People may say, and I know they have written this and said it in private and in public about me: How could I allow this to happen to Alice—to us? How could I allow Father and his lawyers to destroy what Alice and I had together and disgrace our love for each other? How could I let my father ruin any chance we had for a life as husband and wife?

I ask myself these questions every day. I lived with them in excruciating mental torment all during the trial, and especially during the terrible time while the jury was out. My only answer is, and this is something no man ever wants to admit to himself: I allowed it to happen because I am a coward. I am afraid of my father, afraid of his wrath, afraid of what he would do to us if

Alice and I had defied him and stayed married. Afraid of how he would have done everything imaginable to destroy Alice and her family if I refused to allow him to bring the lawsuit.

So why, one might ask, why did I marry Alice in the first place? If I knew she was of mixed race, which of course I did, and if I was aware of what it would mean to my father, and how he would react? Why not just have an affair? Or keep her as a mistress, which would have been seen as perfectly acceptable for a gentleman? Why marry the girl and allow it to become known to the public? I wrestled with these questions countless nights and particularly all during the trial. In the end, I believe I married Alice because it's what she wanted, and what she deserved out of the love and respect I had for her. She wanted to be my wife and to have a family, what nearly all women want. She wanted to be respectable.

To that degree, that much was true as to the facts alleged in the lawsuit. Alice wanted to be my wife. She loved me, and she wanted our love to be recognized and accepted. She wanted us to have a family. I married her out of my regard for her and for the love we had for each other. We were married in our hearts and in our souls; we still are. No matter how the jury decides the case, no matter what my father says and does, no matter what happens to Alice and to me, we will always have that time together, and we will always be Mr. and Mrs. Leonard and Alice Rhinelander; and in our hearts we will always be together no matter what my father, or the lawyers, or even what the jurors have to say.

* * *

After Mr. Brooks testified, I called Alice's family members, first her sisters: Emily, then Grace; and finally the matriarch: Elizabeth Jones, who had been sullied so nastily by Mr. Mills in his opening remarks. Emily Jones confirmed that her parents had disapproved of her marriage to Robert Brooks chiefly due to her age; to Mr. Brooks's unsettled position in his career; and that both her mother and her father had urged her to wait to marry, but that "Robert's race had not been an issue." She said that she and Robert had at one time both worked at the same hotel, and she never had any question that he was a Negro. Furthermore, when I asked, Emily told the jury that she also considered herself to be colored. "We—my sisters, all three of us—we never tried to pass as white. We let people think what they would when it came to our color. Some saw us as white; others as colored. But we were all aware that our father is a colored man."

The third Jones sister, Grace Miller, made quite an impressive appearance. Clearly she saw this as her opportunity for a star performance. All the Jones sisters were pretty, even remarkably attractive; but it was clear Grace was the most outgoing—one might even say flamboyant—of the three. She waltzed in wearing a close-fitting, sleek black dress, with a boa wrapped around her neck, and a plumed crimson toque hat, which I asked her to remove as I wanted the jury to see Grace's hair, which, I believed, with its glossy black color and rather coarse texture left no doubt as to her mixed race.

If there were any question, Grace, in her outspoken and charming fashion, smiling for the men on the jury, and looking up at Judge Morschauser with a coquettish tilt to her exquisite head, Alice's younger sister testified that although her marriage certificate to her husband, Mr. Miller, listed her as white, she considered herself to be, as she put it with characteristic flair, "a colored girl, and not ashamed of it."

When I asked how it happened that her marriage certificate listed her as white, Grace explained that the clerk assumed she was white based on her appearance, and due to the fact that her husband was white; or, as Grace put it, "of Italian descent." She went on to say that at the time she hadn't bothered to correct the clerk because she believed it was a simple enough mistake. Furthermore, she said she never would have imagined a situation where her or her sister's color or supposed race would become a matter of consideration before a jury in a lawsuit.

"None of us girls could ever have foreseen having to testify at a trial where one of us would be accused of lying about her color. Our father taught us to be honest, respectful, and proud of who we are. I know my sister. I know Alice would *never lie* about her color. Besides, Leonard knew, from the very beginning, when he first met me, and when he came to our home and met my father, when he met and became friendly with Robert Brooks: Leonard knew that we had colored blood. We never tried to hide who we are."

"He knew?" I asked to thwart the objection I knew Mills was about to raise. "How are you able to say Rhinelander *knew* you are colored?"

"Well, of course he knew. Because he met my father. It is obvious when you meet our father that we are not pure white. We discussed it."

"You discussed what exactly?"

"We discussed the fact that our father is a colored man."

I asked, "Do you mean to say you discussed it *with Mr. Rhinelander?*"

"With Len, yes. We spoke of our parents being a mixed couple. Len said he had no prejudice; he assured us he wasn't like that. He said he loved Alice and that was all that mattered."

* * *

Elizabeth Jones's appearance had been eagerly anticipated after Mr. Mills's disgraceful attack on her character in his opening remarks. A matronly, middle-aged English lady with a broad Midlands accent, she told the jury that her son-in-law, Robert Brooks, was welcome in their home after the marriage, that she and her husband, George Jones, were aware Mr. Brooks is a Negro; but that for a time they—particularly Mr. Jones, who is strict about such matters, as he is a hard-working man who puts a lot of emphasis upon making one's way in the world—Mr. Jones urged Robert to find a better-paying job and to get a place of their own for his wife and daughter. He even offered to help Robert with the funds needed to get started making a home for the young couple now that they had a child, whom, Mrs. Jones told the jury, both she and her husband adored; but their home was not large. The child needed a room of her own.

"So it was all a matter of those *practical considerations*," I asked. "Living space and such. No other obvious concerns?"

"It was not a question of Mr. Brooks's color," Mrs. Jones said and looked at the judge, and then at the jury. "We are not prejudiced people."

Mrs. Jones affirmed that Kip as well appeared to have had no discrimination as to skin color. I asked her, "Did Rhinelander ever ask about color? Either Mr. Jones's color, or that of the girls?"

"No," Elizabeth said. "It was never an issue in our home."

"You remember, Mrs. Jones, when the newspaper published stories and called your husband a Negro?"

"I do, yes."

"Were you surprised?"

Mrs. Jones said, "We were all surprised. We didn't expect headlines to read as they did. We expected him to be called *a colored man*."

"Something I'd like to clear up, please, madam: In all the time Mr. Rhinelander lived in your home, in any discussions of Alice's background, did Mr. Jones ever tell Mr. Rhinelander that he was *of Spanish descent?*"

She shook her head and said, "No, never. That would be untrue."

"What did Mr. Rhinelander say while he was living in your home during the week beginning November 13, 1924, the week the newspapers published stories about Alice and Mr. Jones? Do you remember?"

"Leonard said, 'Never mind. *I married the girl I love.*'"

Mrs. Jones went on to say that Leonard was always accepted and even loved as a member of the family.

"How did you and your husband—when you discussed it among yourselves—how did you and Mr. Jones view Mr. Rhinelander's courting, and then marrying Alice? Did you see it as your golden opportunity to gain a rich and socially prominent son-in-law?"

"*Not at all,*" Elizabeth Jones stated emphatically. "Mr. Jones in particular was *concerned.* Of course we liked Leonard; he's a very nice and respectful boy, and we certainly welcomed him into our home. But Mr. Jones worried that it was just a *dalliance* on the boy's part; that Leonard's intentions toward our daughter might not be wholesome; that he was just chasing after her, well, for what all boys want from a girl."

This comment brought smirks and giggles from the audience, and smiles to the faces of a few of the jurors.

I asked, "Did you or Mr. Jones ever attempt to *dissuade* Alice from continuing to see Mr. Rhinelander? Or did you or Mr. Jones attempt to *forbid* Alice from seeing Mr. Rhinelander?"

"Mr. Jones spoke with Alice about it; he spoke with Mr. Rhinelander as well. I had my talks with Alice, with all our girls when they came of a certain age. Mr. Jones, at first, he was *dead set against it.*"

"Is it *true* that you and Mr. Jones *plotted to entrap* Rhinelander in marriage with Alice so that your family might prosper as a result of having Alice marry into a wealthy family such as the Rhinelanders?"

"*No, that is not true; certainly not!*" Elizabeth Jones asserted. "Mr. Jones and I believe in working for what we may achieve. We do not wish to gain by attaching ourselves or our daughters to someone of wealth or high social class. That never works to anyone's benefit. Just the opposite."

I then asked Mrs. Jones to recount to the best of her recollection the events around Mr. Jacobs and Mr. Strong arriving at their home to take Leonard away. She made it clear that Jacobs lied to Leonard; he assured Leonard that his father merely wanted to speak to him so as to know his son's intentions, and that Leonard would then be free to return to his wife. She recalled when Jacobs came to serve Alice with the lawsuit; and she told of the note from Leonard urging Alice to fight. Finally, Mrs. Jones confirmed what the jury had already heard from the reporter Miss Reynolds: that Rhinelander remained in the Joneses' home and lived with Alice as husband and wife for some time *after* the news of the marriage became public; that Leonard told them that whatever happened he would not let his father or his father's lawyers destroy their marriage.

I made it a point to look directly at Rhinelander after Mrs. Jones said this, and I repeated her words while scowling at the boy. "So, young Kip, the plaintiff, the gentleman seated with his lawyers: he told you THAT HE WOULD NOT LET HIS FATHER OR HIS FATHER'S LAWYERS DESTROY THEIR MARRIAGE. *Is that what the boy said?*"

"He did, yes."

"Well," I said, still looking at Rhinelander, "*I wonder what happened.*"

Rhinelander looked back at me and flushed with shame.

* * *

Mrs. Jones continued and testified that as a young woman she had made some mistakes; perhaps, she said, that is why she was careful to bring her daughters up as proper young ladies and not as the tramps Mr. Mills had described them as. She said she and her husband immigrated to this country because they hoped to raise their daughters with what they understood to be true: that in the United States all people from all over the world were welcome regardless of skin color, of family background, or of religion; and they hoped to bring their girls up in a country where everyone was considered equal and available to opportunities to advance their station in life. She stated that she and her husband had been welcomed in New Rochelle. George Jones had made a good business for himself and his family with the taxi stand and later buying commercial property. The family attended the local Presbyterian Church; and they had no remarkable incidents of racial discrimination or hatred until after Alice married Rhinelander; and, more recently, after she admitted she had some Black blood; then, Mrs. Jones recalled, "All hell broke loose."

Their lives had been turned upside down. She told of how they were pursued and terrorized by Klansmen and other racist bullies. Paving stones with hate-filled notes had been thrown through their windows. Mr. Jones, Alice, and even her sisters had been refused service in several local businesses that were pleased to take their money and treated them as everyone else until the trial and acknowledgment of Alice's mixed blood.

"*Why*," Mrs. Jones wondered for the jury. "Hadn't they seen it before? The same shopkeepers had been pleased to take George Jones's money and to accept his services? *What changed?*"

Mrs. Jones professed to being deeply hurt and disturbed by the outcry, as well as by the treatment she and her family—and in particular her daughter Alice—had been forced to endure since the marriage was revealed in the newspapers and made into such a notorious spectacle. All this was quite new to the family, and, sadly, brought to them by young Rhinelander, whom Mrs. Jones professed to love. She said she forgave Leonard for initiating the lawsuit against her daughter; which, she believed, had been solely instigated by Rhinelander Senior.

"I know Leonard loves Alice. And *he knew*, he was well aware of Mr. Jones's color. Leonard told me that it mattered not at all to him what Alice was. All that mattered, he said, was that they loved each other."

"Thank you, Mrs. Jones." I turned to Mr. Mills. "Your witness."

Holding a document in his hand, Mills began his cross-examination. "The shipping manifest I have here shows that you and Mr. Jones brought a child to this country named Ethel. *Was that child yours?*" he asked with a malicious scowl and a disgusted sneer to the tone in his voice.

Mrs. Jones replied, "Yes." She flushed, realizing where Mills was going with this line of questioning.

"Was Mr. Jones the father of Ethel?"

I stood. "*Are you really going into this?*" I demanded. I was upset that Mills would again sink so low as to attack this woman for something that had taken place more than thirty years ago. My face reddened, my voice quavered, and my hands trembled with rage. "*Your Honor*—"

Mills turned and glared at me as he said, "Here is a question of whether this woman guarded, as you contend, these young people—"

"*Thirty-six years ago!*" I cut him off. "Seriously, I must protest, you are not going into this and—"

"Just a moment, sir!" Mr. Mills exclaimed. "*You will not tell me how to conduct my*—"

I ignored him. "Your Honor, *I object.* This is a clear effort on behalf of counsel to persuade the jury against this witness by raising incidents that are *decades old* and that have no relevance whatsoever to the case at trial."

"Overruled," the judge said. "Mr. Mills is within legal rights."

Mills turned back to the witness. "*Who was the father of Ethel?*"

Elizabeth Jones looked steadfastly back at Mills and said, "I do not wish to answer."

"Now she is within *her* legal rights," declared Judge Morschauser.

Mills was not about to let it go. "Was *Mr. Jones* the father of Ethel?"

"No, sir. He was not."

"Who was Ethel's father if not Mr. Jones?"

"I do not wish to answer."

"She is within her legal rights," His Honor repeated.

"Were you married before you were married to Mr. Jones?"

"Your Honor," I objected, "this is pointless, irrelevant, and quite tedious. Does Mr. Mills not see that he is putting the jury to sleep with all this ancient history? Can we move on to questions that perhaps have some bearing upon the case at trial?"

Mills would not give up. "Did you ever have another child, now living in England, named William, before you married Jones?"

"No, that is not true."

"Is Ethel the only child you had before you married Jones?"

"Yes."

I stood and addressed the court. "Your Honor, again I must object to this entire line of questioning. He's badgering the witness. What possible relevance could any of this have to do with whether Leonard Rhinelander was defrauded into marrying his wife, Alice? Mr. Mills is trying to upset this woman and doing everything he can think of to defame her good name. I am sorry to have to see such a mean display of counsel's heartless treatment of this witness. I beg the court to call a recess and give us all a break from this insulting conduct."

Court was adjourned for ten minutes.

Elizabeth Jones stepped down from the stand and stood shakily before she was quickly embraced by all three of her daughters, who then tried to shepherd their mother through the throng of reporters and photographers jostling each other to get at the witness. I asked the judge to order the photographers to back off and let the lady leave, which Judge Morschauser did, demanding that he would ban them all from the courtroom if they did not behave in a more civilized and respectful manner.

* * *

When court reconvened, I announced: "The defense calls the plaintiff, Leonard Rhinelander."

Mills objected. "You Honor—*what now?* This must not be allowed. Mr. Davis has had his opportunity to question Mr. Rhinelander."

"That was *before* the plaintiff filed his amended complaint," I countered. "There are now *some new specific questions* I wish to ask in reference to new charges he alleges in this late filing."

Judge Morschauser agreed it was proper. Rhinelander stood and resumed the witness stand. He was reminded that he was still under oath.

"You know, do you, that your complaint against your wife has been amended?" I asked Rhinelander.

"I do, yes," he answered.

"And you are thinking clearly today? No trouble with your brain?"

"*No*," Kip snapped.

"Sir, you now complain that your wife deceived you by saying *nothing* as to her color, is that so?"

"Yes."

"Curious, *what?* Well then, was the deception you contend by saying that she is white?"

Obviously growing confused, Kip again said, "Yes."

"She said she is white; now you say she kept quiet. How can both be true?"

Kip shook his head, looked around nervously, and then answered, "I don't know anything about that."

"*Of course you don't*," I insisted, ready to pounce given the boy's complacent pose. "You don't know what's going on in this case, *do you?* Perhaps your lawyers can explain this oxymoron: how Mrs. Rhinelander was able to say she was white, and at the same time say nothing?

"Never mind," I waved the question away. "Let me ask you, with regard to the family chauffeur, Ross Chidester, you and Mr. Ross were friendly, weren't you?"

"I think so . . . yes," Leonard admitted; and then he suddenly scowled as though he realized where this was headed.

"You two chatted as he drove you about in your limousine. Have you seen Mr. Ross Chidester lately? He left the family employ, *no?*"

"My family's limousine, not mine."

"There you go again, correcting me. You love these distinctions. With regard to your driver, Chidester: When did he leave the family employ?"

"Nearly two years ago, I believe."

"May I approach, Your Honor?" I picked up an expensive lady's watch from our table and held the watch aloft for all to see. "I would ask to show this lady's watch to the plaintiff and inquire if he can identify it."

Judge Morschauser said, "You may approach."

I showed the watch to Leonard. "Sir, is this the watch you bought and gave to your wife, Alice, for Christmas at around, I believe it was 1921?"

"Yes, I . . . It is, yes."

I turned my back on the bench and announced in a stentorian voice: "BRING IN THE WITNESS!"

There was an expectant stir in the courtroom as the doors were opened and everyone turned to see the Rhinelander family's former chauffeur, Ross Chidester, a slight, unassuming man dressed in khaki trousers and a white shirt, who strode importantly to the well of the court.

Rhinelander blanched upon seeing Chidester enter; he was excused and left the stand clearly in a state of dismay at the prospect of his former driver testifying; no doubt racking his brain to recall whatever secrets he shared that the man might divulge. Kip took his seat at the plaintiff's table as Chidester was sworn in and settled on the witness stand.

I had Chidester establish for the jury that he had worked for Philip Rhinelander as a driver for three years before leaving the family's staff. "So, of course, you know the plaintiff, Leonard Kip Rhinelander, correct?"

"Yes, I do."

"Do you know him well, sir?"

"I'd say so, yes."

"Would it be fair to say that you and Mr. Rhinelander were, let us say, somewhat better acquainted than simply employer to family staff? Can you describe your relationship with Mr. Rhinelander?"

"I'd say we were as close as one can be given the . . . my position. I often drove Mr. Kip, and we talked about different things. He'd ask my opinion about whatever might be going on in his life. And that was very often girls—or I should say women."

"Ah, yes, girls, and women. Always on a young man's mind—*what?* Speaking of girls, do you know the defendant in this matter, Alice Rhinelander, Kip's bride?"

"Yes," Chidester said and looked at Alice with undisguised contempt.

"How do you know Mrs. Rhinelander? Or, let me be more specific: When did you first meet Alice?"

"When Kip asked me to pick her up in New Rochelle."

"Did you see her face at that time?"

"Yes."

"Where did you take them?"

"To the Hotel Marie Antoinette on the West Side."

I showed Chidester the watch I had previously had Leonard identify.

"Can you tell us if you recognize this lady's watch, sir?

"Yes, I know it, I believe."

"How do you know it?"

"I believe it's the watch Mr. Kip showed me and told me he intended to give it to the Jones girl as a gift—as a Christmas present."

"When was this, exactly, if you remember?"

"It was the same day I picked her up in New Rochelle with Kip and drove them to Manhattan, just before Christmas 1921."

"By 'her' you mean *Mrs. Rhinelander?*"

"Her," Chidester said and pointed at Alice.

Judge Morschauser said, "Let the record reflect that the witness has identified the defendant, Alice Rhinelander, as the person he picked up just before Christmas in 1921. You may continue."

"Thank you, Your Honor."

I addressed the witness. "Sir, what did you say to Mr. Rhinelander when he told you he intended to give Alice this gift, the watch?"

Chidester said, "I asked him *why*. I said, 'You mean to tell me you bought her a Christmas present? You know her father is a colored man?'"

"How did you know? That Mr. Jones is colored?"

"*I'd seen him*. Another time, I saw him through the window at the Jones home when I picked Kip up there."

I turned to the jury and gave them a facial expression as if to say, *Well, if the driver could see it through the window, then surely . . .*

"What did Mr. Rhinelander say when you asked him this?" I asked Chidester while still facing the jurors. "If *he knew* Alice's father was a colored man?"

"He said, '*I don't give a damn.*'"

"Those were Mr. Rhinelander's words: '*I don't give a damn*'?" I asked and turned to look first at Leonard and then back at the jury. "He said he *didn't give a damn that Alice's father was a colored man? Are you sure?*"

"Sure as I'm sittin' here lookin' at you," Chidester said with certainty and then turned to face the jury. "That's what the boy said. Why, I had a notion to take him out in front of the school and *kick the shit out of him!*"

This statement caused a few of the ladies to gasp, and the men to chuckle and shake their heads, no doubt thinking they too would have liked to give Rhinelander a good beating. Judge Morschauser looked down from the bench and told the witness to remember that he was in a court of law and to be aware of his use of foul language.

Chidester looked up at the judge and said, "I'm just telling you what happened, and what I was feeling."

I said, "You were upset."

"You're damn tootin'. I knew his father wasn't gonna like it either."

"And then, if you recall, what did you say?"

"I said, 'But surely you know . . . *that makes her a nigger!*' "

This unvarnished racist slur brought muted exclamations from the gallery. I noticed a slight smile play on Mr. Mills's face as I turned from the witness and looked at the men seated at the plaintiff's table. This was exactly the testimony Mills would have liked to get before the men in the jury: the specter of bias and race hatred spoken by the witness with no attempt to hide his animosity; and here it was coming from *our* witness.

Judge Morschauser interrupted to remind the witness that he was in a court of law, to which Chidester replied, "I know where I am, Judge. The man asked me a question, and I give him an honest answer."

"What else did you say?" I asked him.

"I said, 'Don't you know, *it's wrong!*' He, Kip was just a boy, and not too smart. Or so I was told. He seemed smart enough to me. He knew what he was doing with the girl. But his head was filled with crazy ideas."

"What kind of ideas?" I asked.

"When I asked him how he could court a girl like Miss Jones, and give her expensive Christmas presents—a *colored girl!* Kip said it made no difference to him. He said, she's beautiful, which I couldn't argue about that. And she was nice to him. That I seen with my own eyes. I could see them in the rearview, all the way into the city, they was at it hot and heavy. I was disgusted with the way they was goin' at it in the back seat of the car. I knew how his father would be . . . well, for Philip Rhinelander's son to be going around with a nigger girl, necking with her and all up under her dress! *It was not right! No, sir!* I knew his father was gonna be very upset, and very angry. So I was angry. I knew Mr. Rhinelander wouldn't want me drivin' these two, drivin' her around with his boy, and them doin' that in the back seat of his car. But what could I do? The boy refused to listen to me. He went on seein' this . . . person." Chidester pointed at Alice, who looked right back at him. "I knew it was gonna be trouble. The boy's father was upset when I told him where I took them."

"Where did you take the couple?"

"Like I said, to the hotel. The Marie Antoinette on Broadway in Manhattan. When they got out of the car in front of the hotel, the girl gave me a five-dollar bill like she was the lady of the family."

I asked, "Did you accept the five-dollar bill?"

Chidester said, "You're damn tootin' I took it."

"Sir," Judge Morschauser said.

"Sorry, Your Honor. I keep forgettin'."

I said, "Thank you, Mr. Chidester."

I turned the witness over to Mr. Mills, who was clearly nonplussed by the appearance of this surprise witness and yet determined to turn his appearance to Rhinelander's benefit. First he made a showing of objecting to Chidester having been called without prior notice, "sprung upon the court," as he put it, though it was clear the testimony had cut both ways: damaging to Rhinelander while enhancing the sensitive issues of prejudice and racial mixing. I argued that plaintiff's counsel was aware of this witness, but that we only just heard from him. Mills made a tepid attempt to impeach Chidester's testimony, suggesting I hired him to fashion his evidence to get back at the Rhinelanders for dismissing him. No, he'd not been fired; Chidester said he left on his own. He went on to say that after he read about the trial in the newspaper, he called Mr. Jacobs and left him a message. But Leonard's lawyer never returned the call. I sought Chidester out and found him employed as a driver and salesman for a local bakery. Chidester claimed that when I inquired if he would be willing to appear for the defense, he said he believed it to be his civic and moral duty to tell the truth of what he knew about Kip Rhinelander's pursuit of Alice; of the boy's knowledge as to her mixed race; and the warnings Kip had been given by his father and others, including himself, to cease pursuing what was clearly an unacceptable relationship for a white man of Rhinelander's family pedigree.

Appearing frustrated when his repeated attempts to impeach the witness failed, and yet pleased with the man's obvious racial prejudice as an issue he was happy to use to influence the jurors, at last Mills turned to the judge and announced that he had no further questions.

Chidester and Leonard exchanged a meaningful look as his former driver stepped down from the witness stand and walked past the plaintiff's table on his way from the courtroom. Chidester shook his head when he looked at Rhinelander as if to say, *I told you, boy. You should have listened to me.*

For his part, Leonard blushed noticeably and quickly looked away. Mr. Mills stood and asked to call Leonard to rebut Chidester. The judge checked with the clerk as to the hour; then said he would allow it solely for the purpose of rebuttal and not in an effort to elicit new testimony.

Rhinelander strode to the witness stand and resumed his seat. The judge reminded him that he was still under oath.

"Mr. Rhinelander," Mills demanded, "you have heard your *former driver* testify that he confronted you with the affirmation of Mr. George Jones's, Alice Jones's father's skin color, and reminded you that Mr. Jones was a colored man. Is that a true statement, sir? Did your driver—*the family chauffeur*—did he ever speak to you about having observed Alice Jones's father's skin color? And then *warn you* not to pursue a friendship with the girl?"

"*Absolutely not*," Kip replied with his most certain and self-satisfied composure so far exhibited. "That is *perfectly preposterous.* I would *never* be on such friendly terms with a man who was a mere employee that he would *dare to assume* he could speak to me in that fashion."

Here at last was the self-satisfied rich boy asserting his class privilege.

"Just a moment," I said, as the judge appeared ready to excuse the witness. "I have just one question in response."

Judge Morschauser nodded. Mills fumed. I approached the witness determined to take some of the wind from his sails.

"But tell us, Mr. Rhinelander: If the jury is to believe that you are an intelligent man with good eyesight, as you have testified; and if you saw Mr. George Jones, Alice's father, on numerous occasions, *countless times both before and after you married his daughter*—how then can you sit there and insult the intelligence of the men on this jury and expect them to believe that you couldn't see that Mr. Jones is a colored man? You couldn't see *what your driver saw through the window*, even though you lived in the home with Mr. Jones? Why, that, sir, *is preposterous*."

Mills jerked to his feet. "Your Honor, please ask learned defense counsel to refrain from editorializing on the testimony. It is up to the men on the jury to determine the credibility of the witness."

"Yes, so it is," Judge Morschauser responded. "Mr. Davis, let the witnesses speak for themselves. Confine your comments to your closing statement."

"Of course. Thank you, Your Honor."

I turned and sat down. There was no doubt in my mind that Chidester's testimony had been damaging to the alleged fraud of

Rhinelander's case, which by now no longer seemed a credible issue. At the same time I knew that at least some of the jurors, perhaps even most of them, would sympathize with the racist sentiments the driver had expressed. They might want to take Rhinelander out behind the courthouse and give him a good thrashing; but would they vote to keep him married to a Black girl?

Here was the crux of the matter: how to get the men on the jury to separate their beliefs about race from the facts in evidence. I would have ample opportunity to ponder how I might bring about this distinction.

* * *

Judge Morschauser chose this opportunity to recess court for the weekend with notice that the trial would resume the following Monday morning at the usual time. He reminded the jurors that they were not to discuss the case, not with one another, and not with friends or even their closest family members. They should also refrain from reading about the trial in the newspapers; not listen to reports on the radio; and generally endeavor to keep an open mind until all the evidence was before them, when it would become their responsibility to decide upon a verdict.

As I left the courthouse and made my way through the crowds, my sense was that we could not have ended at a more auspicious moment for our side: first with Mr. Mills's ill-advised and disgraceful cross-examination of Mrs. Jones, which already had provoked harsh disapproving notice in the press; and then with the powerful if double-edged testimony of Ross Chidester; and last, with Mr. Mills's obvious failure to impeach the witness, and Rhinelander's superior attitude toward his former driver. I recall Mr. Mills speaking to reporters after Chidester's testimony, and he called the witness's surprise appearance a "godsend" for Rhinelander. And I wondered, *Is this man observing the same trial and hearing the same evidence as I?* How could he possibly have interpreted Chidester's testimony as having been beneficial for his client? The man made it clear that Rhinelander was aware of Alice's mixed blood well before he married her, and he told his driver that he didn't give a damn. And then I remembered: of course, Mr. Mills was not seeing the same trial I was seeing. I understood once more that most important issue that kept slipping away and hiding its ugly presence from my mind in the heat of argument as to how the Rhinelander lawyers had decided to play their hand. Facts were to be downplayed. What Kip knew or didn't care to know didn't matter. Racial prejudice was their only cause, nothing more; and white fear of miscegenation was all they would offer to the jury as reason to nullify the marriage. Even the idea of supposed social class superiority had been turned on its head by Rhinelander's own lawyers' depiction of him as a witless dupe in combination with his poor showing in his appearance on the witness stand. Now Rhinelander's defenders welcomed any opportunity to stoke the fires of prejudice and fear; first with Mr. Mills's heartless treatment of Elizabeth Jones as the white wife of a colored man, mother of three mulatto girls; and then with Chidester saying he'd wanted to "kick the shit" out of young Rhinelander for pursuing an affair with a colored girl—as one might imagine a few of the jurors also wished to do for any number of reasons. Rhinelander's lawyers bargained that the jurors would relate to Chidester and not to Rhinelander no matter what the driver said about Rhinelander's knowledge of Alice's Black blood; they would see Chidester as a working white man not unlike themselves; and when he had called Alice a "nigger" girl, and warned Kip to cease courting her, yet the boy persisted, they might easily perceive this as proof of the Rhinelander counsel's argument that Kip must have been infatuated, mesmerized, and become enslaved by the older, sexually experienced Black vamp. There was now no doubt in my mind that Kip's lawyers believed the boy's only hope of winning when all the facts were against them was for them to appeal to the jurors' racial prejudice and fear of mixing the races in marriage. White America must be protected at all costs from the wiles of seductive Black women. That was their entire case.

How many times must I be reminded? As weak as Rhinelander's case may have been on the facts, it was that strong on the emotions.

* * *

Rest? Well, not quite: there would be no repose for the lawyers over two full weekends. With the case nearly ready to go to the jury, I would need to spend a good amount of time conferring with co-counsel as to how to proceed, and then composing and perfecting my closing statement. I'm certain Messrs. Mills and Jacobs were similarly occupied. As I'd purposely left the possibility of Alice testifying open, even in my own mind, and done so knowing that Rhinelander's attorneys would not be able to focus their entire attention on their closing statement as long as the possibility of Alice appearing as a witness existed, and with the need to cross-examine her that it would require, I had a slight hidden advantage.

My co-counsel, Judge Samuel Swinburne, Richard Keogh, and I had spent several long hours arguing the merits and potential pitfalls of calling Alice to the witness stand to have her testify in her own defense. Both of these learned men of the law advised me to examine Alice. However, I wavered; and, in the end, every instinct I had nurtured and developed as a trial lawyer in case after case over the years and in questioning countless witnesses told me no, don't do it to her, don't subject her to what I knew was coming from the other side: a veritable deluge of bile and filth. It would not only be traumatic for Alice and upsetting to her family, it could also be devastating to our case. With her beauty and subtle charms, if Alice were to appear on the stand as the demure and mysteriously seductive woman I knew her to be—"the eternal feminine," in Johann Wolfgang von Goethe's words, "a manifestation of the ineffable, mysterious, and desirable"—the men on the jury might feel disarmed and threatened by her allure and then choose to side against her out of fear of their own hidden desires, even as they had been shown her naked body but would never be able to touch such a woman. As with everything in this case, with deep emotions probed and moved, every idea, every tactic, every witness, and every question posed to each and every witness had to be seen as its potential opposite in how it might influence each and every man on the jury; and so I determined to keep Alice off the witness stand.

* * *

Over the break, Alice told me she enjoyed a family feast at the Joneses' home surrounded by her loved ones and in-laws. She said that it had been forbidden to talk of the trial during the meal; but that once they were all fed and sitting comfortably around the living room in the Joneses' home, the conversation was concerned with little else. I met with Alice for a time on Friday evening, then again on Sunday after church services we met for coffee. The girl was so emotionally drained and overwrought that I was convinced the decision to not call her to testify was the right one, although she said she was ready if need be. This had long been my choice given the emotional toll it was obvious that the trial was taking upon Alice; and knowing full well how vicious Mr. Mills's cross-examination was bound to be; with him undoubtedly unearthing and asking the girl to admit and describe every sexual encounter she'd ever had not only with young Kip, but also with anyone else she would be forced to recall.

It might be expected that Alice should take the stand in her own defense. But then I thought, *No, why not let the girl's personality remain a mystery; her charms mute? Let her appearance speak for itself and say, Now, gentlemen find your verdict for the defendant based on what you have seen with your own eyes. There is no more proof you need. Yes, my skin is dusky. The boy is a liar. His lawyers are liars. Don't be swayed by their obvious ploy of raising the specter of racial mixing. That's not the issue in this case. The issue is: Was Kip defrauded? Look at the evidence and only at the evidence. Look at me! See me for who I am. I am a demure and quiet girl of mixed race. It is this lawsuit that is fraudulent.*

Such was the language that came to mind as I began to compose my closing statement.

When court reconvened on that Monday morning, with the men on the jury all looking rested from the weekend break, I recalled Alice's mother, Elizabeth Jones, to the witness stand. Treating her with all the deference and kindness that I knew would stand in marked contrast in the jurors' minds to how Mr. Mills had purposely attacked her in an attempt to disgrace the lady with his nasty cross-examination, I said I had only one question I wished to ask her. This was a question I had prepared solely for the mood I hoped to establish while preparing to rest our case—indeed, "rest" being the operative word.

"Mrs. Jones," I asked, "can you tell the gentlemen of the jury—who have seen your daughter's body exposed—has Alice's skin tone, has her *color* remained the same from her time of birth until now?"

"Yes," Mrs. Jones replied. "It hasn't changed since she was a baby."

I thanked Mrs. Jones, and Alice's mother stepped down. All eyes were upon me, and on Alice seated beside me. She looked as lovely as always and perhaps more beautiful even though haunted with unrelenting stress.

I stood to address the court. I put my hand on Alice's delicate hand. I squeezed it as though to comfort her for what was coming. I then turned and walked to the podium—a place I rarely chanced to visit during trial, preferring to argue from the well of the court or directly before the jury box. No doubt everyone in the room anticipated that as my next witness I would call Alice, or possibly George Jones and then Alice.

Instead, I looked and nodded knowingly to the men seated in the jury box as if to show that they were my allies in this tactic I was about to employ; as if they knew there was no need for further evidence: they had seen the girl's naked body; what more evidence was needed? And then, after a prolonged hesitation, I turned back, and announced to the room:

"Your Honor, acting entirely upon my own discretion as an attorney, and upon my own responsibility as an individual, *the defense rests*."

There were audible cries of surprise, gasps, and an increasingly noisy commotion filled the room as stunned spectators and anxious journalists realized that, after nearly a month of testimony and argument, the Rhinelander trial was over but for closing statements, the judge's charge to the jury, and finally the long-anticipated verdict.

Mr. Mills jumped up to question "this unexpected announcement."

Judge Morschauser as well appeared taken aback by our abrupt decision to rest. Reporters rushed out to file their stories. His Honor banged his gavel and called for order. He referred to his calendar; had a brief side discussion with his clerk;

and, perhaps piqued by my sudden end to the testimony, announced that he expected counsel to be prepared to commence closing statements immediately following the noontime recess.

Mills and Jacobs both glowered at me as though wishing to cause me some remorse for having blindsided them with our sudden decision to rest—which, of course, they understood was not sudden at all but instead plotted well in anticipation of catching them unawares.

Ah, yes, I reflected, *serves you fellows right for all your attempts at deceit and trickery—and for bringing this shocking case in the first place.*

One takes pleasure in employing such deft tactics at the trial lawyer's disposal—and meant to thoroughly discombobulate one's opponents.

CHAPTER THIRTY

The Vamp and the Dupe

I began my summation following the noon recess. Fortunately, I had been composing my closing statement in my mind for weeks, and only just put pen to paper once I knew the trial's end was imminent.

This final address to the finders of fact before they retire to deliberate is undoubtedly the most significant speech a lawyer is called upon to present to his jury. After days and weeks of conflicting and often confusing testimony from a parade of good and not so good witnesses; and after hours upon hours of tedious legal argument, numerous recesses over weekends and holidays, the men of the jury need to be reminded of the evidence; and they must be given a summary of the important legal issues for them to decide. With a case such as *Rhinelander,* given the scandalous and inflammatory evidence before the court, as one might expect; and the impassioned public debate not only in the streets around the courthouse, but also in the newspapers and on the airwaves and in barrooms and living rooms and bedrooms all over our divided nation on issues of race and sex and class and the steady dissolution of the hitherto accepted lines separating white from Black, upper-class from lower, even calling into question accepted sexual relations between a man and a woman in the privacy of the marital bed as against filthy, debased, criminal sex acts: the Rhinelander case had it all. Now it was up to me to help the men of the jury see their way clear through all this controversy, all this extraneous evidence of social disorder and changing mores and smut and name-calling to the heart of the matter; simply this: love between a boy and a girl. The case at the bar was about nothing more. Their verdict, I had to make the jurors understand, was only about these factual questions: Did Rhinelander love Alice and marry her knowing full well and accepting the fact that she had colored blood? Or did Alice lie, tell him she was a pure white girl; alternatively, as per the amended complaint: Did Alice defraud Rhinelander by remaining silent about her mixed race?

* * *

"May it please the court and gentlemen," I began before a rapt jury, "I do not know if you men can realize the feelings that are coursing through my body at this moment—this long-awaited moment—and the thoughts that occupy my mind as I stand before you gentlemen. For, *upon my shoulders rests a tremendous responsibility*," I announced. "As Alice Rhinelander's defender, *I alone* stand between this young girl"—here I gestured to Alice, who looked even more lovely than ever as she sat watching me speak—"yes, I call her a girl, though she is practically in the beginning of womanhood—*and I am THE ONLY ONE to stand between her and absolute ruin.*

"These men," I turned and pointed an accusing finger first at Jacobs; "Leon Jacobs, the Rhinelander's lawyer from Manhattan;" then I pointed at Judge Mills; "and my mentor and colleague Isaac Mills—both esteemed and respected members of the legal profession—these men, acting as advocates in the employ of the high and mighty millionaire Philip Rhinelander—perhaps they were enticed by the family fortune, I don't know, but what I do know is that *they have torn from this young girl ruthlessly every scrap of respectability that a woman loves most.* They have attempted to *sway* you good and intelligent men with what is a *travesty of justice*; yes, and it is an *insult to basic human decency!* They have fought *viciously to defame* Alice, attacking her mother and her family; and they have tried *assiduously, relentlessly* to delude you good and wise men into *believing the lie* that this young girl, Alice, the person you see sitting here as she has sat here day after day during this awful trial and repelling with her beauty and her grace *all of the filth these men have thrown her way* to try to prove to you that she is nothing but a conniving, wanton vamp! *Yes! That is their purpose.* They want you to believe *Alice Rhinelander is a sexual predator* who seduced the feebleminded dupe, this man"—here I pointed to the plaintiff—"Leonard Kip Rhinelander—who, oh, gentlemen, I hasten to add how we have proved with *indisputable evidence*, including his own testimony, you heard him declare that his mind is good, that he is no stuttering nut, no innocent idiot as his lawyers wished to make you believe; no, in fact the plaintiff in this matter, Leonard Kip Rhinelander, is well educated, he is intelligent, and he is far from the innocent young man as his lawyers have tried to portray him. *On the contrary*, Leonard Rhinelander is *the son*, he is *the scion* and the *heir apparent* of one of New York's wealthiest and preeminent social families. Leonard Rhinelander, as we have proved, is also a *sexually aggressive* and *randy rich boy* who—he would have us believe—is *entitled*; yes, I say, *entitled*—to drive up from his private school in his brand-new roadster car bought for him by his absent father; and here, upon our streets, to collect a young girl hailing from our environs—yes, a local girl, Alice Jones—and to turn her head and infatuate her with romantic drives in his fancy roadster auto; and then to carry her off to a hotel suite in Manhattan, register them under false names as husband and wife, and there with only one goal: to have his debased, *filthy criminal sexual ways with her.*

"Let us not forget Kip's filthy letters! You heard the evidence of his *perverted sex acts*; and you heard him testify that he found such activity '*normal.*' And then, lo and behold—he married her! Yes, he did; Kip did the right and proper thing and he made Alice his wife.

"He is to be commended for behaving as a gentleman and marrying the girl. Ah, but alas, what happens when *Papa* learns whom the boy married, and when *Papa* disapproves of his son's wife, when His Majesty Sir Philip declares the bride unworthy and unacceptable, and he then sets about to dissolve the marriage. What does the spoiled rich boy do? Does he stand up to his father and say, '*No! I love her! I married her because I am deeply in love with her! I am a man, turned of legal age, and I shall be the ruler of my own destiny!*'

"Oh, how I wish the boy had *the courage, the decency* to say that, for I think we all know that is how he felt in his heart. *But no!* The story does not have a happy ending because young Kip, the lad, hasn't the . . . You know, gentlemen, I have thought about this a good deal over the weeks and months that I have been retained to defend Alice Rhinelander. *What happened to Kip?* Surely the boy loved Alice; that's apparent. But what was the essential *failure in his character* that allowed him to stand helplessly by while his father, while Philip Rhinelander *ruined the love* these two young people felt for each other? That is a mystery we may all contemplate as long as we live. It is the essential question each man and woman must ask themselves throughout their lives. Keep that question in your minds, gentlemen, for I will return to it before I finish.

"First, let us consider the boy's actions. What did Kip do? How did he react when his father called him to explain himself and to defend his marriage to Alice? Did he say, 'Father, I love her. Alice is my wife and I will not allow you to separate us'? No, he did not. He cowered before his father; and he promptly *cast his bride aside*; he allowed her to be insulted and disgraced; and then he wished to make her go away; he attempted with the aid of his father's lawyers to cause Alice to *cease to exist as his betrothed* and to be forever *shamed and condemned* as a *liar and a fraud.* Kip lost his nerve and he allowed his father to seek *to destroy the girl he loves as if the marriage*, and as if *the love he claimed to have for his bride*, as if it were all just his way of having some fun with a common girl.

"*How*, I ask you good men, *how does one* who claims to be a decent, educated man—*indeed, a gentleman*—how could Rhinelander do that to a young girl he claims to love and who obviously loves him deeply; a woman who gave herself to him wholly out of true and abiding love? Yes, it shocks the conscience. It astounds our sense of what it means to be a gentleman. Why, *it's horrid.* And it's painful—not what this young girl or any of her loving family has done—*no, never!* These are good and honest people," I said as I indicated first Alice, then her mother and father, as well as her two sisters sitting in the first row of the spectators' benches.

"These are our neighbors. These are our fellow parishioners. *But remember what was done to them by the rich boy from Manhattan!* Consider how this good family has been *maligned and attacked* by the *wealthy and powerful* Philip Rhinelander acting through his son.

"Oh, in all truth, I don't blame the boy, Leonard, or Kip, as they call him. I cannot blame him. Why blame him when he is merely the unwitting tool of his father's arrogance and disdain;

his father's sense of superiority; that he and his ilk, wealthy and proud Manhattan aristocrats, believe themselves to be the masters of the world; and that his poor, terrified son is nothing but his puppet, his toy to dangle and order about in his name and as he chooses. Never mind what the boy may have felt for Alice, that he may truly have been deeply in love with the woman he married—no, his father made up his mind *that it was not to be!* And the son did not have the *strength of character* to oppose his domineering father.

"You men all saw Kip as he sat here in his three-piece, Saville Row English suit and his owl eyeglasses, his fine shoes with their spotless spats; you watched Rhinelander enter the court accompanied by his retinue of bodyguards and attendants, and you saw him take the stand as he tried with his father's lawyer's connivance and upon his father's orders to *throw away his wife* as though she were a used receptacle for his disgusting sexual adventures. You gentlemen have all seen Mr. Kip Rhinelander swagger into this courtroom surrounded by his bodyguards and handlers whenever he felt like honoring us with his presence; and with barely a nod or gesture to acknowledge the woman he seduced and professed to love, his wife, Alice Rhinelander, whom he has now dragged into court to be humiliated and brutally cast aside."

Here I hesitated as though struck with a new thought.

"*But wait!* No—that is not accurate: Alice *is* Kip's wife. Alice is *his lawful spouse.* Indeed, Alice is the woman *Kip did love!* I'm sorry, of course he did, young Rhinelander loved Alice *deeply*—I believe he did. I believe he was as madly in love with her as she was with him *until* . . . until his imperious father, high and mighty Philip Rhinelander"—here once more I stopped and looked around the courtroom as though to see if Rhinelander Senior had stooped to join the proceedings.

"*Is he here?*" I asked. "Is the wealthy Manhattan aristocrat here among us common folk? Has he dared to brave the disgrace brought upon his family by his son? No, of course he hasn't; perhaps cowardice is a family trait." (This, I realized even as I said it, unscripted as it was, this was a serious insult, and one for which I would be roundly condemned.) "But Rhinelander did see his way clear to step into his adult son's affairs and demand: '*No, Kip! You must not! You cannot love her! For her father is a colored man! And you are a Rhinelander, a proud member of the aristocratic, white Anglo-Saxon ruling class!*'

"Oh! God forbid! Lord Almighty . . . *Where is he?* Is His Majesty, the Rhinelander patriarch here? *No!* But look who is here, George Jones, Alice's father, is here, and he has been here *every day of this trial to support his child.*"

I turned to indicate George Jones, who sat in the spectators' benches and looked for all the world as the delighted and dignified dark-skinned man that he is, proud sire of Alice and her sisters, bearing no shame for who he and his family are, and as a witness to his daughter's defense.

"And you see her, Alice," I said, now moderating my tone. "You gentlemen have watched Alice here in this courtroom *day after day* as she has been *attacked viciously* by the plaintiff's counsel. *Vilified. Slandered.* She is a lovely girl, Alice Rhinelander—of that I believe we can all agree. Alice is a most beautiful and charming young woman *WITH DARK SKIN!* Oh, yes, it is true: her skin is dark. You men all saw it. It is skin that any man with working eyesight and a functioning brain can see has a taint of the tar brush, to put it in common terms. *She's colored!* Why, you might not notice it at first, particularly when she is fully clothed, and dressed in the latest fashions, and wearing a smart-looking hat. You might mistake her for a dark-complected Spanish girl or even a southern Italian girl. We've all seen dark women and men who are not Negroes; not strictly speaking of the African Negro race; but noticeably dark-skinned. *But when you see Alice's body,* as I had you gentlemen look at a portion of what he, what the Rhinelander scion saw—the rich boy having his way with a dark girl—why, you men all saw Alice's back above the waist. You saw her breasts. You saw a portion of her upper leg. He, the Rhinelander boy, when he was . . . *having his way with her,* oh, of course! He saw *all of her body*; he not only saw it—*he explored her body* time and time again as he made love to her—as he put it—as he had intercourse with her *several times a day* while they were ensconced at the Hotel Marie Antoinette for their assignation. And then . . . *and then!* . . . *What?* Need I remind you? *No, I will not say it!* Not with ladies present! But you men all heard it, *what the boy did to this girl, his wife. The debased sex acts!* And his lawyers say he is a simpleminded boy who never kissed a girl before he met Alice. *What nonsense!* Well, *kissed her where?* I ask you. And now you are going to tell me that he never suspected Alice had colored blood. *Oh, please, what rubbish!* That is what he testifies to! Are we to believe the boy is blind? Not only blind but also that he has no feelings? Not even physical feelings in his tongue and lips?

"*You gentlemen saw her body with your own eyes. Why, a boy of twelve could see that colored blood was coursing through her veins.* And so there *can be no question in your minds* after having seen her as Rhinelander saw her and—well, not only did young Kip see her, but, as we have heard, he bathed her, and . . . well . . . with his tongue and lips—*no! I will not go there! Not again!* I cannot allow it with women present in the courtroom. You gentlemen will remember it, and the scandalous letters written by the plaintiff describing *bestial and debased sex acts he performed on this young girl. Oh, no!* I will not go there. I need not remind you men of these things with women present.

"We are asked to believe that this boy, the plaintiff, Kip Rhinelander, was the innocent dupe in all these shenanigans and sex games. Why, you heard the boy's letters read to you. And you have the letters in evidence. You can read them yourselves. Does that seem like the writings of a sexually inexperienced boy? *No, it does not.* It is the writing of a young man who made *a study of lewd and obscene sex acts*, and then included them in his repertoire, and practiced them on this young girl even before he took her as his wife.

"But what these men, what Philip Rhinelander's lawyers—and make no mistake about it, *Philip Rhinelander, the rich and powerful landowner and not his weak-minded son*—no, let me amend that. The boy, Kip is not weak-minded at all. We've shown that for the lie it is. Leonard Kip Rhinelander is a boy of *weak character.* He has a well-functioning brain, but he does not have *the will* nor *the courage to be a man and stand up to his father.* Leonard Kip Rhinelander *does not have the courage to take responsibility for his own actions*, or none of us would be here in this courtroom having to bear witness to what these . . . what Leon Jacobs and Isaac Mills are hoping to have you men *do to this innocent young girl.*

"No, gentlemen. Please, make no mistake about it. What the Rhinelander lawyers are asking you to do, let us be clear: *they want you to utterly ruin the girl*; they want you to *destroy her good name for the rest of her young life and even into her dotage* . . . all the way to her grave. They want you to send her back out into the world labeled *a fraud, a cheat, a conniver, a disgrace to the white race and to the Black race:* to be shunned by both. What these men have already done to this girl is despicable enough. They have dragged her here before you and smeared her and her family by claiming every imaginable wicked intent behind her marriage to the Rhinelander boy. There is not any other thing they can do to this girl *except one.* There is *one more dreadful thing* the

Rhinelander millionaires can do to Alice, and that is for you twelve men to come into this courtroom and add the last straw and say, *'Alice Rhinelander, you go out into this world a fraud.'*

"*No*, I tell you, *it must not be.* For I trust you good and true twelve men to put a stop to this fraud, to the real fraud of how Alice Rhinelander—*and that is her name!*—how Alice Rhinelander has been slandered and accused of being a female predator; she has been defamed and lied about; and now she has *proved beyond any doubt* that she is in fact NOT GUILTY of anything but being a loving and true wife to her husband, a loyal wife to the weak and spoiled son of wealth and class superiority, the reluctant plaintiff, Leonard Kip Rhinelander."

I took a breath, I composed myself and looked intently at each of the twelve men seated in the jury box and who were all wide awake and looking back at me. Then I continued in a composed and moderated tone.

"So you see, gentlemen, it is a terrible responsibility I assume to stand between this girl and such a verdict at your hands. But where, I ask you to consider, and to discuss with one another when you retire to decide your verdict—*this the most important question you will have to answer*—I ask you: *Where is the evidence?* Gone. Not here for you to consider because *there was no evidence to begin with.* It's not here; never was—like the mastermind of this case, Philip Rhinelander, is not here. He, Philip Rhinelander, brought us in here to attempt to prove that Alice Rhinelander, his daughter-in-law, is a liar and a fraud; that she deceived the boy Kip Rhinelander into marrying her by lying about her race and inveigling him with promises of sex orgies; but Rhinelander forgot one important matter. *He forgot you, gentlemen.* Rhinelander and his minions, his factotums—and I know Mr. Jacobs resents it when I call him that, but that is what he is—Rhinelander Senior *forgot* that his lawyers needed *actual evidence* to convince intelligent and independent-minded men to find this girl guilty of their *supposed and concocted* fraud. Yes, in their arrogance, their Manhattan sense of superiority, they imagined that they could come in here to our county courthouse in White Plains and impress us with their millions, the plaintiff, Kip, with his Seville Row English suits and with his bodyguards hustling him in and out as though he were a movie star; the Rhinelander family with their social status and their millions; and they believed that they could simply have their way with you gentlemen, as the boy had his way with this girl; and they expected *to lie the boy's way out* of his marriage to Alice without needing *actual real evidence* to prove their case. *What arrogance! What contempt* for you gentlemen of the jury for them to believe that they could do this and pull this on you without *one scintilla of actual and believable evidence.* Why, it shocks and greatly disturbs one's sense of fair play, of social responsibility, and even of legal credibility.

"Because, let us look at the evidence—*their so-called evidence*—and ask: Did they provide one iota, one believable fragment of actual evidence from any single witness to prove their case? No, they did not. And that is because they—the Rhinelander lawyers, Philip Rhinelander himself; and not his boy, not young Kip, who simply does whatever Daddy orders him to do, or what Daddy's lawyers order him to do—and you all heard him testify how Daddy's lawyers ORDERED him to swear to and sign the suit while they were huddled out of sight in a Manhattan subway station like so many perpetrators of a fraud, and swearing to allegations that *they knew were false* rather than in a law office with an honorable and true cause.

"The evidence, *their* evidence, gentlemen, I would take you through it and describe it for you to remind you what they are alleging, BUT THERE IS NO EVIDENCE TO PROVE THEIR

CASE! IT IS ALL JUST ONE THING and ONE THING ONLY: IT IS PREJUDICE! IT IS RACIAL HATRED! And FEAR, *fear of racial mixing!* That's all they have brought into this courtroom to prove their case. That is all they have to try to strike fear in your hearts and to convince you men to bring in a false and despicable verdict against this girl based on *fear* and with *not one shred of believable evidence* to prove their case. *Nothing* . . . you heard it all and it was all nothing but nasty hate, fear, and disdain.

"Kip, the plaintiff, whimpers, 'Oh, poor me . . . Alice told me she was not colored. And I believed her.' That is their evidence. *What nonsense* . . . It is nothing but an attempt to *bamboozle*—you gentlemen all know that word and what it means; I like the word 'bamboozle.' I love these interesting words of our wonderful English language, as I'm sure you men have noticed by now. *Bamboozle:* it is a word that sounds like what it means, and it's a common term, an informal word, not the highfalutin language my esteemed opponent Mr. Mills likes to use, the language of lawyers, fifty-dollar words, so to speak. But we all know what it means, to try to bamboozle someone; to deceive them; to attempt by trickery and by deceit to make someone believe something that is not true, something that does not hold up when looked at and considered honestly. I am sure you have all had the experience. Someone tries to *bamboozle* you, to trick you into believing something that is false, or tries to bamboozle you into buying something that is of shoddy quality.

"Well, gentlemen, make no mistake about it: THAT IS EXACTLY WHAT THESE MEN HAVE ATTEMPTED TO DO TO YOU! They are trying to *bamboozle* you into believing that this girl, Alice Rhinelander—and I call her that, Alice Rhinelander, and not some other name, for that is who she is, the lawful wedded wife of the plaintiff, Leonard Kip Rhinelander, whose lawyers are attempting to *bamboozle* you men into believing their lies about Alice, their disgusting and patently false allegations that this good woman, this young girl—and Alice is both: a good woman and a young girl—that she *deceived* her husband, the scion of a rich and socially prominent family, the Rhinelanders with all their millions; these New York City lawyers have come up here to White Plains, Westchester County, and our good court, and they tried to bamboozle you men into believing the lie that this young girl *tricked* Rhinelander; she made him believe what his eyes told him was untrue; she bamboozled him with her sex—and remember, you saw her body! You men saw the flesh of this girl's body that Rhinelander had before his eyes when he . . . well, I need not remind you how he did those things, those filthy sex acts that he did to this young girl when he had her under his control while in the Hotel Marie Antoinette, and then again in their hideaway on Cape Cod. Remember. You saw her as he saw her. You heard his letters read to you. Do I need to remind you of the debased and *criminal* sex acts he delighted in writing to her *in vivid description?! No, I do not!* There are women present. We have heard enough.

"Do these men, Rhinelander's lawyers—you see them there, high-priced lawyers from Manhattan, Mr. Leon Jacobs and my colleague Mr. Mills who—excuse me, Judge Mills is a local fellow, brought in as local counsel—do these men really believe that you gentlemen of Westchester County are also innocent dupes? Brain-tied idiots like they want us to believe of the plaintiff, Kip Rhinelander? Do they really believe that they can BAMBOOZLE you fellows into believing that this girl, Alice—whom you have watched here in this courtroom over the past several weeks; you've seen her with her family; you heard her mother and her father—whom we all know as the proprietor of the local taxi stand—and her sisters—whom we also know as good and proper young ladies—how they told you what they knew of the girl Alice and of her affair and marriage to Kip; you heard and you know the truth. Now these men, Mr. Jacobs and Mr. Mills, would attempt to deceive you men on the jury into believing that Alice and her mother *concocted this whole scheme*, that they entrapped the innocent Rhinelander boy, duped him into marrying Alice, and that they did this purely, they would have you believe, for her and her family's financial gain. I ask you, Do they think you men are brain-tied idiots? Or do they think you are blind, as Mr. Rhinelander would have us believe he is, THAT HE COULD NOT SEE WITH HIS OWN FUNCTIONING EYESIGHT WHAT YOU MEN SAW: THAT HIS WIFE HAS COLORED BLOOD! THAT IT IS APPARENT IN THE COLOR OF HER SKIN! AND IN THE SKIN OF HER FATHER!

"*Ridiculous! Absurd!* Mark my words: it would be laughable if it were not so serious, if these allegations of fraud were not—as false as they are on their face, they are real. If you allow them, they will do *irreparable harm* to this young girl and her family. And if you gentlemen allow yourselves to be swayed by the argument I am certain my learned adversary Mr. Mills will present when it is his turn to address you; he will have only *one truth* to try to convince you of, *only one fact*, and that is the truth, the shameful reality *and the fact of racial prejudice and racial hate based on skin color.* Nothing more. Pure and simple—but powerful. Oh, yes, it is very powerful. So powerful here in America that our great nation fought the terrible, bloody Civil War over this subject. Vast numbers of people have perished and continue to be disenfranchised because of this racial hatred. Innocent men and women have been lynched, hung by the neck to be murdered over this issue of race. As Americans we are all still cursed by the sins engendered by this horror and the treatment of other human beings based on skin color; that we would *steal them* from their homeland; *turn them into slaves*, into *commodities to be bought and sold*. It is the *appalling original sin of our nation*. And my learned adversaries will be up here next to try to convince you gentlemen *that it is right* and *proper* for you to find Alice guilty of fraud FOR NO OTHER REASON THAN that: *RACISM!* Call it what it is! Prejudice! Hatred based on nothing more than the color of one's skin!"

I shook my head and gasped with disbelief. "But . . . oh, no, I'm sorry, it's based on much more than that. I have been thinking deeply about this subject over these past weeks and months since I first met Alice Rhinelander, when her father, George Jones—whom I know as the proprietor of the taxi stand, as a fellow parishioner at our church, as a decent, hardworking man with three lovely and respectable daughters and an English wife—when George Jones, Mrs. Jones, and Alice first came into my offices and engaged me to represent Alice; since that time I have been thinking deeply, meditating upon these issues of race in America, and even going into my own beliefs and questioning ideas and feelings about this sensitive and deeply resonant subject that is so incendiary and emotionally charged and important as to the future of our great country. And as I have come to know Alice, come to respect her, come to find in her a woman of uncommon strength of character and depth of feeling, all this has caused me to consider these issues of race from an entirely different perspective—from Alice's perspective. That is, for Alice to face the world as she does. I have tried to see our country and our fellow Americans through Alice's eyes—from the perspective of someone who is not Black or white; yes, it is true, Alice is not white and she is not Black—*she is both!* The future of these great United States—and the word "united" is important here, gentlemen—the future of this great country is not white or Black; like Alice Rhinelander, IT IS BOTH! It is not rich or poor, IT IS BOTH. It is not male or female, IT IS BOTH. It is not Protestant, Catholic, Jew, Arab, Chinese, English, African, and on and on; it is all of the above! As it was intended by our Founding Fathers to be, this land and the freedoms it offers are for *everyone* from all over who comes to these shores seeking liberty from racial bias and prejudice whether or not they came here of their own free will, or if they were brought here as slaves stolen from their families and their homes. Our nation is BOTH BLACK AND WHITE AMERICA, and I would say, we should be proud of that, we should enjoy such diversity as it is the very soul of what it means to be an American; and if that is not to your liking, if you do not want to live in a country such as the United States of America, where we welcome the peoples of all over the world and where all our forefathers came seeking freedom, and where there are more than one race of people, then you should go elsewhere, for this is what America stands for: *freedom and justice for all.* Not just the white race. And not only the rich. *But everyone.*"

Here I paused briefly to let these ideas, these crucial American ideals and values we've all been taught but perhaps not always believed nor practiced, to let these profound thoughts of what it means to be an American resonate in each and every member of the jury's heart and mind.

"And this is what you men as members of a jury in these great United States have been called upon to decide: Are we racists or are we Christians? Are we racists or are we Americans? Do we love our fellow man and woman—for let us not forget this woman, this—I call her a girl, but Alice Rhinelander is every bit a woman, a strong and determined woman who came here and asked me to prove her case, her honesty. *Do not forget her.* And I will tell you that it was *my choice not to call Alice* to the witness stand to testify on her own behalf. *Why?* I know some of you may be wondering why I chose not to call Alice. And I know this subject will come up when you retire to deliberate and reach your verdict. *I chose not to call Alice to testify because I don't trust my adversaries*; yes: because I know them too well after having seen how they have chosen to fight their case; when I saw what they tried to do to Alice's mother, reprehensible as that was, I knew what they would try to do to Alice; how they would stoop to every vile and low trick to try to hurt her, to try to have you gentlemen see her as they have attempted to portray her—as a wanton, unscrupulous Black she-devil who ruined an innocent, upstanding boy of the white Anglo-Saxon race; indeed, a Huguenot, a Rhinelander, a millionaire's son; and not as he is truly—a spoiled boy who would have his fun playing with a dark-skinned girl, marry her, and then seek to throw her away. They would try all their lowdown tricks to try to hurt Alice even more than they have already, and how they chose to hurt and defame her mother. *Who does that?* I ask you, Who attacks a girl's mother? Shameful, I say . . . and that is why I chose not to put Alice on the witness stand to give these men another opportunity to hurt and disgrace the girl any more than they already have. It was my choice and my decision based on what I know of the tactics used by my adversaries."

I began on a new tack. "You know, gentlemen, actually, to tell you the truth, I feel badly for the Rhinelander boy; really I do, as I'm sure you might . . . as we see Kip seated there now looking down at his shoes with their fine, spotless spats. Yes, I feel badly for young Kip for, even with all his money—his family's money; and for all the cars and drivers and mansions and special schools and vacations in Havana and Bermuda—I feel sorry for Kip for two reasons: one, because I believe he really loved Alice, and perhaps he still does love his wife; and second and more important, because he is NOT HIS OWN MAN.

"Now, you men all know and understand what is meant by that phrase, when I say of Rhinelander, or when we say of any man, that he is *not his own man.* And it is something important, something terrible to contemplate, that one is ruled by others, that one does not have free will, so to speak; and I will ask you all to keep very much in mind as you retire to the jury room to deliberate, because perhaps nowhere in the world and in our lives as citizens in a free country is it of more importance that each and every one of you remember to continue to BE YOUR OWN MAN. That is, to believe what *you* believe, and to be true to the facts in evidence and how *you* see them and not to be swayed or influenced by any others no matter how convincing your fellow jurors may be. *Be your own man.* Each and every one of you, no matter how they may raise the false issues of race, false in the sense that they *are not issues that you have been asked to consider.* These issues will come up. My learned adversary will see to that; he will stand up soon and do all within the considerable sway of his eloquence to try to convince you men NOT TO BE YOUR OWN MAN but to be sheep and hatemongers and to follow others who may not themselves be men of conscience but rather men of prejudice, men ruled by fear and hate and not by reason and by facts and not by evidence.

"Here, then, in the case before you: the evidence is overwhelming, gentlemen. The evidence is clear and true. The evidence clearly absolves Alice Rhinelander of any trace of fraud, or any lie and deceit in her presentation of who she is either to her husband or to you men on the jury. Alice Rhinelander is no liar, no perpetrator of fraud. And so I implore you to each *be your own man* in that jury room. Base your verdict *on the facts in evidence* as you saw them presented to you in this trial and not upon racial bias and prejudice.

"Yes, it is true that, as angry as I am with young Kip Rhinelander for allowing this false case to be brought against his wife, I must admit, I do feel sympathy for him. Yes, I do. I believe the boy fell in love with Alice knowing she had some Black blood; but that, just as he admitted to the reporter, and you men will remember her testimony, the testimony of Barbara Reynolds, whom Kip told that he knew Alice's father was colored, and that he realized that meant his wife also had colored blood; but I believe his words when he said that *it made no difference to him*. The boy loved her. I believe that, and it makes me feel sympathy for the boy. It must be a terrible thing, a great emotional wound not to be free to love the woman your heart tells you to love. This was the woman young Kip fell in love with and married—perhaps the one brave and original thing the boy has done in his entire sheltered life. But I feel sorry for Kip because the boy DOES NOT HAVE THE STRENGTH OF CHARACTER TO LIVE UP TO HIS OWN CONVICTIONS. THE SON DOES NOT HAVE THE WILL TO STAND UP TO HIS POWERFUL AND PRIDEFUL FATHER. HE DOES NOT HAVE THE STRENGTH OF CHARACTER TO *BECOME HIS OWN MAN!*

"There you have it. That's all it is, all this case is about. You see, I believe that young Rhinelander is not a boy who lives in the kind of racial fear and hatred that his lawyers have sought to use, and that rule his father's life—and that they will try again to use to influence you men. No, Kip is a modern boy in many ways, a good-hearted boy, or at least he *wanted* to be. He saw himself as without racial prejudice. You heard Mr. Brooks testify. Young Kip was happy to play poker and drink tea with Brooks and his Negro friends. He felt no racial hatred, and for that I admire the boy. For that, he was able to love Alice as much as, if not more than he would love a girl of his own color and social class. That may be shocking, but it *was his choice*. Made freely until thwarted by his father.

"And let us not forget that other issue, the issue of social class, which is perhaps not as emotionally charged as is the issue of race, but still very much a fact of life and a fact to be considered in this case. Leonard Kip Rhinelander is the son—the only remaining son still living under his father's control—in a wealthy family that prides itself on being in the top two hundred families in the social register of rich and la-di-da aristocratic New York families—a list upon which I know my name does not appear, and that I trust is a list that has excluded you men as well. But the Rhinelander name is on that list. Wonderful, yes, oh, it is wonderful! And we are all very impressed. *Except Alice.* It was brought to Alice's attention, and you heard her words to the reporter. She said she did not marry Leonard to get her name on any list. It meant nothing to her. She married Leonard because she loves him. And yet young Kip—not only does he not see race; he ignores class differences as well! Most impressive for a boy of his aristocratic background. Why, Kip is a *true American.* And he is a thoroughly modern man . . . in some ways, important ways, I might add—modern ways, open-minded ways. Kip is a boy who saw no race, saw no class; who saw only a beautiful young girl he fell madly in love with and who he chose to make his bride.

"Yes, and that's fine. I can't help but to feel sorry for Kip, indeed for the Rhinelander family, that their pride, their arrogance, their social disdain are such that they would deny their boy the woman he loves as his bride. This whole case—the love affair, the marriage, these ugly, false allegations against Alice—*is a tragedy, a tragic love story.* But do not—I will ask you gentlemen again—*do not let this become a tragedy you men must participate in and perpetuate by bringing in a false verdict of fraud against this young girl. That would only serve to perpetuate the tragedy.* That would only serve to sanction and prolong the tragedy. *Let it end here.*

"Let the shame of this attack on Alice Rhinelander end with your verdict of NOT GUILTY!

"One last thing I must ask you before you retire to deliberate, I ask you to remember Kip Rhinelander's letters to Alice. Mr. Mills chose to read you Alice's letters. You may remember I did not want to read the private letters of these young people. I was aware of what was in Kip's letters to his wife. I knew how shocking and vile his letters are, and I did not wish to have such subjects discussed openly in a court of law, certainly not with women present. Mr. Mills was determined to read Alice's rather innocent letters, but he certainly wasn't pleased to have Kip's letters read to you—was he? An innocent dupe, aye? Well, *I think not.*

"Rhinelander's lawyers would have you send Alice Rhinelander from this court out into the world *as a fraud.* I say *no, no, gentlemen!* I say LOOK AT THE EVIDENCE. There is only one fraud in this case. REMEMBER HIS LETTERS. And that fraudster, the only one guilty of fraud is the *plaintiff himself!* Yes, the spoiled and effete scion of the rich and powerful Rhinelander family; Leonard Rhinelander, a boy of weak character who lives in the shadow of fear cast by his domineering and prideful father.

"By the way, may I ask again: Where is Philip Rhinelander? Has anyone seen him make an appearance at the trial for an annulment brought in his son's name against this girl? *No.* He does not deign to appear. Philip Rhinelander is too high and mighty to rub shoulders with the good people of New Rochelle and White Plains, or even to show any moral support for his morally deficient son. Perhaps Rhinelander is too embarrassed to show his face in this courtroom. *I should think so.* Mr. Jacobs—well, after what we did to him on the witness stand, Mr. Jacobs should just go back to Manhattan with his tail between his legs!"

(This comment elicited bursts of laughter from the spectators, which Judge Morschauser quickly sought to extinguish. Jacobs flushed with anger.)

"Let Mr. Jacobs run back to Manhattan and report to His Majesty at the Rhinelander mansion and inform his nibs that he failed miserably to bamboozle—there's that word again—he failed to bamboozle you intelligent and sensitive men of Westchester County. For that is all this case is, gentlemen, pure and simple: *It is a lie*, and, yes, *it is a fraud*. But make no mistake: the fraud was not perpetrated on behalf of this young girl—NOT AT ALL. Alice Jones Rhinelander, this lovely and sincere person whom I have come to know well over the course of this heinous attempt by the Rhinelanders to defraud you good men—*Alice is blameless*. She is innocent. Alice is the person who is defrauded in all this. Alice is the one who was seduced by a rich and sexually aggressive young man, and, gentlemen, *remember the letters!* Rhinelander's letters! Need I remind you how he performed the most—*need I say it?* No. You remember the letters. Of course you do. Do I need to say the word? I think not. You gentlemen have heard enough of the plaintiff's vile smut in the pornographic so-called love letters he wrote and mailed to this young girl. And, I ask you, whose plan was it to engage in these bestial acts? Remember, gentlemen, it was young Kip Rhinelander who came prepared with a manual of esoteric sex practices when he brought the girl to the Hotel Marie Antoinette in his limousine—while, as we heard him testify, *playing with the girl's vagina* to arouse her so that she would succumb to his desires to have sexual intercourse. *An innocent dupe, you say?* Leonard Kip, one who has come down through a long family line, surrounded from birth by everything that is comfort afforded by wealth, and given a fine education; you are asked to believe that this grown man has *less excuse* than a boy who is born in a hovel, and who has not a long family name behind him. *So much for the Huguenots!* Well really, gentlemen, Rhinelander's lawyers must believe that you men are all innocent dupes if they expect you to find in Kip's favor and ruin this good and innocent girl and her family based on this . . . *this tripe, this rubbish.*"

I held up the lawsuit document and dropped it into the trash bin beside our table. "That is all this is, gentlemen, rubbish, and that's where this lawsuit belongs, in the trash, below anyone's contempt. Not even worthy of your time to consider these outrageous false claims."

Then, abruptly, I whirled around and pointed at Mrs. Miriam Rich, wife of the proprietor of the furniture store, who was seated in the gallery.

"*Where is she?*" I called out. "Oh, look, *there she is!* In the spectators' benches. Stand, please, Mrs. Rich. Stand and show yourself to the jury!

"Remember this witness?" I asked the jurors as the stunned woman rose to her feet. "Alice's false friend, who said she did not want to hurt this girl. But here she is in court—*what a place for a woman!*—as a vestige of the old gladiatorial days, she wanted to be in at the death! She wanted to see the victim sacrificed. *Shame that she sits there smiling as she hopes to see Alice ruined.*

"You, gentlemen, remember her. Now she's come back, she hopes, to gloat. To say, 'There, Alice, my friend, let my *spiteful lies* and *obvious jealousy call you a fraud!'* Frankly, I'm surprised the lady has the gall to show her face in this courtroom after her cheap and baseless testimony. I said to my co-counsel, 'What a mistake my opponents made by putting *that person* on the witness stand!' Miriam Rich and Rhinelander's lawyers should be *ashamed of themselves!* This is their evidence? They would seek to defame this girl with their paltry, insignificant so-called evidence. What did she say, Miriam Rich? Do I need remind you? They, these men, Jacobs and Mills—*I'll get to them*—they bring in a witness and put her on the stand to tell you men that Alice invited her along with her henpecked husband, invited them to dinner and to the theater in Manhattan, all paid for by her husband, Leonard Kip. 'Oh, yes,' she says, 'of course we believed her when she said she was white. Or was it Spanish? Because we, like Rhinelander, *we are blind.* We can't see color. We couldn't see that her father, George Jones, whom everyone in New Rochelle knows is a colored man, but we couldn't see it, BECAUSE WE WERE BLINDED BY THE COLOR OF ALICE'S HUSBAND'S MONEY.' *Go, on, Mrs. Rich.* Tell your tales somewhere else, for such lies have no place in a court of law. *I have pity on your husband!*"

Then I turned to Mr. Mills. "And here, gentlemen, here sits my esteemed colleague—indeed, my mentor, Isaac Mills—a tried and true practitioner of the lawyer's arts of, well, let us just say of charm, for we know Mr. Mills can be charming when he wants, and when it suits his goal of persuading you men seated in the jury box; and of near legendary oratorical skill; a man who could charm the birds out of the trees with his mellifluous basso profundo voice. He will talk to you gentlemen next, and he will do what he and his colleagues have done *throughout this despicable travesty*: he will try to convince you men that this trial is about a girl, Alice, deceiving a boy, young Kip, into believing she is of all-white Anglo-Saxon blood.

"I ask you to remember and to keep foremost in your minds this one important fact: *racial prejudice has no place in a court of law.* Certainly in the United States of America it does not. The verdict before you to determine must be based on *the facts as presented to you* over the weeks of testimony. It is to be based solely upon *the overwhelming evidence* presented in defense of this girl; it is not to be based on racial prejudice, on hatred, or on the class disdain that Mr. Mills will attempt to convince you of; and I warn you: Mr. Mills is as cute as a fox when it comes to—let me use their own word here—when it comes to *duping* a jury into believing something that *is not supported by the evidence.*

"You men have seen how the Rhinelander lawyers, and in particular Mr. Mills, how he attempted to sway you by dragging Alice's entire family through the muck, and most deplorably her mother, Elizabeth; by spewing slime and dragging her through the mud. *Was that really necessary?* Did you need to do that, sir, to prove your case against the daughter? To disparage the mother? What on earth does that prove except that Mr. Mills is seeking to inflame you men with bias? Elizabeth Jones's past of three decades ago? What could that possibly have to do with this case except to be used in the hope to arouse base feelings against the woman and against her daughter, against Alice? For—and here is an important point for you men to remember—when the facts of a case are weak, as they are most woefully for the plaintiff in the case before you; when the facts do not support their cause, the attorney will seek to base his case on emotions. And that is what Mr. Mills hopes to do, how he hopes to sway you men into voting based *not on the facts*, but *on the emotions* he has been working most diligently to evoke throughout this trial. Mills attempted to evoke sympathy for the Rhinelander lad by mentioning—no, *harping on*—his mother's tragic death. Yes, death by fire is indeed tragic. I doubt if death by burning is not preferable to the living death put upon this little old woman, Mrs. Elizabeth Jones, and her entire family.

"Gentlemen, let us consider this family, the Jones family. They live in New Rochelle, not Manhattan. They live in a home we all heard described as warm, simple, and welcoming. Even Rhinelander said he found the Joneses' home comfortable—comfortable enough to stay there after the marriage was made public, and after his wife was called a Negress, and the family was under siege. Remember that. It is important. Rhinelander *did not leave his wife* when the news broke of Alice's color. His testimony on that issue was clearly false. He did not leave the Jones home until *after* this man, Mr. Jacobs came and lied to him, told him that his father wanted to see him, and that he would be allowed to return. The Jones home is not a Park Avenue mansion bustling with household staff like the Rhinelander mansion; it's a family dwelling where one could sit and relax and feel at home while served a strong cup of English tea by Mrs. Jones. Rhinelander was happy in that home. The Jones sisters came in to support Alice, their adored sibling. George Jones, whom many of you gentlemen may know or have seen as the proprietor of the taxi stand in New Rochelle, Mr. Jones has been in court *every day of this trial*, never missed a session. Once again I ask: *Where is Philip Rhinelander?* Has anyone seen his nibs? No, of course not. Why, Philip Rhinelander is too high and mighty to stoop to enter the court where his son, his remaining male heir, is claiming to have been defrauded by this girl into marrying her by lying about her color. Philip Rhinelander was too proud to visit his stuttering son when he had him sent off to a special school. Perhaps that is where it all began, with young Kip shunted away and hidden by his father. Now it has come to this; Kip has become the man who would allow his father to call the girl he loves a fraud and curse her for the rest of her days. Oh, sad, so very sad, yes, a tragic story of love destroyed by racial and social pride. I have pity on the boy's soul.

"*Don't let them get away with it!*" I implored the men of the jury. "*No! Don't let them sway you with racial hate!* The Jones family are good and honest people, decent people, people who regardless of the color of George Jones's skin are not ashamed to hold their heads up high and to come here to court to support their dearly beloved girl Alice. They don't lie about the color of

Mr. Jones's skin—*why, that is simply absurd!* They don't pretend they are something they are not. That is an insult to your intelligence, gentlemen. They are not ashamed of who they are. One merely needs to look at George Jones, Alice's father, *to know he is colored.* And, yes, that makes his daughters colored as well, which is why Alice admitted she had some Black blood at the outset of this trial. Because *it is obvious to anyone who has eyesight.* And the Jones girls—see them seated there in the benches—lovely girls, all of them, they are not ashamed of who they are or of the color of their father's skin.

"In summing up, I beseech you gentlemen to recognize in your deliberation that this lawsuit brought against this young girl is *without merit; it is void of valid, factual evidence.* It is, as I said, *rubbish*, and it is *an insult to the intelligence* of you men seated on this jury. I firmly believe that you men will see that the facts of this case, the evidence before you simply does not even come close to proving that Alice Rhinelander in any way seduced, lied to, tricked, or silently mislead Kip Rhinelander into believing that she is of fully white blood. *No, impossible.* Alice's mixed color is obvious. You heard several witnesses testify, including the local reporter Barbara Reynolds; you heard her say that Rhinelander knew his wife was colored when he married her, and that it made no difference to him because he married the woman he loved; and you heard Rhinelander's driver, Ross Chidester, you heard him say that when he questioned Rhinelander about his pursuit of Alice given that her father is colored, Rhinelander replied that he 'didn't give a damn.'

"Does that sound like the words of a brain-tied dupe? An innocent boy entrapped by a lascivious older Black woman? *I think not!* And again, may I remind you: remember Rhinelander's letters. Oh, no, we can't forget his pornographic epistles. *Shocking! Disgusting.* From a naive dupe? *Hardly!* Recall how he wrote, well, I won't say it; there are ladies and young people present. I won't go into detail of how Kip admitted that he sought to stimulate his wife's sexual desires by writing to her of the debased sex acts he—"

At this point, Rhinelander suddenly stood up, he nearly upset the chair he had been sitting in, and he ran from the courtroom; he bolted out the door and was gone.

There was a moment of stunned silence, then an outburst of noisy chatter and confusion. Judge Morschauser demanded order. I looked to Jacobs, then at the Rhinelander bodyguards seated in the front row of the gallery. These men quickly rose and followed their charge from the room.

His Honor then addressed me and said, "You may continue."

Continue? It took a moment for me to recollect my thoughts. The men in the jury as well appeared stunned by Rhinelander's hasty retreat. What might this mean for the lawsuit? And for the marriage? By the evening news, speculation was rife. Would Leonard emerge to denounce his father's efforts to annul his marriage and seek to renew his vows? Would—could—Alice take him back after what she'd been forced to endure? Was there any prospect of a happy future for either of these two young people? What would the jury think of Rhinelander's sudden flight? And where was Philip Rhinelander in all of this? Reporters were said to be lurking outside the Rhinelander mansion in Manhattan hoping to catch the father coming or going and speak to him.

I thought of making some snide remark about the boy's sudden departure; but decided it would be in bad taste; better to ignore it, to act like it was an insignificant event to have the plaintiff in a lawsuit suddenly flee from the court. I chose instead to bear down on the essential elements of the case, believing that the jury had heard enough.

"Gentlemen, here are the questions you must decide, and

these are the only questions that are before you as the finders of fact in this case: Did Alice Rhinelander voluntarily tell her husband that she is white? Did she declare that she has no Black blood in her veins? And did Rhinelander believe her to be of fully white blood when he married her? Or, alternatively, as per the amended complaint: Did Alice simply fail to acknowledge to her husband what was as plain as the skin on her body, skin that you men all saw? You know the color of her body and you know whether any man with working eyesight could be deceived by the color of Alice's skin into believing that she has no Black blood. Did she fail to inform Kip of this fact? Or did she lie to him about it and claim that what was apparent was not true? These are the only questions you must answer in your verdict. We all know the truth, which is that Rhinelander knew his wife's color and he liked it in spite of his family name.

"Finally, before you gentlemen answer the questions posed as to who committed the fraud in this case, I must remind you as well as everyone following this trial that *regardless of your verdict*, which I know you will find in favor of Alice, but nevertheless, this marriage—which I believe we all know was founded on mutual love even in the face of class and race differences—this marriage of two young people who were obviously very much in love, *it cannot and it will not survive.* No, the Rhinelander marriage *is doomed*; it is over, finished, done, and through; it cannot and it will not survive regardless of what you men decide. *Too much damage and shame have been inflicted upon this young couple and their blameless love for them ever to hope to enjoy a life as husband and wife.*"

I halted, shook my head sadly, looked back at Alice, who was once again weeping into her handkerchief, and I continued. "This is a tragedy, yes; it is a tragedy of a pure and simple love between two young people that has been destroyed. But not because Alice lied to her husband about her color. Don't go into your jury room and say, 'Here, we won't tie this man up with one with colored blood.' You are not being asked that question. Remember it. And remember, when you retire to your jury room, that what has happened in this courtroom has destroyed any possibility of Alice and her husband, Kip Rhinelander, ever living together again. No, their marriage is ruined; it is tainted, yes, tainted with lies and shame for only one reason, and nothing to do with Alice: the marriage is over because Kip's lordly father, his imperial majesty, Philip Rhinelander, *disapproved of his son's choice for his bride.* Philip Rhinelander seeks to end this marriage and not the boy who just ran from the courtroom *because he couldn't stand to hear any more of this rubbish!*

"You see what is going on here, gentlemen. Rhinelander has torn the Joneses' home down over their heads. He has destroyed his boy's hope of true love. He tore it into pieces as he does with everything that confronts him. He wrecks everyone in sight, including his own boy. And he has thrown this girl into the sewer and slime, and she has only one thing left: *to be saved from the charge of being a defrauder.* That is what you men are charged to do. I ask you to bring in a verdict that is *based on the evidence,* that is *uninterfered with by prejudice,* and give this girl—and I don't care what her color is, just as I believe you men will not, as you give her *clearance of this charge of fraud.*

"I will admit, yes, I do; I feel sympathy for the Rhinelander boy, sympathy tinged with regret, as I'm certain that had these two young people been left alone to live together and love each other and respect one another in the marriage and before God as they both desired, *none of this would ever have come to pass.* The girl you see sitting here beside me in tears loves the man who just ran from the courtroom. But they both know that their marriage was over the moment Philip Rhinelander decided to end it. Alice Rhinelander has been irreparably injured by this trial. She is almost a total wreck. When she walks out of the courtroom she will be shunned by the colored race; she will be shunned by the white race.

"Do you realize as you sit there that you, and each one of you, constitute the foundation, literally speaking, the very foundation upon which our present form of government rests? By your verdict in one case—in this case that is now before you—you could tear out a portion of that foundation and set a precedent for others to follow. *In this case you are the only tribunal that can say to this young girl, 'You are a fraud.'*

"And, speaking frankly, if there is any man in this jury that has any feeling of race hatred in his veins, applicable to this case, you cannot be fair unless you cast it aside. Let us try this case on the evidence and not on sympathy or feelings of passion or prejudice.

"Now I say to you that, based solely upon the evidence you have heard over the weeks of this trial, on the facts and nothing more, you should bring in a verdict *clearing Alice Rhinelander on the charge of fraud!*

"May your verdict before God and man be fair."

With that, I sat down. Judge Morschauser seemed to come out of a deep reverie; he looked up, took note of the hour, and adjourned court until the following morning when, he told the jury, they would hear a final statement from the plaintiff's lawyer before His Honor would charge them, and they would retire to decide the case. Then, as he always did, the judge reminded the jurors of their responsibility and their promise not to discuss the case with anyone, including each other, until after they heard from Mr. Mills and from His Honor in his charge on the law as the last words they would hear before retiring to deliberate.

"All rise!" commanded the clerk. Judge Morschauser left the bench, and court was adjourned for the day.

* * *

I wish I could say that I had a relaxing evening knowing that the bulk of my work on Alice's defense at this stage in the trial was completed; but it was not to be. As we left the courthouse, Alice was besieged by frantic members of the press seeking a statement on how she regarded her husband's sudden flight from the courtroom. *What did she think? Why had Leonard run away? Was she secretly in touch with him?* And so on. We made them a promise that once the trial was over and once the verdict was in that regardless of the outcome, Alice would agree to speak to members of the press for the record; but that now with the jury still impaneled and about to hear the closing argument from the plaintiff, it would not be right for her to comment upon the trial or even to speculate as to Leonard's reasons for his abrupt departure.

Did Alice believe that if she were exonerated she and Leonard would get back together? she was asked. No, she said, sadly, as was pointed out by her lawyer: it was too late for that. Their marriage had been ruined. She would answer any other questions only after the verdict was in.

Surrounded by her family, Alice left the courthouse and made her way back to the Joneses' home. Rhinelander had not been seen in or around the courthouse since he beat his hasty retreat during my summation. In fact, the plaintiff had all but disappeared; no one in our party or from the general public or the newspeople would see or hear from Kip Rhinelander for some time to come.

* * *

Come the following morning, after a fitful sleep, as I sat in court and watched my learned adversary take his place at the podium, had there been any doubt in my mind as to the basis for the plaintiff's case, or of the strategy Mills and Jacobs planned to employ during trial in pursuing victory in the Rhinelander lawsuit—and by this point in the proceedings there wasn't any question in anyone's mind—still I was not prepared for the vitriol and the sheer nastiness of the racially poisoned bile and hate Mills spewed forth in his closing remarks to the jury. I was appalled.

Mills began innocently enough by telling the men of the jury that he as well as counsel for the defense felt the need for us all to put aside any trace of race prejudice, and to "join in the American sentiment to treat all men and women equally regardless of their race or religion."

Then, still taking the high road, he addressed the subject of the missing father, Philip Rhinelander, from the proceedings—without mentioning that the son as well was no longer in attendance.

"My colleague, Mr. Davis, whom I think we will all agree is a skillful practitioner of the trial lawyer's art of argument, Mr. Davis has asked this question time and time again: Where is Philip Rhinelander? Where is the boy's father? It is a good question, and one that needs to be answered. I admit that Philip Rhinelander's absence from this courtroom in his son's hour of need certainly smacks of elite indifference. But let us remember: Philip Rhinelander abandoned his son not only now when the boy needs him most, but over his son's entire lifetime. Philip Rhinelander may well be a man who is so concerned with profits for his companies and with the opinion of the elite social circles that he frequents that he left his boy, throughout the boy's life, he left Leonard without his presence, without his fatherly love and guidance; he abandoned the boy not only now but he left Kip to be raised and nurtured by others, by nannies and tutors, and with no parental love or guidance after the boy's mother's tragic death. Philip Rhinelander assumed that money could take the place of fatherly love and guidance; it is a common mistake made by wealthy parents.

"Why did Philip Rhinelander do this to his boy? He did it because in his son Philip Rhinelander saw a failure, he saw a disappointment. So he has distanced himself from his own child. He ordered his boy to do this and to do that, as it were, from afar. He distanced himself from the lad. He rejected the boy. It is sad, yes.

"But I say to you gentlemen: Is that valid cause for us all to desert Leonard and to leave him in the hands of a conniving Black wife? Is that now reason for us—for you good men—to add insult to injury by forcing the Rhinelander boy to continue in this unholy marriage?

"No, of course it is not! I don't believe it, and I don't believe that you men as well see this as reason to also abandon the boy to the wiles of a predatory family such as the Joneses. I believe that there is not a father among you who would do this to his own boy. That may be how Philip Rhinelander chooses to treat his son, but it is not what we would do with our own offspring. *We are better than that!*"

Brilliant, I thought, *a stroke of genius by Mr. Mills. Of course, take the weakness—take the truth, take the facts—and turn it all on its head so that it implies its opposite, as only a seasoned practitioner of the lawyer's art of verbal contortion can accomplish.*

"And we are intelligent men," Mills continued. "We were not born yesterday. We do not live in a plush Manhattan mansion removed and protected from the real world. We men know how these things work. The boy was *vulnerable.* He lost his mother in a horrific, tragic accident. Burned to death while the boy sought valiantly to save her from the flames. And then his father shunts him off to boarding school for socially awkward boys; and we feel in our hearts what that says about the boy when his father *does not even go to visit his boy once while he is there! Never visits the boy!* I think we all winced with the emotional pain we knew Leonard must have felt when we heard that. The boy falls in with a conniving hired man at the school who leads him astray. In his wanderings, he meets this woman, Alice Jones, as she sits there looking as innocent as a schoolgirl. But we are not deceived by her virginal looks; we men know how women of that race are sexually aggressive. They are mothers at fifteen. Women of that race mature earlier, and they gain such beauty as they may have earlier than fair-skinned women. And they use such beauty as they may have to entice young white boys such as Mr. Rhinelander into a scandalous affair in their hope and expectation of gaining some monetary benefit.

"Oh, this is an old story; we know the plot of this story. The Jones girls were out strutting their stuff on the streets of New Rochelle to do precisely what Alice did: to entice and entrap innocent, sheltered, wealthy white boys such as Leonard Rhinelander, a boy left to fend on his own by his distant father; a boy with no understanding of the wiles of Black girls; and such a boy who is no match for the worldly sex tricks of women of this stripe: women who use their bodies to entrap a young man into an unacceptable liaison; then get themselves pregnant; and finally force the boy to marry them all to gain access to his family's money and social status. That is all that happened here, gentlemen—please do not be deceived into thinking this was a true romance. It was nothing of the kind. It was a bold attempt by this half-breed woman and her conniving family to gain access to the Rhinelander family's money and social standing."

I cannot say that I was surprised. Yes, it is remarkable that, after having opened with his statement as to the importance of putting the issues of race and prejudice aside, and then, after that initial claim, *every single point* that Mills raised in the remainder of his long-winded and hate-filled diatribe was about nothing but stoking the fires of racial fear and hate. But how might I say that this surprised me when I knew that the Rhinelander lawyers had no other facts with which to argue their case?

Mills commanded the men of the jury to see this as "a case of life and death. You might as well—gentlemen of this jury—you might as well take and bury that young man." Here Mills pointed to the empty chair where Rhinelander had been sitting. "Yes, take the boy out and bury him six feet deep in the soil of the old churchyard as to consign him to be *forever chained to that woman!*" Mills ranted and now brought his attention to focus on Alice, who looked back at him without a trace of anger or insult.

"For, I declare that, and I believe this to be true," Mills continued, turning back to face the jury, his voice mounting with scorn, "*there isn't a father among you*—and you remember I sought to get fathers on this jury—*there isn't a father among you who would rather not see his son in his casket than to see him wedded to a mulatto woman!*

"And let us make no mistake," Mills affirmed, as though he were an expert on the opinions of the Negro race, "feelings of race separation do not belong to whites alone. Decent Blacks have the same feeling; they do not wish to see their sons or daughters married to whites any more than you would want to see your sons or your daughters married to Blacks."

Had Mills forgotten what he just said? That Alice and her colored sisters, her colored father, had all connived to become race traitors?

"*There is not a mother among your wives who would not rather see her daughter with her white hands crossed above her shroud than to see her locked in the embrace of a mulatto or Black husband!* And every one of you gentlemen knows that in this respect I speak unto you *the words of truth and soberness.*

"It is shocking enough when the girl is simply common, when she uses sex to entrap a naive boy of the upper classes. We try to overlook that, when a boy of Rhinelander's social class runs off with a vulgar girl. But then a marriage becomes *notorious*; it goes against *everything we hold dear in preserving the white race* when it is done by a woman *who knows she is colored* and yet who *hides that fact as she passes for white* and then uses her sexual powers to entice and entrap a wealthy and socially prominent white man in an unacceptable marriage.

"*This is an outrage!*" Mills bellowed. "*This is unacceptable. This is criminal fraud* as I'm sure you men all agree. And we cannot, no, WE MUST NOT allow such deceit to go *unpunished*. We must not allow this kind of *passing* and *trickery of race and class* to exist let alone to be rewarded by social advancement.

"*The future of the white race is at stake here,* gentlemen: *nothing less!*" Mr. Mills promised. "Think about it: If a woman such as Alice Jones can trick and entrap a boy such as Leonard Rhinelander into believing she is of pure white blood, and then to marry him, and to perhaps bear children of this unholy alliance, children who would then go on to continue this mongrelization of the Rhinelander bloodlines and of the white race, then I declare to you men that NO ONE IS SAFE. *The white race is not safe.* The future of this great country is at stake and cannot survive such dissolution of the ruling white race. *What next?* Where do we go from here with this mixing of the races? My learned brother at the bar is correct. It is in your hands, and with your verdict, you have a grave responsibility to preserve the foundations of this nation's pride and to keep the bloodlines pure and the boundaries of social class and color discrimination sacrosanct.

"I do not excuse the Rhinelander boy's behavior. No, we may call it what it is: foolish, even reckless to begin with, a boy in his fancy new car bought for him by his distant and unloving father, and led astray by an older, married man, both out looking for excitement with vulgar girls. Leonard meets Alice, and she is an experienced woman, expert in the techniques of seduction. She teaches the boy how to kiss her and to pet with her. Soon *he is beyond the pale, utterly, hopelessly enslaved by sex*—yes, a slave to this woman's sexual desire, and entrapped by a wanton Black girl with mastery in the bedroom. You heard how he was enslaved by the sexual exploits of an older, oversexed colored woman who used her considerable skills at seduction to blind him not only as to her color, which she hid from him, but also as to the plan she and her mother had contrived, which was to catch a rich white boy in marriage as their means to exploit his family and make their move into white society—for that was their final goal here, gentlemen, make no mistake: the goal of the defendant and her conniving mother was to insinuate themselves into white culture and community and thereby to gain access to the Rhinelander fortune and social status. That's it, incredible and criminal as it may seem: *that was their plan to infiltrate white American society.*

"It was this girl, with her beauty—we won't deny her that—and more particularly with her sexual attraction and skills in lovemaking who was the seducer, the aggressor; not the inept and inexperienced, lonely schoolboy Leonard Kip Rhinelander—who, you will recall, admitted that before he met this woman he had not so much as kissed a girl. He was a rank beginner when it came to matters of making love to a girl; Leonard had no idea how to go about it. But that was *her high art*, and that became a clear example of the man following the woman—oh, we've heard of this, and we've seen this before with men, or boys, rather, of the boy being led by the woman while all the while believing that *he* is in control. It's very clever how they do this. Soon after they met, certainly by the time she lured him to the Hotel Marie Antoinette, she already had the boy so discombobulated that he did not know—could not see Black from white. Yes, my learned adversary is right when he asks that of Mr. Rhinelander. Because, by that time, steamed up as he was in the back of the car, he did not have control of himself. He had lost his ability to think straight, which, as we have heard, was not fully developed to begin with. So he certainly was not able to see clearly. But once this sexpot got him into the room and into the bed at the Hotel Marie Antoinette—oh, well, gentlemen, need we guess what happened to the boy? *Why, it was all over.* The woman had made her conquest. The boy, Rhinelander, no matter his bloodline—*his blood was on fire!* And he lay at her feet; he was her captive. Her will was his law. Yes, *he was her slave . . . her sex slave.* Call it what it was: she owned the boy body and soul. Young Kip Rhinelander, the descendant of the noble Rhinelanders, the boy was so enslaved by this woman's sexual prowess that he forgot who he was! He forgot his station in life. He was so stricken down, so terrified that he might lose her when he read her letters alluding to the possibility that she might choose another man, he was so jealous of the other suitors she mentioned time after time in her letters to arouse his jealousy and his fear of losing her that he, Kip Rhinelander, began to fear *that he was not good enough for her!* Can you imagine, gentlemen? That is how topsy-turvy this whole affair had become: the colored girl of humble origin had convinced the wealthy young scion of a socially prominent family that *he was in danger of losing her!* The boy was in a muddle. So to save himself from what he had come to imagine was a great and terrible thing, he rushed back, upon turning twenty-one and coming of age, lured by her lurid sex letters, the boy rushed back to have his fill of her. But, by now, having fully captivated the boy, she laid down the law: 'Make me your bride; make me a Rhinelander; give me access to your name and to your family's place in society *and to your money*; then you can have more of me.

You can have me every day and night if you wish . . . until I tire of you.'

"Of course, this woman, Alice Jones, did not just suddenly spring out of nowhere and with no social skills in her plan to entrap a rich young white man into marrying her. No, we know she did not. *Alice was schooled in the arts of seduction.* She had her mother, with her vast experience in trapping men, as her trainer—her mentor, as it were— showing her how to dress, how to make herself attractive to the white fellows from the higher social classes. Mrs. Jones instilled in her daughters Alice and Grace her own vaunting ambition to move into the white world for all the comforts, status, and wealth it offered. She sent her girls to Sunday school at the white church the family attended, and she continually urged her daughters to meet and marry white men. This white woman, who married a Negro hack driver, wanted better for her—"

At this, Alice's father, George Jones—who had remained quiet and reserved throughout the trial even while hearing his wife and daughter ignominiously sullied by Rhinelander's lawyers, and while hearing the most disgusting filth read from the letters—Mr. Jones suddenly leaped to his feet and lurched at Mr. Mills as though he would throttle him. Upon hearing himself described as a "hack driver," he'd had enough.

Mr. Mills appeared unshaken.

"I'm not a hack driver!" George Jones stood and managed to express.

"Take your seat and remain seated! This is a court of law, not a free-for-all," Judge Morschauser commanded from the bench.

"If I may continue, Your Honor," Mills resumed his statement once the court had come to order. "This woman, Alice Jones—and this is most important for you men to keep in mind—*she was able to pass as white*; in fact, she is practiced at it.

She is a chameleon who makes it her practice to move comfortably and easily in either white or Black society; and there is the heart of the matter, gentlemen; for this is how she was able to practice her seductive ways and to hoodwink young Kip. She had been trained by her white English mother how to behave in such a way as to further confuse anyone who was unable to discern her race simply by looking at her. She speaks, she dresses, and she comports herself *as a white girl* and not *as a Negress.* Leonard was not alone in being fooled by Alice into believing she is white. That list of people who were unable to see Alice's racial taint includes the desk clerk at the Hotel Marie Antoinette, or Alice would not have been allowed at the respectable hotel; as well as any number of hotels the couple stayed at during their trip throughout New England. And let us not forget the clerk at the mayor's office who listed Alice as white on the marriage license because he assumed by her appearance that she is white. Alice was also able to convince Miriam and Joseph Rich that she was of Spanish descent. All these people were fooled by her—and now you are going to judge Leonard Kip Rhinelander, who was so besotted, so befuddled with love and desire for sex with the girl, who wrote that letter from the very depths of his soul—are you going to blame him for taking her as white when these unbefuddled, independent witnesses also saw her as white?

"And, actually, gentlemen, if I can ask you to recall the original answer the Jones woman's lawyers, Mr. Davis and Judge Samuel Swinburne, filed in response to the Rhinelander lawsuit: they as well had been fooled by the Jones woman into believing she is white.

"Then you are called to consider the Jones girls' father, Mr. George Jones, consider his face. What I say in regard to his face is that every feature of his face is distinctly Caucasian—except the color. I say that, if by some miracle you could change the color of his skin as he sits there he would pass anywhere for a white man. Let us see. He has got the nose of a white man. His nose is far more aquiline than mine. He has got the same nostrils as a white man, thinner than mine. He has got the high cheekbones that do not belong to the African race. He has got a narrow face. He has got a long face, not the round face of colored blood.

"And to look at Alice Jones, she too has got the features we commonly see in members of the Caucasian race. To look at her, she inherits from her father the aquiline nose, the high cheekbones. Her lips are not different from her father's lips and are as thin as my lips. That is her facial appearance. You have seen her color. You saw her body. And yes, it was shameful what her lawyer Mr. Davis made her do, to display herself, to bare her body before you men: *shocking and disgraceful*, nothing less. You may recall that I argued against allowing this shameless display of the defendant's naked body before you gentlemen. She had every right to cry, and I have no doubt her tears were genuine. But with the buoyancy of her race, she has recovered. And I too saw her body. I cannot say it is markedly darker than her face, and no less ambiguous as to her race. You see her now. You see her face. You see her neck, her hands. Her appearance by herself would not condemn her anywhere as being of colored blood. So you see, and we all see as we sit here and look at Alice Jones: *it is not a simple matter to say she is white or she is Black*. But, in the end, we know, we know now that she has Black blood and she may have passed time and time again as white; but, in the end, and with your verdict, gentlemen, you shall answer once more that ancient question put in Holy Writ, *'Can the Ethiopian change his skin?'*

"I do not wish to attack the girl's mother, Mrs. Jones; that is not, and it has never been my intention. But it is clear that this mother has caused the need for this trial. For, in her love for her girls, and from her ambition to move them into a higher station in life, Mrs. Jones entered upon that problem: Can the Ethiopian change his skin?

"*It cannot be done. Black cannot become white. Negro cannot become Caucasian.* Your answer, gentlemen, to that ancient question, by your verdict, must be in the negative. *No, it cannot be done. It is against nature.*

"And finally, I might ask, where was the defendant when she might have been called to testify? She was here. We need not ask, 'Alice, O Alice, where art thou?' But we may ask why she was not given an opportunity to speak for herself.

"Now, gentlemen, I'm at the end. God knows I have given this young man, Leonard Kip Rhinelander, the utmost that is in me in prosecuting his annulment suit. May I remind you, and urge you to keep this in mind as you reach your verdict: *There is only one person here to be judged before you men*; only one person who *needs to be punished for her deceptive actions*; and that person is this woman, Alice Jones: *the racial trespasser!* The woman who would ensnare and entrap the Rhinelander boy, using her sex skills, and mesmerize him, coerce him into taking her and her family into his family through deceit and fraud. *It must not be allowed!*

"I now give you gentlemen your long-awaited opportunity to free this young man, Leonard Rhinelander, free him from an indefensible and unacceptable, fraudulently achieved wedlock; set this boy free from this curse of love, a curse that has taken him to the gates of hell, and free him from this accursed marriage to live again as a *white man* and to pursue a *good and normal life with a woman of his own kind*. I thank you."

Mr. Mills turned from the jury and sat down.

* * *

My goodness—why, I had to take a moment to steady my nerves before I stood to make the standard, perfunctory motion to dismiss the case on grounds the plaintiff failed to prove a material fraud, which His Honor promptly denied and noted for the record.

Judge Morschauser, aware that the Christmas holidays were close upon us, given the pressures to end this trial, and in hopes to avert another recess before excusing the jury, His Honor announced that he would proceed with his charge to the jury immediately. He told the jurors that he expected they would be given the case, and then be allowed to retire to begin their deliberations following the noon recess.

This announcement resulted in the usual scurrying about of the reporters intent on filing their stories for the evening editions.

"Gentlemen," His Honor commenced his charge, "now, you have sat patiently through a long and a most difficult trial—an emotionally charged trial of this young person, the defendant, Alice Rhinelander. You have heard the evidence presented by both sides in this lawsuit, and you have heard both these learned men summarize their cases for you to consider. *Now it is your time to take over this proceeding.*

"The case is now *yours to decide.* Your verdict is the final word. And here, in this final phase of the process, you men who have sat quietly, patiently, often for long hours when nothing much seemed to be happening, but while the court had to make a determination upon an issue of law or of procedure in what has been a most unusual trial—*need I say it?*—a trial of national and international fascination as well as of unprecedented events taking place both inside and outside the courtroom, and with the eyes of the world focused upon the outcome.

"And yet it is *your responsibility, and your duty alone* as the jurors in this case *to determine the long-awaited and much-anticipated verdict*.

"Now it is your turn to fulfill your most important role in this process, gentlemen: that of the *finders of fact*. For, much of what you heard presented in this case before you is *opinion*; it is testimony that has come to you through the words and the opinions of the witnesses and presented through the skills of the lawyers. Now it is your job and your duty to wade through the morass of conflicting opinions and beliefs to determine *the facts* as *you heard them*; and, upon the finding of those facts and those facts alone as they pertain to the issue of *material fraud* before you, it is only those facts that you are to base your verdict upon—not opinions, not questions of race or mixing the races—only upon the facts that are in contention, which facts I will elucidate.

"It is my responsibility as the jurist charged with overseeing this trial to inform you of the questions you are charged to consider; and consider *only* those questions; and include them as answered with your verdict. I handed each of you my written charge; you may read it along with me, and you may take it with you into the jury room while you deliberate.

"There are in fact *seven questions* included in the charge. However, over the course of the trial, two of them have already been answered. They are: question one: 'At the time of the marriage of the parties, was the defendant colored and of colored blood?' This question has been conceded by the defense, answered in the affirmative, and therefore you must answer in the affirmative. Alice Rhinelander's lawyers have admitted that she has colored blood in her veins for the purpose of this trial. Therefore you need not consider the first question. As well, question number seven has been answered in the affirmative by the plaintiff, Mr. Rhinelander, who testified that he continued to live with the defendant as man and wife in the Joneses' home *after* Mrs. Rhinelander was identified in the newspapers as the daughter of a colored man. So that question as well has been answered.

"That leaves as remaining questions two through six in the charge I have prepared for you. I will now instruct you on those questions and ask that you consider each of the questions *separately*, and that you answer each of them either in the *negative* or *positive separately.*

"The remaining five questions are: question two: *Did the defendant before the marriage by silence conceal from the plaintiff that she was of colored blood?* Question three: *Did the defendant before the marriage represent that she was not of colored blood?* Question four: *Did the defendant practice said concealment or make said representation with the intent thereby to induce the plaintiff to marry her?* Number five: *Was the plaintiff by said concealment or by said representation, or by both, induced to marry the defendant?* Number six: *If the plaintiff had known that the defendant was of colored blood, would he have married her?*

"Those and only those are the questions that your verdict must answer.

"Now, gentlemen, may I also instruct you as to the law that defines 'colored'; it is as such: Colored blood really means, when you get to it, is her skin colored? We can't expect you to pass judgment on her blood except as it is reflected in the color of her skin. You saw her body. It is for you to decide whether the defendant concealed her Negro blood. As you gentlemen have been afforded the unusual opportunity of a visible inspection of the evidence of the defendant's skin color in those parts of her body that might otherwise not be visible with her fully clothed, and as you have had the opportunity to make your own judgment as to whether her color is and was of the colored race and obvious to her husband—the plaintiff, Leonard

Rhinelander—you are also charged with making your own determinations as to the color of the defendant and as whether that was obvious to the plaintiff in determining if the plaintiff had been, as alleged in the lawsuit, if he was *defrauded* by the defendant's representing herself as of pure white blood. You understand the question: In looking at the defendant's body, is it obviously the body of a colored person? It was an unusual demonstration to be sure, and I had to consider it carefully before allowing this evidence to be submitted. Upon consideration, and after consultation with counsel representing the defendant, I was convinced of the reliability of the evidence and its admissibility. I allowed it in for you men of the jury to consider in reaching your verdict.

"This is the extent of my charge. You men are now given the case and will retire to deliberate and to reach your verdict. However, because of what you have heard in this courtroom, and as well due to the intense debate over the issues in this trial that is taking place in the newspapers and on the radio, I must remind you that as you assume this weighty responsibility as the finders of fact, it is of vital importance that you remember and keep in the forefront of your mind that we live in a nation of laws. We are not a nation of men who are ruled by emotion when it comes to deciding the validity of something as important, as sacred, and as revered as the institution of lawful marriage between a man and a woman.

"As well, I will remind you that, in this state, in the State of New York, *the law does not preclude marriage between men and women of different races*. Therefore, that Alice Jones Rhinelander has admitted she does have colored blood is in itself *not a valid cause to annul this marriage*. It is, however, only a valid cause for annulment if you men determine that in fact, based upon the evidence you heard and you saw with your own eyes, that you determine Alice Jones Rhinelander *defrauded* Mr. Leonard Kip Rhinelander into marrying her either *by lying to him about her race*, or *intentionally deceiving him into marrying her by not revealing that she has some Black blood.* Either of these findings that she had fraudulently concealed her race would constitute *material fraud.*

"Now, I also wish to make it clear that you men are not here seated upon this jury and with this awesome responsibility, and we are not here in this court to judge whether or not it is right for two people of different races to marry. *That is not a question you are asked to answer.* Your personal feelings and ideas upon the subject of mixing of the races in marriage *are not to be considered upon reaching your verdict.* As the lawyers of both sides have done in their summations of their respective cases, and I do the same: you are instructed to leave any personal issues you may have as to race and the mixing of the races in marriage outside the jury room when you retire to deliberate. If you allow yourself to be influenced by your sympathies or prejudices, you do the parties an injustice. I say it another way: to let your emotions determine your verdict, you are failing in the given responsibility as *the finders of fact in this case.* Sentiment, passion, prejudices or other influences should not interfere with honest determination. An honest, courageous determination upon the evidence is all that is required of you by your oath.

"I cannot stress this enough because it is so important for each one of you to keep this understanding in your minds as you discuss and arrive at your verdict. I say it again: we are a nation of laws, and the law in this case and in this court at this time *is not to* determine the validity of this marriage on the issue of race. It is only to determine the *validity of this marriage on the issue of fraud*, as I have explained, and that issue as I have written out for you to refer to in my charge.

"You all know what fraud is, and you have heard the legal

definition of fraud given you at the outset of this trial; I will remind you of it here. Fraud is the *intentional misrepresentation of material existing fact* that is made by one person to another person *with knowledge of its falsity* and for the purpose of *inducing the other person to act*, and upon which the other person *relies with resulting injury or damage.* The question of whether a fraud took place in this case is very clear, as explained by the lawyers. The question of fraud comes down to a simple matter, and that is whether Mrs. Rhinelander *defrauded her husband into marrying her by concealing or by lying about her race.* That's all. Nothing else need be considered or discussed as you reach your verdict. Did Alice Rhinelander lie to Leonard Rhinelander and tell him she was of the pure white race? Or did she conceal the fact of her mixed blood in an effort to deceive him into marrying her without the knowledge that she is colored?

"You have only to answer those questions left for you to decide based on what you saw and what you heard in evidence in this courtroom during the trial. Nothing else must influence your verdict. Whatever you might have seen or heard outside this courtroom, or whatever you may have read in the news or heard broadcast on the radio is not to be considered in rendering your decision. You must base your verdict *solely upon the evidence presented at trial.*

"Therefore, in addressing these remaining questions with regard to determining if in fact the defendant defrauded the plaintiff into marrying her, you may consider these facts presented in evidence: that the plaintiff, Leonard Rhinelander, saw the colored father and brother-in-law of the defendant; that he saw and knew the surroundings of the defendant; that he slept at her father's house; that he saw the white mother and the defendant's sisters; that he was on very friendly terms with them; and that he saw the defendant's body, and all of it; and that was exhibited to you as well. You heard the plaintiff testify that those parts of her body you saw are of the same color as when he saw them on previous occasions.

"Therefore, knowing all of this, you may ask: 'Did he not realize she was of colored blood and she was not a fully white woman?' If the plaintiff had the ability—that is, the eyesight, the opportunity, and the ordinary intelligence of a man his age—to determine the truth of the defendant's color, then it follows that he was required to do so, and he cannot make a true showing of fraud.

"I wish to thank you gentlemen for your time, for your patience, and your attention in hearing the evidence put before you by both the plaintiff and the defendant; and I entrust each of you to your own intelligence and conscience in considering and arriving at your verdict.

"Gentlemen, the case is yours. You may retire."

Security guards accompanied the jurors from the courtroom and to their private sanctum, where they were to commence deliberations. There was a brief hush in the courtroom as the solemnity of the moment settled in and quickly passed. The trial was finally over but for the verdict. Then, with the jury out and His Honor having left the bench, chaos ensued.

Reporters rushed out to file their stories; photographers pushed and jostled to get into position to take photographs of Alice and her family; spectators milled about to get a closer look at the now infamous defendant. And everyone wondered: *Where is the plaintiff? What has become of Leonard Kip Rhinelander?*

We formed our circle around Alice and escorted her from the courtroom. Given the swelling crowds, and with the ongoing reports of violent episodes in and around New Rochelle and White Plains (there had been a number of fights between Blacks and whites, and even whites against whites outside the courthouse and in town; stones were thrown through the Joneses' home windows; members of the Klan demonstrated and threatened violence to Alice and her family), an additional 150 Westchester County men were deputized, given truncheons, and placed on duty outside the courthouse. We made our way through the increasingly boisterous and agitated crowds to the law offices across the square from the courthouse, and there we settled in to await the verdict.

* * *

It has been said that hell is being made to wait. If that is so, then waiting for a jury to bring in their verdict is best described as not unlike the Christian concept of purgatory: one is in limbo between heaven and hell, between exoneration and conviction, between guilty and not guilty while waiting to be judged. Even after so many years of sitting or standing about, smoking countless cigarettes while pacing the halls of courthouses all up and down this great state, and upon coming to the end of a long career as a trial lawyer, I had still not become accustomed to, or rather inured to, the mental discomfort of waiting for a jury to render its verdict.

We wait. We wonder. We argue among ourselves about what we did or didn't do that could be the deciding factor in the case. We speculate on what the men in the jury room are saying to one another about what they heard and what they believe they understood from the evidence presented during trial. We who are in purgatory discuss the different aspects of the individual jurors, and we make our conjectures based on what we think we saw of their comportment, their facial expressions, and their bodily movements during testimony. We agonize over what we may have forgotten to tell the jury in our summation, or what we may have failed to explain adequately. We apologize to ourselves and to our colleagues for our presumed miscalculations or our obvious missteps or lapses of judgment in presenting our evidence.

Or we simply say and do nothing but sit and wait with our minds as dull as empty space.

I was made to reconsider and to question every aspect of our case, every decision I had made as I presented Alice's evidence to the jury. Should I have listened to the urgings of my co-counsel and called Alice to the witness stand? Vexed as I was by this question, I felt it my responsibility to think first of the girl and what it might do to her if she were made to testify. This may sound insincere given how I had caused Alice to suffer by having her stand naked and display her body before the jury. But it is one thing to have your body revealed and let it speak for itself; it is quite another to have a gifted and vicious trial lawyer strip you of any shred of dignity and self-respect by making even your most innocent or noble acts look like mean-spirited selfishness or base immorality.

Should I have called George Jones? I was aware of his explosive temper, having seen him confront a group of racists demonstrating outside the courthouse. We had all seen how angry he became with Mr. Mills's characterization of him as a hack driver during his summation. George Jones is what one might describe as a slow burn. He appears quite composed, and indeed he is a sedate and dignified man until one gets his back up; and then, as we saw, he's ready to attack whomever he believes is out to hurt him or his family. And I fretted over my cross-examination of young Kip Rhinelander. As Alice feared: Had I been too hard on him and perhaps evoked sympathy for the spoiled rich boy? Or should I have gone harder and fulfilled my vow to ruin him? And so on and so forth: Had I not adequately defended Mrs. Jones's dignity from Mr. Mills's cruel assault on her character and therefore left her unfairly shamed without convincing rebuttal? The debate over the use of Alice's physical body as an exhibit placed in evidence raged on outside the courthouse and in the newspapers and on the radio while the jury was out. Had I gone too far? No man seemed to think so; the women I spoke to chastised me; and yet most agreed that it had been the one definitive piece of evidence that could not be denied, misinterpreted, or argued into irrelevance.

While these doubts and questions played havoc with my peace of mind, the deliberations continued.

* * *

But then, on the first afternoon of deliberations, Tuesday, December 23, only minutes after the jurors returned from their lunch break, the parties were summoned to return to the courtroom. We were surprised to learn that the jury was in. Could there be a verdict so soon? We were made to brave a freezing rain as we rushed back to the courthouse only to learn that it was not to hear a verdict.

The jury foreman, Clarence Pietsch, told the court that the jury had sent out a note with a question they wanted answered before they could continue their deliberations. Mr. Pietsch handed Judge Morschauser the note, which His Honor read to himself, and then aloud to the lawyers. The jury asked if Leonard's attorneys had questioned Barbara Reynolds, the reporter from the *New Rochelle Standard Star*, when she testified that Leonard admitted to her that he knew he had married the daughter of a colored man, and that it made no difference to him because he had married the woman he loved. I recalled that there had been no dispute of this testimony offered by Leonard's lawyers, and Mr. Mills concurred that Miss Reynolds was not cross-examined on this aspect of her evidence. Judge Morschauser advised that the record reflected Miss Reynolds's statement had not been disputed, nor had her cross-examination by plaintiff's counsel impugned her testimony. The jurors then withdrew to resume deliberations.

We perceived this question as clear indication that the jury tended toward a finding in favor of Alice. However, a jury is a fickle, twelve-headed creature, and it is never wise to seek to divine their verdict based on anything they might do or their queries sent out before their actual answers are before the court. Nevertheless, we were encouraged. Clearly, if the men deciding the verdict believed Barbara Reynolds, a reporter covering the case, and someone with no obvious bias either way; and if there had been no attempt by Leonard's lawyers to challenge this witness when she testified that Leonard admitted knowing Alice's father was colored but that it didn't matter to him because he loved the girl he married regardless of her color, then the men on the jury apparently had focused on the most important consideration in an effort to reach a verdict: Leonard's state of mind, his knowledge of Alice's mixed race, and his acceptance of her color, all of which refuted his testimony and severely undercut any allegations of fraud.

* * *

There were conflicting reports of sounds coming from the jury room: loud voices raised in heated argument; hands slamming on tables; and yet the jurors all appeared calm and resolute when half a dozen county deputies escorted them back to the courthouse from their evening meal. My colleague, Judge Swinburne, reported hearing a rumor that they had actually reached their verdict and only continued deliberations until after dinner so as to enjoy another meal at the county's expense.

Still the evening wore on with no word from the jury.

Alice and her parents, her sisters, and Mr. Brooks all went home. Given the hour and the foul weather, the crowds that had gathered outside the courthouse gradually began to thin out as it looked as though there would be no verdict that night. Only half a dozen reporters lingered inside; twice that many spectators lurked in the shadows outside.

* * *

I was at home and ready to retire for the night when at nearly midnight I received word that a verdict had been reached. I was told that the judge ordered the verdict sealed, and the jurors had been sent home. Judge Morschauser, reached by telephone at his home, instructed that the verdict would remain sealed; he said it would be read by His Honor and announced in open court the following morning at ten o'clock when all parties had been reached and were in attendance.

We had no choice but to try to get to sleep that night knowing there was a verdict, but not what that verdict was.

CHAPTER THIRTY-ONE

Tuesday, December 23, 1924

Dear best friend!

It's over! Well, not quite. The trial is over, now it's only the verdict to be decided. Only the verdict! Is that all? Only the question of whether I am to be branded a liar and a cheat who tricked Len into marrying me, a horrible person who used sex and lies to trap Len in a marriage to be declared illegal and forever treated as though it never took place. All we can do now is wait for the verdict that will either name me as a liar and a fraud or—*what?* As Mr. Davis has said so many times, and as I still don't want to admit to myself, whatever happens, Len is lost to me forever. Our marriage is over no matter the jury's verdict.

You can't believe the things Leonard's lawyer Mr. Mills said to the jury about me! It was so horrible, so mean and nasty! What I was thinking, and it is what Mr. Davis has said to me all along, the only reason they are doing this, Len's lawyers—calling me these names and saying these terrible things about what I supposedly did to Len—is because they know their claims against me are not true, not even believable when you look at the evidence. Still, it hurts. It is unbelievably painful to sit there in court day after day and listen to all these things Len's lawyers or different witnesses have to say about me—like that horrid Miriam Rich, whom I thought was a friend! Well, you certainly find out who your friends are when you are put on trial with all these people coming into the courtroom to say whatever things they want about you.

Len has disappeared! You must know how strange this is. He left the courtroom, after his time on the witness stand, which I know had been difficult for him because Mr. Davis was cruel the way he attacked Len. I asked him not to do it, but he did it anyway, and everyone said what he did was right. Of course, that was nothing compared to my having to take my clothes off in front of the jury! Can you imagine? Standing there in front of a room full of men in nothing but Mother's overcoat and then having to expose different parts of my naked body so the men could look at my skin and decide whether I had lied about my race! It is so humiliating! And then Len's letters! Oh, nothing can compare with those letters! It was upsetting, yes, but also I thought, *Good, let them hear it, serves them right for bringing this into court in the first place. It's our business, our marriage, and it never should have been made into a lawsuit for a jury to hear in public. That's all the Rhinelanders' fault, so let them suffer the embarrassment of Len's letters.*

And Len—typical Leonard—he just got up and walked out of the courtroom and no one has seen him since! That's my Len. You never know what that boy will do. He gave me the loveliest smile—truly a smile like he used to give me, a smile of love and kindness as he left the witness stand and walked out of the courtroom and disappeared into thin air. Funny boy, my strange and unpredictable boy. Who can ever know what goes on in that mind of his?

Will I ever see Len again? Is it really over, our love, our marriage, and will we never be together again as husband and wife? O God, I am about to cry. I try to accept that it is finished and that I will never—I can't even write it here, but I must. I don't think I will ever see Len again, not as the man I once knew and loved, because, although I still love him, the truth is that I no longer respect Len. I want to love him as I once did, but when you no longer respect someone it's impossible to love them as you did before you lost respect. Now I feel sorry for Len—truly I do. And that is no way to feel for someone you love as a man, as your husband—that you pity him, that you have lost respect.

It hurts to admit this, I probably wouldn't say it to anyone but to my trusty and faithful diary, but that part of me that was so deeply in love with Len, it's just . . . it's gone. I don't know if that part of me can forgive him for leaving me, for letting this happen, and for allowing those men to say those horrible things about me. It's so sad for me to admit this.

My dear Leonard, wherever you are, however you will go on from here and live in this world, my heart goes out to you and, yes, I still love you, but it is with a different love from what I felt before. It is a sad love, a deeply unhappy love, and a sadness that lives in my very spirit.

Because I loved you so deeply, my boy, my Greek god, that is how deeply you hurt me.

CHAPTER THIRTY-TWO

The Verdict

The early morning editions of the New York tabloid newspapers on Wednesday, December 24, 1924, preemptively declared Alice the winner even before Judge Morschauser read the official verdict. Whether some intrepid reporter had wheedled or bribed the court clerk into revealing the verdict, or if it was all merely speculation, no one knew for certain as we assembled in the courtroom to hear His Honor announce the verdict.

The courthouse was mobbed. Half a dozen court officers stood at the doors to the hallway to keep the clamorous crowd outside and prevent them from barging into the courtroom; nevertheless, it was jam-packed.

At exactly ten o'clock, the door to the judge's chambers opened and Judge Morschauser, dressed in his judicial robes but looking as though he'd only just left his bed, His Honor strode in to take his place on the bench. With a stern expression, he referred to some papers on his desk, then he looked up and gazed out at the tense crowd as he declared: "While this court is in session, I want you all to know *this is no circus*. There will be *order in this court throughout the reading of the verdict*. Anyone making the slightest attempt at a demonstration when the jury's answers are read will be charged with contempt of court."

Alice sat quietly looking from His Honor on the bench to the white handkerchief she kept folding and unfolding in her delicate brown hands. She appeared remarkably composed for a woman about to hear whether she was to be declared a fraud and forever stripped of her rights as a lawful wife; and then sent out into the world utterly disgraced and broken.

There was still no sign of Rhinelander; no one had seen him in White Plains since he fled from the courtroom. Nor was Rhinelander's Manhattan attorney, Leon Jacobs, present to hear the verdict. Isaac Mills sat alone at the plaintiff's table. He gazed down at some papers before him and looked utterly exhausted. From the newspaper reports, and from the general consensus around the courthouse, Alice had been exonerated. No one knew if this were in fact the true result, or from where the information had come, and on what grounds.

"Bring in the jury," His Honor declared.

The twelve men charged with deciding Alice's fate filed in and took their seats in the jury box. They sat stone-faced, doing their utmost not to betray any evidence of their decision. They looked tired, perhaps a bit rumpled, and even nervous; but they gave no indication of relief or of comfort at having served their duty and arrived at what was bound to be a controversial decision no matter which way it went.

Once the jurors were seated, His Honor bade them a good morning, and thanked them for their service. Then he asked: "Have you reached a verdict, and been able to answer all of the questions in your verdict?"

Jury foreman Clarence Pietsch said, "Yes, Your Honor, we have."

He handed a sealed verdict to the clerk, who then gave it to the judge. Judge Morschauser read the verdict to himself; he made no facial expression as he read. He then looked up, and I noticed that he appeared to give a sigh of relief that the trial was finally over. Sometime later, after he retired, Judge Morschauser would remember the Rhinelander case as the most difficult and exhausting of all the cases he had been called upon to adjudicate in his more than thirty years on the bench. He attributed this difficulty to the still pertinent and painful issues of race in America, and particularly when concerned with the mixing of the races in marriage.

"Question one," His Honor began to read the verdict, "as stated, this question is answered in the affirmative by the defendant, Alice Rhinelander, who admitted for the purposes of this trial that she has some Black blood. As to question two, *Did the defendant before the marriage by her silence conceal from the plaintiff that she was of colored blood?*

"To this question the jury has answered: *No.*

"Question three, *Did the defendant before the marriage represent to the plaintiff that she was not of colored blood?*

"To this question the jury has answered: *No.*"

His Honor paused and looked up at the expectant crowd.

"We come now to question four," he continued. "*Did the defendant, Alice Jones Rhinelander, practice said concealment, or make said representation, with the intent thereby to induce plaintiff Leonard Kip Rhinelander to marry her?*

"To this question the jury has answered: *No.*"

There was a gasp of relief or surprise or dismay from the spectator's benches and a rustling of movement as reporters began jockeying for position to dart out of the doors as soon as the final questions were answered.

Judge Morschauser rapped his gavel and said, "I will remind you: let there be no outbreak of commotion. I have asked for everyone in this room to show the proper respect for these proceedings, and to the parties as the final questions are answered.

"As to question number five," he continued, and you could hear the proverbial pin drop, "which question asks, *Was the plaintiff by said concealment or by said representation, or by both induced to marry the defendant?*

"The jury has answered: *No.*"

Now the crowd could barely contain themselves. Women wept openly. Men shook their heads and sighed. Journalists furiously scribbled notes as they shouldered their way toward the doors.

Judge Morschauser continued, "And finally, as to question number seven which question asks: *If the plaintiff, Leonard Kip Rhinelander, had known that the defendant, Alice Beatrice Jones Rhinelander was of colored blood, would he have married her?*"

The judge put down the verdict sheet from which he had been reading, and he looked up at the crowd.

"As to this final question, the jury has answered: *Yes*," His Honor said.

Judge Morschauser then banged his gavel three times and announced, "You have now heard the verdict as decided and recorded by the jury. I hereby *dismiss the jury* and rule that by this verdict the jury has declared a *complete exoneration for this defendant*, Mrs. Alice Beatrice Jones Rhinelander, on the charges of fraud brought against her in this annulment suit."

Then he addressed Alice: "Mrs. Rhinelander, the court hereby *dismisses* this action upon a verdict in your favor and excuses you."

No one moved or made an audible sound. Then Alice said, "Thank you, Your Honor." And her whole body seemed to go limp with relief.

I put my arm around her shoulder and whispered, "It's over."

Alice nodded barely perceptibly and then she looked up at me and said, "Thank you. And God bless you."

Mr. Mills stood and made the standard request to the judge that he set aside the verdict on the basis that it had not been proved by the evidence. He requested a new trial alleging that the jury had been unfairly prejudiced against the plaintiff by the judge's charge. Morschauser grimaced at the accusation and promptly denied the motion. Mills then asked to have the jury polled. Judge Morschauser scowled; he turned and addressed each member of the jury individually, and asked: "Are the answers as read in the verdict in keeping with the decision you reached of your own accord?"

Each and every man on the jury answered yes, that they were.

"I believe we've heard enough," His Honor announced and declared, "This court is now adjourned."

At last, as I gathered my papers and prepared to leave, Isaac Mills turned to me, his onetime protégé, and said, "Congratulations, sir, on a job well done."

The stillness that had persisted in the gallery was suddenly and loudly shattered as the judge left the bench and the journalists rushed for the doors to file their reports. The photographers crowded in to surround Alice and began snapping their photos. Upon my advice, and in keeping with our promises to the reporters, now that the trial was finally over and the verdict announced, Alice agreed to sit for an interview to take place in our offices across from the courthouse.

* * *

Alice took a seat in our law library with her parents standing on either side next to her, and all smiled for the photographers. It was noted that Alice was still wearing her wedding ring.

"Well," she said when asked, "I am still married to Leonard."

Grace Robinson from the *Daily News*, whose stories had consistently favored Alice, asked Alice if she expected that, given the verdict, she would return to live as husband and wife with Leonard.

Alice's smile quickly faded. She shook her head slightly,

looked down at her hands, then looked up with sadness in her eyes and answered, "I can't say that." She thought a moment and then she added, "No, I don't think so."

Had she spoken to Leonard or seen him since he left the courtroom? another reporter asked her. Again Alice answered no. When asked how she felt about her win at trial, Alice replied in a low voice quaking with emotion, "Naturally, I am relieved that it's finally over. I am happy the jury decided in my favor, but I was not happy over the torture I went through. I was hurt, deeply hurt. I still feel terrible over losing my husband, losing Leonard, the man I love, and all that has happened since he left me. It has been an awful time for me and for my family. And I will never be happy—of course, because I can never be happy about how our marriage . . . how it has been treated by people who don't know us, who don't see our hearts, and can't seem to understand that Leonard and I loved each other. And, through it all, we only wished to be left alone to live together as husband and wife as other couples do.

"We are not different. We are just people," Alice said and trailed off.

Grace Robinson asked, "Do you still love Leonard . . . after what he put you through?"

Alice's eyes glistened with tears. She nodded, dabbed her eyes with her handkerchief, and said, "Yes. I do love him . . . *and no . . . I don't* . . . I don't blame Leonard; it's not his fault. I will never stop loving him and cherishing what we had together. But I still can't forget some of the horrible things that were done to me, and to my family, some of the things that were said . . . about me, and my family, particularly my mother. It was terrible. I can forget some of the misery that came with the torture of the past few weeks. I'd rather remember other things. I'd rather remember how happy we were, Leonard and I when we were together, before all this began; and how we made plans for our future life together. I'd much rather remember that, those times we shared together, and that Leonard's love and mine was a wonderful thing, and not at all how they made it seem."

At that point, seeing Alice was on the verge of breaking down, with her eyes swollen with tears, and with even a few of the reporters appearing deeply moved, I ended the interview and asked that Alice be left alone and allowed to rest and recover from what had been an ordeal no woman should ever have to go through.

"This has been an awful strain on Mrs. Rhinelander. She is bereft of her husband, the man she loves," I said. "She's been horribly slandered by Rhinelander's lawyers. She and her family have been threatened and attacked by angry racist mobs. And now, if you will, Alice wishes only to be allowed to live a quiet and peaceful life."

* * *

I read where Rhinelander was finally located, by a couple of indefatigable reporters hours after the verdict was announced as he left his rooms and checked out of the Gramatan Hotel in Bronxville. Apparently Kip had been holed up there since his abrupt flight from the courtroom. When asked by reporters, Rhinelander said that yes, he had heard the verdict; but he refused to answer most of the other questions asked by reporters, saying only that he was in a hurry to return to Manhattan.

"Were you surprised by the verdict?" a reporter shouted as Rhinelander got into his chauffeur-driven limousine.

"No," Leonard answered without a second thought. "*I expected it.*"

"What will you do now that you are still married to Alice?" the reporter asked. "Do you expect the marriage to continue?"

Rhinelander made no answer. He sat in the rear of the car and looked straight ahead as he was driven away.

CHAPTER THIRTY-THREE

Under a Gibbous Moon

I found Alice sitting alone in the garden outside her family home on an evening a few years following the verdict, and looking up at the moon. I had papers for her signature: the final executed agreement between Alice and the Rhinelander estate.

"There's a name for that," Alice said, referring to the moon. "Len once told me. When we were on Cape Cod, in Provincetown. It's when the moon is just past half full, and it sort of bulges."

"Yes," I said. "It's called a *gibbous moon*."

"Yes, that's it . . . *gibbous* . . . what a funny word. Len said it's like the moon is pregnant. . . . He called me his 'gibbous girl.' "

"What happened, Alice?" I asked.

"I lost the baby. . . . Len's lawyers—I know they tried to make it look like I had . . . like I got rid of the baby, but that's not true. And I'm glad it was never allowed to come in the trial, even though Len's lawyers did everything they could to make it appear that I had an abortion. Len knew the truth. I had a miscarriage. I don't know if it's because I was so upset when those men took Len away or . . . well, whoever knows why these things happen? It just wasn't meant to be . . . like our marriage, I suppose. . . .

"You know, Mr. Davis, I still miss Len—I miss him every day," she said. "His smile . . . his laugh. He was so much fun. . . . I wasn't surprised when I heard that Len had died. Of course I was upset. I knew he was ill. They say he died of pneumonia. I don't believe it. Leonard died of a broken heart.

"I remember thinking . . . when I heard that Len moved out to Nevada, and when the divorce was finalized, I read somewhere that a reporter had found him in Nevada working as a woodcutter.

"*A woodcutter?* I thought. *Len?* That didn't make any sense. What on earth would Len be doing working as a woodcutter? And what exactly does a woodcutter do? Cut wood all day? I think it's called a sawyer. . . . I couldn't imagine it, not as something for Len, in any case.

"But then, of course, as you know, he got sick, and they brought him back to New York. He went into the hospital. They said it was pneumonia. They can say what they want. The truth is, as I said, Leonard died of a broken heart. No one will ever convince me otherwise. He loved me. We loved each other, and it broke his heart when his father . . . did what he did, and made Leonard leave me and then—well, you know all the rest. . . . It hurt him as much as it hurt me, perhaps even more. At least I had my family's love and support through it all. Len had no one. I believe everyone turned on him for marrying me. And he was heartbroken. It killed him.

"I can't blame him for what he did, and I don't. *I never will* . . . I . . . *I can't.* I try to understand him. But it was—I don't want to say it, but it was Len's fault. No—that's not right. Len didn't *make* it happen, but he *let* it happen; that's different. He let his father, and his father's beliefs—all that, Len let it control him. And I'll never understand—not completely, anyway, though I think about it all the time and I wonder why—*why he let it happen.*

Wasn't our love strong enough? Why he didn't just say, '*No. Alice is my wife. I love her, and that's the end of it*'? I think everyone would have respected him for that—except perhaps his father.

"For the life of me, I've thought about this so much over the years, and still I can't understand why Len just *allowed* his father to do what he did to us and then, even after the trial; why Leonard never even tried to save our marriage. It baffles me, and it saddens me so much. I don't know what to think, *that he never really loved me?* No, I don't believe that.

"I suppose it's as you said, Mr. Davis: too much damage had been done. I don't know if our marriage ever could have been saved . . . but, O God, how it hurt. How it still hurts . . .

"I know Len never remarried. I've heard he never even . . . saw any other girls or . . . he just . . . he moved to Nevada to get the divorce and he . . . well, I don't know, he went on to become a woodcutter. Please tell me, Mr. Davis, if you can: How does that make any sense? A man who never—as you put it during the trial—a man who never worked a day in his life; not that kind of work, anyway. Now he moves out to Nevada to cut wood. . . . I thought Nevada was a desert. How much wood could there be in the desert in Nevada for Len to cut? None of it makes any sense except this: *Len had a broken heart.* Yes, his heart was broken, and so he cut wood—whatever wood there was out there in the desert for him to cut—he cut wood to take his mind off of the pain he felt at allowing his father to do what he did to us . . . and to our marriage. . . .

"*It was wrong.* Oh, I said it then and I say it now," Alice grieved. "A boy—a man—no man should ever allow his father to rule over his life as Philip did over Len. It never works. And a father—a father who loves his son should never try to make his son into something he's not. It always turns out badly for both father and son. How do you think Philip Rhinelander felt when he saw his son die of a broken heart when Len was still a young man—just thirty-four years old? What father wants to outlive his boy? Do you think Philip said to himself: *This is my fault; I did this to my son*? I doubt it. And I find it all so hard to understand. . . .

"Of course I miss Len. Yes, I miss him terribly. I think of him every day. And even more: *I miss the children . . . the family we never had.*"

Alice dabbed her eyes and shook her head.

"Sometimes . . . I daydream about . . . what I call my *imaginary family*—the children Len and I would have had in our family. How big and strong the boys would have been. You know, Len was tall, six feet, and my father, George Jones, was a strong man, so our boys would have been tall and strong . . . and with fair skin, thank God, so they would never have to go through what we Jones girls went through; or maybe they would, it's all so upsetting and confusing with people constantly asking or wondering, *Are you Black or are you white?*

"And our boys, the sons we would have had, the boys in our imaginary family would grow up to be good men and respectful to their parents, but free to live their own lives because of the love we would have shown them . . . as well as the discipline, and the teaching to follow their hearts. And they would treat everyone with respect and kindness no matter what color they were.

"You know, sometimes I think that even Philip, Len's father—as much as he fought against me and my family, and we know how he tried so desperately to hurt us; *why?* Because of my father's skin color? Or because we are . . . not of the same social standing? All that nonsense about the social register or whatever it is. Who will care about any of that a hundred years from now? That's what Father always said when one of his girls got upset over something: 'What difference will it make a hundred years from now?'

"But—imagine if we had been allowed to live our lives together as we wanted; then, think of it, there could have been children, our children's children still alive and doing great things for the people of this country a hundred years from now. I like to think that even Philip Rhinelander would have come to love our children, particularly the boys, because they would have been hardworking men like my father (not like Len, who was really spoiled as a boy, I think, and lazy, even if he did become a good woodcutter, whatever that is). Our boys would grow up to be men like George Jones, a good, honest, hardworking man who never asked for anything for nothing and was always kind and respectful—although Father did get angry and lose his temper sometimes. And who cares if our boys' skin would have been a bit darker than that of the other boys? What does it matter? Why *should* it matter? As my father used to say, and he could be a bit vulgar at times, 'It doesn't matter what color a man's skin is; we all got to take down our britches to do our business.'

"Our sons could have gone to work for the Rhinelander Real Estate Company . . . or not, if they wished to do something else. I named the first boy in my imaginary family George after my father, may he rest in peace—the peace I was never able to give him during his life, poor man. He suffered so much during the trial and even after it was over with those horrible men, the Klan or whoever they were—they wouldn't leave us alone! They gave my father a terrible time until he finally knocked one of them out and they all ran away. My mother and I finally had to leave town. We went on a cruise ship to England and visited her family. Later, I heard, they—the Klan—they thought I was in Florida, and they sent some men down there looking for me. Actually, I never was in Florida. . . .

"But getting back to my imaginary family: how sweet and lovely our girls would be! We would name the oldest girl Adelaide, after Len's mother. You know, it's the strangest thing, Mr. Davis. Now . . . honestly, I don't believe in ghosts or spirits of the dead coming back to haunt us; but for some unknown reason, maybe because of how Len used to talk about Adelaide, his mother, I feel so close to her sometimes, to Len's dead mother, almost as though her soul would comfort me when I had terrible thoughts about all the pain and upset Len and I caused to his family, and mine, because of our love for each other and our marriage.

"Len always told me that Adelaide would have loved me if she'd been alive when Len and I met. I have no idea if that's true. Other people have said that the Kip family is just as high and mighty as, if not more so than, the Rhinelanders, though I can't imagine how anyone could be so full of himself as Philip Rhinelander to cause his son so much heartbreak. But then, Len's mother died when he was still very young and he may have remembered her in his own way and not as she really was. . . .

"It's another thing, like our imaginary family, something we will never know. . . .

"My God, when I think of it, when I think of what they put us through, the Rhinelanders! *Why?* Why would anyone do that to their own son? Because of their pride? Their only remaining son still in the home, for that matter. I don't understand Philip Rhinelander. And Len's sisters! O God, they were horrible. Even after the trial ended. First one appeal, which upheld the verdict. Then they appealed that decision up to the higher courts. As you know, by the time we were through, practically all the money I was awarded had to go to pay the lawyer's fees. And then, after Len died, his sisters tried to have the court take away even the small amount I was awarded. Not that I minded, not really. I was never an expensive girl. I still live in my parents' home—this home in New Rochelle. It's now my home, and I'm quite comfortable. But it's more the principle of the thing. Why should they deny me this small amount? It's not like they need it. It's just spite; they do it to spite me . . . for the pain that Len's own family caused.

"People wonder why I never remarried. They ask if it's because whatever money I get from the Rhinelander settlement would stop if I were to marry. No, that has nothing to do with it. My marriage to Leonard was never about money, and to this day I don't make decisions of the heart based on money. I could never live that way. I loved Leonard because of the way he treated me . . . first of all. He was so kind and gentle, so caring, so . . . well, I've said it before, but I'll say it again, he was respectful. He treated me like a lady. He was polite. He was sweet . . . never mean. And he was funny! He made me laugh. We had so much fun together. I never cared about the money, and I still don't. And, well, I never remarried because I never met another man I love like I loved Len.

"To me, the way I see it, there were two Lens—that's the only way I can understand him. There was the Len I knew and loved when he was with me: a gentle man, loving and caring; and there was the other Len, the man he was when he was away from me and around his family or just other people, as though he had to pretend to be someone else, a person he believed that everyone expected him to be—*a Rhinelander*—and not the good-hearted man he really was.

"I've met some men, of course, and I've gone out a few times. Some of them were nice; others were boring or so full of themselves; and some were just plain rude; or they were after me because they thought I have money. But I never met anyone who made me feel as happy as I felt when I was with Len. I loved Len; I truly loved him. I've never felt anything like that for another man, and I doubt if I ever will.

"In a way, I suppose, and I've heard it said, *It is better to have loved and lost than never to have loved at all.* I believe that. At least I know what we had; and the love we knew for each other can never be taken away even with all the Rhinelanders' money, and with all they did to try to spoil it. Len and I will never grow tired of each other; never get on each other's nerves—they say that happens to couples sometimes, though I never saw it with my mother and father. Mother could be difficult at times and take her moods out on my father; but he was always kind and respectful. I know they say he had a temper; I saw it a few times; but never with Mother.

"Len as well—he never remarried; did I say that? Oh, yes, I did; but it's something to think about. Of course, you know that. A man like Len all by himself, well, and there he was . . . all alone . . . out there in the desert in Nevada cutting wood, until he got sick. Then they brought him back to New York. And they treated him for the pneumonia, but not for his broken heart; and by then it was too late, and that is what killed him.

"If only I had been allowed to go to him then . . ." Alice closed her eyes and shook her head. Then she looked up at me with tears still brimming in those remarkable brown eyes.

"And here I am, still living at home," she said and gestured toward her home, "still in the same house I grew up in, and where Len and I lived together during those . . . those terrible days after the news of the marriage was in all the newspapers and everything began to go wrong. . . .

"Of course I'm lonely. . . . Yes, I do have a cat; and I do

have my sisters and their families, all the nieces and nephews. But sometimes I feel terribly lonely. It's when I miss Len, and I imagine I'll die an old maid. And when I think of the children Len and I never had, when I think of my imaginary family with Len: those strong boys and lovely girls. I see them so clearly in my mind's eye. And my dream of life continuing with our love even after we have gone."

Alice shook her head, she looked at me and said, "It all dies with us."

ACKNOWLEDGMENTS

I learned of the Rhinelander case while reading *The Art of Cross-Examination* by Francis L. Wellman, a classic text for trial lawyers that includes excerpts from Lee Parsons Davis's brilliant cross-examination of Leonard Rhinelander. Before reimagining the case as a novel, I read three books on the infamous trial: *Property Rites: The Rhinelander Trial, Passing, and the Protection of Whiteness* by Elizabeth M. Smith-Pryor; *Love on Trial: An American Scandal in Black and White* by Earl Lewis and Heidi Ardizzone; and *According to Our Hearts: Rhinelander v. Rhinelander and the Law of the Multiracial Family* by Angela Onwuachi-Willig.

For my own interest in the law and its practitioners, and for his expert advice, I thank Ivan S. Fisher, Esq., an esteemed defense attorney who represented me before the Second Circuit Court of Appeals and won an important decision that set me free, and who then employed me as a forensics specialist.

Thomas Heffernon, Esq., a childhood friend who became a criminal defense attorney and won two cases on my behalf, also read early drafts of the book and offered his insightful advice.

Thanks to Steve Glick, my dear friend and former agent at William Morris Endeavor, who has been with me on this journey for more than thirty years.

And I thank Patrik Bass, my editor at HarperCollins, who was already familiar with Alice Rhinelander's story, and who has given me his heartfelt advice, enthusiastic encouragement, and invaluable editorial guidance in bringing the novel to completion.

As well, I give deep respect to the memory of my longtime friend and mentor, Norman Mailer, who taught me to practice discipline in my work as well as to revere the craft of writing.

To my family, friends, colleagues, and supporters whom I did not mention by name, thank you all for being a part of my life.

And finally my wife, Antoinette, who listened patiently for hours while I rambled on about the characters in this story, and who then urged me to stop talking and go back to my desk and write. Antoinette is my inspiration.

ABOUT THE AUTHOR

Richard Stratton is an award-winning writer and filmmaker. His fiction and journalism have appeared in numerous magazines, including GQ, *Esquire, Details, Newsweek, Rolling Stone, Spin, Playboy*, and *Story* magazine. His collection of journalism includes *Altered States of America: Outlaws and Icons, Hitmakers and Hitmen*. Stratton's article "Godfather and Son," published in *Playboy*, won the 2011 New York Press Club Award for Crime Reporting. He is the author of the memoir trilogy: *Smuggler's Blues: A True Story of the Hippie Mafia; Kingpin: Prisoner of the War on Drugs*; and *In the World: From the Big House to Hollywood.*

Stratton wrote and produced the feature film *Slam*, which won the Grand Jury Prize at Sundance and the Camera d'Or at Cannes. Stratton also wrote and produced *Whiteboyz* for Fox Searchlight as well as producing a number of documentary films for HBO. He created, executive produced, and was the showrunner for the Showtime dramatic series *Street Time.*

He produced and directed a four-hour documentary series for A&E based on his magazine article "Godfather and Son" about John Gotti Sr. and John Gotti Jr. Stratton lives in New York City with his wife, Antoinette, and is the father of five children.

Here ends Richard Stratton's
Defending Alice.

The first edition of the book was printed and
bound at LSC Communications
in Harrisonburg, Virginia, October 2022.

A NOTE ON THE TYPE

The text of this novel was set in Bembo, a typeface dating back to one of the most famous printers of the Italian Renaissance, Aldus Manutius, founder of the Aldine Press. In 1496, Manutius used a new roman typeface to print *de Aetna*, a travelogue by popular writer Pietro Bembo. Prolific punchcutter Francesco Griffo designed the type; he was one of the first to depart from the heavier pen-drawn look of humanist calligraphy to develop the more stylized look we associate with roman types today. In 1929, influential British typographer Stanley Morison and the design staff at the Monotype Corporation used Griffo's roman as the model for a revival type design named Bembo, which is noted for its quiet presence and graceful stability. The characteristics of many other well-known typefaces such as Garamond® and Times New Roman® can be traced back to the Bembo typeface.

HARPERVIA

An imprint dedicated to publishing international voices,
offering readers a chance to encounter other lives and other
points of view via the language of the imagination.